RICHARD LAYMON

DARK MOUNTAIN

LEISURE BOOKS   NEW YORK CITY

For Bob, my brother,
who trekked with me
the trails of our youth

A LEISURE BOOK®

March 2009

Published by

Dorchester Publishing Co., Inc.
200 Madison Avenue
New York, NY 10016

ISBN 10: 0-8439-6138-4   LAYMON
ISBN 13: 978-0-8439-6138-6
E-ISBN: 1-4285-0612-8

The name "Leisure Books" and the stylized "L" with design are trademarks of Dorchester Publishing Co., Inc.

Printed in the United States of America.

10 9 8 7 6 5 4 3 2 1

Visit us on the web at www.dorchesterpub.com.

DARK MOUNTAIN

Beware on your journey,
Tread softly with care.
Beware of the hag
In her dark mountain lair.

Speak only in whispers,
Don't wander alone.
Take heed of the shadows—
Watch out for the crone.

She waits and she wants you.
She knows you are there.
Don't wander alone,
Tread softly with care.

PART ONE

CHAPTER ONE

Cheryl heard it again—the soft, dry crunching sound that a foot might make in leaves. This time, it was very close.

She lay rigid in her sleeping bag, barely daring to breathe, gazing straight up at the dark slanting wall of the tent and telling herself to stay calm.

It's probably just an animal. Maybe a deer. A few days ago, camped in a meadow below the pass, they'd been awakened in the night by a deer wandering near their tent. Its hooves had crashed through the foliage, snapping branches and shaking the ground. Bambi the Elephant, Danny had called it.

This was different.

This was stealthy.

She heard it again, flinched, and dug her fingertips into her bare thighs.

Maybe something falling from a tree? Pinecones? They could make sounds like that, she supposed. Plenty of wind out there to shake them loose.

That's it. That has to be it. Otherwise, somebody is standing just outside the tent, and that can't be.

They'd seen nobody for two days. They'd reached Lower Mesquite Lake early in the afternoon. Except for this small patch of woods, the glacial lake was surrounded by barren rock. They'd hiked completely around it. They'd explored the woods. They'd seen nobody.

Not even when they hiked over a small ridge to Upper Mesquite.

Nobody.

Cheryl took a deep breath, trying to calm herself.

Go to sleep, chicken-shit.

Cheryl consciously relaxed her legs and rump and back, settling down into the warmth, and turned her head to stretch her taut neck muscles. She felt like rolling over. She wanted to turn facedown and burrow deep, but she was afraid to move that much.

A monster under the bed. Just like when she was a kid and *knew* there was a terrible monster under the bed. If she lay absolutely still, it would leave her alone.

I'm eighteen. I'm too old for this.

Slowly, she started to turn over. Her bare skin made whispery, sliding sounds against the nylon bag, almost loud enough to mask the other sound. She went stiff. She was on her side, facing Danny. The other sound came from behind her—a quiet hissing sigh, a sound such as fingernails might make scraping along the tent's wall.

She flung herself against Danny, shook him by the shoulders. Moaning, he raised his head. "Huh? Wha—"

"Somebody's outside," she gasped.

He pushed himself up on his elbows. "Huh?"

"Outside. I heard him."

"Who?"

"Shh."

Neither of them moved.

"I don't hear anything," he said in a groggy voice.

"I did. God, he's right outside the tent. He *scratched* on it."

"Probably just a branch."

"*Danny.*"

"Okay, okay, I'll go out 'n' have a look."

"I'll go with you."

"No point both of us freezing our asses. I'll go." He rose to his hands and knees, still in the double sleeping bag, letting in the cold night air as he searched through the clothes and gear at the head of the tent. He pulled his flashlight out of his boot. "Just be a minute," he said.

Cheryl scooted away. Danny climbed from the bag and

crawled to the foot of the tent. Kneeling there, naked, he pulled at the zipper of the mosquito netting.

Cheryl sat up. The cold wrapped around her. Shuddering, she hugged her breasts. "Maybe you'd better not," she whispered. "Come on back."

"Nah, it's all right."

"Please?"

"I've gotta take a leak anyway," he said, and started to crawl through the flaps. He was halfway out when he stopped. He uttered a low groan. One of his feet reached backward.

Cheryl heard a wet thud. Spray rained against the tent flaps.

Danny's legs shot out from under him. He bounced up and down, knees pounding the tent floor, flopping in mad spasms that seemed to last forever. At last, he lay motionless.

Cheryl stared in horror as Danny began to slide through the flaps. His buttocks vanished. His legs dragged along as if he were being sucked slowly into a dark mouth.

Cheryl was alone in the tent.

But not for long.

CHAPTER TWO

Meg staggered into the living room, a strap of her negligee sagging down her arm. "Good grief, hon, what time is it?"

"Nighttime," Karen said.

"Tell me. Christ, tell me. Call this a vacation?"

"I sure do."

"Yeah, guess you would." She flopped into a chair, hooked one leg over its stuffed arm, and stretched to reach for a pack of cigarettes. "What time's he picking you up?"

"Five thirty."

"Gug. Want me to put on some coffee?"

"I don't want to be peeing."

"Shit. Car full of kids, you'll be stopping every five minutes anyway." She lit a cigarette.

"They're not exactly kids," Karen said. "Julie's sixteen. Benny's thirteen or fourteen."

"Even worse. Christ, kiddo, you're in for it."

"They're okay." Karen propped the backpack against the sofa and shoved in the mummy bag.

"Who's this other family?"

"The Gordons. Never met them before."

"They have kids, too?"

"Three."

"Oh, you're gonna have a *swell* time. Hope you're not planning to screw the guy."

"We'll see." Karen buckled the leather straps of the cover, picked up the backpack, and carried it toward the front door. She leaned it against the wall.

"Sure sounds like loads of fun. Wish I was coming."

"You were invited."

"Give me a break. I need a campout like I need a third boob."

Karen dropped to the sofa and started to put on her hiking boots. They were Pivettas, scratched and scuffed. They had stood in the back of her closet, unworn since the summer she finished her MA four years before, but they felt comfortable and familiar, like good friends from the past— friends with stories of dusty switchbacks, the cool wind of mountain passes, desolate lakes, icy streams, and campfire smoke. She finished lacing them, and slapped her bare knees. "This is gonna be great."

"You're a masochist," Meg said, and stabbed out her cigarette.

"You don't know what you're missing."

"Sure I do. Sack time." She pushed herself off the chair, yawned, and stretched. "Well, have fun if you can."

"Right. See you next Sunday."

"Give my regards to the chipmunks." With a wiggle of her fingers, she turned away and left the room.

Karen glanced at her wristwatch. Five twenty-eight. Leaning back, she stretched out her legs. Her plaid shirt was gaping open at the belly. She fastened the button, then checked the fly of her cutoff corduroys. All set. She yawned. Maybe she should've taken Meg up on that coffee. She inhaled, a deep breath that seemed to fill her whole body with a light, pleasant weariness. As she let it slowly out, she shut her eyes.

A whole week in the mountains with Scott. Kids or no kids, it would be wonderful. They would find time to be alone, if only at night. It'd be cold, and they'd snuggle together with the wind whapping the tent walls. . . .

The blare of the doorbell shocked her awake. She shoved herself off the sofa and hurried to the door. She pulled it open.

Scott, standing under the porch light, smiled at her through the screen.

"Take your *Watchtower* and shove it," she said, and shut the door. When she opened it again, his face was pressed to the screen.

"I want your body," he whispered.

For an instant, face mashed out of shape, he looked like a stranger. Karen felt a tingle of fright. Then he stepped back and was Scott again, handsome and smiling. "Ready for action?" he asked.

"Yep." As she pushed open the screen door, she leaned out and glimpsed his car in the driveway. The headlights were on. The car's interior was dark. "The kids there?" she asked.

"Just barely. It was murder getting Julie out of bed. Benny was raring to go. I'm not sure he even slept last night. Then he decided he couldn't live without his binoculars and we couldn't find the damn things."

"Did you?"

"We did. But it screwed up our departure time."

"You're forgiven."

"Thanks," he said. He took Karen into his arms. He smelled of coffee and aftershave. With his mouth pushing gently against hers, she felt so comfortable that she thought she might doze off. Until his hands went under her shirt. She was wide awake as they moved up her back and under her armpits and closed gently over her breasts. They circled. They caressed. Her nipples stiffened under their touch.

"Think I'll send the kids home," he muttered.

"Mmm. I've missed you."

He kissed her again, hugging her tightly. "We'd better get it in motion. You all packed and ready?"

"All set."

She bent to pick up her backpack. "Allow me," Scott said. As he lifted it, Karen hurried to the coffee table. She grabbed her handbag and floppy felt hat, and followed him out the door.

The morning air wrapped around her bare arms and legs, seeped like chilly water through her shirt. Shivering, she waved at the dim face peering out through the backseat window. In the blue-gray light, she couldn't tell whether it belonged to Julie or Benny.

"You can get in," Scott said.

She shrugged, preferring to wait rather than enter the car without him. They went to the trunk. She stood with her shoulders hunched, arms folded across her chest, legs pressed together, jaw tight to keep her teeth from chattering.

Scott smiled back at her as he unlocked the trunk. "The heater's on."

"The fresh air feels good."

He laughed, and placed her backpack on top of the others. Then he swung the lid shut. "Forget anything?"

"Probably."

He leaned back against the trunk, looking relaxed and warm. Of course, he was wearing long pants and a flannel shirt. "Sunglasses?" he asked.

"Got 'em."

"Jacket?"

"In my pack. Wish I had it on."

"Let's go."

Karen headed for the passenger door, taking her time, waiting until Scott was in the driver's seat before she opened the door. She ducked inside and smiled over the back of her seat. "Morning," she said.

"Hiya, hiya," Benny said, winking one eye in time with the words. He raised a closed hand to his mouth as if holding a microphone. "And a good good morning to you and thanks for tuning in. Have we got a show for you!"

"Can it, Bonzo," Julie said. She gave Karen a quick, tight-lipped smile and turned her face toward the window.

Karen sat down. She pulled her door shut. The heater blew against her legs. She sighed and settled back, enjoying the warmth as Scott backed out of the driveway.

"All right if I drive?" Nick asked.

His father shoved the station wagon's tailgate into place. "Can you keep it under sixty?"

"If you don't care when we get there."

"Well, our ETA's two thirty. I think we can make it without breaking any speed records. You start getting tired, though, let me know."

"Right."

They climbed into the car. Nick started the engine.

His father twisted around. "Any last-minute pit stops?"

"Gross," Heather said from the backseat.

"Vile," said Rose.

"I think we're all set," Mom told him.

"Sunglasses? Hats? Tampax?"

"*Dad!*" the twins blurted in unison.

"Arnold!"

"High altitudes," he said, keeping a straight face. "Bleeding occurs."

"*Nose*bleeds," Rose said.

Heather giggled.

"Whatever," Dad said. "Can't be too careful. 'Be Prepared,' right, Nick?"

"I've got mine."

His father burst out laughing, and slapped his knee.

"I hope you fellows get it out of your systems before we meet the O'Tooles."

"Scott's no prude." He glanced at Nick. "San Diego Freeway. Runs right into 99 just the other side of the Grapevine."

Nick pulled away from the curb.

"Everybody buckled up?"

Near the corner, Nick flipped on the turn signal though no other cars were in sight. With his father beside him, he planned to drive by the book. He slowed almost to a stop before making the turn.

"What's his girlfriend's name?" Mom asked.

"Sharon? *Karen*. Karen something. He ran into her at a Sav-On."

"A checkout girl?"

"No, no, she was in line with him. I think he said she's a teacher."

"Oh, yuck," Rose said.

"What does she look like?"

"A real bow-wow. Floppy ears, hair on her face, a wet nose. Nice tail, though."

"What *do* you know about her?" Mom asked.

"Not much. You know Scott. Keeps his cards close to the vest."

"I hope she plays bridge. June was so fantastic."

"Don't start on her."

"Well, she was."

"I don't think we want to discuss that person in front of the girls."

"I don't know why you're so angry. She didn't run out on *you*."

"My best friend. Same difference. Now I think it would be wise to drop the subject. You have a green arrow," he told Nick.

Nick made the left-hand turn and headed down the freeway on-ramp, embarrassed that he'd let his mind drift away from the driving. In the past, he'd heard a few references to the O'Tooles' breakup, but never anything so close to an argument. He was intrigued. It was none of his business, though. Driving was his business, and he'd better pay attention or his father would take over.

Nick liked to drive. He wished they were taking the Mustang instead of this clunker, but it would've been a tight squeeze with all of them plus five backpacks. Besides, Dad wouldn't want to leave it sitting out in the middle of nowhere for a week. Last year, up at Yosemite, someone had broken a window of the station wagon and had a party inside. They'd come back to find beer cans and a pair of torn, pink panties on the floor.

The break-in had frightened Nick, and he felt uneasy thinking about it now. It was bad enough that some creeps had fooled around in the car, but what if you ran into them on an isolated trail? What if they stumbled onto your camp?

Nothing like that had ever happened to them, but it

could. Nick was glad that the O'Tooles were coming along this year. Like Dad, Scott O'Toole was a big man. If any trouble came up, they'd be able to handle it.

With a feeling of relief, he checked the side mirror, signaled, and slipped into the right-hand lane. He sped up on the overpass. Before it curved over the Santa Monica Freeway, he eased off the accelerator. He picked up speed again on the way down, signaled a left, and drifted across three deserted lanes of the San Diego Freeway.

His father leaned across the seat to check the speedometer. The needle hovered between 55 and 60 miles per hour. With a nod of approval, he settled back. "You get tired, let me know."

Benny leaned forward. "Hey, Karen?" he said to the back of her head. She turned in her seat and looked around at him. Her face, so near to his, made him feel funny—excited and warm and a little embarrassed. He stared at her, forgetting what he'd planned to say.

He'd never seen her from so close. Her eyes were clear blue like the water of the swimming pool. He noticed, for the first time, the light golden hair barely visible above her upper lip. His cousin, Tanya, with dark hair, had more of a mustache there. Hers looked a little gross, but this on Karen looked so soft and fuzzy that he wished he could touch it. Maybe there wasn't even enough to feel, not over her mouth anyway, but it looked a little heavier on her smooth, tanned cheeks.

"Do you know how to get down off an elephant?" he asked.

"No, how?"

"You don't. You get down off a duck."

Karen smiled and shook her head slightly.

Then she turned away. He could no longer see her face. Sitting back, he stared at her. The rim of an ear showed through her hair. He wished she would look around again, but first he would have to think of another joke.

He'd only seen Karen once before today. Usually, his father drove off to meet her. But last Saturday, she came over for barbecued ribs. She'd worn white shorts and a loose shirt of shiny red with green and white flowers, and she'd looked beautiful. When Dad introduced him, she shook his hand and said, "Very nice to meet you, Benny."

She had a pale scar curved like a horseshoe on her forearm. He'd wanted to ask her about it, but didn't have the guts.

That day was overcast, so nobody went into the pool and he didn't get to see her in a swimsuit. She sat across the table from him at dinner. It wasn't dark yet, but his father had lit candles. The light from the flames made her hair shine like gold. He thought she was very nice. Julie acted creepy, though. After dinner, Tanya took him and Julie to a movie. By the time they got home, Karen was gone. Dad said she would be coming along on the camping trip, and Julie went crazy. "What do we need her along for? I don't even like her! I don't want to go if she's going." Dad, looking unhappy, asked why she didn't like Karen. "Oh, never mind!" she snapped.

"I think she's nice," Benny had said.

"So do I," Dad told him.

Sometimes, Julie could be a real jerk.

"Anyone hungry?" Dad asked.

"Me!" Benny said.

Julie shrugged and kept on reading her book.

"Julie?"

"I don't care."

"I could use a bite," Karen said, looking toward Dad. Benny saw the side of her face for a moment before she turned forward again. He sighed. Gosh, she was beautiful.

"Well," Dad said. "We'll be at Gorman in a few minutes. We'll stop there and have some breakfast."

"Look out there," Flash said, keeping his voice calm but pressing a hand to the dashboard as a semi swung into their lane. It was moving up the steep grade toward Tejon Pass at half their speed. They were closing in fast.

Nick slipped over one lane to the left, and sped past the truck.

"Stupid fucking bastard," Flash muttered. He lowered his hand from the dash. Nick was looking nervous. "You all right?"

The boy nodded, and licked his lips.

"That . . . He had no business coming over." Flash took a few deep breaths, and slipped a White Owl from his shirt pocket. His fingers trembled as he tore open the cellophane wrapper. He plugged the cigar into his mouth and lit it, then cranked open his window to let the smoke stream out.

"I tell you, Nick, Vietnam was safer than these freeways. Goddamn truckers. Run you down as soon as look at you. Best thing to do is stay out of their way."

Nick glanced at him. The boy still looked shaky. "Too bad this isn't an F-8," Nick said. "We could blow them off the road."

"Thataboy. I tell you, we did our share of that, Scott and me. Nailed whole convoys along the Ho Chi Minh Trail. Blasted the shit out of 'em."

"Arnold," Alice complained from the backseat. She'd heard that one. He glanced around. The twins were asleep, Rose slumped against the door with Heather leaning against her.

"I'll keep it down," he said in a quiet voice.

"Keep it clean."

He tapped off a length of ash, and took a long draw on his cigar. Smoke swirled around his face. *Smoke filled the cockpit.* "*Blue Leader, this is Flash. Caught a hot one.*"

He shook his head sharply, trying to dislodge the memory as his heart began to thunder and his stomach twisted into an icy coil. Oh, Christ!

The station wagon nosed downward, picking up speed.

"Take it slow," he warned.

Nick looked at him and frowned. "Are you okay, Dad?"

"Sure. Fine." He wiped the sweat from his face. He started remembering again. "Well well well," he said quickly to block off the thoughts. "We're over the hump now. The old buggy made it over the Grapevine once again. Gonna be hot as blue blazes in the valley. Good thing we've got our air-conditioning."

CHAPTER THREE

"I offered 'em down, Ettie."

She gazed at the naked bodies of the young man and woman stretched out side by side in front of the tent. The man was facedown, a terrible wound across the back of his neck. The woman, on her back, was bruised and torn. Ettie saw bite marks on her mouth and chin, on her shoulders and breasts. The left nipple was missing entirely.

"I offered *him* with a hatchet," Merle said, rubbing his hands on the legs of his jeans and trying to smile. "The gal, I plain choked her."

"Looks like you did more than that," Ettie muttered.

"She was pretty."

"Merle, you haven't got the sense of a toadstool."

Her son tugged the bill of his faded Dodgers cap down to hide his eyes. "I'm sorry," he said.

"What're we gonna do with you?"

He shrugged. He toed a pinecone with his tennis shoe. "*You* do it," he argued.

"Only when He speaks to me."

"He spoke to me, Ettie. Honest He did. I never would've done it, but He asked me to."

"You sure you weren't just feeling horny?"

"No, ma'am. He spoke to me."

"I saw you yesterday spying on these two. I was afraid you might pull a stunt like this, but I trusted you, fool that I am. I should've known better." She glared at Merle. The bill of his cap rose for a moment as he looked at her. Then it dipped down again. "What did you promise me?"

"I know," he mumbled. "I *said* I'm sorry."

"What did you promise me?" she repeated.

"Not to do it again without asking."

"But you went ahead and did it anyway."

"Yes, ma'am."

"This is gonna make it hot for us, Merle."

In the shadow of the ball cap, she saw a thin smile. "You just can't take me anywhere."

"Wipe that smile off your face."

"It isn't *that* bad, Ettie. I already looked through their stuff. They didn't have any fire permit."

"So?"

He tipped back the bill, no longer afraid of meeting Ettie's gaze. "If they'd checked in with a ranger, they would've got one and said where they were going. But they didn't. So the rangers don't even know they're here."

"Well, that's something."

"Even if someone knows they're gone, nobody's gonna have the first notion where to look. We'll just bury 'em and take their stuff to the cave, and we'll be okay."

Ettie sighed, folded her arms across her bosom, and stared down at the bodies. "I'll put out a spell to ward off searchers, just in case."

Merle looked doubtful. "Maybe I better."

"I can still conjure circles around you, boy, and don't you forget it. I got us safe out of Fresno, no thanks to you. If you'd had the sense to fetch me what I needed—"

"I was seen."

"Wouldn't have taken you half a minute," she said. Merle stood silent, watching as she knelt beside the man's body. She untied a leather pouch from her belt and opened it. "Never should've taught you the Ways."

"Don't say that, Ettie."

"Made us no end of trouble." She wrapped her fingers

around a lock of hair, and yanked it from the man's scalp. She pressed the hair into the raw gorge at the back of his neck. Thick blood coated the strands. She twisted them into a string, knotted them once in the center, and poked them into her pouch. Then she lifted his hand. The fingernails were chewed to the quick. She unsheathed her knife, pressed the blade to the cuticle of his index finger, and removed the entire nail. She dropped it into her pouch and stepped over to the woman.

Squatting beside the body, she ripped out a ringlet of hair. She squeezed the breast to force more blood to the surface, and dabbed the hair in it. She tied the sticky cord into a knot. She flicked it into her pouch, then picked up a hand. The plum fingernail polish was chipped. One nail was broken, but the rest were long and neatly rounded. She pared off the tips of four, catching them in her palm, and brushed them into her bag.

"Now, that's all there is to it," she said, looking up at Merle. "Wouldn't have taken you half a minute, and I could've laid down a dandy spell and we'd still be in Fresno today. You didn't even have to take blood. If you'd just had the good sense to bring me hair and nails, I'd have had the essence to throw a cover on us."

"I like it here fine," he mumbled.

"Well, I don't." Her knees crackled as she straightened up. "I like my creature comforts, Merle. I like a good meal and a cold beer and nice clothes and a soft bed."

"And men," he added, showing a sliver of a smile.

"That's the truth." She pushed her knife into its sheath at the side of her dress, and started tying the pouch to her belt. "You deprived me of all that 'cause you were horny and careless."

"I told you, Ettie. He spoke to me."

She didn't believe him. "Don't go laying off your blame, Merle. Now, you take care of the burying and bring up their things to the cave. I'll come along and check before sundown, and I want to see this place looking like nobody was ever here. Do you understand?"

"Yes, ma'am."

"And if you ever offer down again without my say-so, you'll be the sorriest young man that ever walked on two legs."

He looked down at his feet. "Yes, ma'am."

Leaving him there, Ettie made her way along the rock-bound shore. At the narrow, southern tip of the lake where its feeder stream splashed down from Upper Mesquite, she crouched and cupped water to her mouth. Even after spending a month up here, she still couldn't get over the cold, fresh taste of it. Hard to believe that water could be so fine. She knew she would miss it in September, when they had to leave. Wouldn't miss anything else, though: not the heat steaming off the rocks, or the mosquitoes, or the wind that tore around at night so loud it often kept her awake, or the cold when the sun went down, or the hard ground she slept on. She'd be glad to leave all that behind. Not the water, though.

She unsnapped the canvas bag of her canteen, and pulled out the aluminum bottle. After twisting off its cap, she upended it. The old water burbled out. She held the empty canteen under a lip of mossy rock, gripping it tightly as fresh water washed over her hand. When the bottle overflowed, she capped it, then slipped it back into the case. It felt heavy and good against her hip as she stood up.

Staying close to the stream, she climbed up pale, broken slabs of granite to the ridge between the two lakes. She turned slowly, scanning the slopes that rose high above her. Then she peered toward the trail slanting down from Carver Pass beyond the northern end of Lower Mesquite. Once every few days, backpackers hiked by. Until yesterday, when those two stayed and camped, Merle had been just fine.

Blast Merle. Damn and shit!

The trail was deserted now. More than likely, if anyone

should show up today, it wouldn't be till the afternoon. The pass was a hard, three-hour climb from the nearest lake to the east, so Merle should have plenty of time to take care of the mess. Besides, there was the spell. . . .

Stepping onto a flat surface of rock, Ettie unbuckled her belt with all its gear. She set it at her feet and opened the buttons of her faded, shapeless dress. She pulled the dress up over her head. Except for her heavy socks and boots, she was naked. She felt the sun on her skin, the caress of soft breezes. The air smelled hot. It smelled of scorched pine needles, of baking rock.

Bending over, she spread her dress across the granite. Then she sat on it. Through the thin layers of fabric, the rock felt hard and rough. The heat seeped through, stinging her buttocks as she removed her boots and damp socks.

When they were off, she untied the leather pouch from her belt. She crossed her legs and sat upright, with her back arched, her head straight forward. With both hands, she clasped the pouch to her breastbone.

"Into darkness," she whispered, "I commit the essence of my foes. As their essence is obscured, so let all traces of their presence be banished from this canyon, that those who seek them might find no cause to trespass here."

Lowering her head, she opened the drawstrings of the pouch. She pulled out a bloody lock of hair and placed it into her mouth. She chewed slowly, working it into a sodden clump, and swallowed it. She did the same with the second coil of hair. She washed them down with water from her canteen. Then she dumped the fingernails onto her palm, raised them to her lips, and ate them. She drank some more water.

The rock was rough and hot through her dress. The hair felt thick and heavy in her stomach.

But she was done.

She smiled. She raised the canteen and poured its cold water over her head. It streamed down her face, her shoulders. It rolled down her back. It spilled over her breasts, dripped from her nipples, ran down her belly and sides. Moving the canteen, she let the water fall onto her crossed legs, her groin. She sighed at its icy touch.

Too soon the canteen was empty.

She stared at the glinting blue of Upper Mesquite. Why not? She deserved a treat. Leaving everything, she skipped over the searing rocks to the shore. She waded in, shivering and gasping, and hesitated only a moment before plunging headlong.

CHAPTER FOUR

They stopped at a gas station in Fresno. Rolling down his window, Julie's father asked the teenaged attendant to "fill her up with super unleaded and check under the hood."

With the window open, heat rushed into the car. Julie fanned her face with her book.

"Guess I'll make a pit stop," Karen said.

"Me, too," said Benny.

They both climbed out.

"Julie?" Dad asked.

"I'll wait till they're back." She watched them walk through the glaring sunlight toward the side of the station. Benny was smiling up at the woman, grinning and talking.

"Benny seems to really like Karen," Dad said.

"I noticed." The two disappeared around a corner of the garage.

"I think you'd like her, too, if you gave her half a chance."

"What have I done?" Julie blurted.

"It's your attitude."

"I can't help it if I'm not crazy about her. What am I supposed to do, worship the ground she walks on?"

"There's no call for sarcasm."

"*I* didn't ask her to come with us."

"Well, *I* did, and I'd appreciate it if you'd get your act together. You've been miserable all morning."

"I am miserable." Her throat tightened. She suddenly felt as if she might start blubbering.

Dad looked around at her. "What's the matter, honey?" he asked in a gentle voice.

"Nothing," she mumbled.

"What is it?"

"I don't see why I even had to come." Tears filled her eyes. She stared out the window at the gas pumps. "I should've stayed home with Tanya. You don't want me here anyway."

"Of course I do."

"No you don't. You've got Karen. You don't need Benny and me."

"Look, if I'd wanted to be alone with Karen, would I have insisted you come with us? I could've left you home easily enough, but I wanted you and Benny along. Hell, it wouldn't be half as much fun without you two. Now come on, buck up, old girl. Let's see a smile."

Julie wiped her eyes, but didn't try to smile.

"Come on."

The squeak of a squeegee drew her eyes to the young attendant. He was grinning down at her through the passenger window as he scraped away the dirty water.

"Here they come," Dad told her. "Why don't you go on ahead?"

With a nod, she opened her door. She slid out and stepped toward the rear of the car.

"It's around back," Karen said as they passed.

"Thanks." Walking away, she glanced over her shoulder. The boy at the windshield met her eyes. She smiled at him, and continued on her way.

The heat brought sweat to her forehead. She wondered if the boy was watching, admiring the way she looked in her T-shirt and tight white shorts.

The restroom was shadowy and stifling. She quickly relieved herself. At the sink, she splashed tepid water onto her face and looked at herself in the mirror. Her eyes were rimmed with red from crying. Her hair was slightly mussed. She wished she'd brought her brush along. She combed her fingers through her hair and patted the swept-back sides.

Her T-shirt looked loose and baggy. Opening her shorts again, she pulled it down firmly and tucked it in. She looked down at herself. The shirt was taut over her breasts, emphasizing them. The white lace of her bra was clearly visible through the stretched fabric.

She smiled at her reflection. She winked at herself. Then she stepped out of the restroom into the glaring sunlight.

The car was still at the pumps, but the boy was gone. She spotted him through the windows of the office. At the car, she put her hands on the sill of Karen's open window and looked in. "Dad, could we get some Cokes or something?"

"Yeah!" Benny said.

"Sure. Why not?" Dad shifted his weight to reach for the wallet in his back pocket.

"Let me," Karen said. "My treat."

"No," Dad said. "That's—"

"I insist." She took a billfold from her handbag. After a moment of searching, she said, "I guess I don't have any change," and gave Julie a five-dollar bill. "Why don't you pick up some chips or something, if they've got 'em?"

"I'll come with you," Benny said, and burst from the car.

"What'll you have, Dad?"

"Root beer or Coke."

"Karen?"

The woman smiled at her. "Mountain Dew, or Dr. Pepper. If they haven't got one of those, a cola'd be fine."

Benny raced ahead of her to the office, and planted himself in front of the soft-drink vending machine. Julie, feeling a flutter of anticipation, took a deep breath and entered. "Hi," she said to the boy behind the desk.

He got to his feet and swept a hank of brown hair away from his forehead. "Hi. Can I help you?"

Julie held the bill out to him. "Could we have some change for your machines?"

He smiled. "Sure thing." He leaned over the desk. As he reached out, his eyes lowered from Julie's face to her breasts to her extended arm. He took the money. "You'll be wanting quarters," he said. He broke a fresh roll of them into the open drawer of the cash register. The patch above his shirt pocket read TIM. "Are you from around here?" he asked.

"From Los Angeles. We're on our way to the mountains."

"Yeah? Camping?"

"We'll be backpacking out of Black Butte."

"No kidding? I've been there. That's real nice country." He counted out quarters, and dropped them four at a time into Julie's palm, his fingers sometimes brushing her.

"Thank you, Tim."

He beamed, and nodded.

Turning away, Julie gave the coins to Benny. "Here, you get the stuff. You know what everybody wants?"

"Sure." With the quarters clutched in his hand, he stepped up close to the soft-drink dispenser. Julie went back to Tim.

"Do you work here all the time?" she asked.

"Whenever I can. My dad's the owner."

"Don't you get awfully hot?"

"Oh, you get used to it."

"I don't think I would."

"It's not so bad." He stepped around the desk and sat on its edge. "You've got a nice tan," he said, looking at her legs.

"Thanks."

"I bet you go to the beach a lot, being in Los Angeles and everything."

"Yeah." She considered explaining about their backyard swimming pool. Tim might think she was bragging, though. "I really like the ocean," she said.

"We've got the river," he said, "and some lakes. I'll go over to Millerton or Pine Flat. They aren't far. We take the boat over when—" The double ring of a bell interrupted him. He peered out the window. A pickup was rolling to a stop beside the pumps. With a sigh of disappointment that pleased Julie, he pushed himself off the desk. "Well, I've gotta go. Have a good trip, now. Stop in on your way back if you get a chance."

"Okay. 'Bye, Tim."

He left the office. On his way toward the pickup, he looked over his shoulder and waved. Julie waved back.

Benny had set the four soft-drink cans on the floor to free his hands. He punched a number on the snack machine. Inside the display window, a clamp opened, dropping a small pack of barbecued potato chips into a trough.

Julie picked up the chilly, wet cans. Benny gathered up four packs of chips and Fritos. Together, they left the office.

At her door, Julie watched Tim lift the hood of the pickup. "So long," she called.

"Stop by again," he said.

Then she climbed into the car. She passed around the drinks, poured the remaining change into Karen's hand, and thanked her.

As they pulled away, she looked out the rear window. Tim was wiping a dipstick with a red rag.

"He seemed like a nice young fellow," Dad said.

"His father owns the station," Julie said.

"Oh? Checked him out, did you?"

"I didn't 'check him out.' We were just talking, that's all."

"Baloney and liver sausage," Benny said.

"He looked like he was about Nick's age," Dad told her.

"Nick?"

"Flash's son. You remember him? The company picnic?"

"Unh-uh."

"Well, that was about five or six years ago. I think you ran the three-legged race with him."

"Oh, *him*." She smiled. "We won that. He's Mr. Gordon's son?"

"Yep. He's seventeen now."

"Oh, yeah?" Maybe this wouldn't turn out to be such a rotten vacation after all.

"Ow!" Heather cried, clutching the back of her hand.

"Rose, play nice."

"I didn't hit her hard."

Alice Gordon gave her daughter a warning scowl. She considered calling a stop to the game, but Heather had already hidden her hand behind her back, ready to continue.

"One, two, three," Rose said. Her open hand darted out.

Heather, at the same instant, swung her hand into view with two fingers extended. "Aha! Scissors cut paper!"

Rose presented her hand. Heather slapped it hard, getting even.

"Didn't hurt," Rose taunted.

They got ready for another match. "One, two, three," Rose said.

Heather came out with scissors again. As Rose's flat hand swung forward, it closed into a fist. "Rock breaks scissors," she declared.

"No fair!" Heather cried out. "You cheated. Didn't she, Mom? You saw her! She was paper!"

Nick looked around from the passenger seat. "Is Rose cheating again?"

"Yes!" Heather blurted.

"I think we've had enough of this game," Alice said. "Why don't you find something nice to play? Twenty Questions or Hangman."

"I get to slap her!" Heather protested. "She was paper!"

"No more slapping."

"But I won!"

"Kids!" Arnold snapped. He was driving and didn't look back. "Do as your mother says."

"But, Daaaad!"

"You heard me."

Heather sighed as if the world were unfair. She narrowed her eyes at Rose. "Cheater."

With a long-suffering smile, Rose offered her hand. "Go ahead and give it to me."

"Mom, can I?"

"Oh, I don't care. Just once, then I want you both to find something better to do."

Heather slapped downward. Rose's hand shot out from

under the path of the blow, and smacked the back of Heather's descending hand. "Hey!"

Rose laughed. So did Nick. Heather punched her sister's knee.

"That's enough!" Alice snapped. "Stop it!"

"I think I'll pull over and tan some hides," Arnold said.

"No!" Heather yelped.

"We'll be good," Rose said. "Promise."

"All right then. Now, do as your mother says and play something nice."

"Better yet," Nick said, "take a nap."

Rose rolled her eyes upward. "Are we almost there yet?"

"A couple more hours," Arnold told her.

The idea of a nap certainly appealed to Alice. She took the pillow from the space between her and Heather, fluffed it up, and placed it behind her head. Snuggling back against it, she closed her eyes. In quiet voices, the twins were discussing whether to play Hangman. She heard a rustle of paper. Good. That should keep them out of mischief for ten or fifteen minutes.

She wondered if Arnold had remembered to set the lamp timer before they left. No point bothering to ask, though. If he'd forgotten, it was too late now.

Her mind drifted to the last time she'd seen Scott O'Toole. They'd gone over for dinner and bridge. Scott had complimented her on her perm. That must've been over a year ago, closer to two. How could June walk out on a man like him? Must be more to it than meets the eye. Maybe he was fooling around on the side. Sure had plenty of opportunity, being away half the time. And those flight attendants. Everyone knows how they are. June was no slouch, not by any stretch of the imagination, but a guy like Scott'd be a real prize for lonely stews. A lot of temptation there. Take a strong man to resist.

Thank God Arnold stopped flying. He might have to work nights when the shift bid didn't go his way, but at least he came home to his own bed and wasn't alone in hotels all across the country. Would've been nice for him to have a pilot's pay and prestige, but she'd rather have him as he is. They got by just fine, thank you, and she didn't have to spend all her time worrying.

Poor June must've been worried sick, wondering if he'd go down or get himself shacked up with some stew. Who was that—Jack?—no, Jake. Jake Peterson. Had a whole second family in Pittsburgh. Must've come as quite a shock to his wife—*both* wives. Wasn't even a Mormon, not that that would've made it right, but ... Alice's thoughts slipped away as sleep overtook her.

The road up the mountainside had once been paved, but winter snow, spring runoff, and summer sun had broken up the asphalt, leaving a dusty shambles. The car bounced over ruts and potholes as Scott steered slowly up the grade.

Ahead, a Volkswagen appeared around a bend.

"What now?" Karen asked.

"He's small." Scott eased the car to the right until branches squeaked against its side. He stopped.

"Hope he's careful," Karen said. She was gripping the armrest.

"If he's not," Scott told her, "he'll have a very thrilling ride for a few seconds."

A girl in the passenger seat of the VW had her head out the window. She was looking down, apparently contemplating just such a ride. From her perspective, Scott imagined that the sheer drop-off must look bottomless. After a moment, she pulled her head in and said something to the driver.

The VW crawled closer. The young bearded man behind the wheel grinned at Scott as he inched alongside. "Lovely day," he said.

"Yep," Scott agreed. "How far to Black Butte?"

"Take you an hour."

"The road get any better up ahead?"

"No. Tell you what, though, there's an RV about a mile behind me."

"Thanks for the warning."

"Have a good one, friend."

"You, too."

The Volkswagen finished passing, took to the center of the narrow road, and sped off with a cloud of dust.

"A camper?" Karen asked. She looked sick.

"What'll we do?" Julie asked from the back.

"I guess we'd do well to find a wider place in the road before he shows up."

"No sweat. Right, Dad?" Benny asked.

"No sweat," he said, and pulled away. He drove slowly, looking for a place to turn out. Ahead, the road bent back in an uphill hairpin. He took the curve. Now *they* were on the outside, the slope dropping away sharply to the right. "Maybe a little sweat," Scott admitted. He picked up speed. The car lurched and jarred as it rushed up the grade.

Should've played it safe, he thought. Should've stopped back at the bend. But now he was committed. What he could see of the road ahead didn't look good. The mountainside rose up steeply to the left, leaving no room for turning out. To the right, there was no more than a yard's width before the ground fell away. Even if he parked at the very edge, he doubted there would be room for a recreational vehicle to squeeze through.

"What'll we do?" Karen asked.

"If worse comes to worst, we can always back up."

"Oh, wonderful."

Scott's foot jumped off the accelerator as the camper came down the center of the road straight at them. In a reflexive move, he pulled at the wheel as if to raise the nose and shoot above the oncoming vehicle. His car remained earthbound. He stepped on the brake, and eased to a halt.

The camper moved over close to the mountain's wall and

stopped, blocking two thirds of the road. An arm poked through the driver's window. It waved Scott forward.

"Can you make it?" Karen asked.

"Sure," he said. "Just to be on the safe side, though, I want you out." He looked over his shoulder. "Everybody out."

"I'm not scared," Benny said.

"No arguments."

With a sigh, Benny opened his door. When he, Julie, and Karen were outside the car, Scott unbuckled his seat belt. The trio walked ahead of him, Karen nodding and speaking to the man behind the wheel. At the rear of the camper, they stopped and turned around to watch. Karen straddled the road's edge, her eyes fixed on his right front tire. Her lips were drawn back in a grimace. She wiped her hands on the sides of her corduroy shorts.

This must be really bad for her, Scott thought as he inched forward. Karen knows no one's immune to an accident. She'd barely escaped death in a car crash three years before, and her fiancé had been killed.

With the fingers of his left hand curled around the door lever, he steered alongside the camper. He watched its gleaming side as he slid past it, no more than an inch away. If the car should start to tip, he realized, he wouldn't be able to get his door open.

Not at first anyway. He might find an instant, though, just before the car slipped over the edge.

He glanced at Karen. Her hand was covering her mouth. Benny looked relaxed. Julie was squatting down, hands on knees, staring at the tire.

Ice fishing when he was a kid, Scott drove out on the frozen Saint Lawrence River with his father. Sometimes, the ice creaked and groaned under the weight of the pickup truck. They always kept their doors open for quick escapes. Everyone did, driving on the river. Everyone but fools.

He wished he had his door open now. A little precaution like that could save a man's life.

The front of his car was even with the rear of the camper. He fought an urge to speed up, and kept to a steady crawl until he cleared the vehicle. Then he swung to the left and stopped in the road's center.

Benny climbed in first. "Boy, Dad, that was really close."

"A piece of cake," he said, and backhanded the sweat off his upper lip.

"Hope we don't have to go through *that* again," Julie said.

Karen slumped in the passenger seat with her knees against the dash. She stared straight ahead. Her lips were a tight line.

Reaching out, Scott rubbed the side of her neck. "You okay?"

"I guess," she muttered.

After another traverse, the road curved around the mountainside to a high, wooded valley. A weathered sign, caught in a patch of sunlight, read BLACK BUTTE RANGER STATION, 6 MI.

CHAPTER FIVE

The forest, pressing in close on both sides of the unpaved road, opened up. Karen saw two cars ahead, parked under trees. One, a dusty Mazda resting at a rakish angle, had a rock at the base of each rear tire to keep it from rolling.

"Guess we beat them to it," Scott said.

"What do they drive?" Karen asked.

"Probably the Plymouth station wagon."

Karen imagined a station wagon trying to squeeze past the RV on the thin strand of road along the mountain slope, and her stomach tightened.

Scott swung off to the left. He pulled forward slowly, the tires crunching over fallen limbs and pinecones. He parked with the bumper close to an aspen, and shut off the engine. "Let's leave everything here for now, and check out the ranger station. We can pick up our fire permit while we're waiting."

They climbed out of the car. After the air-conditioning, the heat outside felt stifling to Karen. But the air smelled sweet, and a soft breeze stirred the trees. She took a deep breath. She stretched, arching her stiff back, sighing with pleasure as her muscles strained. Then she followed Benny around the rear of the car, the thick mat of leaves and pine needles springy under her boots. "This is really wonderful," she said, joining Scott and Julie.

"Warm," Scott said. He took off his flannel shirt, rolled it up, and tossed it into the trunk. His T-shirt was tight across his chest, with a slight rip at the shoulder seam. "Well, let's see if we can scout up a ranger."

They walked alongside the tire tracks toward a small log cabin in the clearing ahead. A Jeep was parked close to the cabin's side. The snort of a horse drew Karen's eyes to a corral at the left, where a man in a uniform was currying a brown stallion. "That's probably the ranger," she said.

They walked toward the corral. The man saw them and waved. He slapped the horse's haunch, tossed aside the curry brush, and climbed over the fence. "Hello there," he called in an eager voice. "Hope I didn't keep you waiting. I was out on the trails, just got back."

"No," Scott said, "we just arrived ourselves."

"Well, that's good." He smiled at Karen and Julie, winked at Benny. He looked to be barely twenty, with short blond hair and cheerful eyes. Though he wore a badge on his uniform shirt, he was unarmed and had a casual manner that put Karen at ease. "Come on over to the office," he said. "We'll take care of your wilderness permit and get you on your way."

They followed him toward the cabin.

"Where you folks from?" he asked.

"Los Angeles," Scott told him.

"Dad's a pilot," Benny said, looking proud.

"Oh? What do you fly?"

"L1011s, mostly."

"No fooling? The big birds. My old man's a crop duster. He flies a replica of an old Fokker DR-1. The triplane?"

"Sure. Von Richthofen. The Flying Circus."

"Yeah. My old man calls himself the Green Baron. He works out of Bakersfield."

"Sometimes I wish I had three wings," Scott said, stepping onto the porch after him.

"All that airfoil, he can glide for miles. Sometimes has to."

They entered the dim, shadowy cabin. The young man

stepped behind a counter near the door. On the wall was a huge topographical map of the area. A poster of Smokey the Bear hung over a two-way radio. Benny nudged Karen's arm, and pointed to a rifle rack on the wall across from them.

"Whereabouts are you heading?" the ranger asked.

"We're hoping to make it over to the Triangle Lakes area."

"Some good fishing up there. Here's an *Angler's Guide* for you," he said, and spread open a leaflet on the countertop. "This map's a bit sketchy."

"We'll be meeting some friends. They've got topogs of the area."

"Fine. This one'll give you a nice overview, but it's weak on detail. You've got a nasty ridge here, for instance." He tapped his ballpoint against a bare spot on the map. "Looks like an easy jaunt from Wilson to Round, but don't you believe it. It'd take an hour of hard climbing. The topogs'll take care of that for you."

He tapped the counter three inches from the bottom edge of the map. "Okay. You're about here. You'll want to take the Juniper Lake trail. It's two miles to Juniper." As he scribbled directions on an edge of the map, he said, "That'd be a fine place to spend the night. Some nice campsites all around it. When you head out of there, you just follow the trail you came in on. It branches out at the head of the lake, and there's a marker there for Triangle Lakes. You just stay on it, all the way. Here's where it comes onto the map." He drew a line along the trail. He circled a lake. "This is Tully. It's beautiful, has a real nice waterfall at the western end. Just a couple of miles farther, you've got Lake Parker. They're a good day's hike from Juniper. I'd stick to one or the other if I were you. Once you leave Parker behind, you've got Carver Pass to look forward to. You'll want to be fresh when you tackle that. It's a good three- or four-hour climb, takes you up to eleven thousand feet."

"Yuck," said Julie.

The ranger grinned at her. "About halfway up, if you're like most folks, you'll start wishing you were back home watching a ball game." He marked zigzags on the map. "You've got switchbacks you think'll never quit."

"I'm already exhausted," Karen said, "just hearing about it."

"A great view from the top," he told her. "And a good, cool wind." He lowered his eyes to the map. "Right here, on the down side, you'll run into the Mesquite Lakes. I don't recommend you bother with those. You'll know what I mean when you see them."

"The pits?" Julie asked.

"That's exactly what they are." He drew his line along the trail. "Wilson's just an easy three miles beyond the Mesquites, and it's fabulous. Wooded, good campsites." He circled Lake Wilson. "From there, you've got an easy shot to the Triangles. Get an early start from Wilson, and you should be there by noon."

"Sounds terrific," Scott said.

"Shall I put you down for Juniper, Parker, Wilson, and the Triangles?"

"Fine by me."

He took out a form and began to fill in the information. "So, we've got you into the Triangles on night four. How long will you stay there?"

"We'll want to be within an easy hike of here by next Sunday. Maybe spend Saturday night back at Juniper."

The ranger marked it down. "If you want to see some new scenery, you can make a circle by following the Postpile trail south out of the Triangles." He marked the trail, describing the lakes along the way, explaining that the return route was shorter and mostly downhill.

"So, we'll figure on two nights at the Triangles, then a night at Rabbit Ears, a night at Lake Tobash, and then back to Juniper. Should be a fine trip." The ranger reversed the permit form and pushed it toward Scott. "Would you please read this and fill out the rest?"

Scott studied the sheet. He wrote his name and address, and the number of people in his party. He signed it, and paid the permit fee. The ranger tore off a section and gave it to him.

"Okay, you're all set." He pointed at the screen door. "About a hundred yards that way, you can pick up the trail."

"Thanks for all your help," Scott said.

"That's what I'm here for. Have a real good trip."

They all thanked him and left the cabin.

"Well," Karen said. "That was painless."

"The pain starts when we put our packs on."

"He was neat," Benny blurted. "Did you see those neat rifles?"

"He had a nice Winchester in that rack," Scott said.

"Do you suppose he lives up here all the time?" Julie asked.

"Should've asked him."

She shrugged.

"I imagine he goes down before the snow closes the road."

"It's probably beautiful here in winter," Karen said.

"Yeah, at Christmas," Benny added. Hurrying ahead of the others, he turned around and walked backward. He raised his hands like a choir leader. " 'Dash-in' through the snooow,' " he started to sing, waving his arms.

"Forget it, Mitch," Julie muttered.

He ignored her and continued to sing until she hurled a pinecone at him. It bounced off his shirt. Laughing, he whirled away and ran the final distance to the car.

"He's so juvenile," Julie said, as if to herself.

Scott smiled. "Must run in the family." He patted Karen's back. "Do you think you can stand this for a week?"

"No sweat," she said.

When they reached the car, Scott opened the trunk and lifted out a pack. His T-shirt rode up as he crouched to set the pack down. Karen glanced at the revealed strip of bare skin and the band of his jockey shorts. She remembered Meg's remark, *Hope you're not planning to screw the guy.* We'll see, she thought, we'll see.

He took out the other packs and propped them upright against the rear bumper. He handed Karen her floppy felt hat. She put it on, and turned up the front brim.

"Gabby Hayes," Scott said.

"Gee, thanks."

As he opened the top of his Kelty bag to put his shirt away, Karen heard a car engine. She looked up the shadowy road. A station wagon appeared, bouncing over the ruts.

"Is it them?" Benny asked.

"Yep," Scott said. "Looks like they made it."

The driver, a broad-faced, florid man with a bald crown and a red fringe of hair over his ears, pulled in beside them and stopped. "How'd you beat us up here?" he asked as he climbed out.

"Sheer skill," Scott told him.

They shook hands.

"Karen, this is Arnold Gordon."

"Call me Flash," he said.

"Nice to meet you," Karen said, and shook his big hand.

The others climbed from the car: a thin teenaged boy with his father's freckles and a full head of red hair; a short, rather chubby woman with a pixie haircut; two slim girls, maybe ten years old. Though twins, the girls were dressed differently; one wore her blonde hair in pigtails, while the other had a ponytail. That should help me keep them straight, Karen thought.

Scott and Flash introduced everybody around. Karen repeated the names to herself, and called up associations to help her memory. Flash Gordon was easy. Nick was Nick Adams of "The Big Two-Hearted River," a Hemingway story she'd taught last year. Alice was a toughy. Alice, mal-ice, phallus—no, no. Well, she'd have to work on that one. Rose and Heather, flowers. Careful you don't call them

Tulip and Dandelion. "My Wild Irish Rose," Scottish heather. Remember, Rose has the ponytail. Rosy pony. *The Red Pony.* That should do it.

". . . three-legged race at the picnic," Julie was saying to Nick.

"Oh, I remember that," he said, blushing. "And the egg toss."

"Sure. It broke all over you."

With a nod, he excused himself and turned away to help his father unload the car. The entire family had matching red Kelty packs: two huge ones like Scott's, a slightly smaller one for Alice, and a pair of child-size packs for the girls.

"Arnold tells me you're a schoolteacher," Alice said.

"Yes, that's right. High school."

"Our Nick's quite the student. He makes straight A's in math and science."

"That's very good."

"I was at the top of the class in math myself when I was in high school. Of course, that was a long time ago. I planned to be a teacher, too, but then Arnold came along and I never got around to finishing college." The challenging look in her eyes made Karen uncomfortable. Did she expect a reprimand for giving up school?

"From the looks of your children," Karen said, "you made the right choice."

The hardness left Alice's eyes, and she smiled. "Well, thank you."

"We've already secured the fire permit," Scott told Flash.

"They got a head around here?"

Scott pointed to an outhouse nestled in the shadows of trees a short distance away. "All right, gang, let's hit the facility. Enjoy it, ladies. It'll be your last look at a toilet seat for the next week."

Alice made a face at him.

"Gross," said Rose of the ponytail.

Benny met Karen's eyes. He looked amused.

The entire group started toward the stone building.

"Is it all right to leave the gear over there?" Nick asked his father.

"Who's around to meddle with it?"

"How was your trip up?" Scott asked.

"That one-lane death trap was a bitch. Poor Alice, she nearly laid an egg. Did you happen to run into a camper the size of a bus?"

"Did we."

"I had to back halfway down the mountain to let it by. A real bitch."

"Wasn't much fun," Scott agreed.

Nick watched Julie waiting by the outhouse. Soon the twins came out, and she pushed in. When the door banged shut behind her, Nick turned away. He looked toward the two cars to make sure nobody was tampering with the packs.

There was no one in sight. For all he knew, the valley was deserted except for the nine of them and the ranger. But somebody had to belong to those other two cars, so it couldn't hurt to keep an eye on the equipment.

The last time he'd seen Julie she was just a skinny kid, a tomboy. Now she had breasts and everything. She was as cute as any cheerleader at Samo, and she would be camping with him for a whole week.

The thought of that made Nick very nervous. If only she were plain, or fat, or even ugly, he might be at ease with her and they'd have a good time. How could he manage to be himself, though, with someone like Julie around?

She would probably spend the whole week ignoring him.

Probably goes steady with a football player. Messes around a lot, too. Girls like her always do. Just not with guys like me.

Who needs her?

Behind Nick, the door banged. He looked around. Julie was striding toward her father, her long legs slender and tanned, her hands flat inside the front pockets of her shorts, the white of her bra visible through her T-shirt. She glanced at Nick, but looked away quickly. Her hair bounced and swayed as she walked.

"Don't wear your eyes out," his father said, coming up behind him.

Nick's face grew hot. "I won't," he muttered.

They headed for the car, walking well behind the others. "She sure is something to look at."

"She's all right."

"All right, my ass. She's a knockout, and you know it. Now if I was in your shoes, I'd be right in there striking up an acquaintance."

"Yeah, well . . ."

"You don't want her thinking you're stuck up."

"I'm not stuck up."

Approaching the car, Nick watched Julie pick up her backpack. She lifted it by the straps and swung it onto the trunk of her father's Olds Cutlass. Balancing it there, she turned around. Her eyes met Nick's for a moment, as if to make sure he was watching. Then she leaned back, hooking one arm through a strap, twisting, slipping her other arm into place. She leaned forward. The pack tipped against her. She stood up straight; the pull of the straps drew her shoulders back. Nick found himself staring at her breasts, which seemed more prominent than before.

He turned away to put on his own backpack. When he looked again at Julie, she was wearing aviator sunglasses and a red beret that made her seem like some kind of commando.

That's a sharp hat, he could tell her. Sharp? She'll think I'm a turkey. An awesome hat. That's better. But he didn't say it. Instead, he picked up his walking stick.

"Hey," Julie said, "is that a real blackthorn stick?" She walked toward him.

Blushing, he nodded.

"Can I see it?"

He handed it to her.

"Hey, this is nice." She ran her hands along its polished, knobby shaft.

"I got it in Ireland."

"Really? We've been there. Where did you buy it?"

"Some gift shop near Blarney Castle."

"No kidding? We were there. Benny got a shillelagh at that place. Blarney Handicrafts?"

"Yeah, that's the place."

She returned his stick.

"Did you kiss the Blarney Stone?" she asked.

"Sure."

"How about the stairs going up there?"

"Pretty hairy."

She laughed. "Kissing the stone was a cinch after those stairs. Did you get the gift of gab?"

"I'm not sure it worked on me."

"Let's get this show on the road," Dad called.

Julie stayed beside Nick as they walked over to join the rest of the group. With Mr. O'Toole and Dad in the lead, they hiked across a meadow. Ahead, Nick saw a wooden trail sign.

"Have you ever been up in this area?" Julie asked.

"Not around here. We've been into Mineral King, Yosemite, lots of places. Parts of the John Muir Trail. How about you?"

She shook her head, making her blonde hair sway. "I think it's really neat to go where you haven't been before."

"Yeah, like exploring."

"And you never know what you'll find."

They reached the trail, a wide dusty track leading into the forest. The sign beside it read JUNIPER LAKE, 2 MI.

"If it's all right with everybody," Mr. O'Toole said, "we'll stop there for the night."

"Fine by me," Dad said.

The arrow pointed to the left. They started to walk. The straps felt snug on Nick's shoulders. The pack, though heavy, rode easily on his back. He took a deep breath. The hot air smelled of dust, and flowers, and pine, and he caught a hint of perfume from Julie. She stayed beside him as they walked.

She's not so bad after all, he thought. This could turn out good.

Chapter Six

Ettie's leg muscles trembled from the strain of squatting. Finally, she straightened up. She looked at what she'd done. With both hands, she scooped up loose soil. She sprinkled it onto the pile of her feces. "Into the dirt," she said, "I commit the essence of my foes. As their essence is obscured, so let all traces of their presence be banished from this canyon, that those who seek them might find no cause to trespass here."

She brushed her hands on her dress.

"That'll do it," she muttered.

She backed out of the crevice and sat on a block of granite. This high on the slope, she was still in sunlight. The shadow was not far below, creeping slowly upward as the sun sank closer to the opposite ridge.

There was already a nice breeze. It made her sweaty dress feel cool. Raising her arms, she let the breeze chill her sodden armpits.

Merle appeared, off to the right, mounting the crest of the small ridge that separated the lakes. He wore one blue backpack, and carried another. As Ettie watched, he started climbing the shadowy slope. He didn't get far before abandoning the pack in his arms. With the other still on his back, he made his way higher, leaving the shade behind. He clambered over boulders, scurried up steep granite slabs, and finally vanished. From where Ettie sat, it looked as if he'd stepped through solid rock. She couldn't see the fissure that led into their cave.

A few moments later, Merle reappeared. He sprang down the slope, going to retrieve the second pack.

Though still angry with him, Ettie had to admit she looked forward to checking out the booty. If the couple's tent was any indication, they'd come well equipped. Probably had a camp stove and a couple of nice sleeping bags at least. A stove would come in real handy. Wouldn't put up smoke like the cook fires they sometimes built in the cave. And their ratty old sleeping bags weren't much good against the night's cold. There'd be food, too. Probably enough to keep them going for a few more days anyway. They'd been talking about another raid on campers over by Lake Wilson, just to snatch some food, but there was always the danger of giving themselves away, pulling stunts like that, so it was good not to try it too often.

In spite of the advantages, she wished Merle would learn to control himself. He was just like his father that way. Poor man got a taste of the power, and just couldn't stop. Took a policeman's bullet to stop him. She should've learned her lesson from that, and kept Merle ignorant. Seems a man just hasn't got the same control a woman does. It's that pecker, of course. Once that pecker gets heated up, nothing else matters.

I offered 'em down.

The gall of that boy, laying blame on the Master. The only call he got came from right between his legs.

She should've stopped him. When they saw those two swimming, she'd known Merle might go after the gal. She'd warned him against it. He'd promised to leave her alone. Ettie knew how weak he was. She had to admit she'd half expected him to break his promise. But when he fell asleep after dark, she'd figured it'd be all right. He must've been playing possum, just to put her at ease so she'd sleep and leave him free to sneak down.

Well, he wouldn't trick her that way again. Next time—if there was a next time—she'd keep herself awake all night.

As Merle disappeared again into the cave, Ettie stood up. Her rump was numb from sitting on the rock. She rubbed it, and the feeling returned with an aching tingle. Then she started down the slope.

She was eager to get to the cave and see what Merle had brought in. First things first, though. She'd have to give the campsite a close look to make sure all the traces were gone.

Halfway down the slope, she left the sunlight behind. In the shade, the breeze felt chilly. Ettie hoped those folks had some nice parkas with them. Her sweatshirt up at the cave wasn't nearly warm enough once the sun went down.

She didn't descend all the way to the lake; that would mean more climbing. Instead, when she was about level with the low ridge at the northern end, she traversed the slope. She reached the ridge, leaped across the gap where the stream, far below, tumbled toward Lower Mesquite, and made her way down.

At the clearing among the trees where the campers had been, she found nothing. Even the circle of rocks piled up by previous visitors as a fireplace had been scattered, the ashes covered over. Where the tent had stood, the ground was now littered with pine needles and pinecones, sticks, and a few charred rocks from the fireplace. Merle had done a good job. But what had he done with the bodies?

Ettie wandered among the trees, saw nothing that looked suspicious, and returned to the campsite. Her eyes settled on the flat place where the tent had been. She stepped over to it. With the edge of her boot, she scraped a swath through the debris. She squatted down and pushed her fingers into the loose, grainy soil. Dropping to her knees, she started to dig. The hole deepened quickly as she scooped out handfuls of dirt.

At least if they're here, she thought, Merle planted them down far enough.

Her fingernails raked something soft. She cleared a small area at the bottom of the hole, uncovering an island of skin. Her nails had gouged furrows in it. Widening the hole, she discovered a navel. The skin around it was nearly hairless, so she figured this must be the girl.

She crawled forward, dug some more, and found the man's hip. Satisfied that Merle had buried them both, she filled in the holes. She stomped down the soil. She scattered pine needles over the area until it looked undisturbed.

She didn't much like the fact that Merle had buried them smack in the middle of the lake's only camping area. They were better than a foot under the surface, though. She supposed it'd be all right.

CHAPTER SEVEN

Back at the trail sign, Benny had thought two miles would be easy. After all, two miles was the distance from school to home, and he'd walked it a few times. He didn't remember it being hard. That was without a pack, though. And that was without an uphill climb that seemed to go on forever.

At first, he'd been able to keep up with Dad and Mr. Gordon. When the trail started upward, though, his pack got heavier and heavier. The straps felt like hands on his shoulders, trying to shove him into the ground. Sweat made his glasses slip down his nose. Finally, he stepped off the trail. He dug into his pocket for the elastic band he used in gym class to keep his glasses from falling off. While he was busy attaching it, Karen and Mrs. Gordon came along.

"Is it going okay?" Karen asked. She didn't look tired at all.

"Oh, my glasses," he said. "I'll catch up."

"No hurry." With a wave, she continued up the trail, walking slowly with long strides, leaning into the slope. Benny put on his glasses. He watched the backs of her slender legs.

While he was staring, the twins came up the trail. He nodded a greeting to them, and the one with the ponytail gave him a look like she thought he was a clod. What had he done, he wondered, to deserve that? After they passed, she whispered something to her sister, and both girls giggled a little.

Blushing, he made sure his zipper was up. It was.

They must've been making fun of him because he was resting. Or maybe because of his glasses. Four-eyes is pooped out.

He'd show them who's pooped.

Quickly, he pushed the loop of the elastic band onto his other earpiece. He glanced down the trail. Julie and Nick were coming toward him. He wouldn't give *her* a chance to knock him. Hanging onto his shoulder straps, he leaned into the weight and hurried up the trail.

He took long, steady strides like Karen. He closed in on the twins. "Beep-beep," he said. They glanced back, looking startled, and Pigtails fell in behind her sister to make room. He lunged past them.

One muttered, "Turkey," as he left them behind. He didn't look back.

Karen came into view as he rounded a bend. He kept up his speed until he was only a couple of yards behind her, then slowed his pace to match hers.

Turning sideways, she smiled back at him. Even in that funny hat, she was beautiful. "Do you want through?" she asked.

"No, thanks. This is fine."

It was real fine. He stayed behind her, watching her walk, listening to her voice as she talked with Mrs. Gordon. He couldn't make out many of the words, but that didn't matter.

His shoulders hurt. His back was sore just above his rump where the pack rested. His leg muscles trembled. Sweat dripped down his face. His shirt and underwear felt glued to his skin. He was huffing for breath. But he didn't slow down. He stayed close behind Karen, well ahead of the snotty twins, and Julie and Nick.

No matter how awful he felt, he wouldn't fall behind. He wouldn't let himself.

Finally, the trail leveled out.

Then it sloped gently downward. He scanned the valley to the left, but saw only thick woods.

The lake's gotta be here someplace, he thought.

Two miles, the marker had said. They must've already hiked five. So where is it? Maybe the sign lied. Maybe there was a number one in front of the two and it was covered with dirt or something, and Juniper Lake is twelve miles. No, the ranger had said . . .

"Here we are," came Mr. Gordon's voice. He and Dad had stopped just ahead.

"How's it going?" Dad asked Karen.

"Whew," she said. She took off her hat. It had matted down her hair. The strands across her forehead were wet and dark.

"It was a doozy," Benny said.

She smiled at him, and wiped her forehead with the back of her hand.

"You did real good," Dad told him. "That was pretty tough going."

He shrugged, and managed not to wince as pain streaked through his shoulders. "It wasn't so tough," he said.

While they waited for the others to catch up, Mr. Gordon showed them the trail sign. It read JUNIPER LAKE, but gave no distance. The arrow pointed to the left, where a narrow trail joined the main one and dropped away from the slope. Benny peered into the trees. He saw no trace of a lake.

"Where's the lake?" the ponytailed girl asked, frowning at her mother.

"Down there," Mrs. Gordon said.

"I don't see it."

"Me either," said the sister.

"Right *there*," Benny told them. He pointed down the trail at the shadowy forest. "Can't you see it?" he asked.

"No. Where?"

"See? Through there?"

Both girls scrunched up their faces and squinted into the trees.

"Maybe you need glasses," Benny suggested.

"Do not."

Quite a while later, well after reaching the bottom of the

hill, Benny spotted a pale area through the trees ahead. The lake surface. About time.

"There it is!" cried one of the twins.

He grinned to himself, and kept on walking.

"Well now." With a sigh, Flash slung his pack to the ground.

Scott took off his pack, too. The clearing, at the foot of the trail, was close to the shoreline. It had obviously been used often as a campsite. There were logs laid out as benches around a fireplace. There was a small pile of firewood. Plenty of flat area for sleeping.

Listening carefully, Scott heard the breeze stirring the leaves, the quiet lap of waves. But he heard no running water that would indicate a nearby stream.

"Why don't you all take a load off," he suggested. "I'll scout ahead. There might be a better place farther on."

"This looks all right to me," Flash said.

"Well, I'd rather be near a stream. Running water."

"Good point," Flash said.

"I'll come with you." Karen swung her pack off, set it down, and joined him.

Benny, sitting on the ground against his pack, started to get up.

"You wait here," Scott told him. "We'll just be gone a few minutes."

Looking disappointed, the boy settled back.

Karen followed Scott along a path near the shoreline. Without his pack, he felt nearly weightless. He walked with a springy step. The breeze was cool against his damp T-shirt. And he was alone with Karen, at least for the moment. He turned to her. "Howdy, stranger."

She ducked under his outstretched arm, and leaned against him. He cupped her shoulder. They walked along the path, holding each other. "Now, this is nice," she said.

"You surviving the kids all right?"

"Sure. They're fine. Benny's quite a guy."

"I think he's fallen for you. Can't blame him."

"I've fallen for him, too." She patted Scott's side. "Good thing for you he's just a kid."

"I wish Julie'd shape up. Maybe she will, now that Nick's around."

"They seem to be getting along okay."

"Yeah." He sighed.

"What's wrong?"

"Well, I've been thinking about the sleeping arrangements. I really don't see how we can manage . . ."

"I know. I've thought about that, too. I guess I tent with Julie, huh?"

"I can't figure any way around it, what with the kids and the Gordons."

"That's all right. Maybe we'll be able to sneak off, sometime."

"You can bet on it."

Karen's hand moved down, and pushed into a rear pocket of his trousers. It stayed there, curved against his rump, caressing, as they walked along the path.

"If Julie gives you any trouble," Scott said, "let me know."

"I'm sure we'll be fine. It'll give us a chance to get to know each other."

"She's really not a bad kid. I've been trying to figure her out. It hit her pretty hard when her mother split. But it was never. 'How could she do that to me?' She only seemed upset that I'd been dumped on. She really holds it against June, won't even talk to her on the phone. Both kids are pretty bitter about what she did, but with Julie it seems to have spilled over onto you. It's not you personally. She'd have the same feeling toward any woman I got serious about. I'm sure of that. She seems to feel it's her duty to protect me."

"Maybe she'll get over it once we know each other better."

"I sure hope so. I feel bad, though, that you have to be put through this kind of thing."

Karen smiled up at him. "Hell, you're worth it."

"Is that so?"

"That's so."

They rounded a bend in the shoreline, and Scott heard the sound of rushing water.

"Success!" Karen said. She squeezed his rump, withdrew her hand from his pocket, and stepped ahead through a narrow passage between two trees. Scott watched her hurry forward. She bounded up a small, rocky rise, glanced down, then whirled around. "*Voilà!*" she cried.

Scott climbed up to join her. A few feet below, a stream tumbled and swirled over rocks on its way to the lake.

They stepped down to it. Kneeling, Karen dipped a hand into the water. She cupped some to her mouth, and drank. "It's luscious," she said. As Scott tried the chilly water, she splashed her face. Then, to his amazement, she unbuttoned her blouse. She spread it open, scooped up water with both hands, and flung it against herself. He watched it splatter her bare skin. It slid over her breasts, dripped from the jutting tips of her nipples, rolled down her belly. Bending over, she cupped more water to her mouth.

Scott reached across her back. He lifted the hanging side of her blouse out of the way, and curled his fingers around her breast. The skin was wet and cool, the nipple springy against his palm. She turned her face to him, and they kissed. "We'd . . . better not."

He kissed her again, then let go. As Karen buttoned her blouse, he caressed her back beneath it. Then they stood up. Scott filled his lungs with the fresh air. "Well, let's see if there's a decent place around here to pitch camp."

They leaped across the stream, walked up a low slope of broken granite, and looked down at a clearing. "All *right*," Karen said.

They made their way down to it. In the middle stood a nicely built-up stone fireplace with a grate across the top. Large, flat-topped rocks and smoothly sawed logs for stools were placed around it. Someone had even gone to the trouble of lashing branches together in the semblance of a table. Best of all, Scott saw plenty of level ground for the tents.

"It looks ideal to me," Karen said.

"Me, too."

They headed back to tell the others.

"Let's get organized here," Flash said, rubbing his hands together. "Nick, you help me with the tents. Alice, why don't you and the girls scout around for firewood? We'll get this show on the road."

"Benny," Scott said. "You want to go with them?"

The boy shook his head. "I wanta do the tents."

As Alice led the twins into the trees, Flash turned to Scott. "Where do you want to set up? You should get first choice, since you found this place."

"Makes no difference to me," Scott told him. "Right here's fine for one. Maybe pitch the other over there." He nodded toward a level area closer to the lake.

"You want one that far off?"

"Sure. Why not? Give everybody a little breathing room."

"Breathing room, eh?" He winked.

Scott looked amused as he pulled a tubular plastic bag from his pack.

"Which place do we get?" Benny asked.

"We should let the ladies pick."

"How about it?" Karen asked Julie.

The girl shrugged.

"Over by the lake?"

"I don't care."

"I wanta be close to the fire," Benny said.

Karen grinned. "You've got it. Julie and I'll take the scenic tent." For a moment, her eyes met Flash's. There was mischief in them. Fooled you, they seemed to say.

Flash was fooled, all right. If he'd been in Scott's shoes, nothing in the world could've kept him from tenting with a woman like Karen. He hadn't put it quite that way to Alice, when they'd discussed it last night. He'd simply bet her a dinner at Victoria Station against a dinner at Casa Escobar that the couple would share a tent. "I don't know about the girl," she said, "but Scott isn't that way." Flash had smiled at that. He managed to refrain from telling about the time in Saigon when he and Scott, bare-ass and side by side, humped the daylights out of a couple of whores—then traded. No point in tarnishing Scott's image. Hell, Scott was about the only friend of his that Alice approved of. "Aside from just good manners," Alice had continued, "he wouldn't put Julie and Benny together. They're too old to be sleeping together." That point nearly succeeded in changing Flash's mind. Still, he hadn't called off the bet. Maybe they'd show up with three tents, one for each kid and . . .

"Over here?" Nick asked.

Flash turned around. His son was standing in a six-foot space between two spruces, a rolled-up tent in his arms. "That'll be fine. Hold up a minute, though, till we clear the ground."

Together, they brushed away the twigs and pinecones littering the area. Then they rolled out the red tent, and spread it flat. They joined the fiberglass wands, slid them in at the four corners, inserted the tips into eyelets at the top and bottom, and lifted the roof. In less than five minutes, the tent was up. All that remained was to tie out the guy lines and stake it down.

"I'll get the hatchet," Flash said.

He headed for his pack. Scott, Karen, and Benny had nearly finished setting up a blue, two-man tent similar to his own. Julie was crouched by the fireplace, pouring fuel from an aluminum bottle into the base of a Primus stove.

Flash rummaged through his pack. As he looked for the hatchet, his stomach growled. He tried to remember the menu he'd worked out with Scott, but couldn't recall what was planned for tonight's meal. One of the Dri-Lite stews, probably. With pudding for dessert—either vanilla or chocolate. He hoped for vanilla. Nothing could beat that vanilla pudding, especially when it didn't get mixed up real good and still had some of those lumps in it.

He found the hatchet. As he walked back toward the tent, he saw Nick staring into space. No, not into space. At

Julie. The girl was holding the small stove high, waving a lighted match under its base to warm the fuel for priming.

Wouldn't that be something, Flash thought, if Nick and Julie got together? He wondered if Scott would approve. No reason why he shouldn't. Nick's a fine lad, an Eagle Scout, a good student, and my son. The girl could sure do worse.

So could Nick. A lot worse. As far as Flash knew, the boy had never dated a gal half as attractive as Julie.

She shook out the match, turned a metal key to start the gas jetting, and frowned.

"I'll take care of the stakes, Nick. Go on over and see if Julie needs a hand with the stove."

The boy shrugged.

"Go on. Maybe the nozzle's clogged."

"Well . . . okay. Be right back." He walked toward her. Julie smiled when she saw him approach. "Having some trouble?" he asked.

"This thing doesn't want to cooperate."

"Here, let me take a look."

Go to it, boy, Flash thought, and picked up a stake.

CHAPTER EIGHT

Crouched by the stream, Karen shivered and gritted her teeth. Only a couple of hours ago, she'd been splashing herself to cool off. Then the water had felt like ice on her hot skin. Now, with the sun down and a chilly breeze blowing, the water seemed almost warm.

Except for Benny, everyone else had already finished washing their cook kits and returned to camp. He stood on the opposite bank, shaking and waving his aluminum dish to dry it while Karen scrubbed out the big pot. He was smart. He'd put on a jacket before coming over. Karen was still in her shorts and thin blouse. The blouse did no good at all. The cold breeze passed through the cloth as if it weren't there.

Benny sat down on a rock across from her. He wiped the dish across a leg of his jeans. "Aren't you awfully cold?" he asked.

"I'm one giant goose bump."

"You want me to get a jacket for you?"

"That's all right, I'm about done. Thanks, though."

"It's funny how it gets so cold."

"The altitude, I guess. You bake during the day and freeze at night."

"Yeah. It's weird. It sure isn't like home."

"That's one of the great things about camping," she said. "Home looks so good after you've been out here a while. You start dreaming about a hot bath, a soft bed . . ."

"Yeah!" Benny leaned forward, elbows on knees. "Last year, we were out for a week and I got so I *had* to have a chocolate milkshake. I wanted one so bad I couldn't stand it. Then Dad stopped at Burger King on the way home and . . . gee, I think that was the best milkshake I ever had. I can taste it, just thinking about it."

"Just thinking about it makes me cold." Karen rinsed out the pot, stood up, and shook the water from it. "Right now, I could go for some coffee."

"We've got cocoa, too," Benny said. Standing up, he brushed off the seat of his jeans. "And marshmallows."

"Maybe I'll have a marshmallow in my coffee."

He laughed, and hopped across the stream.

"Thanks for keeping me company," Karen told him as they walked up the granite slab.

"Ah, that's all right."

The clearing ahead shimmered with firelight. Most of the others were seated close to the fire.

"Thought we'd lost you," Scott called.

"Save me some coffee," Karen called back. She handed the pot to Benny, and carried her cook kit down a gradual slope to the tent. "Right with you," she said over her shoulder.

Her backpack was propped against a rock near the tent entrance. She lifted the flap, dropped her kit into the darkness, and dug through the equipment trying to find her jeans and parka. They were near the bottom, of course. What you wanted was always at the bottom.

Clamping the jeans between her legs, she quickly shook open the parka and put it on. She sighed with relief at its warmth.

Then she crawled into the tent. It was very dark inside, but she didn't need her light for this. She sat on her soft, down-filled sleeping bag, took off her boots, and changed from her shorts to the long-legged jeans. Pushing into her boots, she left the tent. She hurried toward the fire, hoping she wouldn't trip on the laces.

Her cup was still on the stump where she'd left it after dinner. "All set," she said.

"Coffee?" Scott asked.

"You bet." She held out the cup. Scott spooned in granules of instant from a plastic bag, then poured hot water into her cup and gave it a stir. Steam rose against Karen's face as she took a sip. "Ah, that's good." She sat on the stump, and drank more.

Benny, she saw, already had cocoa with a couple of marshmallows floating on the surface.

"How about some songs?" Alice suggested.

They started with "Michael, Row the Boat Ashore." Then it was "Shenandoah." Flash led them in "Danny Boy," to which he knew all the words, and seemed almost tearful as he sang of the boy returning to his father's grave.

"Let's get into something more upbeat," Scott said when that one ended. In a loud baritone, he started "The Marine Corps Hymn" and everyone joined in, their voices booming.

"'The Caisson Song'!" Nick called out.

Then "The Battle Hymn of the Republic," then, "Dixie." When that was done, the Gordons sang a song about a logger who stirred his coffee with his thumb.

"That puts me in mind of Robert Service," Scott said. "'There are strange things done in the midnight sun . . .'"

"'By the men who moil for gold,'" Karen said along with him, smiling that they both knew the same poem. They continued with it, line after line, one remembering what the other forgot until they finally got Sam McGee cremated on the marge of Lake LaBarge.

Their performance drew applause, and a two-fingered whistle from Julie.

Alice urged the twins to recite "Stopping by the Woods on a Snowy Evening."

"Sissy stuff," Flash said when they finished. "How's about this one? 'You may talk o' gin and beer/When you're quartered safe out here,/And you're sent to penny-fights and Aldershot it . . .'"

Karen knew "Gunga Din" by heart, but she kept silent as he proceeded. He messed up the middle badly. Nobody seemed to notice, though.

"Bravo!" Scott called, clapping as he finished. "Benny, why don't you do one?"

The boy shrugged. He glanced shyly at Karen.

"Come on," she urged him.

"Well. Is 'The Raven' okay?"

"Great! I love Poe."

Benny leaned forward on his rock, and set his empty cup on the ground between his feet. "Well, here goes." He began to recite the poem in a low, ominous voice. When the raven spoke, he screeched its "Nevermore" like a demented parrot.

Rose giggled. Heather elbowed her for silence.

Benny ignored them. He spoke slowly, a haunted look on his firelit face as if he'd become the lonely, tormented man of the poem. He grew frenzied, then furious. "'Quit the bust above my door!'" he cried out. "'Take thy beak from out my heart and take thy form from off my door!'"

When he finished, there was silence. Everyone looked a bit stunned. Until he stood up, grinning, and bowed. Everyone clapped. Even Rose. Even Julie.

"Terrific," Karen told him. "That was great!"

"Do you know some others?" Rose asked.

"Maybe," he said. "Maybe tomorrow night."

"Let's tell stories," Julie suggested. "Anybody know a really scary one?"

"How about 'The Hook'?" Nick asked.

Rose wrinkled her nose. "That's an old one."

"I could tell you something," Karen said, "that happened to a friend of mine. It happened just a few years ago when she was camping with some friends—not very far from here."

Heather's eyes widened. She looked frightened already. Flash leaned forward, took a burning stick from the fire, and lit a cigar. Benny turned to face Karen.

"We don't want to give the kids nightmares," Scott told her, smiling.

"I'd better not tell it."

"Come on," Nick said.

"Yeah," Julie said. "You can't quit now."

"Well . . . they were camping in the mountains not far from here. It was a cold night, with the wind howling and moaning through the trees. Sandy—that was her name—sat close to the campfire with her two friends, Audrey and Doreen. I would've been along, but I'd sprained my ankle a few days earlier and had to stay home. Lucky for me, as it turned out."

"Is this really a true story?" Benny asked.

"Let her talk," Julie said.

Karen leaned closer to the fire. She felt its heat on her face, the cold on her back. "The three of them huddled close around the fire to keep the cold away. They sang and told ghost stories, none of them wanting to leave the fire's cheery warmth. Slowly the flames dwindled. Sandy put on the last piece of firewood. Soon, that, too, was nearly gone. 'Well,' Sandy said, 'why don't we hit the sack?' The others were against it, though. They'd frightened themselves so much with the ghost stories that the tent, off in the darkness, looked like a creepy shadow.

" 'What if someone's hiding inside?' Doreen asked.

" 'Oh, that's ridiculous,' Sandy said."

Karen glanced at Benny. He was staring, wide-eyed, at his tent across the clearing.

"Well, they decided to stay up for a while longer. But the fire was nearly dead, only a few flickers still lapping around the charred remains of wood. If they were going to stay up till their jitters passed, they would have to replenish the supply of firewood. Since nobody wanted to go alone into the dark woods around the campsite, they decided to all go together.

"But they had no flashlight. The flashlight was in the tent. 'I'm not going in there,' Doreen said.

" 'Me either,' Audrey said.

"Sandy was frightened, too, by this time, but she told herself it was silly. So she volunteered to get the flashlight. She left Audrey and Doreen sitting by the fire, and crossed the dark clearing toward the tent. She crouched in front of it.

Her heart was pounding like crazy, but she wasn't about to let herself be scared off. Then she got an idea that made her grin. She almost laughed, but kept quiet and lifted the tent flap. Inside, it was as black as a cave. She almost lost her nerve, but took a deep breath and crawled in.

"Suddenly, she screamed. She screamed again, a piercing shriek of terror so loud it made her ears hurt. 'No!' she cried out. 'No! Please! NO!' And then she let out a howl of horror and agony that made her own flesh crawl."

"What was it?" Benny whispered. "What got her?"

"Not a thing," Karen answered. "This was Sandy's idea of a practical joke. Like lots of practical jokes, though, this one backfired. Once she was done screaming, she found the flashlight. She crawled out of the tent, all set to yuck it up about the great gag she'd pulled on her friends. But they were gone."

"She scared 'em off," Nick said.

"That's what Sandy thought. She walked around the clearing, calling out to them. 'Hey you guys!' she yelled. 'I was kidding! Come on back!' But they didn't come back.

"Sandy sat by the campfire. Only a glow remained, by now, and she was cold. 'Come on,' she finally called. 'Enough is enough.' But Audrey and Doreen still didn't return.

"At last, she left the campsite and walked into the dark woods, calling out for her friends. With each step, she half expected the girls to leap out at her screaming, to pay her back for the scare. But they didn't. She kept searching, wandering farther and farther from the camp.

"Finally, she spotted them in a moonlit clearing. They stood motionless as she hurried toward them. 'What're you doing way out here?' she asked. They didn't answer. They didn't speak a word. When she reached them, she stared. She began to whimper.

"The two figures wore the clothes of Doreen and Audrey, but the arms and legs were made of sticks. They were scarecrows with heads of bloody fur."

"Yuck," Rose muttered.

"Somehow, Sandy found her way back to the camp. She sat by the dead fire. The wind moaned around her. She stared into the darkness. She waited and waited. Audrey and Doreen never returned."

"Never?" Benny asked.

"Never. Some hikers wandered into camp a couple of days later and found Sandy still sitting there, her wide eyes gazing into the woods as if looking for her lost friends."

"What *did* happen?" Nick asked. "To Audrey and Doreen?"

"Search parties looked everywhere for them. They were never found. Nobody will ever know what became of them after they ran out into the woods that night. Maybe it's best that way."

There was silence. Heather peered over her shoulder. Rose leaned closer to the fire.

"On that cheerful note," Flash said, "I think it's about time to call it a night."

CHAPTER NINE

"Hey," Nick said. "I'm gonna sleep under the stars tonight. You want to?"

"That'd be neat. I'll have to ask Dad first." Turning around, Julie spotted him with Karen and Benny. The three were heading away from the campsite, apparently on their way to the stream. "Wait up!" she called, and ran after them. She quickly caught up with her father. "Can I sleep outside tonight?" she asked.

"Do you have a choice?"

"I mean by the fire. Instead of in the tent. Nick's gonna sleep out, too."

"Just the two of you?"

"I don't know." She sighed. "Jeez, Dad, we're not gonna *do* anything. I hardly even know the guy."

"I wasn't thinking about that. Now that you mention it, though . . ."

"*Dad.*"

He laughed softly. "No, it's fine with me."

"Great!" She whirled away and rushed to tell Nick. She found him crouching over his backpack, pulling out his sleeping bag. "It's okay," she told him.

"Fantastic."

"Meet you by the fire."

Well away from the campsite, in the woods beyond her tent, she brushed her teeth and washed her face using water from her plastic bottle. As she capped the bottle, she heard a quiet crunching sound. Not far away. A footstep?

Holding her breath, she stared through the trees. She saw only black trunks, bushes, a few dim clusters of stone.

Nobody's there, she told herself.

Still, she felt exposed standing in a bright patch of moonlight. With a sidestep, she moved into the dark. She listened. She heard only the breeze in the treetops, the quiet lapping sound of the lake, a few indistinct voices from the camp.

"Damn story," she muttered. Karen's story, and nothing more, was responsible for her jitters. "Wasn't even scary," she said.

But as she lowered her pants and squatted, she scanned the darkness. Ridiculous. Dumb story. She was a jerk to let it bother her.

Here I am, a jerk. Staring into the woods like a fool, half expecting Audrey and Doreen to dash by. Dumb.

She stared and shivered. This was taking forever. Why the hell had she drunk so much coffee?

Finally, she finished. She hurried back to camp. Nick, in his sleeping bag near the fire, waved at her. "Right with you," she called.

In the darkness of her tent, she changed into the hooded warm-up suit she'd brought along for sleepwear. She put on clean wool socks, then slipped into her sneakers. She rolled her mummy bag into a loose bundle, grabbed her foam-rubber mat, and crawled outside.

Nick watched her approach. She felt self-conscious, naked under her snug jacket and pants. He can't tell, she thought. Besides, she was holding the bulky bag in front of herself.

"You ought to put down a ground cloth," he suggested.

"Yeah. I'll get my poncho." She spread out the rubber mat, piled her bag on it, and walked back across the clearing. Let him look, she thought. Nothing to see. For all he knows, she could be wearing long johns under her suit. Her uneasiness, however, was mixed with a tingle of excitement at the idea that he might be watching and wondering.

She crouched over her pack. The pants drew taut against

her rump and slipped down a bit. She felt a strip of cold above the elastic band. Nick can't see. It's dark.

She took out her poncho, water bottle, and flashlight, and fastened down the cover flap for the night. Standing, she hiked up her pants. Then she returned to the fire.

"Can you use a hand?" Nick asked.

"That's okay. I'll just be a minute." She spread her poncho over a fairly smooth patch of ground several feet away from Nick's bag. He was wearing a T-shirt. "Aren't you cold?" she asked.

"Just what you can see. I'm toasty warm from there down."

"Toasty warm?"

"Snug as a bug in a rug."

"Good grief," she muttered.

Nick laughed.

Knees on the poncho, Julie straightened out her rubber pad. It was just wider than her shoulders, just long enough to cushion her from head to rump. She spread her sleeping bag over it. Sitting on the puffy surface, she pulled off her shoes. She placed them near the head of the bag, propped her water bottle between them, and slipped her flashlight inside one. Then she lowered the zipper of her bag halfway. She drew back the top as far as she could and struggled to get in, rolling onto her back and drawing up her knees nearly to her chin before she could work her feet under the edge. "Graceful, huh?"

"Yeah."

She used the inside tab to pull the zipper up. Then, nestled in warmth, she sighed.

"Okay." It was her father's voice, a short distance away. "See you in the morning."

"Bright and early," Karen answered.

"'Night," Benny said.

"Go on ahead, I'll be right with you."

Raising her head, Julie saw Benny turn away from the adults. They walked toward Karen's tent, the one she would've been sharing with Julie. In the darkness near its front, they embraced. They kissed. Julie turned her face away.

"'Night," Benny said as he walked by.

"Yeah," she muttered.

"Good night," Nick said.

Dad came along a while later. At least he didn't go in the tent with her. "Sleep tight, you two," he said as he passed.

"'Night, Dad."

"Good night, Mr. O'Toole."

"From here on, it's Scott. Okay?"

"Sure. Good night."

Soon Dad reached his tent. Julie heard his voice and Benny's, but she couldn't make out the words. Quiet voices also came from the tent where the twins were. They had a flashlight on, its beam making a pale disk that showed through the red wall. Julie smiled.

"Something funny?" Nick asked.

"I think that story really threw a scare into the twins."

"Yeah. They scare real easy." He scooted down until only his head was visible. "You know what'd be neat? We oughta get up and run behind their tent."

"Are you kidding?"

"It'd scare the hell out of them."

"Cold out there," Julie said. She felt cozy in her sleeping bag, but the idea of rushing through the woods with Nick sent a shiver of excitement through her.

"It'd just take a minute," he told her. In the shimmering glow of the firelight, his face looked eager.

She grinned back at him. "We'll get in trouble."

"I don't mind."

"Me either. It'd be worth it. But we've gotta do Benny, too."

"What about Karen's tent?"

"Why bother?"

"Just the two tents, then."

"Right. Let's do it."

Slowly, as if someone might be watching, they unzipped

their mummy bags. Julie's throat felt tight. She clamped her teeth together to stop her chin from trembling, and sat up. As she reached for her shoes, she saw Nick swing his bare legs free of his bag. He was wearing blue shorts. Boxer underwear? No, she decided, must be gym pants. He wouldn't dare run around in nothing but his undies. "You're gonna freeze your tail off," she said in a shaky whisper.

"You're telling me." He turned toward her and started putting on his shoes.

She noticed, with a mixture of relief and disappointment, that the shorts had no fly. She caught herself trying to see up the leg holes, and quickly lowered her gaze. She stared at her shoes as she put them on.

"All set?" he asked.

Julie nodded. She stood up, feeling the cold seep into her clothes. As she tugged at the bottom of her jacket, she saw the thrust of her nipples through the tan fabric. Nick saw, too. He was staring. "Take a picture," she muttered. "It lasts longer."

He met her eyes for a moment, looking stunned and hurt, then turned away. He shook his head.

"Hey," Julie whispered.

"Never mind, let's just forget it." He knelt on his sleeping bag.

"Come on, don't chicken out on me."

"It was a dumb idea." He reached back to pull off a shoe.

Julie squeezed his shoulder. "Come on. I'm sorry. It wasn't your fault. I was a jerk."

"No you weren't."

"Hey, you can look at me all you want. I was looking at you."

"You were?"

"Sure. Come on, let's scare the crap out of everyone."

The flashlight no longer beamed through the side of the twins' tent. Julie heard no talking. "Hope they're not asleep," she whispered.

Nick took the lead, striding quietly across the clearing.

They stopped beside the tent. He began to pound his feet on the earth. Julie joined in. Shoulder to shoulder, they ran in place, their shoes crunching the dry pine needles and twigs and pinecones. Through the noise, Julie heard frantic whispers from inside.

In a high, trilling voice, she called, "Helllllp meee. Pleeeease hellllp meeeee."

Screams erupted from the tent.

Nick slapped a hand across his mouth, apparently to hold in a giggle, and dashed into the trees just behind the tent. He cut to the left, Julie close on his heels. Running through the dark, with the girls still screaming, she felt a strange quivering tightness in her chest as if she needed to scream herself. They passed the tent of Nick's parents, then raced toward the rear of her father's tent.

"Helllp meee!" she called in a shrill voice. "Hellllp meeeee!"

Their feet crashed through the undergrowth.

"Pleeeease hell—"

"It's all right," came her father's voice. "Julie!" he yelled. "It's not funny!"

"It's Doreeeeen!" she cried, and rushed by.

As they raced for their sleeping bags, Mr. Gordon scurried out of his tent. "What the fuck's going on!" he bellowed.

Julie dived for her bag. Nick hit his, laughing, and burrowed inside.

"For Chrissake," Mr. Gordon said. "No more of that, Nick, or you're in for it." He muttered, "Infantile."

Peering out of her sleeping bag, Julie saw him crouch at the entrance of the twins' tent. "It's all right, girls," he said in a loud voice. "Just a couple of morons."

"He called me a moron!" Julie whispered.

She heard Nick laugh.

Scott listened to Benny's slow, deep breathing. Finally asleep. About time. Julie's stunt had thrown quite a shock into him, keeping him awake for a long while afterward.

Good old Karen. She really opened a can of worms with that story of hers.

Good old Karen.

He opened the side of his bag so slowly that the zipper popped open with quiet, individual clicks. Then he silently climbed out.

If Benny wakes up, he thought, I'll just tell him that nature is calling. Won't even be a lie; nature *is* calling.

Naked except for his jockey shorts, he shivered as he crawled to the foot of his sleeping bag. He relaxed his muscles, and the shaking stopped. That's it. Calm. Stay calm. He opened the mosquito screen and crept through the opening. On hands and knees, he scanned the camp. The fire was out. Except for a few pale tatters of moonlight, the area was dark. The two sleeping bags were black bulges near the low stone circle of the fireplace.

He stood up and brushed off his knees. Then he walked quickly to Karen's tent. He unzipped the front and crawled in. Her sleeping bag was stretched lengthwise along the right-hand side. Her face was a vague blur at the far end. Her breathing was slow and steady.

He lay down on the cold floor of the tent, and kissed one of her closed eyes. She moaned. "It's me," he whispered.

"Mmmm." She rolled onto her back.

Scott found the zipper at the side of her bag, eased it down, and slid his arm into the warmth. He touched her. She was wearing something loose and thick and soft. A sweatshirt? His hand moved over it, feeling her heat through the fabric, feeling the smooth curves of her belly and ribs and breasts.

Without warning, a hand grabbed his wrist. "Password?" came a whisper.

"'Open sesame'?"

"'Pumpernickel.' Close enough." She raised her head. "What are you wearing?"

"Not much."

"So I gather. Jeez, get in here." She lifted the cover of her sleeping bag, and Scott crawled in. She snuggled against him. Her lips brushed his as she said, "How nice of you to join me."

"Very thoughtful of Julie to sleep outside."

"Yes." They kissed. Karen flinched as he slid a cold hand under her sweatshirt. She pushed her tongue into his mouth. She touched the band of his shorts, slipped her hand in, and caressed his buttocks.

She sighed when he touched her breast. He stroked its smoothness, filled his hand with it, gently squeezed. She sucked a trembling breath as his thumb pressed her nipple. Then she pulled off her sweatshirt. She was bare and warm and sleek to the waist. She squirmed, rubbing herself against him.

His erect penis felt trapped in his tight shorts. She freed it. Her fingers curled around it, slid down the length of it and up again. Scott moaned as the sensation threatened to break his control. He moved lower, easing out of her hand. His mouth went to her breast. He kissed the rigid nipple, tasting the slight tang of salt on her skin.

Karen rolled onto her back, and he tongued her other breast while his hand roamed down the velvety skin of her belly. He plucked at the drawstring of her sweatpants, opening the bow. He slid his hand down. He felt the soft coils of hair. Her thighs parted to make room. She was warm and slick. Her breath became ragged. She clenched his hair, forcing his mouth hard against her breast as she raised her knees and writhed under his sliding fingers. "Oh, God," she gasped. "Oh, my God."

He took his hand away. She let go of his hair, and he rolled aside. While she struggled out of her pants, he shoved his shorts down and tugged them off. Then he was on top of Karen, thrusting his tongue into her mouth, squeezing a breast, pushing into her. She sheathed him, tight and slippery. She whimpered as he slid in deep. "Hurt?" he whispered.

"Oh, Jesus!"

"Is that a yes?"

"No," she gasped. "It's a no." She dug her fingers into his

buttocks, pulled, and shuddered as he pushed the rest of the way in.

A few endless moments of mad lunging, burying himself in her dark hugging warmth, in her and enclosed by her and part of her; she strained against him for a deeper joining as if she ached for him to penetrate a secret place just out of reach. Scott sought that place. He plunged for it. He rammed for it. Just beyond him and now he couldn't hold back. He pumped, spurting into her, and knew that his fluid was finding that secret place, making that connection, joining them. Karen quaked under him. Then she held him motionless and tight.

CHAPTER TEN

"Keep on going," Ettie muttered. "Don't you stop here."

Dropping to her rump, she scooted down the steep side of the boulder she'd been standing on. The granite felt like hot sandpaper through her dress. She pushed off, fell a short distance into a nook among the rocks, and stretched out flat on an uptilted slab. From there, she watched the hikers stride up the distant trail.

They were heading up toward Carver Pass. Three of them. This far off, they were no more than tiny shapes. Something about the way they walked made Ettie suspect they were girls, but she could only be sure about one; the figure of that one made it obvious.

The person in the lead, who wore a cowboy hat, stopped and turned around, waiting for the others to catch up.

"No," Ettie whispered when the leader pointed down at the lake.

The three stood close together on the trail, gesturing and nodding, apparently discussing the matter. Then the one in the cowboy hat started down the steep path toward the lake. The other two followed.

"Damnation," Ettie muttered.

Squirming forward on the sun-baked granite, she spotted Merle. He was far below, seated on his favorite rock, fishing. With a high outcropping to his right, he was hidden from the intruders, at least for now. They would need to come halfway up the opposite shore to notice Merle in his recess. By then, he was sure to hear their voices and take cover.

"You better behave, boy," she said. "You better just leave 'em be, or I'll skin you."

Before yesterday, there hadn't been much cause to worry on Merle's account. Folks had come down every now and again to rest by the lake, explore it, take a swim, or do some fishing, but Merle always stayed out of sight and left them alone. He'd even behaved the few times campers stayed the night. None of the overnight people had been pretty young women, though, until that last. Easy enough to behave when there's no temptation. But the first pretty girl comes along, he rapes her and kills her and lays it on the Master.

I offered 'em down.

Bullsquat.

Ettie turned her gaze to the hikers. They were already at the bottom of the slope, walking single file along the lakeshore. They were heading toward the area where Merle had buried the bodies. With its trees and shade, it stood out like an oasis in the desolate basin. No one came down without settling there.

A fine place to plant those folks, Ettie thought. We oughta dig them up and stick them someplace out of the way.

Sure enough, the three hikers stopped in the shadows and swung off their packs. One red pack was lowered within a yard of the graves.

As they opened their packs, Ettie heard them talking and laughing. From the sounds of their voices, she was sure that all three were girls.

Merle must hear them, too. She looked toward the boulder where he'd been sitting. He was on his feet, leaning out, trying to see around the jut of rock. He stood motionless for a few moments, then leaped across the narrow band of water, set down his fishing pole, and scrambled up the slope. Near the top, he crouched low, then raised his head enough to see over.

Only the width of the lake separated him from the girls. That couldn't be more than a hundred feet, Ettie figured.

Merle could swim the distance in half a minute, if he had a mind to.

"You just let 'em be," Ettie whispered.

She looked at the girls. They were sitting close together on rocks, passing a couple of small bags back and forth, eating the contents.

Stopped for lunch, Ettie thought. She hoped that was all, that they would finish up quickly and be on their way.

The one in the cowboy hat, who sat with her back to Ettie, took off her checkered blouse. The straps of her bra were white against her tanned skin. She stood up and stretched, as if she liked how the breeze felt. Bending over, she set her hat on a rock. She rubbed her short brown hair, then turned away from the other two girls and walked to the shore. There, she knelt and flipped a hand through the water.

Ettie looked for Merle. He was gone.

The girl returned to her friends. Moving her hat off the rock, she sat down again and began to untie a boot.

"Oh, you fool," Ettie muttered. She studied the opposite shore, but still couldn't see Merle.

One of the other girls, a skinny thing in jeans and a faded blue shirt, got up and stuffed a bag into her pack. Then she took off her shirt. Her breasts were small mounds, white except for their dark tips.

"Oh, Merle, Merle." The temptation would be too much for him.

She considered rushing down to the girls, yelling and trying to scare them away. That might ruin everything, though. They'd be sure to tell someone—maybe a ranger— about the wild woman who chased them off. A spell might take care of that, but why take chances? A good spell's hard to call down, and you can't always count on one to take care of business.

Be better off to find Merle and stop him before he did something foolish.

She looked at the girls. The one who'd tested the water was on her feet, pulling down her shorts. The buxom one had her T-shirt off, and was reaching behind her back to unhook her bra. The skinny one sat right where Merle had planted the bodies, and tugged off her boots.

Ettie still couldn't spot Merle. She guessed he was across the lake from the girls, spying on them, probably hard as a club by now and going crazy.

She scurried across the slope, staying low. She squeezed through crevices, slid down steep slabs on her rump, ducked behind every rock cluster offering any concealment, making her way slowly across the end of the lake. When she paused to catch her breath, she found all three girls stark naked. The one in the lead was knee-deep in the lake, walking backward, urging her friends to come in. The skinny one eased in a foot and jerked it out quickly. The other squatted down, breasts bulging against her knees, and tried the water with her hand.

Ettie left the sheltering rocks. The area ahead was a barren slab of granite that angled slightly downward. It offered no protection. If the girls happened to look toward the end of the lake, they would see her crossing. She squirmed along on her belly, watching them.

The girl in the lake had started to swim. The one crouched on the bank was scooping up water and rubbing it on her shoulders and breasts as if to get used to its cold. The skinny one, cringing and hugging herself, was wading in slowly. None of them so much as glanced in Ettie's direction.

She reached the end of the open space without being seen, and crawled behind a rock. She peered over its top. The small inlet where Merle had been fishing was no more than thirty feet away. Plenty of shelter between here and there. As quickly as she could, she rushed down to it. From the recessed shore, the girls were out of sight. She heard splashing and voices, then a sudden outcry that knotted her stomach before she recognized it as a shriek of laughter.

They're having a great time, stupid bitches. If they knew . . .

She hopped across the water on stepping stones, and crouched at the base of the outcropping. Merle's abandoned fishing pole lay against the rocks in front of her, a shriveled bit of beef jerky on its hook.

Ettie worked her way up the slope, then peered over the top, first at the swimmers, then at the rocks along the bank. From this height, she expected to see Merle crouched behind a boulder.

She didn't see Merle. But she saw his scattered clothes.

A movement caught her eye. To the left. In the water. Just below a jutting clump of rocks. All she saw, at first, were rings, rippling outward as if a stone had been tossed in. Then there was the pale blur of a body sliding along beneath the surface.

Rage seized Ettie. She wanted to scream and yank Merle from the water. The fool! The *fool!*

She scrambled to the top of the outcropping and stood up straight. The first girl was floating on her back, arms out to the sides, her wet breasts shiny in the sunlight, her matted pubic hair glistening as she kicked closer and closer to the long, gliding form of Merle. The boy couldn't be more than a few inches below the surface, but he hadn't come up for air, yet, and none of the girls knew he was there.

"You!" Ettie shouted. "Girls!"

Three wet, astonished faces snapped toward her.

"Get out! There's snakes! Poison snakes. Water moccasins!"

Two of the girls screamed and started splashing for shore even while Ettie yelled. The third, the one who'd started it all by leading her friends down to the lake, trod water and looked around. "I don't see any," she called.

"There!" Ettie snatched up a stone and hurled it. The girl turned to her right as it smacked the water. Not far to her left, Merle's head broke the surface. "Right there! See it?" His head turned toward Ettie, then quickly submerged.

He knows he's found out, she thought. Sure enough,

the pale blur of his body turned beneath the water and started back.

"Tracy!" called one of the girls.

"Come on, Tracy," yelled the other. "Let's get out of here!"

Both girls stood on the far shore, cowering and clutching themselves, trying to hide their nakedness from the intruder as they yelled to their friend.

Tracy frowned up at Ettie. "You're some kind of a nut," she said. Then she swam casually across the lake.

Merle, still underwater, reached the cluster of rocks where he'd started. His head popped up. "Stay down," Ettie snapped.

The girl waded ashore on the far side. Before rushing to join her friends, she thrust her middle finger at Ettie.

"Mom?" Merle sounded pathetic.

"Stay down. I'll tell you when to come out."

He waited, only his head out of the water, while Ettie watched the girls get into their clothes, swing their packs on, and start toward the far end of the lake. "Okay now?" he asked.

"No. Stay where you are."

The trio, often glancing back, reached the footpath and started striding toward the main trail. Ettie turned away. She climbed down the rocks, snapped the baited hook off the line, and picked up the springy stick Merle used as a fishing rod.

She carried it up the slope. When the girls were out of sight, she stepped down and walked along the shore to where Merle was waiting. "Okay," she said. "You can come out now."

"You gotta look away."

"Get out!"

He sighed. "Yes, ma'am." He stood in the waist-deep water and waded ashore, both hands cupped over his groin.

"You haven't got no sense at all, boy."

"The Master, He—"

"Don't you go laying it on the Master! Weren't nothing but your pecker wanted those girls. Bend over."

"Ettie, please."

"Do what I say." He bent over, and she swung the fishing pole hard against his rump. Crying out, he clutched his buttocks. "Move your hands." He was sobbing. As his hands dropped away, Ettie saw a red stripe across his skin. Her throat constricted, and Merle went blurry as tears filled her eyes. She drew back the switch to strike again, but instead of swinging, she threw it down. "Go on and get dressed," she said in a shaky voice. "And don't you ever do nothing like that again, or you'll be the sorriest man that ever walked on two legs."

"Yes, ma'am."

Ettie walked away.

CHAPTER ELEVEN

"Hey, look!" Julie's arm swung up, and she pointed.

Nick gazed up the shadowy trail. Off to the side, he saw a small cleared area between two trees. It was a patch of raised ground, roughly rectangular, enclosed by a border of small stones. A weathered plank of wood tilted from the earth at its far end.

"A grave," Julie whispered.

"Naw."

"Sure looks like one."

Leaning into the straps of his heavy pack, Nick hurried toward the mound. Julie stayed close to his side. He was nervous and excited, as if they were the first ever to discover this forbidden site. He stopped at its foot. The hump of ground was roughly the size of a small man. Words had been carved into the wooden marker. His eyes followed them as Julie read aloud in a hushed voice: " 'Beneath this earth lies Digby Bolles. Poor man ran out of Dr. Scholl's.' "

Nick felt a mixture of relief and disappointment. "It's a joke," he said.

"I guess so."

"Somebody went to a lot of trouble for a practical joke."

"Some people do," Julie said, and gave him an amused look. "*Doreeeen*," she called softly. "*Audreeee*."

Nick nodded. He thought of their brief, wild run behind the tents, the screams of the twins, how daring he'd felt through the whole experience. Running in only his T-shirt and shorts, Julie close to him in the dark. The way he'd wanted to grab her and pull her tight against him, and kiss her.

"We'll have to do that again sometime," she said.

"We'd catch hell," he told her. "I wouldn't mind, though."

"Whatcha got there?" Dad called from behind. He was trudging up the trail with Mom at his side. The girls were a short distance back.

"A grave," Julie said.

"No kidding? Not a *real* grave?"

"Have a look," Nick said. He and Julie stepped aside to make room for them.

"Holy Toledo," Dad said.

"Who is it?" asked Rose, pushing forward.

"A poor guy named Digby Bolles."

Mom read the epitaph aloud.

Heather wrinkled her nose. "Who's Dr. Scholl?"

"It's not a who. It's a brand of foot powder."

"And the guy died when he ran out?"

"No, honey. It's just a joke. Nobody's buried here."

"We oughta get a snapshot of this," Dad said. He swung down his pack. While he opened a side pocket, Rose and Heather stared at the plot of ground.

"Someone's there, all right," Rose said.

"How do you know?"

"I just know."

"A grave," Benny gasped, arriving out of breath.

"Mom says it's not really," Heather told him.

He frowned as he read the inscription. Then he grinned. "Hey, that's neat."

"I better use the flash," Dad said. "All these shadows. Want to make sure the saying comes out." Everyone moved out of his way. He crouched at the foot of the mound. The flash cube made a quick burst of silvery light.

"What's all the excitement?" Scott asked. He was striding up the trail, Karen close beside him.

"It's Digby's grave," Benny explained.

They walked over to it. Karen read the verse aloud, and laughed softly. "That's a shame."

"He should've been more careful," Scott said.

Benny looked up at him. "What do you think's down there?"

"Digby Bolles."

"I mean really."

Julie glanced at Nick. Her eyebrows went up and down. She turned to her father. "What-say we dig it up and find out?"

"What-say we don't?"

"Come on, aren't you curious?"

Half grinning, he said, "Noooo."

"What about you, Karen?"

"I think we should let him rest in peace."

"Now, let's stop all this talk," Mom said. "It's scaring the girls. We all know there's nobody buried here."

"Yes, there is," Rose told her.

"See what I mean? It's just somebody's rotten idea of a joke."

"We've got a lot of ground to cover," Dad said. "I say we haul ass."

"Arnold!"

"Why don't you guys go on ahead?" Julie suggested. "I'll catch up later."

"Julie . . ."

"Why not? What'll it hurt? I'll put everything back just the way it is."

"What are you hoping to find?" Scott asked.

She smiled mysteriously. "Answers."

"Oh, for heaven's sake," Mom muttered. "Nothing's there."

Dad was smiling, obviously pulling for Julie. "Wouldn't hurt to know for sure, though."

"Arnold!"

"I'll stay and help," Nick said.

"This is absurd," his mother muttered.

"Hell, let 'em satisfy their curiosity, Alice. You said yourself they won't find anything."

"That's right," she said. "They won't. But if they want to waste their time and energy, far be it from me to stand in their way."

"Atta girl."

She gave him a quick, humorless smile.

"Don't stay too long, kids," Dad said.

"We'll catch up as soon as we can."

Heather gazed at Nick with wide, frightened eyes. "You gonna dig it up?"

"Probably nothing there but an old shoe," he told her.

Rose narrowed her eyes. "You'll be sor-ry," she said in a singsong.

Both girls turned away and hurried to catch up with their mother and father.

"You want to stay?" Scott asked Benny.

The boy made a face as if he'd been invited to taste a worm. "I don't want to see any stiffs," he proclaimed.

"I don't blame you," Karen said.

Scott turned to her. "Shall we be off and leave Burke and Hare to their grisly chore?"

"I'm with you."

The three of them started up the trail, leaving Nick and Julie by the grave. "Mission accomplished," Julie said. Nick grabbed her pack while she slipped her arms out of the straps. "Thank you, sir," she said, then took it from him and set it down. He swung his own pack to the ground. "I've got a little shovel in here someplace," she told him, propping her pack against his. Crouching, she slid a plastic clamp down its tie cord and peeled back the cover.

Nick stepped behind Julie as she rummaged inside. Her T-shirt clung to her back with sweat. The tint of her skin was visible through the fabric. So was the narrow white crossband of her bra, and the thin straps running up to her shoulders. He could see the bumps of her spine pushing out the material and remembered the way her nipples had shown last night. *Hey, you can look at me all you want. I was looking at you.*

"Here we go." She stood up, a green plastic trowel in her hand.

"Perfect," Nick said.

They stepped over to the mound. "Where'll we dig?"

"In the middle?"

"Good a place as any." She smiled, looking a bit nervous, and knelt beside the border of stones. Nick stepped around her, and dropped to his knees. Her shoulder brushed against him as she reached out with the trowel. Using its edge, she scraped away a layer of pine needles to expose a patch of earth. With its point, she scratched out a pair of crossing lines. "X marks the spot," she whispered. She pushed the plastic blade into the soil, and hesitated. "You don't . . . you don't really think anyone's down there, do you?"

"Naw."

"Me either." She pried out a heap of dirt, and dumped it next to the small hole. "I mean, who'd bury someone out here?"

"I don't know." Nick's mouth was dry. His heart beat fast. He didn't know whether he felt so tense because of the grave or because Julie was so close to him.

"What if we *do* find a body?" she asked, frowning at the tiny hole.

"It's unlikely."

"It's possible, though." She turned her face toward him. Her eyes were so blue that even the white seemed to have a faint bluish color. There was a smudge of dirt on her cheek. Her tongue curled out from a corner of her mouth and caught a trickle of sweat. "It is possible," she said.

Nick felt breathless. "Yeah," he managed.

"Oh, what the hell." Her face turned away, and she reached out with the trowel. Its tip hovered above the hole, quivering slightly. She sighed. "You know, I'm not sure this is such a hot idea after all."

"We don't have to do it," Nick told her.

"We said we would."

"That doesn't matter."

"They'll say we chickened out. Not that I give a rat's ass what anybody says, but . . . I don't know, if there's a real-live actual corpse—"

"A *live* corpse?"

"Okay, a dead one. It'd be sacrilegious to mess around with it."

"Not to mention gross."

She laughed softly. "Yeah, that too." She looked at him again. Her eyebrows lifted. "What do you think?"

"Let's forget it."

She shook her head a bit. "This is really weird. I mean, we both know there's nobody under here. So what're we afraid of?"

"I don't know."

With the edge of her trowel, she brushed the small pile of soil back into the hole. She patted it down. "There you go, Digby. Rest in peace."

They stood up. Julie brushed dirt and pine needles off her knees. "I guess that's that," she said.

"Guess so."

They returned to their packs. Nick watched her crouch down to put away the trowel and close her pack. Like before, he stared at the way her T-shirt clung to her back.

I'm a chicken, all right, he thought. If I weren't a damn chicken, I would've kissed her.

Do it now.

No. I can't. I just can't.

"That's quite a scar you've got there," Flash said, taking a trail cookie from the bag in Karen's hand. The scar was a pale horseshoe on her forearm. "How'd you pick it up?"

"A car accident," she said. She looked away quickly, and offered a cookie to Benny, who was sitting at the other end of the fallen trunk. "Want to pass them around?"

Benny took the bag. "Was it a *bad* accident?" he asked.

"Very bad," she said.

Benny got up from the log, and gave cookies to the others

sitting on the ground against their packs. There was an uneasy silence. Flash bit into his cookie and chewed. Obviously, he shouldn't have mentioned Karen's scar. "I've got a couple of doozies myself," he said. He started to tug his shirt out of his pants.

"*Arnold*," Alice said in her warning voice.

Ignoring her, he pulled up his shirt. He stood up and turned so Karen and Benny could see the small puffy crater in the flesh just above his hip. Karen wrinkled up her nose. Benny looked impressed. "That's from an AK-47 bullet I caught in 'Nam." He turned around. "See there? That's the exit wound."

"How'd it happen?" Benny asked.

"Well, your dad and I were on a strafing run when I caught a SAM. A surface-to-air missile. Knocked me right out of the sky. I hit the silk—ejected, you know—and found myself behind enemy lines." His head suddenly felt light. He let his shirt fall, and took deep breaths, fighting the dizziness. "Anyway, I spent nine days alone in the jungle . . . working my way south, dodging pa—" He blinked. Benny's silhouette was surrounded by a brilliant blue-silver halo. Shit, he thought, I'm gonna . . . He staggered backward, sat down heavily on the log, and lowered his head between his knees.

"Are you all right, honey?" he heard through the loud ringing in his ears. Alice. "I knew he shouldn't get started on that. He tries to put on that it was a big adventure, but—"

"Stop," he mumbled.

"Well, you shouldn't have brought it up."

He felt a hand on his back. "Here." Scott. "Drink some water."

Flash nodded. The ringing faded. He raised his head, and blinked. His vision seemed okay again. The girls, beside Alice, were staring at him with wide eyes. Alice was frowning. "Just a little dizzy spell," he said. "Probably the altitude." He took the canteen from Scott, nodded his thanks, and drank a few swallows of cold water.

"Maybe you'd better lie down," Alice suggested.

"I'm fine. Think I'll just . . ." He gave the canteen back to Scott and stood up. He still felt shaky, but the dizziness was gone. Walking carefully, he made his way to the shore of the lake. He stepped out on some low, flat rocks. Crouching, he dipped his hands into the chilly water and splashed his face.

Damn, but he'd made a fool out of himself back there. Should've known better.

He heard the crunch of footsteps behind him. Scott stood on a rock to his left. "You okay?"

"Shit."

"What was it, the sweats?"

"Yeah. Happens now and again. Shit, you'd think fifteen goddamn years'd be enough to get over it. The damn thing's fucked up my whole life."

Scott tossed a pebble into the water. It made a soft *plip*. "I guess none of us got out of it unscathed. I have plenty of bad times myself, and I wasn't even shot down."

"God, I used to love to fly."

"You were one of the best."

"I'd probably be a captain, now, like you, if . . . You know what really gets me? It's all in my head. All in my fucked-up head, and there's not a thing I can do about it. Like there's some damn stranger inside here." He tapped his fingertips against his temple. "Just hiding in here, scared shitless, and every once in a while he has to pop up and let me know he's still at the controls." Flash forced a smile. "Could've been worse. I'd been a grunt, I might be scared to walk."

Scott smiled. "Always a bright side."

They stood up, and turned away from the shining lake. As they walked back toward the others, Flash saw Nick and Julie coming up the trail. "Dig him up?" he called out.

"Sure did," Nick said.

"Boy, was he a mess!" Julie added.

Flash sat down on the log and watched the two approaching. Nick's hand was out, closed as if he were holding something.

"He was all dismembered," Nick said.

"What?" Karen asked, looking stunned.

"All cut up in little pieces."

"That's not amusing," Alice said.

Nick and Julie smiled as if it were. Nick stepped in front of the twins, who were resting against their packs with their legs outstretched. "I brought you girls a souvenir," he said. "One of Digby's fingers."

"Nick!" Alice snapped.

"Catch, Rose." He made an underhand toss. His sister shrieked as a finger-sized object fell on her lap. Julie cracked up.

"*Nick!*"

"You creep!" Rose yelled, and hurled the stub of wood back at him.

Heather started to laugh. Everyone laughed except Rose and Alice. "Really juvenile," Alice said, scowling.

"So," Flash said, "what did you really find?"

"Nothing," Nick told him. "We decided to leave the thing alone."

"Poor Digby's been through enough," Julie explained.

"You didn't find out what's buried there?"

"I guess we'll never know," Nick said.

Julie nodded. "One of life's unsolved mysteries."

Flash looked at Scott and shook his head. "Our kids, I'm afraid, are a couple of chickens."

Scott grinned at him. "As my pappy used to say, 'Better a chicken than a ghoul.'"

CHAPTER TWELVE

"Must we?" Alice complained. "Why don't we play cards instead? Do you play bridge, Karen?"

"Not very well, I'm afraid."

"I want a story," Rose protested.

"Me, too," said Heather.

"You girls were frightened out of your wits last night."

"It was *neat*."

"Too windy for cards," Arnold said. He broke a dead branch over his knee, and placed both pieces on the fire. "I'm for a story."

Alice sighed. She didn't want to be a stick in the mud. On the other hand, she certainly didn't want a repeat of last night's shenanigans. The story itself hadn't bothered her. Not much anyway. But her idea of fun did not include being startled from a half sleep by the hysterical screams of her daughters. "It's all right with me," she said. She stared across the blazing fire at Nick. "No funny stuff tonight. Promise?"

"Cross my heart," he said.

"Who's got a story?" Scott asked.

"A real scary one," Benny added.

"Karen?" Arnold asked.

"Someone else's turn. I did my damage."

At least she had the good sense to realize she'd caused all the trouble.

Scott leaned toward the fire, grinning. "There is, of course, the true story of Digby Bolles."

"Oh, Dad." Julie smirked at him.

"Go on," Alice urged. This story should be harmless enough.

"Is it scary?" Benny asked.

"Listen and find out. Digby came to the mountains, insane with grief, to look for his missing daughter, Doreen."

"*The* Doreen?" Karen asked.

"The very Doreen who vanished with Audrey so mysteriously earlier that summer. Well, Digby wandered the trails and woods and the high, barren passes, looking everywhere. Soon, his food ran out. But he didn't turn back. He kept searching. He lived on chipmunks and squirrels, which he ate raw."

"Yuck," Rose said.

"Squirrel tartare," said Julie.

"October came, and a terrible blizzard hit. But Digby continued his search. He couldn't find any more squirrels. He was starving to death. Then one night he saw the light of a campfire in the distance. He trudged through the knee-deep snow, and came upon a lone camper. He staggered up to the man, who was kind enough to offer him a bowl of stew. But Digby had lost his taste for stew. The man, who happened to be a surgeon on a fishing trip, looked very appetizing to Digby. And he tasted as good as he looked." Scott leaned back, folded his arms across his chest, and grinned.

"Is that all?" Benny asked.

"Great story, Pop," Julie muttered, shaking her head:

"What happened next?" Rose demanded.

"Well, poor Digby eventually starved to death. He ran out of Dr. Scholl's."

"Boo," Julie said.

"That's awful," Karen gasped as she laughed.

"Wasn't even scary," Benny complained.

"The best I could do on short notice."

Heather looked up at Alice, frowning. "I don't get it."

"That's all right, honey. It's just as well."

"He *ate* the guy, stupid," Rose explained.

"I know that. What I mean is, if he ate up Dr. Scholl's and then died, who buried him?"

"We'll never know," Scott said. "One of those great, unsolved mysteries of life."

"It's just a story," Alice told the girls. "None of it really happened."

"But we saw his grave," Heather said.

"Don't be a dork."

Alice glared at Rose. "Watch your language, young lady."

"I want a real story," Benny said. "That wasn't even scary. It was okay, but it was just a joke. I want a scary one."

Nick suddenly sat up straight and slapped his knees. "I've got it! Let's all get our flashlights and go on a Doreen and Audrey hunt!"

"Neat!" Benny blurted.

Julie looked eager. "They've gotta be around here someplace."

"Can we, Mom?" Rose asked.

"Not me. I'm perfectly comfortable where I am."

Arnold turned to Scott. "What do you think?"

"I'm all for letting the kids go, if that's what they want."

"Somebody might get hurt," Alice said. She wanted to protest more strongly, but since Scott seemed to think it was all right . . .

"We'll be real careful," Nick told her.

"And no funny stuff. I don't want you trying to scare the girls."

He raised three fingers. "Scout's honor."

"Don't go wandering off too far," Arnold said. "We don't want to lose you."

"We'll just circle the lake."

"Maybe one of us should go with them," Alice suggested. "Just in case."

"Jeez, Mom, nothing's gonna happen."

"Nick's old enough to take care of things," Arnold said.

She sighed. "Well, be very careful. Somebody could fall and break a leg."

"We'll be careful," Nick assured her.

A flashlight shined in Benny's eyes as he hurried through the darkness. "What took you so long?" Julie asked.

"I couldn't find my flashlight." He shielded his eyes from the beam.

"Have you got it?"

"Yeah."

Julie lowered her light. It made a pale disk on the ground at her feet.

"Okay," Nick said. "Let's stay close together." Benny heard a slight tremor in the older boy's voice.

He was shivering himself. It was partly the cold, but he felt shriveled and shaky inside. I'm not scared, he thought. Just excited.

"Now watch where you're walking," Nick said. "We'll catch hell if someone gets hurt, and they won't let us do it again."

"Maybe we can do it *every* night," Benny said, thrilled by the idea.

They started walking single file along a footpath near the shore. Nick was in the lead, with Julie close behind him. The twins followed Julie. With hoods up, their hair was out of sight, so Benny couldn't tell which was which.

Looking over his shoulder toward the clearing, he saw the glow of the campfire. He wished Karen had come along. It would be a lot more fun with Karen, even if she was a grown-up.

He took his flashlight from a pocket of his parka, and turned it on. The beam lit up the red jeans and sneakers of the girl in front of him. He shined it into the trees to his left. The weird, lurching shadows made him nervous. He swung his light down across the path, over pale rocks along the shore, and onto the water. The surface of the lake was rough from the wind. He swept the beam back and forth over the waves. He made curlicues. It was fun at first. Then he thought, What if a hand reaches up out of the water and nobody sees it but me? That's stupid, he told himself. But the image of a dead pale hand rising out of the murky lake wouldn't go away and he began to feel certain he would see it if he kept watching. His skin was prickly with goose bumps. He turned off the flashlight.

"Doreeeen," Julie called in an eerie voice. "Audreeey! Come on, everybody."

Nick took up the call. Then the high voices of the twins joined in. With a shrug, Benny started calling out, too. Their voices rose, mingling with the noise of the wind.

Somebody'll hear, Benny thought. But he kept on shouting, unwilling to be the only silent one of the group. Besides, he told himself, there's nobody around to hear us. Nobody we know about. He glanced over his shoulder, but saw only darkness behind him.

He began to wish he weren't last in line. It'd get him first. Nobody would even know. He'd yell his head off, but with all the others calling for Doreen and Audrey, they wouldn't even hear him. It'd drag him away and . . .

Benny jerked his foot back, but it was too late. The girl yelped and stumbled forward, leaving her sneaker behind. She crashed into the other twin, and they both fell sprawling. "Jeez, I'm sorry!" he blurted.

"Get off me!" snapped the one on the bottom, pushing at her sister.

Benny picked up the shoe.

"What happened?" Nick asked. "You okay?" He and Julie helped the girls to their feet.

"I tripped," said the girl Benny had stepped on. She had to be Heather.

"I stepped on her," Benny admitted.

"Four-eyes!" Rose snapped.

"You klutz!" Julie said. "Goddamn it!"

"I'm sorry."

"Jesus, why don't you watch where you're going?"

His throat felt tight. He fought to keep himself from crying as he handed the shoe to Heather. "I'm awfully sorry."

"It's okay," she told him. "It doesn't hurt much."

"Stupid jerk."

"That's enough, Rose," Nick said. "It was just an accident. You both all right?"

The girls nodded. Heather put on her shoe.

"Okay, let's get going."

"Don't walk so close," Julie warned Benny.

"Maybe I'll just go back to camp."

"Good idea. Why don't you?"

Turning away, he looked down the dark trail. They were near the end of the lake. There was no sign of the campsite.

Someone tugged the sleeve of his parka. "Come on," said a girl's voice. "It's all right." He looked around, and saw one of the twins behind him.

"I'm sorry I stepped on you," he mumbled.

She smiled up at him. "That's okay. Don't go back, okay?"

"I guess not," he said. "Thank you."

They started walking again. Benny grimaced as he noticed that Heather was limping. He was careful to stay well behind her until the narrow path curved upward and vanished in the rocks at the lake's end. There, he stepped up beside her. She looked at him and smiled. Side by side, they walked over the low slabs of granite near the shore.

With no trees to cast heavy shadows, the night seemed very bright. The lake still looked almost black, but the bare rock was pale, as if painted with milk. Benny was amazed that he could see so well. He saw Julie's hair blowing in the wind, the pattern of Nick's plaid jacket, even the three stripes on the side of Rose's left sneaker. No colors, though. He couldn't make out any colors. Even Heather's jeans, which he knew were bright red, appeared to be a dark shade of gray. He wondered about that. You can see colors with a flashlight, but not by moonlight. It seemed strange.

Nick stopped and took hold of Julie's arm. "Look," he said, pointing high.

"What?" Julie asked.

"Way up there. Near the top."

Benny scanned the pale slope. He saw patches of darkness, a few scrawny trees scattered about like solitary, watching men.

"Oh, yeah," Julie said.

"I don't see anything," Heather muttered.

"I do," Rose said. "Are they dogs?"

"Coyotes," Nick explained.

Then Benny spotted a pair of lean, gray shapes strutting stiff-legged across a ledge high on the slope. They had long snouts, and tails as bushy as a squirrel's.

"I still don't . . ." Heather began.

Benny crouched to her level and pointed.

"Oh, gosh," she said.

"Don't worry," Benny told her. "They don't hurt anyone."

"Is that so?" Julie asked. "A coyote killed a four-year-old girl, last year, in her own backyard."

"Where?" Nick asked.

"Back home, in L.A. One of those canyon areas. It just came down from the hills behind their yard and mauled her to death."

"Let's get out of here," Heather whispered.

"It's all right," Nick said. "They're way up there. Besides, they wouldn't try anything with five of us."

"Unless they're hungry," Julie added.

Nick laughed nervously, and started walking again. Soon, Benny saw the glow of the campfire on the other side of the lake. When they were directly across from it, he could see the tents and the adults sitting around the fire.

"Hel-lo!" Julie called.

Nobody answered. The wind must be too loud, Benny thought.

They kept moving. Benny stayed close to Heather. She continued to limp slightly. Sometimes, when they had to climb over clusters of rock, Benny went first and gave her a hand. He liked helping her. She wasn't a snot like her sister.

And she still seemed nervous about the coyotes. Every few steps, she looked back. "I don't like it here," she said after a while.

"There's nothing to be afraid of," he told her.

She glanced behind her. "What's *that?*"

Benny spun around, his heart thudding. "That? Just a bush."

"Are you sure?"

"Sure I'm sure," he said, but he kept staring at the dark, hunched shape. It was barely visible in the shadows of an outcropping no more than two yards away. It *was* a bush, wasn't it? An icy feeling of dread crept up Benny's back. "Come on," he said. He took Heather's hand and pulled her away. She sidestepped behind him, still looking back. They hurried to catch up with the others.

Benny was glad to see that they had almost reached the end of the lake. Just below an outcropping ahead, the forest would start again. They would merely have to pick up the trail there, follow it around a bend in the shoreline, and hike straight back to the camp.

Nick, in the lead, disappeared over the top of the outcropping. Julie followed. Rose waited for Benny and Heather, then started down.

Benny looked back. Nothing was approaching from the rear. He let Heather go ahead of him. As she climbed down, Nick, at the bottom, suddenly lurched backward and swung an arm against Julie. With a yelp, Rose whirled around and began to scurry up the rocks. "It's *them!*" she cried out. "Doreen and Audrey!"

Heather twisted around. Benny saw terror on her moon-washed face. She lunged up and he grabbed her outstretched arm and yanked her to the top.

Julie pressed a hand to her thumping heart. "Christ, you scared the crap out of us."

"We were . . . uh . . . getting a trifle nervous ourselves," said the buxom girl in the sweatshirt.

"We heard you coming," said the one in the cowboy hat. She had a husky, confident voice. Her face glowed as she sucked on a cigarette. "You from the campfire?"

"Yeah," Nick said. Turning away, he called to the twins and Benny. "It's all right! Come on down."

"We didn't know anyone was around," Julie said. "Are you camped here?"

"Just off in the trees," said the one in the hat.

"Don't you have a fire?" Nick asked.

"I wanted one," said the other.

"A fire just makes you colder. And it kills your night vision. And it lets everyone for ten miles know you're there. Not real healthy when you're three girls camping alone."

"Three of you?" Nick asked.

"Barb's back at camp."

"You're not Doreen and Audrey, I take it," Julie said.

"Who?"

"I didn't think so." At the sound of footsteps behind her, Julie turned around. Benny and the twins were coming slowly forward. "They're not Doreen and Audrey," she said.

The girl in the cowboy hat tapped ash off her cigarette. "This Doreen and Audrey, you looking for them or something?"

Julie explained, telling briefly of Karen's story and how they'd used it as an excuse, tonight, to explore the lake's shoreline.

"Something like a snipe hunt," said the girl in the hat.

"More like a ghost hunt," said the other.

"If we'd known, we could've screamed it up for you."

"I almost did anyway. Still jumpy from that nutcase."

"What's that?" Nick asked.

The girl folded her arms across her sweatshirt and looked at her friend. "We'd better warn 'em."

"Which way are you guys heading?"

"Over to the Triangle Lakes area," Nick said.

"Then you'll be heading over Carver Pass, tomorrow. You know the area?"

"Just from maps."

"Well, there's a couple of lakes just the other side of the pass. The Mesquites. We stopped at one of them for lunch today, and ran into some crazy old bag."

"A real weirdo."

"We went in swimming, and she popped up out of nowhere and started raving about water snakes."

"Scared the hell out of us."

"Speak for yourself. Anyway, I didn't see any snakes. I think she was just some kind of lunatic trying to get rid of us. I wouldn't worry much about her, if I were you guys. She might even be gone, by now."

"Might not," her friend countered.

"If you stop there, just don't be too surprised if you run into her, that's all."

"Sounds like a good place to avoid," Julie said. The ranger, she remembered, had already advised them to pass up the Mesquites. Did he know about the crazy woman? That didn't seem likely.

"I mean, we don't want to scare you," said the girl in the sweatshirt. "She didn't *do* anything. Just yelled at us. But she was definitely creepy. She had this look in her eyes. And she wasn't even dressed like a camper. I mean—do you believe it?—she was actually wearing a dress!"

"Sort of a housedress," added the other girl, mashing her cigarette stub on the sole of her boot. "A faded old thing."

"And hiking boots."

"Did you see her knife?"

"Knife?"

"On her belt. Looked like a bowie knife. A *huge* sucker."

"Lovely," Julie muttered. "A crazy woman with a bowie knife. I think we'll stay away from that lake for sure."

Chapter Thirteen

Karen hung upside down in the overturned car, clawing for the seat-belt buckle, unable to find it. "Buckle up for safety, buckle up," the old jingle taunted her. "I'll warm you up," said a voice from the window.

She knew what she would see if she turned her head, and the thought of it terrified her. She didn't want to see. But she couldn't stop herself. Her head turned slowly toward the open window. Go away! she thought. I'll shut my eyes and he'll go away. She shut them, but her eyelids were transparent and she gazed at the charred face. Wisps of smoke curled out of its empty sockets, the hole where its nose should have been, its mouth.

"Turnabout's fair play," it said, blowing smoke into her eyes. The mouth twitched in a blistered grin, cracking the black flesh of its cheeks.

"No!" she cried. "It wasn't my fault!"

He thrust a gasoline spout at her face. The foul liquid gushed out, stinging her eyes, filling her nostrils. She opened her mouth for a breath and gasoline filled it, choking her.

He grabbed her shoulder. She tried to pry the fingers loose. They were dry and brittle, and she knew they would break off if she pulled hard enough.

"Karen!"

She woke up, gasping. Scott was kneeling beside her, a hand on her shoulder. "Are you okay?" he whispered.

"Thank God you woke me."

"Must've been a hell of a nightmare."

"It was." With trembling fingers, she found the zipper tab inside her sleeping bag and slid it down. She rolled onto her side to make room for Scott. He climbed in, pulled the zipper shut, and took her into his arms. Like last night, he wore only jockey shorts. His back was smooth and cold under her hands.

"You're shaking," he said.

"So are you."

"I'm frozen."

"I'm just scared out of my wits." She hugged him tightly.

"Chased by boogeymen?"

"Something like that." She let out a deep sigh. "I haven't had one like that in a long time."

"Sleeping on the hard ground'll do that to you. I've been having some pretty wild dreams myself. Mostly about you."

"Not nightmares, I hope."

"No indeedy." He pulled her sweatshirt up so she was bare against his belly and chest. Gently, he stroked her back. "I'll tell you mine if you tell me yours."

"You don't want to hear mine."

"Might help to talk about it. Maybe we can figure out what it means."

"I know what it means. And what brought it on, too—that business about the scars this afternoon."

His hands stopped moving. They pressed Karen closer against him. "Your accident?" he whispered.

"Yeah. Only it's not Frank trapped in the car, it's me. He was crouched by the window . . . all burnt up. He sprayed me with gas . . ."

"Good Christ."

"You woke me up before he got a chance to light it."

"Must've been awful."

"I've had it worse, sometimes. I usually wake up about the time he strikes the match, but a couple of times . . . I'm on fire and he crawls in through the window and . . ." She suddenly gagged.

Scott stroked the back of her head. "It's all right," he said. "Shh."

"Sorry."

"It's all right. I'll tell you about my dreams."

"Yours are nice, right?"

"Very nice. This morning—yesterday morning?—I dreamed it was raining and you came out of your tent in a clear plastic poncho, and nothing else."

"You're making this up."

"No. Honest. The rain was coming down real hard. Your hair was all matted down. Your face was slick and dripping. Water was streaming down the outside of your poncho, and I could see gooseflesh underneath. And your nipples were erect."

"Like now?"

A hand went to her breast. "Like now."

She sighed as he fingered the nipple.

"One thing was weird, though."

"What?"

"You know how dreams are."

"Weird."

"Right. Well, you didn't have any pubic hair. You'd shaved it off."

"This dream of yours is getting me hot."

"Me, too." His hand slid down, caressing her belly. It pushed inside her sweatpants. Slowly, it moved lower. "Just a dream," he said.

"I could shave it."

"It's nice this way."

"Hey, if you dream it's shaven, that's an expression of a frustrated desire, right? I'll do it. One of these days. It'll be a"—his sliding finger took her breath away—"a surprise."

"Want to hear the rest of the dream?"

"There's more?"

"Sure." His hand moved away, drawing a slick trail up her skin. He started pulling at the bow in her drawstring. "I said,

'You must be cold. What happened to your clothes?' And you told me Julie had stolen them."

"Significant, that."

"She told you she'd hidden them so you'd have to stay in the tent."

"Away from you?"

"Could be." The drawstring loose, he pulled at Karen's sweatpants. She helped by kicking them down her legs. The inside of the sleeping bag felt cool and slippery on her bare skin. Scott caressed the back of her leg. His hand slid up her buttock, held it gently. "Anyway, I said I didn't want you to freeze. We went into my tent so I could get you some warm clothes, but the only clothes you wanted were the ones I was wearing."

"You have very peculiar dreams."

"Don't I? So you made me lie down on top of my sleeping bag. You took off your poncho and knelt over me and started to undress me."

"I stripped you naked?"

"Very slowly."

She hooked her fingers under the waistband of his shorts, eased the elastic away from his body, and pulled downward. She felt him spring free. With the back of her hand, she caressed the underside of his rigid penis. She tugged the shorts lower. Then she curled her fingers around him, feeling his hardness and his heat. "Did I do this?" she whispered.

He answered with a moan.

"And did I use my mouth?"

"Yes."

Her encircling fingers glided up the smooth length of him. "And did you use your mouth?"

"Yes."

"Where?"

His hands showed her where, rubbing, fingers sliding in. She trembled as heat surged through her body. "Unzip the bag," she gasped.

"We'll freeze."

"Did you freeze in the dream?"

"No, but—"

"Wouldn't you like your dream to come true? Better yours than mine, right?"

"You don't know everything we did."

"Show me."

He did.

"This is when I woke up," he finally gasped.

"Oh. Oh, Christ. Well, don't stop now!"

"But . . . this is when I—"

"Ad-lib."

When they were through, Scott pulled the cover of the sleeping bag over them. They held each other, panting and sweaty. "Quite a dream," Karen whispered, and kissed him.

Later, he fell asleep. Karen lay cuddled against his long smooth warmth, feeling his breath on her face, feeling the slow rise and fall of his chest. She was lazy and content. She wanted to let herself slip into sleep and wake up in the morning with him, but she couldn't.

It had always been that way. During their months together, she constantly longed for him to stay, to spend the whole night. In the morning, she would make him breakfast. It would be so wonderful, so complete. Instead, he always had to leave her bed and hurry home. For the kids. She certainly didn't blame him, but she wished it were different. Someday, maybe.

She kissed his eyelids, his mouth. He stirred against her. His hand moved up her side. It closed gently over her breast. "You'd better be going," she whispered.

Scott groaned. "I'd rather not," he muttered.

"I know."

He held her for a long time. He kissed her. Then he eased away and left the sleeping bag. "Woe, it's cooold," he gasped, pulling on his underwear.

"Do you want my sweatshirt?"

"No, that's—"

"Please. I don't want you freezing out there." She tugged it from under her shoulder, and held it out to him. "You can bring it back tomorrow night."

"It's a deal."

As he pulled it over his head, Karen sat up. The cold wrapped her bare skin to the waist.

"Tight fit," he said. Then he leaned closer and hugged her. She felt his warmth through the softness of the sweatshirt. "Sleep well," he said. He kissed her again, then released her and crawled out through the tent flap.

Karen snuggled down in her sleeping bag. She heard his quick footfalls in the leaves, and imagined him rushing toward his tent. She was glad he'd taken her sweatshirt. It was as if part of her had gone with him. She wondered if he would keep it on once he was in his own sleeping bag. Would he wear it and think of her?

Curling up, she reached under her legs and found her sweatpants. She pulled them free. Instead of putting them on, she pressed the limp legs between her thighs. She smoothed the fabric over her belly and breasts. It was soft and warm. With the pants hugged against her, she fell asleep.

Chapter Fourteen

Scott woke up with a bad need to urinate. Lying motionless, he forced one eye open. The tent was murky with morning light. Benny was still asleep, breathing deeply, the red of his stocking cap all that showed of him at the top of his mummy bag.

After returning from Karen's tent, Scott hadn't bothered to put his own cap on. He should've. His head was cold, and the rolled-up jeans he used as a pillow felt hard.

He scooted lower until his head was covered, and brought up an arm to cushion it. A thick, soft sleeve pressed against the side of his face. Karen's sweatshirt. He sniffed it. There was a mild, fresh scent that brought a memory of crawling into her sleeping bag, huddling against her warmth, lifting the sweatshirt up over her breasts. She was without it now. He imagined how she would look wearing only the gray sweatpants. That gave him an erection. Swell, he thought.

He concentrated on how to conceal the sweatshirt. If the kids should see it . . . but Benny was still asleep and he heard no one stirring about the campsite. If he got up now, he could hide it in his pack, which was just outside the tent. He might wrap the sweatshirt in something, just to be safe. No telling whether Julie would actually be asleep.

Hell, if Julie *was* still sleeping, he could take the sweatshirt right over to Karen's tent and . . . no, too risky.

He didn't want to leave the snug warmth. He could just stay here. Take off the sweatshirt and leave it hidden in the bottom of the bag until later. Wait right here until the nice hot sun broke over the ridge. . . . But that might be an hour. My teeth are floating!

Quickly, he pulled off the sweatshirt. He shoved it down low in the bag, unzipped the side, and climbed out. He gritted his teeth so hard his jaw ached. Funny, he thought, how the cold didn't bother him so much when he was sneaking out at night. It's all in the mind, he told himself. Sure. Feels more like it's in the bones. Sitting on the slick cover of his sleeping bag, he unrolled his jeans. He pushed his legs in, and leaned back slightly. He stifled a yelp as his shoulders met the cold, wet wall of the tent. Ducking away, he grabbed his cotton shirt and pulled it on.

He snatched up his hiking boots. Fresh socks were tucked inside them. He willed his hands to stop quaking, but they didn't obey. Finally, he managed to tug the socks over his feet. He shoved his feet into the boots. The cold of the boots, still damp from yesterday's sweat, seeped through his socks.

Why the hell does anyone go camping? he asked himself. We're a bunch of damn masochists.

He tucked the laces under the boot tongues. Even if he wanted to tie them, his hands were shaking too badly.

He crawled toward the tent flap, then remembered Karen's sweatshirt. He glanced at Benny. Still asleep. Reaching into the warmth of his sleeping bag, Scott pulled out the sweatshirt. He tucked it inside his shirt, and crawled outside.

He glanced at the two sleeping bags, some twenty feet away, stretched out side by side near the circled rocks of the fireplace. They didn't seem quite as far apart as the first night. Interesting. The tan hood of Julie's warm-up suit was all he could see of her. He quickly opened his pack, stuffed the sweatshirt deep inside, and rushed off into the trees behind the tents.

When he returned, he felt a lot better. If he could just get a fire started, he knew he would feel terrific. Fooling with it, though, he'd be sure to wake up Julie and Nick.

Their sleeping bags were no more than a yard apart. Very interesting, that. He was glad Julie seemed to like the boy. The way the trip had started, he'd been afraid of a disaster. Since meeting Nick, however, she'd been acting civil. Her resentment of Karen's presence seemed to have faded to the point where it was hardly noticeable. He supposed he could thank Nick for that.

And for picking up Julie's spirits in general. After getting dumped by that turkey, Clemens, she needed a friend.

O'Toole the matchmaker.

He took a small satchel and towel from his pack, and walked silently past the tent, heading for the stream. He smiled as he walked.

Julie would croak if she knew he'd planned it this way. When Flash first mentioned taking his family on a week-long backpacking trip, Scott had imagined spending time in the high mountains alone with Karen. It'd be a shame, though, to leave the kids home. Maybe a trip would help to pull Julie out of her depression. . . . Then he thought of Flash's son, a handsome, reliable kid, a bit on the quiet side, but only a year older than Julie. If the two should hit it off at all, Julie might forget about that rat Clemens and start enjoying life again. So he'd suggested to Flash that their families join forces for the trip, and Flash had jumped at the idea.

Seems the little scheme had paid off.

The two kids were getting along pretty well—even better than Scott had expected. They didn't act smitten, but it was obvious that they enjoyed each other's company, and who knew what might be going on in their minds? Better, maybe, not to know. Just be glad Julie's back to normal.

At the stream, he spotted a place where sunlight slanted down through a gap in the trees. The bright swath, hazy with dust motes, fell upon a cluster of rocks not far away. He tramped through the bushes and stepped out onto the rocks. For a long time, he stood motionless, letting the warmth seep into him.

When he felt sufficiently thawed, he took off his shirt. He crouched low and cupped the cold water into his mouth. Then he brushed his teeth. He managed to raise a thin lather on his face, using a biodegradable soap, and began to shave with a straight razor.

"You're a terrible disappointment."

He looked downstream. Karen, in her sweatpants and parka, was standing on a log bridge, arms folded across her chest, staring at him. "Come on over here where it's warm," he called. He continued to shave while she hurried toward him. She leaped onto a flat rock beside him.

"Oh, this is better."

"And why am I such a disappointment? Or don't I want to know?"

"Using a razor," she said in a mocking tone. "I would've expected a macho guy like you to shave with a dull knife."

"Tried it once. Half my face came off with the whiskers. This is far superior. Gives a nice, close shave without the inconvenience of a bloodbath." Smiling up at her, he said, "Did you come by for a shave?"

A blush darkened her face. "My legs, you mean?"

"Also your legs, if you like."

"Nasty man."

"Is that a no?"

"Other people are up and around."

"Damn." He swirled the blade through the water, wiped it dry across a leg of his jeans, and folded it shut. He splashed water on his face. When the soap was rinsed off, he picked up his towel. "Sleep well?" he asked as he dried his face.

"Like a rock."

"No more dreams?"

"Not bad ones. How about you?"

"I'll tell you about mine tonight."

"Oh ho-*ho*!"

"When I bring back your sweatshirt." He stood up and lowered the zipper of her parka. She wore nothing under it.

He slid his arms inside and around her back, and pulled her against him. She was smooth and warm.

"Good morning," she said.

He kissed her.

Then there were voices in the distance. Reluctantly, Scott eased away from her.

"Nobody's here yet," she said, and lifted his hands to her breasts. She held them there. Her nipples were firm under his palms. She sighed and her head tilted back, eyes shut against the sun.

"Wanton woman," Scott whispered.

"Wantin' you," she said. She pressed his hands firmly against her, then let go.

Scott moved his hands down the undersides of her breasts, down her ribs, inward as her velvety skin sloped to her belly. Then he pulled together the lower corners of her parka and fitted the zipper into its slot. He raised the tab about three inches. "There."

"Oh, charming."

Someone came tramping through the bushes. With an exaggerated look of alarm, Karen jerked the zipper to her throat. The footfalls grew louder.

Scott had time to turn away, crouch, and slip his razor into the satchel before Flash appeared downstream near the log bridge. The man was already dressed in his knit shirt, plaid shorts, and boots. His mussy fringe of red hair was the only clue that he'd just crawled out of his sleeping bag. He squatted by the stream and dipped an aluminum pot into the water.

"Morning!" Karen called.

He looked over and waved. "Tally-ho, mates!"

Scott grinned up at Karen. "Mates?" he asked.

"Nautical jargon," she said quietly.

"Ah. Afraid he was being a wise guy." Standing up, Scott yelled, "Ahoy and avast, are ye of a mind to weigh anchor?"

"Ain't had me coffee yet," Flash called back.

"Then we'll sail for Java." To Karen, he said, "Shall we be off?"

"Aye, matey."

"Meet you in the galley," Scott called.

They made their way back to camp. Julie, still in her warm-up suit, was feeding sticks to the fire. Nick's sleeping bag was empty, but he was nowhere to be seen. One of the twins was walking into the woods with a roll of toilet paper. Alice, bundled in her coat, was tearing open a plastic bag of powdered eggs with her teeth.

"Back in a jiff," Karen said, and headed for her tent.

In his own tent, Scott saw that Benny was still asleep. "Up and at 'em," he said, finding a foot through the down-filled bag and giving it a small shake. The boy raised his head and looked around, one eye covered by his red stocking cap. "Sleep well?"

"Yeah." Benny reached into the boot by his head, and pulled out his glasses. The lenses were fogged up. He tugged off his cap and put the glasses on anyway, then scrunched up his face as if that might help him to see better. "Where'd you go?"

"What?"

"I woke up and you weren't here."

"I've been up for a while," Scott told him.

"No, I mean last night."

Oh, Christ, he thought. He couldn't lie to his son, but how could he tell the truth? "I took a little walk," he said.

"See any coyotes?"

"Not a one. You better haul yourself out of there and get dressed. Breakfast'll be ready before you know it." Before Benny might be tempted to question him further, he backed out of the tent.

"Ahoy!" Flash said, walking by with a full pot of water.

"Avast," Scott said. "I'll get my stove going." He took his Primus stove from his pack and carried it over to the fire.

Julie was there, stretched out on her sleeping bag to

squeeze the air out before attempting to mash it into its stuff bag.

"Have a good night?" he asked her.

"My feet froze, but aside from that . . ."

"Maybe wear an extra pair of socks." Hanging onto its key chain, he dangled the stove over the flame to heat the fuel. Thank God that Julie, at least, wasn't aware of his nighttime forays. The truth probably wouldn't upset Benny, but Julie . . . If Benny should mention his disappearance last night, she'd guess at once what he'd been up to. She might not throw a fit, but her resentment would surface and she would do her best to make everyone miserable. Probably even start sleeping in the tent just so it wouldn't happen again.

Should've just tented with Karen in the first place. Well, with the Gordons along they couldn't have done that anyway.

He swung the stove away from the campfire flames, and set it inside its aluminum holder.

"You got that sucker going yet?" Flash asked, coming up behind him.

"Stand back and get ready to duck."

Flash scraped the last of his scrambled eggs and bacon bits from the bottom of his dish. "Ah, that was good stuff. Want me to polish off yours for you?" he asked Rose.

"No."

"Aw, come on. It'll only weigh you down."

"Daddy!"

"Let her finish it," Alice said. "Have some Grape Nuts if you're still hungry."

"Bleah."

"It's good roughage."

"So is bark. Doesn't mean I want to eat a tree." He looked at the twins. "Everything out of your tent?" They nodded as they shoved forkfuls of egg into their mouths. "Let's get to it, Nick."

Nick, on the other side of the fire, took a sip of coffee, nodded, and stood up. They went over to the tent and started taking it down. They worked in silence, pulling the guy lines, Flash holding the front upright while Nick folded the rear forward, then easing the front backward. When the tent was flat, they removed the collapsible rods, pulled out the stakes along its sides, and folded it into thirds. Flash rolled it up with the rods inside. Nick held the plastic stuff bag open, and Flash shoved the tent into it.

They stepped over to the other tent, and began to repeat the process.

"So long, over there," a voice called.

Looking up, Flash saw three teenaged girls through the trees. They were on the main trail, hiking single file.

"'Bye," Nick yelled. "Have a good trip back."

"Watch out for the crazy woman," warned the girl in the lead. Then the three vanished among the trees.

Nick eased the rear of the tent forward.

"Those the gals you ran into last night?" Flash asked.

"Yeah."

"What's this about a crazy woman?"

"Nothing much," Nick said. He shrugged as if it were unimportant, but his eyes looked worried. "They told us they ran into some weird old lady yesterday at a lake the other side of the pass. I guess she yelled at them, or something."

"What for?"

"I don't know. They just thought she was crazy."

"Takes all kinds, I guess."

"Hope we don't run into her."

"Don't worry about it. Any crazy old bag gives us any lip, we'll stomp her. Right?"

Nick gave a nervous laugh. "Sure thing."

Heather grimaced, lips drawn back and teeth clenched, as she pushed her left foot into her boot. "What's wrong?" Alice asked.

"Nothing."

"Let me see." She squatted down beside the girl. "Take your boot off."

"Really, Mom, it's all right."

"I'll be the judge of that."

With a reluctant sigh, Heather pulled off her boot. She peeled the wool sock down her ankle. The skin above her heel was gray, as if smudged with dirt. She winced when Alice pressed it. "Arnold, would you come over here?"

He was crouched over his pack, securing its flap. He looked over his shoulder. "What's wrong?"

"We have an injury here."

"Oh, shit," he muttered. He hurried over.

"A bruised Achilles tendon," Alice said.

Arnold gently rotated the foot. Heather's face showed pain. "It's all right," she insisted.

"How did this happen?" Alice asked.

Heather shrugged.

Rose, who'd been sitting on a rock nearby and watching, said, "I'll tell you. It was that klutz, Benny. He kicked her last night."

"He didn't *kick* me, he *stepped* on me."

"Shit."

"Arnold!"

"Does it hurt much?" he asked.

"No. Really."

"I thought I saw you limping," Alice said. "Good heavens, Heather, why didn't you tell us about it?"

The girl shrugged, and pulled up her sock.

"I bet," Rose said, "she just didn't want to get Benny in trouble. She's got a crush on him."

"I do not!"

"Do, too."

"Knock it off," Arnold muttered. He frowned at Heather. "You can walk on it okay, though, right?"

"Yeah. It's fine."

"Well, we'll try to take it easy today. If it gives you too much trouble, we'll figure something out."

"Let's leave her behind," Rose said. "So the coyotes can eat her."

"That's enough out of you, young lady."

"All right," Arnold said. "Let's haul it. I've got a feeling this'll be a long day."

Chapter Fifteen

Nick stopped at the trail sign. It read CARVER PASS, 2 MI. Leaning against a rock to ease the weight of his pack, he looked down into the valley. Lake Parker was there in the distance, as blue as the sky, its north shore hidden among the trees. The south shore was mostly barren rock. He spotted the outcropping he'd climbed down last night, and felt a small tremor of the fear that had numbed him when he came unexpectedly upon the two girls. Then he smiled, remembering Rose's shriek and the way she'd scurried up the rocks. It had been quite a little adventure. Damn it, though. Poor Heather. They should've just stayed in camp after all.

"Hand me my water bottle?" Julie asked.

"Sure."

She turned away. Nick unzipped a side pocket of her pack, and pulled out the green plastic container. He watched Julie tilt the bottle to her lips and drink. Her face was burnished with sunburn, her nose peeling a bit. The leather band of her beret was dark with sweat. When she finished drinking, she offered a drink to Nick. He took a few swallows, and slid the bottle back into her pack.

"This is gonna be a bear," she said.

"Yeah. Especially for Heather."

"That idiot brother of mine."

"Looks like it'll be switchbacks from here to the top."

"Don't you just love switchbacks?"

"On the bright side, it'll all be downhill to Lake Wilson."

"If we can just make it to the top."

Down the trail, Scott and Karen appeared, hiking side by side through the shadows. "Let's hold it up," Scott called. "Wait for the others."

"How's Heather doing?" Julie asked.

"Holding her own."

They waited. Soon, Nick saw Rose coming up the trail. His father and mother were a short distance behind the girl. Dad was carrying Heather's red backpack like an unwieldy grocery bag. Nick hurried down. Taking the pack from his father, he saw Benny and Heather. They were far back. Heather, limping along with the aid of Nick's blackthorn stick, laughed at something Benny said. A good sign. At least she wasn't whimpering with pain.

Nick turned away. He trudged up the trail ahead of his parents.

"Is that pretty heavy?" Julie asked.

"Not as bad as ours."

Karen stepped toward him. "Let me feel." She took Heather's pack from his arms. "Why don't we split up what's in it? We'll each carry some, and nobody'll be stuck with lugging around a full pack all day."

"Not only pretty, but brilliant," Dad said. "Any objections?"

Rose wrinkled her face, but nodded with defeat. Everyone else acted as if it were a great idea. Heather watched, looking embarrassed, while packs were opened and rearranged to make room for her belongings. When her father started to lash her empty pack to his own, she finally objected. "I can carry that."

"No trouble," he told her.

"I'll carry it," Benny said. His voice was a little whiny. "It's all my fault."

"Hey, those things happen," Dad consoled him. "Don't blame yourself."

Benny looked around as if searching for a hole to crawl into. Finding none, he let out a deep sigh. "I'm sorry, everybody."

"No sweat," Scott told him.

"Sure," Julie said. "It'll be fun carrying a little extra weight."

Scott scowled at her.

"I knew we shouldn't have let them go off last night," Mom said. "Nobody listens to me. Next time—"

"Let's get this show on the road," Dad interrupted. "We've got a mountain to climb."

Shouldering their packs, they started up the trail again. The trees thinned out, leaving fewer patches of shade, then no shade at all.

Nick and Julie, in the lead, paused often to wait for the others to catch up. Finally, near noon, they stopped at one of the flat areas where the trail turned back on itself in its zigzag up the mountainside. They shed their packs and sat on a boulder. Scott and Karen were a distance down the trail, slowly trudging closer.

"Who ever said backpacking's fun?" Julie asked.

"Not me."

"Shit." She lifted the front of her T-shirt and rubbed her sweaty face. Nick glanced at her bare midriff. She pulled the shirt down again. It clung to her. "Feel like I'm gonna die."

"At least there's a little breeze."

"How'd you like to dive in a swimming pool about now?"

"I'd dive into anything that's cold," Nick said.

"You and me both. Man, this is the pits. How'd we get into this? We could be home right now, having iced tea by the swimming pool."

"A hamburger and chocolate shake at Burger King."

"On the other hand . . ."

"What?"

"Well." Julie looked at him, and shrugged. "If we weren't up here in this godforsaken armpit of a wilderness, we wouldn't . . . I wouldn't have got to know you. I mean, I'm glad about that anyway."

The words made Nick's heart pound fast. "Maybe when

we get back, we could—I don't know—go to the movies or something."

She met his eyes. She smiled slightly. "By then, you'll be sick of me."

"Maybe," he said.

Julie laughed.

"I doubt it, though."

Karen called, "Where's the top?"

"Up there someplace," Julie answered.

"That's the rumor," Nick added.

"You guys are really burning up the trail," Scott said.

Julie nodded. "Regular roadrunners."

Scott and Karen took off their packs. Scott looked as if the strenuous hike had barely fazed him. He wasn't even breathing hard. Karen looked just as good. She fluttered the front of her plaid shirt, then opened the three lower buttons. She gathered up the shirttails and made a knot just below her breasts. "Nice breeze," she said. She lay down against her pack, and fanned her face with her floppy hat.

"We thought," Julie said, "that this'd be as good a place as any to have lunch."

"Sounds good," Scott said.

After a lunch of gorp, dehydrated fruit slices, shortbread cookies, and Tropical Chocolate bars, they resumed the hike. At first, the weight of his pack felt unbearable to Nick. His shoulders and back throbbed with pain, and his legs seemed barely capable of supporting him. He felt like collapsing, but forced himself to take one step after another. Slowly, the torment faded, as if his body were giving up its rebellion, accepting its role as a beast of burden.

He walked behind Julie and matched his stride to hers. Her boots were powdered with trail dust. One sock was slightly lower than the other. The seat of her white shorts had two half-moons of yellow-brown dirt from sitting down, and he could see the outline of her panties through the thin fabric. The panties were very brief. Like a bikini bottom. "Did you bring a bathing suit?" he asked.

"Sure. You?"

"Yeah."

"Water's so cold, though. We'd freeze our butts."

"Those girls swam."

"Must be polar bears."

"Probably not bad, once you're in it."

"Depends. Some lakes aren't so bad."

"Warmer if they're shallow," Nick said.

"Depends on the runoff, too."

"Way I feel, I'd swim in ice cubes."

"We get to Wilson in time, I'd give it a try."

They trudged along in silence. Looking up the slope, Nick could see where the mountainside ended. It didn't seem far above them, but he realized that the view might be deceiving. The area that appeared to be the top from here might turn out to be a shelf, the rest of the mountain farther back and out of sight. He tried not to let his hopes get too high.

He and Julie were still a distance below the apparent top, however, when the trail, instead of switching back, continued forward and curved around the slope. A strong, cool wind blew against Nick. Julie stopped. He moved up beside her. She smiled at him. "What do you know," she said.

"Didn't think we'd ever make it."

Ahead of them, the trail wound over a flat, barren area between two bluffs. Then it dropped out of sight. In the distance, Nick saw peaks shrouded by clouds. A few minutes of hiking took them across the level area. They shed their packs and sat on a block of granite. From there, the trail started gradually downward along a narrow ridge. To the right of the ridge was a deep ravine. To the left was a shallow valley with two lakes. The lower lake, no more than a hundred feet below their perch, was larger than the other, bounded by rocky slopes except for a small stand of pine at its western shore.

The upper lake, just above its southwest end, looked treeless and even more desolate.

"Must be the Mesquites," Nick said.

"The ranger was right. They're the pits."

"I don't see anyone down there."

"The Madwoman of the Mesquites?" Julie asked. "She's probably moved on. I mean, who'd want to camp there? Looks like the backside of the moon."

"I hope Lake Wilson's better than these."

"The ranger said it was nice. Besides, it's about a thousand feet lower."

"What is it, three or four miles?"

"Something like that."

Nick followed the trail with his eyes. It passed above Lower Mesquite, and vanished behind a steep wall of granite. "At least it'll be downhill," he said.

"Sometimes that's worse."

"Yeah. Gets you in the toes."

"And everywhere else."

Scott and Karen arrived. They took off their packs, and settled down on a nearby boulder. Karen lifted her blouse again and tied it in front as she'd done when they stopped for lunch. "Ah," she said, "that wind's terrific."

"I don't like the looks of those clouds," Scott said.

The clouds hugging the distant peaks were thick and gray. Nick figured that they must be at least ten miles away.

"I don't think I'd mind a little rain," Karen said.

"It'd put a damper on dinner."

"Maybe it'll miss us," Julie said.

Scott shook his head. "Looks like they're coming our way. These mountain storms are unpredictable, though. Could pass over us without leaving a drop. Or we might be in for it. Only time will tell."

"Time wounds all heals," Karen said.

"Time's like hiking, then," Scott added.

"Like Benny," Julie said. "He's the greatest heel wounder of all time."

Scott looked pained. "Why don't you ease up on that? Benny feels bad enough without your help."

"He's not here."

Scott ignored the remark and stared out over the valley. Karen leaned back against her pack. She folded her hands on top of her head, mashing the soft crown of her hat. "I wonder," she said, "if Heather can make it as far as Wilson."

Chapter Sixteen

Ettie watched with despair through a crevice in the rocks. Luck had sure turned against them. Maybe the Master was dishing out punishment, paying them back for what Merle did to those other two campers—claiming he offered them down when he did no such thing, but just went at them for his own need and then laid it on the Master.

Then again, maybe Ettie wasn't judging the matter right. Could be a test. Maybe even an offering. She'd have to find out for sure, so she'd know what to do.

One thing was sure: the campers were fixing to stay. They were down in the clearing by the trees, setting up four tents, a kid in glasses rounding up rocks to build a fireplace.

Ettie eased away from the crevice and made her way across the slope to the cave entrance. Turning sideways, she squeezed through the opening. The murky light inside seemed very dark after the brightness, but she saw the dim shape of Merle sprawled out on one of the sleeping bags. She sat down on the other bag. Sunlight from the fissure overhead made a hot band along her crossed legs. She leaned back slightly against the cool granite wall.

"You awake, Merle?"

"Just laying here. I sure like this sleeping bag. It's the softest thing."

"We've got some folks down by the lake."

He sat up so fast that it startled Ettie.

"Just stay put," she warned.

He was almost to his feet, but he dropped down again as if his legs had gone soft. "Can't I see 'em, Ettie?"

"Just sit still."

"Who are they?" he asked.

"How'd I know that?"

"They snooping?"

"They're putting up a camp. One's soaking her foot in the lake. She came limping in pretty bad. I guess she hurt herself in the pass. I figure that's maybe why they stopped."

"A girl?"

"Don't get your heat up. They got three men along."

"Can't I just look?"

"I'll tell you when you can look. We're gonna stay put till I've got it figured out."

"Well, how many are there?"

"Nine."

"Nine, and just three of 'em men?"

"There's some kids, don't look older than twelve. And three women."

"How old are they?"

"Never you mind."

"Are they pretty?"

"Fetch me the coyote skin."

Obediently, Merle crawled past the head of her sleeping bag. He rummaged through a dark pile at the far end of the chamber and came back with the pelt of a coyote he had snared two weeks before. "What're you fixing to do?" he asked.

"Read the signs. Maybe these folks come here by chance, or maybe the Master sent them."

"Think He wants 'em offered down?"

"I don't know what to make of it. Could be we're out of favor and He sent them to punish us."

"Why'd He do that, Ettie?"

"Not saying He *did*. I'm saying He might've. Now you just shush, and let me find out."

She got to her knees and spread the coyote pelt on the sleeping bag. Then she unsheathed her knife. "O great Master," she intoned, "Shadow of the Dark, give us a sign that we, Your servants, may know Your will." With the knife, she carved a crescent on her left forearm. Blood spilled out, pattering on the coyote skin. "Give us wisdom, Master, that we may abide by Your way." She slowly waved her cut arm back and forth over the skin, then held it steady while she sheathed her knife. "Count backward from thirteen," she told Merle. Together, they counted down. When they reached one, she swung in her arm and tied a kerchief around the wound.

She stared down at the hide. The band of sunlight made a bright path across it, showing streaks and pools of blood on the pale skin. Except for the sunlit area, the rest was in deep shadow.

"What'd He say?" Merle asked.

"Get me matches."

He dug a book of matches out of his jeans and gave it to Ettie. She plucked a match free, struck it, and bent low over the hide. By the light of the wavering flame, she studied the pattern of her spilled blood: its trails of shiny droplets, its loops, the way its shiny threads connected larger blotches, the shapes of the small puddles. A cold, sick feeling spread through her as the meaning became clear. She moaned.

"What's wrong?"

"Shh." She shook out the match, lit another, and once again studied the map of blood. No, she hadn't been mistaken. She dropped the match. A spatter of blood killed its flame in a hiss.

"Is it bad, Ettie?"

She stared at her son. He was on his knees, looking down at the pelt. His face was a dim blur in the shadows. Reaching out, she patted his cheek. "Nothing's gonna come of it, honey. It's nothing to fret over. We're just gonna stay hidden here till they go away."

As Merle reached for the pelt, Ettie swept a hand across it, smearing the blood.

"Shit!" he cried.

"It's not for your eyes."

"Wouldn't of hurt nothing," he said in a pouty voice.

Ettie folded the pelt over. She pressed down on the fur with both hands, and rubbed it hard.

" 'Least you can do is tell me what it said," Merle complained. "Must've said more than just stay in the cave."

"*It* didn't say to stay in the cave, *I* did."

"Well, what'd the blood say?"

"Said we better not mess with the folks down there. They brought death."

Merle was silent. He stared down at the pelt for a while, then picked it up and peeled it open and moved it through the path of sunlight, squinting at the red smears. "Is that what it really said?" he asked, sounding doubtful.

"You calling me a liar, son?"

"Well, no. But maybe you didn't read it right."

"I read it right. Now, you got any notions about the women down there, put them out of your head, or you'll get us both killed. Do you understand?"

"I guess."

"That's not much of an answer, Merle." She crawled along her sleeping bag to the dimly lit gap of the cave's entrance. There, she sat down and crossed her legs, blocking the only way out.

"You don't gotta do that," Merle whined.

"I'll do it, just the same."

CHAPTER SEVENTEEN

With a sooty rock in each hand, Julie stepped over to the fireplace. "Here's a couple more for you," she told Benny, and dropped them to the ground beside him.

"Thanks," he muttered. He didn't look up. He lifted one of the rocks and added it to the low, circular wall he was building.

"Don't look so pitiful," Julie said.

"It's all my fault."

"That's right, Bonzo. Look on the bright side. At least you didn't break her foot."

"Thanks. You're real nice."

"Ain't I, though?" Trying to brush the black from her hands, she walked toward the lakeshore. Nick was there, sitting on a rock beside his sister while she soaked her left foot. "How's it going?" Julie asked.

"Fine," Heather said.

"Haven't seen any water snakes," Nick said.

"Well, that's a relief. Any crazy old women?"

"Not a one."

"Terrific." She stepped out onto a low flat rock, squatted down, and washed her hands. The water felt cold, but not numbing. "Still interested in a swim?" she asked.

"Sure."

"Can I swim, too?" Heather asked.

"Better check with Mom."

Julie shook the water from her hands and leaped ashore.

"See you in a couple of minutes," she called over her shoulder.

Benny, still crouched by the fireplace, raised his head as Julie approached. His nose was wrinkled, upper teeth bared, like a snarling dog. Just his way to keep his glasses from slipping off. He shoved them up with a forefinger and stopped snarling.

"We're going for a swim," Julie said. "Wanta come?"

His head tilted sideways. He looked confounded. "Are *you* going in?"

"That's the picture."

"What about the water moccasins?"

"If you're scared, stay here." In front of the tent, she dug into her backpack and dragged out her towel. It was still slightly damp from that morning's washing up. She hung it over a shoulder, and continued to search until she found her bikini at the very bottom.

Dropping to her knees, she crawled inside the tent. The tent had only been up for a few minutes, but already the trapped air felt stifling. Karen's sleeping bag was laid out. It looked thick and soft. Had it belonged to anyone but Karen, Julie would've sat on it while she changed. Instead, she sat on the tent floor, the ground hard under her as she stripped off her clothes.

She was on her back, naked, legs in the air, pulling the small white bottom of her bathing suit over her feet when the tent flap opened. Sunlight spilled onto her.

"Sorry," Karen blurted. The flap dropped, shutting out the light.

Julie muttered, "Shit." Raising her rump, she pulled the pants into place. She sat up. Her heart was thudding. With shaky fingers, she knotted the strings of the top behind her neck, stretched the flimsy fabric of the triangles down over her breasts, and reached behind her to tie the back. "Okay," she called. "You can come in."

Karen ducked inside. She had a one-piece black swimsuit

in her hand. "Sorry about that," she said. "I didn't realize you were in here."

"You could've asked," Julie muttered, still fumbling with the strings at her back.

Karen sat down on the bag, and started to unlace her boots. "Hot in here," she said.

"You going in the lake?"

"Yeah. Benny and your dad are getting into their trunks." She tugged her boots off, and sighed with pleasure. "That water's gonna feel awfully good."

Julie got the strings tied, but didn't move. She watched the woman peel off a sock and inspect her foot in the murky blue light. "Well, no blisters on this one. How're your feet holding out?"

"That's *my* business," she said.

Karen stared at her. In the gloomy light, Julie couldn't tell whether she looked angry or just hurt. "Sorry," Karen finally said. "I was just trying to be friendly."

"Don't bother."

In a quiet voice, she asked, "What are you afraid of?"

"I'm not afraid of you, that's for sure."

"You're afraid of liking me, I think."

"What, you're so irresistibly charming I've gotta be a nut-case if I'm not kissing the goddamn ground you walk on? Forget it. I just don't like you, that's all. I wish Dad had never met you."

"Your father and I . . . we love each other."

"Ain't that just dandy," Julie said through a tightness in her throat.

"You knew that, didn't you?"

"I'm not blind."

"We love each other, Julie, but don't think for one instant that he loves you or Benny any less because of that. You're his daughter. He's been with you all your life, and he'll love you as long as he lives, no matter what. You'll always be part of him in a way I can never be. I'm not taking him away from you. I couldn't, even if I wanted to."

Julie stared down at her folded hands.

"Would you be happier if I stopped seeing your father?"

"I don't know," she mumbled. "I guess not."

"What would make you happy?"

"I don't know." She gnawed her lower lip as tears filled her eyes. "I don't want him hurt, that's all."

"You think I'd hurt him?"

Shrugging, she wiped her eyes. "Everything was fine till you came along."

"Your dad wasn't fine. He was lonely."

"He had us."

"And he had a wife who'd run out on him. That left a big hole inside. Maybe he didn't let you see the hurt because he didn't want to make things worse for you and Benny, but it was there. And it isn't so bad anymore."

"Thanks to you, huh?"

"Thanks to the way we feel about each other."

Julie took a deep, trembling breath. She picked up her towel, and rubbed the tears from her face. "Nick's waiting for me," she muttered.

"You'll make his day when he sees you in that bikini."

"Trying to butter me up?"

"Yep. It's the truth, though. Look, Julie, I'm going to be your friend whether you like it or not. Because I love your father and I like you."

"You like me, huh? Sure."

"I do. And you'll get to like me, too, sooner or later. Before you know it, you and I are going to be buddies. Do you know why?"

"Why?"

"Because I'm irresistibly charming."

Julie cracked a smile. "My ass," she said, and crawled out of the tent. The bright sunlight made her eyes ache. Standing, she brushed some dirt and pine needles off her knees. She felt strange—her mind vague, her muscles weak, her legs trembling. As she walked toward the lake, she tried to make sense out of her encounter with Karen. Her mind couldn't hold steady on it. Maybe everything had changed. Or maybe the talk had just confused her.

Nick, standing at the shore, was watching the twins wade in. He had a towel draped around his neck, and wore blue shorts that looked like the ones he slept in. When Julie walked closer, he turned around as if sensing her approach. He gazed at her. She blushed, uncomfortably aware of her near nakedness and the way her breasts jiggled with the motion of her walk. "All set?" she asked.

Nick smiled thinly, nodded, and quickly turned away.

Julie realized that she liked how she'd felt while he was staring. Beneath her uneasiness, there'd been a kind of thrill. She found herself dashing past Nick, the chill water splashing up her legs. Knee-deep, she spun around, scooped up water with both hands, and flung it at him.

"No!" he cried. He raised his arms to block the cold shower, and cringed as it splashed against him.

Julie stood up straight. She frowned with pretended concern. "Oh, I'm sorry. Did that get you?"

He looked astonished for a moment. Then, laughing, he lunged forward, drove his hands into the water, and launched an icy barrage that pelted Julie from face to knees. Staggering away, she lost her footing. She yelped and fell, flapping her arms and hitting the lake flat on her back. She shuddered as the chill water closed over her. After the first shock, though, it didn't feel so bad. She pushed against the rocky bottom and sat up.

"Are you okay?" Nick asked. He sounded worried.

She wiped her eyes clear, and blinked up at him. "Was it a graceful entry?"

Rose and Heather were giggling.

"Beautiful," Nick told her.

"I'm so glad." Her bikini top felt slightly awry. She made sure her breasts were still in it, gave the front a small adjustment, and stood up. Nick stared as the water streamed off her.

"How's the water?" Dad called from behind him.

"Cold," she answered.

Karen was walking along close beside Dad, holding his hand. Her one-piece black suit clung to her like shiny skin. It was open in front with a wide, deep V that extended down to her belly. The lower part of the suit seemed even more revealing, cut so high at the sides that it left her hipbones bare and formed a long, lean triangle down to her groin.

Benny, off to one side and slightly behind Karen, was agape as he stared at her.

Someone whistled. Julie spotted Flash near one of the tents, his arms loaded with firewood. The whistle caught Nick's attention. He looked over his shoulder at the same time that Karen turned around to say something to Flash. Julie sighed. The suit was backless and almost bottomless, so narrow down the buttocks that it left the sides of her cheeks bare. They were lean, and smooth.

"Come on, Nick."

He kept staring.

"Forget it. She's already taken."

He faced Julie, innocently raising his eyebrows as if he'd been caught daydreaming by a teacher.

"Besides," Julie said, "isn't she a little old for you?"

His eyebrows dropped to their normal level, and the corners of his mouth turned up. "Yeah," he said. "She's sure something to look at, though."

"Tell me about it," Julie muttered, feeling a little sick.

"She's gorgeous, in fact."

"Not to mention irresistibly charming."

Nick opened his mouth to speak, but Julie whirled away and dived, hitting the water flat out and swimming hard. Bastard, she thought. Damn it all to hell. The bitch *is* irresistible. Has Dad head over heels, and Benny damn near swooning. Even Nick's got the hots for her. Parading around damn near naked. Flash whistling at her. He didn't whistle at me. What am I, dog food? Damn her! Wants to be my friend. Sure, sure.

Julie realized she was crying, sobbing into the water. She choked and came up for air.

Wonderful. Drown yourself.

She kept her head above the surface, but continued to swim as hard as she could. She didn't look back. She was near the center of the lake, so she turned to the right and swam parallel to the shore.

She saw a small inlet where a slab of granite slanted out of the water. She sidestroked toward it. When she reached the rock, she crawled up it and lay down flat. She crossed her arms under her face. The surface was hot and gritty against her skin. The sun on her back felt good. She panted for air, and tried to stop sobbing.

Then she heard splashes. Someone swimming not far away. Coming closer.

Go away, she thought. Whoever you are, go away and leave me alone.

Down near her feet, the splashing stopped. She didn't bother looking around.

"You're pretty fast." Nick.

"A regular speed demon," she muttered.

"Mind if I come up and join you?"

"I don't care."

She heard a swoosh of water, then dribbling sounds as he crawled up the rock. He sat down close beside her and leaned back, bracing himself up with stiff arms. His slim belly, streaming with water, heaved as he gasped for breath. "You mad at me?" he asked.

"Why should I be mad?" Julie muttered, and turned her head aside so she wouldn't have to look at him.

"I don't know. Because I made you fall?"

"It wasn't that."

"Then you *are* mad at me. What'd I do?"

"Nothing," she mumbled.

"I don't get it."

"That's okay. You don't have to get it."

"Is it because I was staring at you? Like the other night when you yelled at me?"

"I didn't yell," she protested.

"You said, 'Take a picture. It lasts longer.' If that's it, I'm sorry. Really. It's hard not to stare, though. You're so . . ." He hesitated.

"What?"

"Well, you know—beautiful. I keep trying not to stare, but then you come along in something like . . . like what you're wearing, and . . ."

She raised her head and looked at Nick. He was frowning out at the lake. "You think I was angry because you were staring at me?"

"Well, yeah."

"I didn't mind that."

"Are you sure?"

"I'm sure." Julie rolled over. She folded her hands under her head to cushion it. Her heart was racing, and her mouth was very dry. She licked her lips. Nick continued to gaze forward. "I got upset, if you really want to know, because you were staring at Karen instead of me."

He shook his head as if rejecting the idea, then turned and met her eyes. He seemed to be frowning and grinning at the same time. He looked very confused. "Are you *serious?*"

"I know I shouldn't blame you. I mean, you're a guy and . . . like you said, she's gorgeous. And that bathing suit of hers . . ."

"You won't . . ." Nick paused, shaking his head some more.

"I won't what?"

"Never mind," he muttered, and looked away.

"Come on, tell me."

"It's too embarrassing."

Julie smiled. "Embarrassing for who?"

"Me, I guess. Maybe you, too."

She braced herself up on her elbows. "Go on."

"Well . . . about Karen's suit. When I was looking at her? You won't believe this but I was imagining how it would look on you."

"You're kidding," Julie said. Her voice came out in a

whisper. Her heart was thundering, and she was short of breath. She sat up straight to breathe better.

"I'm not kidding," Nick said. "I mean, it's nothing against your bikini. I just, uh, tried to picture how you'd look in . . . I *told* you it'd be embarrassing."

"A little bit," she admitted.

He leaned forward, put his hands on his knees, and hung his head. "I guess I'm kind of a lech."

"I guess you are," Julie said. For the first time, she noticed the sounds of distant laughter and splashing. An outcropping of rock, however, blocked her view of those in the lake. She put a hand on Nick's back. He flinched slightly, startled by her touch, and looked into her eyes. For a long time, while her hand moved slowly up and down, they gazed at each other. His eyes lingered on hers, studied every part of her face, followed the curve of her neck, glanced at her breasts, and returned quickly to her eyes as if asking permission. A slight smile trembled on Julie's lips. Twisting herself sideways, she reached out and took hold of his far shoulder. She leaned toward Nick as she turned him. She held him motionless, and he stared down, his gaze roaming from one breast to the other. He looked again into her eyes. He reached under her outstretched arm, lay his hand against her back, and eased her closer. His other arm went around her. He turned her some more. Julie felt herself start to tip. Nick's eyes widened with alarm. Then he was flat on his back, still holding her. She lay across his chest. "Woops," she said.

For a moment, he looked as if he might laugh. Then his face went serious. "Julie," he whispered.

She kissed him gently, briefly on the mouth. "We'd better get back in the lake," she whispered.

"Yeah," he said. But when Julie tried to push herself up, he held onto her. "One more?"

"One more."

This time, his hand went behind her head. His fingers thrust into her hair and he pressed her close, kissing her again and again, his lips firm and warm and urgent, as if he had needed to kiss her for a long time and feared he would never get another chance.

Julie mashed her lips against his. She wanted it never to end, but there were those in the lake who might see them. So she turned her face. Nick kissed her cheek, her ear. "We've gotta stop," she gasped.

"Okay." His hand slid out of her hair.

She raised her head. Nick's face was beaded with sweat, his eyes somewhat vague, as if he were in a daze.

"Well," she said.

"Yeah." His arms fell away from her.

She pushed herself up. Nick lay spread-eagled at her knees, his skin glossy with water and sweat, his chest heaving. His damp, clinging shorts bulged as if he'd slid a length of pipe down the front. A thick pipe. A long one. If it were any bigger, Julie thought, it would push right up under the elastic waistband and . . .

"Take a picture," he said. "It lasts longer."

Julie grinned down at him. Nick grinned up at her.

"Come on," she said. "Let's go swimming."

CHAPTER EIGHTEEN

"I gotta pee, Ettie. Let me go out. I won't do nothing."

She shook her head. "Any business you got, you just do it right here. You can't go out till they're gone."

"How you know they're still here?"

"Folks don't put their tents up and move on in an hour. They're staying the night. And you're staying right where you are."

"I gotta *pee*," he whined.

"Use a pot."

"You're here."

"Hon, you got nothing I ain't seen before. I'm the gal used to change your diapers."

"Let me go out. Please."

Ettie pushed herself away from the gap in the wall, crawled forward to the candle between their sleeping bags, and blew it out. The cave went black. "There. Now you don't gotta be shy." She backed up quickly to block the opening. "Go on ahead, Merle."

Though her eyes were open, she could see nothing. She heard him sigh, then the soft hiss of fabric as he made his way along the sleeping bag. A match snicked and flared. Merle, kneeling at the far end of the chamber, was tossing around clothes and plastic packs of food to get at the cooking utensils. With a scrape and clatter, he pulled out a small saucepan. He waved it. "This okay?"

"Just fine," Ettie said.

He shook out his match.

"I'll dump it when you're done."

"You said we have to stay here."

"*I* can go out. You're the one goes around offering folks down for no good reason."

"He told me to."

"Horseshit." She heard Merle's zipper slide down. "Careful you don't miss," she said. "Hold it up good and close."

"Don't know why I can't go out," he muttered as his stream started hitting the aluminum. "I wouldn't do nothing. You just don't trust me, that's all. I'd leave 'em alone." He was talking fast, as if trying to cover the other sound. "I just wanta see 'em, that's all. What'm I gonna try with three men down there? Think I'm a fool? Don't see why we can't both go out, and you keep an eye on me if you think I'm so crazy. I just wanta see 'em, that's all." The splashing stopped.

Ettie waited until she heard his zipper, then crawled forward and lit the candle. Merle scowled at her as she picked up the pan. "I'll be right outside," she said. "You just stay put, you hear?"

"Yes, ma'am," he mumbled.

She backed away on her knees, then got to her feet and squeezed through the crevice, the back of her thick parka whispering against the rock. Outside, she crouched low to empty the pan. She set it down and stood up straight, stretching her stiff muscles.

In spite of the cold wind blowing through her dress, Ettie was glad to be out of the cave. She pushed her hands into the pockets of her parka, and leaned back to block the narrow entrance.

The night was very dark, as if a heavy blanket had been spread across the sky to hide the moon and stars. The only light came from the campfire down by the lake. It fluttered, yellow-orange, and cast a glowing aura that shimmered on the campers seated at its far side. Those on the near side of the fire were black silhouettes.

Staring at them, Ettie felt herself knot up inside. She groaned, and pushed her fists against her belly. If the blood signs had been right . . . Maybe she'd read them wrong. She could've missed something, reading them by match light.

They showed Merle dead. They showed her dead. Killed by some of the folks sitting down there so peacefully around the campfire.

These things are never certain, though. Even if you read the signs right, there's always a little room for doubt, so you take precautions and don't give up hope. If it weren't for that, there'd be no point in hiding away.

Always a chance, at least, that things won't turn out the way the blood signs say. A small chance.

She might go ahead and try throwing a spell to shield her and Merle. She'd given a lot of thought to that, while waiting in the cave, but it hadn't seemed too practical. She was sure the Master sent these folks as punishment, so He wouldn't let her magic work anyway. But what if He didn't send them? He *did* give a warning in the blood signs. Why warn her if he meant the folks to kill them? Just to torment her?

Maybe they weren't out of favor after all, and a spell would do the trick. Sure worth a try.

Ettie picked up the saucepan. She turned it over and gave it a few hard shakes. Then, with a last look at the figures huddled around the distant fire, she entered the crevice. She sidestepped, squeezing through the tight gap. "Merle," she said, "we're gonna cast a Spell of Obscurity over us." He didn't answer.

She was near the chamber now and expected to see a fluttering glow of candlelight. The area ahead was black. "Merle, what happened to the candle?" He still didn't answer. Ettie's heart started thudding.

"You answer me, Merle. None of your foolishness."

The walls no longer pressed against her. She tossed the pan forward. It landed with a soft *whup* on one of the sleeping bags. Her hands free, she dug into a pocket and pulled out a book of matches. Her left ankle was grabbed and jerked sideways. She pitched forward, falling through the darkness. Her parka and a sleeping bag cushioned her impact. As she started to rise, a body dropped onto her back and drove her down. "Merle!" Cold fingers dug into the sides of her neck, squeezed. "No!" she cried out.

She reached up, clutched the wrists, struggled to tear the hands away. Merle was too strong. Her ears were ringing. The blackness in front of her eyes glowed red.

Later, she woke up.

Her head was throbbing with pain. She was lying on her side. When she tried to move, Ettie realized that she was bound with rope—wrists tied behind her back, legs bent at the knees, ankles lashed tight. She attempted to straighten her legs, but her wrists were tugged down as her feet moved.

"Merle?" she asked.

She heard only her own breathing and heartbeat, and the moan of the wind outside.

"Merle, are you here?"

A stupid question, she thought. Of course he's not here. He's gone after the women.

CHAPTER NINETEEN

Flash blew steam away, and took a sip of his coffee. Across the fire, Benny leaned forward with a demented look on his face as he continued his poem:

"And I cried, 'It was surely October/on *this* very night of last year/That I journeyed—I journeyed down here/That I brought a dread burden down here/On this night of all nights in the year,/Ah, what demon has tempted me here?'" His glasses reflected the firelight, hiding his eyes behind leaping flames. "'Well I know, now, this dim lake of Auber—/This misty mid region of Weir—/Well I know, now, this dank tarn of Auber/This ghoul-haunted woodland of Weir.'" He leaned back, took a deep breath, and smiled.

Heather, who'd been gazing spellbound, started to clap. The others joined in. "Terrific," Karen said. Flash clamped his hot mug between his knees, and applauded.

"Did you learn that for school?" Karen asked.

"No, just for myself."

She shook her head as if amazed, and Benny swelled up with pride.

"Sure was a *creepy* poem," Nick said.

Julie turned to Nick, hunched her shoulders, and contorted her face. In a low, moany voice, she said, "'The ghoul-haunted woodland of Weir.'"

Nick made himself look frightened. "Yeeeeahh!" he cried, and covered his face.

"Why is it," Alice said, "that we insist on trying to frighten ourselves? Why doesn't somebody say a *nice* poem?"

Flash grinned. "Nymphomaniacal Jill used dynamite to get her thrill—"

"Don't you dare!"

"Gross," Rose said.

Flash peered at his daughter, surprised.

"Why don't I start a story," Alice suggested, "and we'll go around the campfire and everybody add onto it?"

"Bleah," Rose said.

Nick nodded. "That's a drag, Mom."

"Why don't we give it a try?" Karen said. "Might be fun."

Scott nodded. "Sure. Go ahead, Alice."

Alice looked grateful for their approval. "All right," she said. "Once upon a time, there was a fair maiden who lived in the woods, all alone except for . . ." Pausing, she turned her head toward Rose.

"Mick Jagger," Rose said.

She got plenty of laughs except from Alice. "Be serious."

Rose sighed. "Okay. Except for her mean mother."

Alice rolled her eyes up, and Flash took a drink of coffee to hide his grin.

"One day, the maiden got so tired of her mother always spoiling her fun that she ran off into the woods and met . . ." She turned to Heather.

Heather looked across the fire at Benny as if asking for help. With a shrug, she said, "And met a . . . gee, I don't know."

"The gee-I-don't-know," Nick continued, "was an ugly, hairy thing with one eye where its nose should've been . . ."

"And two noses," Julie added, "where its eyes should've been. The noses were upside down, so it wore a big cowboy hat to keep itself from drowning during rainstorms. Whenever it sneezed, it blew its hat off." She turned to Benny, who stared at her as if she were crazy.

"When the maiden found the gee-whatever-it-is," he said, "it was crawling around looking for its contact lens. She helped it, and finally they found the lens." Shrugging, he looked at Karen.

"With the contact lens back in its eye, the gee-I-don't-know stared at the maiden. She was the most beautiful creature it had ever seen. 'Gee, you're purty,' it said." She grinned at Scott.

"The maiden blushed," he went on. "'You're not too shabby yourself,' she said. 'And with those two noses, I bet you smell a lot better than me.'" He raised his eyebrows at Flash.

"So the gee-I-don't-know picked up the fair maiden and carried her deep into the woods. They came to his hut, and went at it hot and heavy."

"*Dad,*" Rose muttered.

"Before you know it," he continued, "the little hut was crowded with little gee-I-don't-knows, so they packed up and moved to a condo in Palm Springs and lived happily ever after."

"What a dumb story," Rose muttered.

"I thought it was kind of cute," Karen said.

"Why don't you tell a story?" Benny asked her. "Do you know another scary one like 'Doreen and Audrey'?"

"Afraid not. That was my entire repertoire."

"How about you, Dad?" Julie asked.

"My last one didn't go over too well."

Julie wrinkled her nose. "Yeah, that's right. Forget I asked."

"I've got one," Flash said.

Alice raised an eyebrow. "Is it clean?"

"Sure."

"Go on," Nick said. "Let's hear it."

Flash finished his coffee, and set the aluminum cup on the ground between his boots. "Maybe I'd better not," he said. "Your mother has this thing about creepy stories."

"Don't make *me* the villain," she protested. "If you think the story's appropriate, go ahead and tell it."

He grinned. "Well, if you insist." Reaching inside his jacket, he took a cigar from his shirt pocket. He tore off the cellophane wrapper, crinkled it into a ball, and tossed it into the fire. "This happened to me a long time ago, back when I was in high school."

"The Dark Ages," Nick said.

"Right." Clamping the cigar in his teeth, he lifted a twig from the fire. With one hand shielding the small flame from the wind, he lit up. "My dad, my brother, Cliff, and I were on a fishing trip up around Land O'Lakes, Wisconsin. We'd heard about a string of ax murders in the area. Seems some lunatic was running around giving the whack to folks he found in the woods. They called him the Chopper. Maybe a frustrated tree surgeon." Flash grinned at his joke, and stared at the glowing tip of his cigar. "There were four or five bodies they found in the woods. All of 'em were dismembered. Some had arms cut off. Some were missing a leg. Two of 'em were beheaded."

"Arnold," Alice said in a warning voice.

"You said I could tell it."

"I imagined you'd use some discretion."

"Want me to stop?"

"Keep going," Nick said. "It's neat."

Alice sighed. "Just tone it down, all right? There are children present."

"Tone it down, okay. Now, where was I?" He sucked in some smoke, let it drift out of his nostrils. The wind whipped it away. "Oh, yeah. So the Chopper was on the loose, and they'd found some of his handiwork in the woods, but there were a few other folks who'd just disappeared, so they figured the body count would get even higher. We were a little jumpy, camping out in the neighborhood. Dad was packing a .22 revolver, though, so we figured we'd waste the sucker if he showed himself.

"I tell you, though, we didn't get much sleep that first night. We were the only campers on the lake. It was mighty dark and silent. Every now and then, we'd hear a rustle in the bushes. Me and Cliff were sure it was the Chopper sneaking in close. I tell you, that was one of the longest nights I ever spent. Before the war anyway," he added, and felt his chest tighten as he saw himself cowering in the jungle.

"Did he get you?" Scott asked.

"Huh? No. No, we made it through the night okay." Flash took a deep breath. "We spent the next day on the lake. Rowing around and fishing. It was sunny and hot. Real nice. Dragonflies, loons cackling. Real pleasant. And we had a lot of luck, fishing. Brought in a whole string of bluegill and sunfish, a couple of bullheads. We fried them up for dinner, and had a real feast. Then we went out in the rowboat again for some night fishing.

"I guess we were all glad to be on the lake after dark. Out there, we didn't have to worry about the Chopper. My God, it was nice out there. Warm, just a little breeze. The moonlight looked like silver on the water. There were lightning bugs. We were all greased up and stinky with 6-12, to keep the mosquitoes off." He sighed. "Anyway, we were drifting near the north end of the lake, maybe fifty yards from shore, when I felt a sudden tug on my line. Man, I was excited! I started reeling in, thinking I'd hooked a real whopper. Felt heavy, you know? My rod was bent almost double. But I started to wonder, because I wasn't getting any play. You know how you can usually feel the fish flipping around down there? Well, this one didn't seem to be moving at all. Just a dead weight.

"Cliff shined his flashlight on the lake where my line was in. The beam only went in a little way. I remember how dirty the water looked. Like it was full of dust, or something. Then, as I cranked the reel, this pale hand came up like there was somebody reaching for the light. I tell you, I damn near croaked. But I kept reeling in, and Cliff held the flashlight steady, and a second later I had a severed arm swinging from the end of my rod. It was cut off at the elbow. My hook was in its wrist. We all just stared at the thing. It hung there, dripping and swaying."

"My God," Julie muttered.

Alice said, "I thought you promised to tone it down."

"I'm just telling what happened," Flash said.

"This didn't happen," she said.

"Didn't it? Ask Cliff next time he's over."

"How come you never mentioned it?"

"You know how you are about these things."

"Why'd you have to bring it up, then?"

"The kids wanted a story."

"Mother of God."

"May I continue?"

"You mean there's more?"

"I haven't got to the good part yet."

"Oh, for crying out loud."

"Go on," Nick said. He was leaning forward, elbows on knees. "What'd you do with the thing?"

"I wanted to cut my line and get rid of it, but Dad said we had to keep it for the authorities. He told me to swing it over to him. He was sitting in the stern. I swung it over, and he grabbed the line and lowered the arm into the boat and cut the line. Then Cliff rowed us back to camp.

"By the time we got there, most of the shock had worn off. We were all pretty excited, acting as if we'd landed a record-breaking muskie or something. We figured, you know, that it must be the arm of a Chopper victim. Dad put it in a grocery bag. He wanted to take it to the police right away. The nearest town was about an hour drive, though, and we had lots of good camping gear we didn't want to leave behind while we went in. Cliff volunteered to stay and guard the stuff, but Dad wouldn't let him. We finally decided to break camp and take everything with us. We figured, you know, we wouldn't be too eager to stick around another day anyhow.

"We didn't bother making a campfire. I lit the Coleman lantern, and we kept it by the tent while we gathered up our things. We worked real fast, but it seemed to take forever. The car was parked about a hundred yards away. Dad left me and Cliff a couple of times while he carried stuff over. We didn't much like it when he was gone. We kept looking over our shoulders at the bag with the arm.

"Anyway, he was carrying the cooler and tackle box to the car and Cliff and I were busy folding the tent, our backs to the lake, when we heard this splashing sound behind us. Like somebody wading slowly out of the water. We leaped to our feet and spun around. And Jesus, there was a man coming at us!"

Heather covered her eyes.

"He was kind of stumbling along like he was drunk. He was just a dim shape in the darkness at first. When he got closer to the lantern, though, we could see him real well—too well. He was a skinny guy, about forty. He was wearing jeans and a plaid shirt. His sneakers squished with each step. He was dripping from head to foot. The top of his head was split open like a broken watermelon, and his left arm was gone.

"Right beside the lantern, he stopped and stared at us with these blank eyes. Then his mouth opened. He tried to say something, and about a gallon of water gushed out of his mouth like he was throwing up. When the water stopped pouring out, he said in this kind of choked, gurgling voice, 'My arm. I want my arm.'

"Cliff and I ran like hell, too scared even to scream. When we got back to the camp with Dad, the guy was gone." Flash sighed. He tapped a length of ash off his cigar. "We followed his footprints to the edge of the lake. For a long time, we stared out over the water. We couldn't see the guy, but we knew he was out there. Somewhere down below. In the dark, murky water. With his arm."

CHAPTER TWENTY

The struggle had left Ettie's wrists and ankles raw, but the ropes binding her were as tight as they'd been when she started. Her blood made them slippery, but still she couldn't pull free.

Her only chance was to cut herself loose. Either that, or wait for Merle to release her. But he might not come back. If the signs had been right . . . Maybe it was already too late to save him. Or herself. Maybe this is how it would end, with Merle meeting his fate at the hands of the campers and Ettie starving to death, helpless in the cave.

"No," she said into the darkness.

She would get loose. She had to!

She knew, from rolling onto her side, that her sheath knife was gone. Merle must've taken it. But what about the Swiss Army knife they'd found among the gear of the dead campers? If he'd forgotten about it, the knife would be somewhere in the heap of equipment at the far end of the cave.

Slowly, moaning as she strained with stiff muscles, she began to squirm forward. The journey seemed to take forever, but finally she was lying in the jumble of boots, plastic bags, backpacks, cook kits. She felt cloth against her cheek, nudged it aside, felt cool metal. The butane cylinder? She wondered if she might try to burn the ropes off, then quickly abandoned that idea; with her limited mobility, it would be far too risky. Maybe as a last resort.

The packs, she knew, were empty. Merle had dumped out their contents the day he'd brought them in. So the knife had to be lying loose here, someplace.

She continued to search, using her face to push away invisible objects, exploring some with her tongue. She bit and dragged aside soft fabric, a button between her teeth. She lowered her face where it had been, and felt a metallic tube against her lips. She ran her tongue up the ribbed surface. The tube bulged at one end. A flashlight? She rolled it, and felt the switch against her cheek. A flashlight.

They'd used it only once, testing it when it came tumbling from the pack two days before. Its beam had been dusky yellow, the batteries weak, and she'd told Merle they should save it for an emergency. After that, she'd forgotten all about it.

Ettie pushed the switch with her chin. The dim beam spilled out, revealing a rumpled pair of jeans. Gripping the flashlight in her teeth, she struggled to her knees. She turned her head slowly, shining the beam over the packs, a sweatshirt, tennis shoes, a collapsible plastic water bucket, foil and cellophane packets of food, a Primus stove, a wallet, a first-aid kit. Her mouth, stretched wide to hold the flashlight, ached badly. She could breathe only through her nose. She felt as if she were suffocating. She gagged, and her eyes teared, but she kept her bite on the metal.

The red plastic handle of the knife was nowhere to be seen.

Inching forward, she crept into the heap. Her left knee nudged a hard object hidden under a flannel shirt. She pushed the shirt aside, and tucked her chin down to shine the light at her knees. The murky yellow beam fell on a hatchet.

Relief swept through Ettie. She forced her mouth open wide, and let the flashlight drop. It hit the granite floor with a dull thud. The cave went dark.

Ettie writhed and twisted until her fingers found the hatchet. Gripping the blunt end of its head, she pressed the cutting edge between her wrists and began to saw the rope.

Chapter Twenty-one

Nick shoved aside a sawed-off stump and a rock that had been used as seats at the campfire. Then he spread out his ground cloth. He opened the straps, keeping his rubber mat in a tight roll.

"Are we sleeping out?" Julie asked.

He looked over his shoulder. She was approaching from between two of the tents, a toothbrush and tube of toothpaste in her hand, her water bottle clamped under one arm. "Don't you want to?" he asked.

"What about the rain?"

He held out his open hands. "What rain?"

Julie smiled. Her sun-burnished face glowed copper in the firelight. "I'm game if you are," she said. Grinning, she turned away. Nick watched her stride toward the far tent and crouch over her pack. When she vanished inside the tent, he finished arranging his sleeping bag.

His parents were down by the shore with the twins, washing and brushing teeth. He went to his pack, took out his shorts and T-shirt, and crawled into their tent. His shorts felt cool when he put them on, as if they were still damp from swimming. He knew the sun had dried them, though, and his T-shirt had the same moist feel against his skin. Shivering, he hurried outside, stuffed his clothing into his pack, and rushed to his sleeping bag. His teeth chattered as he tugged off his untied boots and his socks. He put them at the head of his bag, and scurried into it. The slippery fabric was cold at first. Slowly, it filled with warmth. By the time Julie came out of her tent, he'd stopped shaking.

"You look cozy," she said.

"I am. Sort of."

She spread her poncho on the ground beside him, rolled out her foam rubber mat, and tugged open the drawstrings of her stuff bag. The sleeping bag bloomed as if inflating when she pulled it free. On her knees, facing Nick, she bent over to spread it out. He watched the way her hair, hanging from under the edges of her hood, brushed against her cheeks like wisps of gold in the firelight.

"You sleeping out?" Scott called. He appeared from behind one of the tents, Karen and Benny at his sides.

"Sure," Julie said. "It's not gonna rain."

"I hope you're right."

When they were gone, Julie unzipped her sleeping bag, crawled in, and pulled the zipper up to her shoulder. She rolled onto her side. She pillowed her head on her bent arm, and smiled at Nick.

"We'll wait till they're all in their tents," he whispered. "Then we'll run around yelling, 'My arm! Where's my arm?'"

She laughed softly. "Forget it. I'm not moving a muscle till the sun comes up."

"Unless it rains?" Nick asked.

"If it rains, I think I'll murder you."

"Hope you two've got your Mae Wests on," Dad said, coming back from the shore.

"You're gonna drown," Rose informed them.

"You people have no confidence," Nick said.

"I'll move in with the girls," Mom said. "If the rain starts, young man, you hightail it into your father's tent."

"Fine," he said.

At last, everyone vanished into tents. Nick lay on his side, staring at Julie's face a yard away. She was looking at him, too. He wished there was more light.

"You ought to wear a hat when you sleep," Julie said.

"I burrow down."

"You're not burrowed now."

"If I burrow, I can't look at you." He could hardly believe he'd said that. But he was glad. As the silence stretched out, he felt his heart beating fast. His stomach was fluttery.

Julie moved her sleeping bag closer. "How's that?" she whispered.

His throat felt tight. He nodded. "Great," he managed. Julie's face was dim in the faint, shimmering glow of firelight, her eyes glistening. He felt the warmth of her breath through the cold air. "Do you know what?" he whispered. His thundering heart felt as if it might explode.

"What?" she asked.

"I . . ." He backed down. He couldn't say it.

"What?"

"I've never known a girl like you."

"How do you mean?"

"I don't know. I'm not very . . . I like you an awful lot, Julie."

"I like you an awful lot, too."

"You do?" He felt a trembling warmth spread through him.

"Yeah, I do. I . . . hell . . ."

"What?" he asked.

Her lower lip curled in. She clamped it between her teeth. Then she let the lip go, and sighed. "I think," she whispered, "that maybe I love you."

The words stunned Nick. He went breathless and dizzy. He felt like shouting with joy, like weeping. He said, "Jesus."

"The name's Julie."

"God, Julie. You really . . ."

"Really."

"Oh, Julie," he whispered. "Julie, I love you." He pressed his mouth gently to her parted lips.

Scott stared at the slanting dark walls of the tent above him, and listened to the sounds of Benny's breathing. He didn't think the boy was asleep yet. As he waited, he stroked the sweatshirt spread over his chest and belly. He imagined Karen wearing only her sweatpants.

"Dad?" Benny asked.

"Huh?"

"Do you think it was true?" The boy sounded nervous. "About the guy and his arm?"

"No, of course not."

"He said it was true."

"It's not. Dead people do not get up and wander around."

"Have you ever heard of zombies?"

"I think so," Scott said, smiling in the darkness.

"They're dead people who get brought back to life with voodoo. They're supposed to really exist. You know, like in Haiti? I've read about 'em."

"You oughta be reading *The Hardy Boys* instead of all that weird junk."

"You don't think there are zombies?"

"I sincerely doubt it."

"What about witches and vampires and werewolves and ghosts?"

He wrapped his arms around the soft sweatshirt. "It's awfully late, Benny. Can't we pick up this conversation in the morning?"

"If you want," he said. He sounded disappointed.

Scott sighed. "I just think it's all people's imaginations. Stuff they made up to frighten each other, like Karen's story about Doreen and Audrey, or Flash's about the guy and the arm. Just stories."

"I don't know," Benny said.

"Well, it's just my opinion. I haven't read a hundred books on the subject the way you have. But I've been around for thirty-eight years and my life's been relatively free of things that go bump in the night. If there are ghoulies and ghosties out there, they've been minding their own business. I haven't lost any sleep over them—until now."

"I guess you want me to be quiet."

"We have a lot of hiking to do tomorrow."

"I'm not very sleepy."

Terrific. "Try to think about something pleasant," Scott said.

"Okay. I'll try. Good night."

"'Night, Benny." He heard the boy sigh and roll over. Turning onto his side, he eased the sweatshirt up against his face. He wondered if Karen was cold without it. No, the sleeping bag would keep her warm. And soon he would be with her. If Benny ever fell asleep.

Karen wondered if he would come tonight. Maybe not. He might be worried about the weather. If he came and it started raining, Julie would catch them. That'd be an embarrassment for everyone.

But he'd whispered, "See you later," when he kissed her good night. He obviously planned to take the chance. He could've changed his mind, though.

It was still early. He couldn't leave his tent until Benny was asleep. He had to worry about Julie and Nick, too. Give all of them time to conk out.

Might be a long wait.

One of her shoulders was cold. She slid down deeper into the bag, the slick fabric making whispery sounds against her skin. She crossed her ankles, folded her hands on her belly, stared up into the darkness, and smiled. Scott would be in for a pleasant surprise when he found her already naked.

If he comes.

He'll come, she told herself. Oh, yes.

She wished she could sleep. Though every muscle ached from lugging her pack up that awful trail, she wasn't the least bit tired. She was wide awake and eager, trembling slightly.

At last, she heard a soft crushing sound behind the tent. It was barely audible over the noise of the wind. It might have been nothing more than a pinecone falling to the ground, but it might have been a footstep. She let out a shaky breath, and listened. For a few moments, she heard only the wind rushing through the trees and mountain gaps. Then came another quiet crunch. She was sure this time that it was a footfall.

He's being very cautious, she thought. Maybe he's not certain Julie's asleep.

With a shaky hand, Karen unzipped the side of her sleeping bag.

The footsteps stopped at the front of the tent. She heard the rustle of the flap being eased aside. Shutting her eyes, she waited. Her heart was pounding hard. She lay motionless, breathing deeply, trying to feign sleep.

He was inside now. She could hear him crawling along the tent floor, coming slowly closer. He stopped beside her.

He smelled bad. Like sweat and urine.

Her eyes flew open. The face above her was a dim, grinning blur in the darkness and it didn't belong to Scott. She opened her mouth to scream. A hand slapped across it. The other hand swept down. Something crashed against the side of her head.

Scott propped himself up on one elbow, and stared at the dark bulk of Benny's sleeping bag. He listened carefully. The boy was breathing in a slow, steady rhythm.

Finally.

He opened his sleeping bag, and felt the cold slide over his skin. He sat up. He folded Karen's sweatshirt and tucked it under one arm. As he started to rise, he heard a soft tapping sound on the taut wall of the tent. Then another. Suddenly, the tent was being pattered by a thousand raindrops.

He muttered, "Shit," lay down again, and zipped himself into his bag.

"Ohhhh crap!" Julie wailed.

Nick's eyes fluttered open. He wrinkled up his face as raindrops smacked it.

Julie kissed him quickly on the mouth. "Better inflate your Mae West," she said.

Then they were both scurrying out of their sleeping bags.

Julie shoved her feet into her boots. The rain soaked through the back of her warm-up jacket as she gathered up her bag. "Oh, damn damn damn damn!" she cried.

Nick grinned at her.

She snatched her rubber pad off the poncho, and raced for her tent. The flaps weren't zipped. She lunged inside, flopped forward, and landed on the soft heap of her sleeping bag.

There was a startled grunt.

"Sorry," she gasped, and raised her face. Beside her, near enough to touch, was a bare rump. The legs were wedged between another pair of legs.

He's screwing Karen! The thought hit her like a punch in the stomach, knocking her breath out. She shoved herself off the bag and crawled backward. He reached out and grabbed her wrist. "Let . . ." Then she saw his face. She screamed and wrenched her hand free. She flung herself away, falling through the tent flaps. Rain splashed her face. She started to squirm away. The flaps flew open and a naked man dived out, a huge knife in one hand. He landed on Julie, slamming her flat on the ground. He clutched her throat, holding her down while he pushed himself up and straddled her hips. He plunged the knife into the earth by her face. He yanked the neck of her jacket, found the zipper, and tugged it down. She bucked with pain and screamed again as a rough hand squeezed her breast. The hand went away. It jerked at her pants. She felt the wet ground under her buttocks. Then he had both her arms pinned down and he was heavy on her and shoving his knees between her legs to force them apart and his mouth was on her, mashing her lips. She heard a yell, and his head snapped back as a bare foot shot past her eyes.

Her father was there, grabbing the man's hair, ripping at it so the head bent back, chopping with his other hand at the bridge of the man's nose. Blood spouted, mixed with the rain hitting Julie's face. The man rolled off her. He scrambled away on hands and knees.

She rolled onto her side. As she pulled up her pants, she watched her father dash toward the man. The man was on his feet now, trying to run, but Dad was gaining on him fast.

Then there was a pale figure sprinting in from the side. *Nick!* In his upraised hand was a hatchet.

Dad slipped on the wet ground. He windmilled, trying to get his balance, and went sprawling headlong. As he skidded, he grabbed for the man's foot. He missed. The man glanced back at him. He crouched and picked up a rock and took a step toward her father, then saw Nick and staggered back. Nick swung. The hatchet caught the stranger high in the chest. Nick tore it free and prepared to strike again. The man took a few wobbly steps backward, and fell.

Nick dropped to the ground and vomited.

Flash, running toward him, yelled, "Stay with the girls!" over his shoulder to Alice. He stopped over the body. "Oh, God," he gasped.

Julie got to her knees. She tried to fasten her zipper, but her hands shook too badly, so she hugged the jacket shut.

Benny was walking slowly forward, unsteady, hands out as if to help his balance.

Dad pushed himself up. He stared for a moment at the body, then ran toward Julie. "You okay?"

She nodded. "He—he hurt Karen."

CHAPTER TWENTY-TWO

Scott fell to his knees. Karen was lying motionless on her open sleeping bag, arms and legs spread wide. He pressed a hand below her rib cage. He felt the rise and fall of her breathing, and he started to cry.

"Karen?" he whispered. She didn't stir.

In a boot near her head, he found a flashlight. He turned it on, and shined the light on her face. Her eyelids trembled, but didn't open. Her left cheekbone was swollen. Her face was slick in places. Teeth marks on her cheek, her mouth. It was all blurry through Scott's tears. Sobbing quietly, he backhanded the tears from his eyes.

"Dad?" Julie's voice. "How is she?"

"Alive."

"Can I come in?"

"Yeah."

Julie crawled through the flap, and knelt beside him. "Is she unconscious?"

"Yeah." He moved the beam down her body.

Julie groaned as it lit wet shiny places and crooked teeth marks on Karen's left shoulder and breast. "God," she murmured.

Fingers had put scratches and red imprints on her skin, but Scott saw no blood, no stab wounds.

"Is everybody okay?" Benny called from outside.

"Yes," Scott answered. "Stay out there."

The marks ended at Karen's rib cage. He nudged Julie. She leaned out of his way and he bent over her body and shined the light on her vagina. There was no blood, no semen. Her legs looked okay.

"Dad?" Julie whispered. "He raped her."

He nodded.

"Do you think she'll be all right?"

"I don't . . ." His voice cracked. "I don't know. Here." He gave Julie the flashlight. "Go over to my tent. Get her sweatshirt. It's in my sleeping bag."

Without a word, she hurried from the tent.

Scott found Karen's sweatpants in the space behind her boots. They were folded neatly.

God, she must've been lying here naked, waiting for him. If only Benny had fallen asleep a few minutes earlier . . . if the rain hadn't come . . . if he hadn't been so damned worried about everyone else, and simply tented with her all along . . .

He stroked the length of her outflung leg, slipped his hand under her calf, and lifted it. He slipped the sweatpants over her foot and drew in her other leg. By the time Julie returned, he had the pants in place. Together, they lifted her to a sitting position and pulled the sweatshirt over her head. Scott worked her limp arms into the sleeves. He lowered her gently, and smoothed the cover of the sleeping bag over her.

Julie was kneeling beside him, staring down at the dark bundle. He put an arm around her. "How are you doing, tiger?"

"Okay."

"Jesus."

"Are *you* okay?"

"Yeah."

"You're gonna freeze."

He realized, vaguely, that he was naked except for his jockey shorts. He was wet and shivering. "I'm okay," he said.

"I guess the guy's dead."

"Yeah. I'm sorry it was Nick. He didn't have to. I—it's too bad."

"I'll go see how he's doing. If you don't need me anymore."

Scott nodded.

Julie eased away. She brought her own sleeping bag over, and wrapped it around him. "Benny and I—we'll stay in the other tent." She kissed him lightly on the cheek, and left.

Benny grabbed Julie's arm as she stood up outside the tent. He stared at her, the rain splashing on his glasses. "Is she okay?" he asked.

"She's unconscious."

"What'd he do to her?"

"He knocked her out."

"I know, but . . ."

"Why don't you go back to the tent? You're drenched."

His chin started to shake. "I gotta know how she is!"

"She'll be fine."

"Goddamn stinking rotten dirty bastard!"

Julie put her hand on Benny's cold, dripping cheek. "She'll be all right. You'll see."

"*He* won't! *He's* dead! I wish *I'd* killed him!" Benny suddenly threw himself against Julie and hugged her tightly. She wrapped her arms around him. He was sobbing out of control. His stocking cap was sodden and cold against her cheek.

Beyond his head, Julie saw Nick sitting on a rock by the dead fire. He was wearing a hooded poncho. He was slumped forward, staring at his feet.

Her own poncho, which she'd left on the ground when the storm hit, was spread over the dead body. It was barely visible through the darkness and sheeting rain. She thought of what was under it, and turned her eyes away.

Flash, in a clear plastic rain slicker, was crouched in front of the far tent, apparently talking to Alice and the girls.

He shouldn't have left Nick alone.

"Come on," Julie said. "Dad's gonna stay with Karen. If you're staying outside, why don't you go get your poncho? And try to find Dad's for me. Okay?"

With a nod, Benny backed away and walked toward the

other tent. Julie went over to Nick. He looked up as she stopped in front of him. "How are you doing?" she asked.

"I still feel a little sick. How about you? Did he hurt you?"

"Bruised me a little. He got Karen pretty bad, though. He raped her."

"God. How is she?"

"Unconscious. He hit her with something. Maybe the knife handle."

"Will she be okay?"

Julie shrugged. "You were great, going after the guy that way."

"I heard you scream," he said. His voice sounded flat, as if his mind were far away. "I saw you on the ground. And your dad hit him. I didn't know what was going on. I just knew I had to get him. I didn't plan to . . . kill him." He stared up at Julie with wide, unblinking eyes. "I don't know. I guess I did want to kill him. I just knew he'd hurt you and I grabbed the hatchet. I feel kind of strange."

She stepped between his knees and pressed his face against her body. "Don't feel bad. If you hadn't done it, I think Dad would've."

"That's what my dad said. He said the guy was 'dead meat.'"

"Here it is," Benny said.

Julie stepped back. She shook open the wrinkled plastic sheet, and pushed her head through its hooded hole. As she snapped the sides under her arms, Flash approached. He squeezed her shoulder. "How're you doing, young lady?"

"Fine, I guess."

"What about Karen?"

"She's beat up some. She's unconscious." With Benny standing there, Julie didn't want to mention the sexual assault. "He messed her up pretty good."

"Well, Nick messed *him* up pretty good. She'll be all right, won't she?"

"I guess so."

"That's good to hear. How you holding up, Nicky?"

"Okay," he muttered.

"I know it's not easy. I've put the nix on a couple of guys in my day. It's never easy. Nothing to worry about, though. A clear case of self-defense. What I think we'll do is get some snapshots of the body. We can't exactly pack it out with us. We'll wrap it up good and tight, and bury it here. Let the authorities come back for it."

Julie watched him reach into his clear slicker and pull an Instamatic from the pocket of his jacket. "You kids can wait here. No need for you to watch."

He walked to the front of the tent where the man had struggled with Julie. The knife was still embedded in the muddy ground. He tugged it free, and went to the dark bundle. With the point of the knife, he swept the poncho aside.

Julie was ready to look away, but the ground where the corpse should have been sprawled was bare.

Benny groaned.

Julie felt a shiver crawl up her spine, squirm on the back of her neck.

Nick muttered, "Holy shit," and leaped to his feet. He ran toward his father, Julie and Benny following close behind.

Flash was walking slowly toward the shoreline. He stopped at the edge of the water. When they caught up to him, he was standing motionless, arms hanging at his sides, eyes staring out at the black ruffled surface of the lake.

"Dad?"

Flash shook his head. His voice came out in a whisper barely loud enough to hear over the sounds of the wind and rain. "He was dead. I know he was dead."

CHAPTER TWENTY-THREE

With a sudden intake of air, Karen sat up straight. Scott put a hand on her shoulder. She flinched and looked at him with wide, pale eyes. "It's all right," he said. She raised a hand to her face, and moaned. Then she lunged forward, scurried out of her sleeping bag, thrust her head through the tent flap, and vomited.

Scott found her water bottle propped up between her boots. He took it to her. She was on her hands and knees, half outside the tent. She'd finished throwing up, and had raised her head. She was staring through the rain. Scott saw four dark figures with flashlights wandering among the rocks and trees to the right.

"What are they—" Karen muttered.

"I don't know." He gave the water bottle to her. As she washed out her mouth and took a long drink, Scott gazed at the place where the body had fallen. He saw a rumpled shape on the ground. Good, they'd covered it. He patted the wet back of Karen's sweatshirt. "Let's get in where it's dry."

She crawled backward and sat down on her sleeping bag. She pulled off her sweatshirt and used it as a towel to dry her hair. Then she lay down. Scott covered her. "Come in with me?" she asked. Her voice was quiet, but pitched high, like that of a child about to cry.

Scott crawled in beside her. He closed the zipper. Rolling against her, he embraced her gently.

"What happened?" she asked in the same high voice.

Scott caressed her back. Her skin was damp and cool near

the shoulders, smooth and dry and warm lower down where the rain hadn't found her. "You don't remember?" he asked.

"I remember waiting for you. I didn't know if you would come. Who did this to me, Scott?"

"I don't know. A stranger."

She hugged him tightly. She burrowed her face against the side of his neck.

"You don't remember any of it?"

"No," she murmured. "I know what he did, though. I . . ." She started weeping. Her tears moistened Scott's neck. She shook with small sobs. "I can . . . feel what he did."

"I'm sorry," Scott whispered through the tightness in his throat. Tears burned in his own eyes. "I'm so sorry, Karen."

"Are they . . . looking for him? Outside?"

"No. I don't know what they're doing. He didn't get away."

Karen stiffened. "Where is he?"

"He's dead."

She pressed herself against Scott.

"He attacked Julie, too."

"Oh, no. Oh, no."

"She's okay. She came in when the rain started, and found him with you. She screamed. I came running, and so did Nick. Nick got him with a hatchet."

"Dear God," she murmured.

"Yeah. I feel bad about that. Nick's just a kid. I feel bad that he killed the guy. It should've been me. I should've done it. Nick beat me to it, that's all."

"Will he be in trouble?"

"Some, I guess. There'll be an inquest, I suppose. Nobody's gonna be arrested, though, not with something like this."

"I guess it's self-defense."

"Something like that. I just hate it that Nick's gonna have to live with killing a man."

For a long time, they lay motionless, holding each other tightly and saying nothing. Scott listened to the patter of raindrops on the tent, to the quiet sounds of her breathing. He felt her warm breath on his skin. Sometimes, when she blinked, her eyelashes tickled his neck. He wished she would sleep and forget, at least for a time, what had happened to her. But her heart was pounding fast. He could feel it against his chest.

Then she whispered, "He didn't come in me. I mean, that would've been worse."

"Yeah."

"I feel so filthy. It's like I can still feel where he . . ." Her voice died. Later, she said, "Will you still want me?"

"Of course. I love you."

"But . . . will it make a difference?"

"I guess it already has. Knowing I could've lost you tonight. He had a knife. I thought I might find you . . . I don't know what I would've done."

"Will you make love to me?"

He fondled her hair. He didn't answer.

"Please. Please, I need you. I can still *feel* him. I want it to be *you* I feel."

"I might hurt you."

"I don't care. You want me, don't you?"

"Of course I do."

Pushing a hand inside her sweatpants, he stroked the warm smooth skin of her rump. He slid his hand up to the curve of her hip, down to her sleek thigh. She stiffened when he touched her pubic hair. "Don't stop," she said. He eased his hand lower, gently cupping her mound, fingers curling in, caressing. She raised a leg slightly, opening herself to him.

She pulled the waistband of Scott's shorts away from his body and down, freeing his erect penis. He moaned as her fingers gripped him.

Then they were both naked, Scott braced above her on elbows and knees, touching her only with his lips while her hands roamed down his back, stroked his buttocks.

"Is something wrong?" she asked.

"I don't want to hurt you."

A hand went away from his rump. Fingers took his penis and guided him lower until he pushed into soft folds. He slid slowly into Karen, deep into her hugging sheath. She sighed. She wrapped her arms around his back, and pulled him tightly against her.

After searching the area around the campsite, they followed Flash to the fireplace. He sat on a stump, rested the bowie knife across his lap, and put his flashlight into a pocket of his slicker. "You kids might as well turn in," he said. "I'll stand watch."

"Do you think he'll be back?" Nick asked.

"Who the hell knows? I thought he was dead. Maybe he wasn't, but I know for damn sure he was too far gone to get up and run off. Might've dragged himself a few yards, maybe even as far as the lake. Or maybe he *was* dead, and somebody carted him off when we weren't looking."

Benny mumbled something.

"What?"

"I said, maybe he's a zombie."

"Give us a break," Julie told him.

"Like the guy in your story who came out of the lake to get his arm."

"That was just a story," Flash said. "It didn't happen."

"What about the woman?" Julie asked.

"What woman?"

"Yeah!" Nick said. "That's right." He looked at Flash. "Remember I told you this morning about a crazy woman who yelled at those girls? They ran into her right here, yesterday."

"The girls said she had a knife like that." Julie pointed at the weapon on Flash's lap.

Nick frowned. "They didn't say anything about a guy."

"He could've been hiding when they were here."

"I've got it," Benny blurted. "The guy and the woman are the same person! Like that guy in *Psycho*. He dresses up—"

"Then who took the body?" Julie asked.

"The woman took it," Nick said. He sounded very sure of himself. "She was a friend of his, maybe his wife. She saw what happened to him. Then she waited for her chance, and snuck over and got him."

"She would have to be an awfully strong woman," Flash said, "to walk off with that guy's body."

"She didn't. She dragged it over to the lake, and towed it away in the water."

"I guess that's possible," Flash admitted.

Julie's face suddenly contorted.

"What's wrong?" Nick asked.

"I just thought of something." Her wide eyes looked from Nick to Flash. "Those girls—they just saw a woman. And we just saw a man."

"So?" Flash said.

"What I mean," Julie continued, "is how do we know there aren't *more* people here? Maybe another man. Maybe a whole bunch."

Flash stared at her. "Damn, I wish you hadn't said that."

"It's possible," Nick said.

Benny started looking around, searching the darkness through his dripping glasses.

"That's all the more reason we'd better keep watch. Even if it's just a woman, we don't know but that she'll try to get back at us. The rest of you go on and hit the sack."

"I'll stay up with you," Nick said.

Flash considered insisting that the boy turn in, but he liked the idea of having company.

"I wouldn't be able to sleep anyway, and if something does happen"—Nick shrugged—"it'd be better if there's two of us."

"I guess you're right. Okay."

The hatchet swinging at his side, Nick walked Julie and Benny to their tent. Benny crawled inside. Julie faced Nick, put her arms around him, and kissed him. The kiss was not brief. Flash felt he shouldn't be staring, so he went over to the poncho he'd used to cover the body. Pools of water had formed on its rumpled plastic. He picked it up and flapped it, shaking off as much water as he could. When he turned around, Julie was gone, and Nick was walking toward him. "This'll help keep us dry. We'll sit back to back so we've got a three-hundred-sixty-degree view."

They moved two stumps together, sat down, and draped the poncho over their heads. The rain made loud, hollow sounds as it struck the plastic. Flash stared through the downpour, moving his gaze slowly over the black lake, the dim pale rocks along the shoreline, the place where the body had fallen, the rocks and trees beyond the border of the clearing, Karen's tent, the pines close behind it, the gap between it and the next tent. Awfully dark behind the tents. A lot of trees. A small rocky rise farther back. Plenty of cover for someone sneaking in. Someone with a knife. . . .

"I'll check around," Flash said. He left the sheltering poncho. With the knife in one hand and his flashlight in the other, he walked to the far side of Karen's tent. He stepped behind it, being careful not to trip over the guy line. He shined his light on the blue fabric long enough to see that it hadn't been rent. Then he swept the beam across the pines, the bushes, the head-high clump of broken granite. The light threw squirming shadows that sent a chill up his back, but he saw no one. He moved on. Behind the next tent, a sudden voice made him jump.

"Who's there?" Julie asked.

"It's me."

"Something wrong?"

"No. Just checking around."

The tent after that was his. He knew it was deserted but he flashed his light across its rear, just in case. It looked all right. He stepped to the last tent. "Just me," he said quietly, in case Alice or the girls should be worried. There was no response. They must be asleep, he thought, but he felt a stab of fear. He put his light on the tent. The red fabric, shiny with running water, was intact.

He made a last check of the trees and rocks behind the

tent, then hurried around to the front. The flaps were zipped shut. He opened them. Ducking low, he swept his light over the three crowded, motionless shapes. They looked okay. He shut the zipper, and walked toward Nick.

"Is everything all right?"

"So far. We'd better check once in a while, though. We're awfully vulnerable back there." He sat on the stump with his back to Nick, and pulled the poncho forward to shield him.

For a long time, Flash stared into the darkness. His eyelids grew heavy. His mind drifted. He imagined he was driving through the rain, fighting hard to stay awake. Alice cried out, "Don't hit him!" and there was a one-armed man staggering up the road, pale in the headlights, a hatchet embedded in his chest. Flash shot his foot at the brake pedal. The heel of his boot skidded on the wet ground and he snapped awake as he started to fall. He caught himself. He wondered how long he'd been out.

Twisting around, he saw that the stump behind him was deserted. He spotted Nick in back of the tents, the flashlight beam sweeping over the rocks and trees.

"Everything shipshape?" Flash asked when the boy returned.

"No problem." Nick sat down and covered his head. "Maybe she won't try anything."

"Sure hope not. We've gotta stay on our toes, though." The warning was more to himself than to his son. He was ashamed of falling asleep. He wouldn't let it happen again.

When he felt himself becoming groggy, he went into his tent for cigars. He returned to the seat, unwrapped a cigar, and clamped it between his teeth. He pulled the poncho forward enough to shield the cigar from the rain. To save his night vision, he shut his eyes when he struck the match. Then there was only the soft red glow of his cigar. Flash smoked slowly. When only a hot, bitter stub remained, he tossed it down and crushed it under his boot. "Still with us?" he asked Nick.

"I'm awake."

"I'll make the rounds."

He stood up, and stretched his stiff back. His light probed the darkness ahead of him. A shape lurched from behind one of the pines, and his heart seemed to jump. Nothing but a shadow. He satisfied himself that no one lurked among the trees or crouched in the tumble of rocks, then turned his beam to the back of the tent.

For an instant, he thought the two-foot vertical slash was another trick of light—nothing more than a shadow. Crouching, he set the knife by his foot and touched the slit. It parted, and his fingers slid in.

He muttered, "Jesus."

Shoving the flashlight through the gap, he tugged the fabric wide. It split more. He dropped to his knees and peered inside.

Scott squinted up at him. He looked alarmed. His forehead was smeared with blood.

"It's me," Flash said.

"What the hell are you doing?"

Karen, beside Scott in the sleeping bag, raised her head. She squeezed her eyes shut when the light hit her. The left side of her face was swollen and discolored. So was her mouth and chin. A speck of fresh blood glistened above one eyebrow.

"Flash?" Scott said.

"Someone was here. I've gotta . . ." He shoved himself away from the tent, staggered backward, and caught his balance. "Nick!" he yelled. "Check Julie!" He rushed past Julie's tent, glimpsing its gashed fabric. His own was the same. He fell to his knees at the rear of the last tent, rammed his flashlight through the split, and yanked a wide opening. Alice lurched upright.

"It's me."

Her forehead was bloody.

"What's going—"

"See if the girls are okay."

Rose was already lifting her head. She blinked into the light. There was blood on her right cheekbone.

Alice shook Heather awake. The girl was buried in her sleeping bag. As she scooted forward, Flash saw a small patch of blood at the top of her head.

Alice touched her daughter's bloody hair, then looked at her finger. "What's going on?" she asked in a low, frightened voice.

"I don't know," Flash said. "Somebody—"

"They're okay!" Nick called. "They're both cut, though."

"Get dressed," he said into the tent. "We're getting out of here."

"Tonight?" Alice asked.

"Right now. As soon as we can break camp."

CHAPTER TWENTY-FOUR

Benny, sitting on top of his sleeping bag, shoved his foot into a boot as Julie slipped a poncho over her head. She started crawling toward the tent flap held open by Nick. Benny blurted, "Don't leave me here!"

"All right. But hurry." She stopped. "Do you know what's going on?" she asked Nick.

"I don't know."

Benny got his other boot on. "Ready," he said. Grabbing his poncho, he followed Julie outside. He stood up and donned the poncho, thrusting his head through the hooded hole.

Mr. Gordon came around from behind the last tent.

"Is everybody okay?" Nick called.

"Just cut. Nothing serious. Christ!"

"They're *all* cut?" Nick asked.

"All of 'em."

"I don't get it."

"Neither do I."

The front of Karen's tent bulged and Dad crawled out, wrapped in a sleeping bag. Karen came out next. She wore gray sweatpants and a quilted parka that reached only to her waist. Her floppy hat covered her head. Her feet were bare.

Looking at her, Benny got a hollow ache in his chest. "Are you hurt much?" he asked.

"Not bad," she said. She slipped a hand from her pocket and held it out to him. He clasped it gently.

"I think we should haul ass outa here," Mr. Gordon said. "What do you think?"

"Is everyone okay?" Dad asked.

"So far. But who knows what we're up against? We're too damn vulnerable here. I say we move out. Once we're on the trail, we can see what's coming. The trip's shot anyway, right?"

"I'd say so," Karen muttered.

"Leave the body here?" Dad asked.

"It's gone," Julie said.

Benny felt Karen's fingers tighten around his hand.

"Either the guy wasn't dead," Mr. Gordon explained, "or someone snuck in and made off with him."

"It had to be that woman," Nick said.

"What woman?" Dad asked.

Nick repeated the story about the three girls who'd been swimming here yesterday until a weird woman yelled at them and frightened them away. "She must be the one who slashed the tents, too," he added.

"Why would anyone do that?" Karen asked. "It'd make sense if she wanted to cut our throats, but . . ."

"Just one woman," Mr. Gordon said, "couldn't have killed everyone. Not with two or three to a tent, and me and Nick on watch. She might've got a couple of us, but we'd have nailed her."

"Why just scratch us, though? What does that accomplish?"

"You don't suppose . . ." Julie's lips drew back, and she shook her head.

"What?" Nick asked.

"It's crazy."

"What's crazy?" Dad asked.

"Well . . . maybe her blade was poisoned."

Benny's stomach knotted. "Curare," he muttered.

"Nobody's got curare out here," his father said. "And if they did, we wouldn't be standing around talking about it."

"Maybe something," Karen said. "Some kind of poison or germs." With her free hand, she touched the cut on Benny's face. "I don't feel any swelling. There'd be swelling with snake venom. Besides, it'd take quite an amount to do much damage."

"Rabies?" Nick suggested.

Julie groaned.

"I don't want to get creepy," he went on, "but all it'd take is some saliva or blood from a rabid animal—"

"I'd say it's pretty unlikely," Dad interrupted. "This had to be a spur-of-the-moment thing. Who's gonna have a rabid animal on hand?"

"A crazy old woman," Julie said.

"Pretty remote chance."

"It's possible, though," Mr. Gordon said. "You'll admit it's possible?"

"Anything's possible." Dad sounded annoyed.

"It does seem a little farfetched," Karen said, "but something like that, at least, would explain why she cut us. Otherwise, what's the point?"

"I don't know," Dad admitted. "I just hate to think that . . . I guess we'd better play it safe."

"We'll hike straight out," Mr. Gordon said. "I bet we can reach the roadhead in a day, if we really push it."

"It's mostly downhill," Julie added.

"Right," Dad said. "We'll lighten our packs. We can leave most of the food behind."

"What about the tents?" Nick asked.

"Forget 'em," Mr. Gordon said. "They're ten pounds each, and they're fucked anyway. We can make better time without 'em."

"I'm with you," Dad told him. "Leave the things. Let's pack up fast and—"

"*Murderers!*" The shrill outcry made Benny jump. Karen jerked her hand away and whirled around. Benny staggered backward a step. Through the sheets of water he saw a woman perched on a boulder near the shore. He felt warm urine spill down his leg, and fought to stop it.

Everyone stood motionless, staring at the woman. She stood with her feet spread apart, dress clinging to her legs, face a thin pale mask streaked with ropes of dark hair, arms raised overhead. The blade of a small knife jutted from one hand. From the other hung a pouch the size of a baby's head.

"*Murderers!*" she shrieked again. "You're cursed!" She shook the pouch. "I have your blood and hair! You killed my son and you'll die, every one of you! Cursed! My curse is on you!"

She leaped off the rock and took a few steps sideways, waving the pouch. Then she turned away and started to run.

Mr. Gordon lunged forward, but Dad grabbed his arm. "Let go! I'll nail her!"

Benny saw the woman dash behind an outcropping.

"Just wait," Dad told Mr. Gordon. "What if she's not alone? What if someone's waiting to pick you off?"

Mrs. Gordon rushed from her tent, Heather and Rose following close behind. They wore yellow slickers and rain hats, and Benny couldn't tell which was Heather until one of the girls waved at him. "Who was that?" Mrs. Gordon asked.

"Some crazy old bag," said Mr. Gordon.

"Apparently the mother," Dad explained, "of the guy who attacked Karen and Julie."

"A witch," Benny said.

The others acted as if they didn't hear him. "What did she want?" Mrs. Gordon asked.

Her husband shrugged. "God only knows."

"Is she the one who took the body?"

"She didn't say."

"She put a curse on us," Benny said loudly. "A death curse. She's a witch."

"Bullshit," Mr. Gordon said.

"Bullshit or not," Karen told him, "that woman did, in fact, put a curse on us. In a way, though, it's a relief. I don't think she cut us to infect us—just to get blood for her hex or whatever."

"That *is* how it sounded," Dad admitted. "The gal's obviously a nutcase. Unless it was all a show to lure us after her."

Benny took a deep breath. His glasses had slipped down

the bridge of his nose. He shoved them back into place, and wrinkled his nose to hold them there. "Do you want to know what I think?" he asked.

"I think we'd better get out of here," Mr. Gordon said. "Rabies or no rabies, the quicker we get back to the cars, the better. We don't want to spend another night out here if we can help it. A loony like that gal, there's no telling what she might do."

"Especially," Julie added, "if she's not alone."

"Can I say something?" Benny asked again.

"What's this about rabies?" Mrs. Gordon asked.

"Probably a false alarm, but—"

"Benny has something to say," Karen broke in.

"Shoot," Dad told him.

"I know I'm just a kid and everything, but I think we better not leave here till we get our stuff back."

"What stuff?" Dad asked.

"Our blood and hair. She's got it in that pouch, I think."

"She's welcome to it," Dad said.

"She'll *use* it. You know, like with a voodoo doll? You need the person's hair or clothes to make it work. If she's got our hair and blood, she can use it like that."

"To make voodoo dolls?" Karen asked.

"Or something. I don't know. I just know she can't mess with us if we take our stuff away from her."

"For cryin' out loud, Benny."

"What if he's right?" Nick asked. "I mean, I'm not saying I believe it, but—"

"You'd certainly *better* not believe it," Mrs. Gordon scolded. "It's blasphemy."

"It's bullshit."

"Please, Arnold."

"Can't we just get out of here," Julie said, "before anything else happens?"

"We can't get away from a curse," Benny warned. "I'm telling you, we'd better—"

"Spare us, okay?"

"Look, Benny," Dad said, "I understand you're worried about this thing, but a curse is in the same category as zombies and vampires and ghosts. It's make-believe. It doesn't really exist. All it can do is frighten us; it can't really hurt us. Guns and knives and hatchets can hurt us, but a curse is just words. Okay? So let's just try to forget about it and move out of here before we have something *real* to contend with."

Benny shrugged. He knew it was pointless to argue. "All right," he muttered. "But we'll be sorry."

PART TWO

CHAPTER TWENTY-FIVE

"Good grief, hon, you're a wreck."

"Tell me about it," Karen said. She swung her pack to the floor, crossed to the couch, sat down, and started to unlace her boots.

"A disaster, huh?" Meg lowered her husky body into a chair, and hooked a leg over one of its padded armrests. She took a cigarette from the side pocket of her housecoat. "How'd you get the shiner? Bump into a tree, or did Scott smack you around?"

"A guy attacked me." Karen pulled off her boots and leaned back against the soft cushions.

Meg groaned as she lit her cigarette. She inhaled deeply and blew smoke out her nostrils. "How do you mean, attacked?"

"He raped me."

"Good Christ! Are you kidding? Are you okay?"

"Mostly bruises."

"My God," she muttered. "Jesus Almighty Christ, that's . . ." She shook her head. Her face was twisted with disgust. "How could it happen? There was a whole army with you."

"I was alone in the tent."

"Must've been . . . Karen, Karen."

"I don't remember any of it. He knocked me unconscious. Scott was with me when I came to."

The cigarette trembled in Meg's fingers as she raised it to her lips. "What happened to the bastard that did it?"

"He was killed."

"Good. I hope he died slowly. I'd have cut off his dick."

"Then I'm glad you weren't there," Karen said. With a moan, she lifted her feet and propped them on the coffee table. She folded her hands on her belly. "I'm sore all over," she muttered. "We hiked out of there in one day—a night and a day. Then spent half a day at the sheriff's office. Then a few hours at some damn hospital for rabies tests."

"Rabies tests? Was the bastard rabid?"

Karen shook her head, wincing at the pull of her stiff neck muscles. "We were worried about his mother's knife."

"His *mother?*"

"Yeah." She explained about the tents being slashed open, the head cuts on everyone except Flash and Nick, the mother showing herself and cursing them.

"Like a fuckin' horror film," Meg said. "What was she, some kind of witch?"

"That's what Benny says. He's pretty spooked about the whole thing."

"And you're not?"

"I'm not gonna lose any sleep over a curse. Sleep, ha! Wonder what that is. Feel like I haven't slept for a week."

"Maybe you'd better hit the sack."

"Funny, I'm not sleepy. Just kind of shaky and spaced out, and like I might vomit. But, anyway, I've gotta take a bath first. Probably turn the water black."

"Can I do something for you? Fix you something to eat?"

"No, thanks. We ate on the road."

"How about a drink? You could probably use a stiff one."

"Yeah. A good belt of Alka-Seltzer. I'll get it." She pushed herself forward, stood up, and limped toward the kitchen. Meg, hurrying ahead of her, turned on the light and went to a cupboard. "Any trouble with the cops?"

"They're sending out a team to search for the body. I guess there won't be an inquest or anything unless they find something."

Meg ran cold water from the tap, and filled the glass.

"Nobody's really sure the guy's dead. We think so, but the way the body disappeared . . ."

"Good Christ."

"We think the mother took it. Anyway, they're investigating the whole thing." She accepted the glass from Meg. "They said they'd be in touch."

"What a mess."

"Yeah."

Meg returned to the living room. Karen carried her glass up the short hall to the bathroom. Leaning against the sink, she opened the medicine cabinet and found a packet of Alka-Seltzer. Her hands shook badly as she tried to tear the foil. Finally, she ripped it with her teeth. She dumped the two tablets into her glass.

While she waited for them to dissolve, she stared at herself in the mirror. She looked as bad as she felt. Her blonde hair was dark and stringy. Her face was puffy and smudged with bruises. There were shadows under each eye. The eyes themselves were like those of a dazed, haggard stranger. She touched the cut above her right eyebrow, and felt the tiny ridge of scab. Combing her hair down with her fingers, she found a swath that was too short.

I have your blood and hair.

The bitch wasn't kidding.

Karen lifted the glass. The cool fizz tickled her nostrils as she drank. When she was done, she stripped off her filthy clothes. Many of the bruises on her neck and shoulders and breasts were shaped like teeth marks.

Beautiful. That's what the female deputy had said while inspecting the marks. Karen had blushed then, and she blushed now at the memory of it. The surge of blood made the pounding in her head hurt worse.

"Beautiful?" she'd muttered.

"The fella would've been an orthodontist's dream. These are nearly as good as fingerprints." Then the deputy had taken an endless series of photos—long shots and close-ups of each injury. "And you're positive there was no ejaculation?" she asked when she finished.

"Does it make any difference?"

"Yes and no. It's rape irregardless, so long as he penetrated without your consent. A semen specimen can be typed, though, if he's a secreter. By that, I mean his blood type can often be determined from a semen sample. That'd be good evidence in court."

"He didn't ejaculate." Scott had. A specimen, if any traces could still be found, would only serve to confuse the situation.

The deputy had shrugged. "We can live without it."

"We can live without it," Karen muttered to the bruised face in the mirror. "Jeez." She turned away. Her head throbbed as she bent over the bathtub and turned the faucets on. When the water was hot, she twisted the shower handle. There was a pause, then water sprayed down. She stepped over the side of the tub, into the hot rush, and pulled the plastic curtain shut.

The water felt wonderful splashing against her, matting her hair and spraying her face, running hot down her body. She turned slowly, sighing as it struck the back of her head, her sore neck and shoulders. Its gentle force massaged her, eased the pain in her head, brought a languor that made washing seem like too much effort.

Finally, she forced herself to shampoo. Her arms ached as she rubbed the suds into her hair and scrubbed her scalp. When she finished rinsing, she stood motionless, arms hanging limp, letting the spray hit her, feeling the hot streams slide down her body. She didn't want to move, except to lie down in the enveloping heat. But she needed to be clean first, to soap away the grime of the trails, her own sweat, the filth of the man who'd soiled her by his touch.

Stepping away from the shower so the water fell just against her calves, she began to rub herself with a bar of soap. Except for a patch of skin out of reach in the center of her back, she lathered herself from neck to ankle. She set the bar in its dish. She felt as if she wore a suit of slick, hugging suds. With a wet washcloth, she began to scrub herself. She did it hard, despite the flickers of pain as she scoured the bruised areas. Squatting, with the spray on her back, she swabbed between her legs. Tomorrow, she thought, she would stop by the Thrifty and buy a douche. She wished she didn't have to wait that long, but the store would be closed by now, so there was no choice.

She stood up and rinsed, cleaned her face and ears, and was done.

Crouching, she stoppered the drain. The sound of the shower changed immediately: a loud sound, hollow and plopping, not unlike the drum of rain on a tent.

It hadn't been raining when the man entered her tent. It had been raining when she came to. When Scott made love to her, the noise of rain smashing the tent was all around them, part of it all, as close to them as the sound of their heartbeats and breathing.

It was a good memory.

Karen sat down in the pooled water and slid herself backward until the spray enveloped all but her outstretched legs. Drawing them up, she wrapped her arms around her knees. She sat there, huddled under the hot shower, the water level rising, the sound like the rain hitting the tent two nights before when Scott was with her, so gentle, so hesitant, afraid of hurting her, finally filling her and making so much of the real hurt go away.

She wished she could be with him now. He'd asked her to come home with him, but it hadn't seemed right. "I'm such a mess," she'd objected. "You'd better take me to my place." Even as the words came out, they'd left a hollow, lonely place inside her. She'd wanted, more than anything, to go home with Scott. She didn't want to leave him. She didn't want to leave Benny or Julie. But they deserved time to be together as a family, time away from her. Even if they wanted her in their home tonight, she knew she would feel like an intruder.

The water splashing on Karen seemed less hot than before. Sliding forward, she twisted the shower handle down. The spray ceased, and water gushed from the faucet. She stopped all the cold, and continued to fill the tub, a hand under the spout until the falling water started to cool. Then she shut it off.

She lay down, her head against the rear of the tub, all but her face submerged in the warmth. The enamel was slick against her back, but she felt the washcloth under her rump. She pulled it free, wrung it out, and spread it over her face.

Wrapped in heat, she felt tranquil and lazy. The soreness seeped from her muscles. Her limp arms were buoyed up. She forced them down, and slid her fingers beneath her buttocks to stop them from rising.

Her mind began to drift. She was crouching by a mountain stream, splashing herself with water so cold it stung. She saw Scott's eager eyes, felt his hand cup her breast. When he pulled off her shirt, she reminded herself that he hadn't done that; they'd kissed and moved on and found the campsite for their first night. But now he did. He pulled off her shirt and kissed the teeth marks on her breasts. There shouldn't be teeth marks, but there were, and he kissed them gently. He plucked open the drawstring of her sweatpants. She'd been wearing shorts that afternoon, but never mind. They were off and she was sprawled naked on a hot granite slab beside the stream, with the spray of the tumbling water icy on her skin, and the sun hot. Scott, standing between her spread legs, wore only a gray sweatshirt. Karen's sweatshirt. It was much too tight. He struggled to take it off, but couldn't, so he slit it up the front with a straight razor. He knelt down. "I've got a surprise for you," he said. Reaching into a bowl, he scooped out a handful of white lather. He spread it on her groin. "Are you going to shave me?" she asked. Scott didn't answer. He rubbed her with the thick, slippery cream, then piled a huge heap of it on her belly. As he smeared it over her skin, he said, "It's not what you think." She asked, "What is it?" He swirled it over her breasts, made tiny white peaks on each nipple, and licked them off. "Whipped cream," he said. "I'm going to eat you up." He raised his face and grinned, but he wasn't Scott anymore but a gaunt, wrinkled old woman with watery eyes and crooked brown teeth. There were dabs of whipped cream on her lips and the tip of her nose. "No! Get away!" Karen gasped. The awful face darted down. She tried to twist away, but the teeth clamped on her breast and sank in. The old woman shook her head like a savaging dog, jerked free, and loomed over Karen's face, chewing a clump of flesh; blood and whipped cream spilled onto Karen's lips. Karen started to scream. Her mouth filled with water.

The choking startled her awake. She spit out a mouthful of water as she lurched upright. The washcloth peeled away from her face. She curled forward, muscles afire as a fit of coughing racked her body.

Gasping and coughing, she thrust herself out of the water. She swept an arm toward the shower curtain, then grabbed a wet fold as her right foot skidded out from under her. The curtain yanked taut, ripped free. Her legs shot out and she was falling. She heard a heavy splash an instant before her head seemed to explode. She slid down. Water covered her eyes, and then she saw nothing at all.

CHAPTER TWENTY-SIX

Kneeling on his bedroom floor, Nick unstrapped his sleeping bag from his pack frame and rolled it aside. Right now, he thought, he would be lying next to Julie high in the mountains, if only . . . "Damn it," he muttered.

He opened his pack and began to empty it, tossing his dirty clothes into a heap for the laundry hamper, setting aside his cook kit, utensils, and water bottle for a trip to the kitchen, making a third pile of equipment—compass, first-aid kit, rope, toilet articles—that would need no attention and could simply be returned to the pack for the next time.

The next time?

After what had happened at Mesquite, he doubted he would ever want to go backpacking again. But you never know. Always in the past, when he stayed away from the mountains too long, he'd been hit with a longing to return, a strong aching need like homesickness. Maybe he wouldn't get that feeling anymore.

Maybe nothing would ever be the same again.

He'd killed a man. He knotted up at the thought of it. Everyone—even the sheriff deputy after hearing the story—had told him it was all right, that the guy had it coming, that Nick had performed a service by ridding the world of him. Nick had told himself the same thing, over and over, and part of him was glad he'd done it—avenged Karen and Julie, stopped the man from attacking Julie's father with the rock, made it so he would never hurt anyone again. But deep inside he felt a steady tight sickness at the knowledge that he had ended a life. The man was dead. Dead. He would never again feel the sun on his face, or . . .

Or rape another woman.

If he'd been dead a week ago, he couldn't have attacked Karen or Julie. He couldn't have messed up their lives, and my life.

And if he'd gotten away, there might've been campers tonight or next week or next year to terrorize, maybe kill.

I did the right thing, Nick told himself. I shouldn't have to feel like shit. It's not fair.

"Nick?"

He looked over his shoulder. His father, dressed in a bathrobe, was standing in the doorway.

"Phone call."

He felt a cold edge of panic. From the look on Dad's face, though, he realized he had nothing to fear. "Who is it?"

"A certain Miss O'Toole."

Nick got to his feet, wincing with the ache of sore muscles, and hobbled down the hallway behind his father.

"You can take it in the den, but stay off the couch in those jeans or your mother'll throw a fit."

"Right," he said.

Dad limped into the master bedroom, and Nick hurried ahead to the den. He snatched the phone off its cradle and said, "I've got it." The bedroom extension went dead. "Hello?" he asked.

"Hi." Her voice sounded slightly different over the phone, but familiar enough to send a warm rush through Nick.

"Hi, Julie. How are you?"

"Long time no see, huh?"

"Yeah."

There was a long pause. Nick tried to find something to say, and wondered if Julie were having the same trouble. Even with the silence, he liked the feel of being close to her.

"I just thought I'd call," she finally said, "and make sure you got home okay."

He smiled. "Afraid the curse might've got us?"

He heard her quiet laughter. "Pardon me while I barf," she said.

"Benny still at it?"

"We had about two hours of peace after we left the hospital. That's because he fell asleep. Then Dad had to stop at Denny's so we could feed our faces, and Benny spent the rest of the time trying to convert us. The kid's warped."

"We're not allowed to talk about it. I brought it up once, and Mom nearly went through the ceiling. You know the first commandment?"

"Whose?"

"God's. You know, to Moses? The stone tablets?"

"Oh, those commandments. I know the eleventh is, 'Don't get caught.'"

Chuckling, Nick started to sit on the couch. He stopped himself in time, and sat on the carpet instead. "Anyway, the first commandment says, 'Thou shalt have no other gods before me'—something like that. According to Mom, that means it's a sin to believe in occult stuff."

"Like curses?"

"Like curses, ghosts, Ouija boards, palm reading, astrology, witches and goblins and gremlins."

"What the hell's a gremlin?"

"I don't know, a fairy."

"Something that lives in San Francisco and lisps?"

"And eats quiche."

"We oughta go on Letterman," Julie said.

"It hurts to laugh."

"Me, too. Gets my stomach muscles."

"Yeah. So stop laughing."

"You, too."

"Right. Anyway, where was I? Oh, yeah, Mom and the curse."

That brought a snort and gales of laughter through the phone. "Oh," Julie finally gasped. "I'm sorry. I"—she giggled—"I think I'm . . . a bit giddy. No sleep." He heard her take a deep breath. "Okay. I'm all right. Continue."

"I think I was done."

"Oh. All right. So. What've you been up to?"

"Just unpacking."

"I'm saving that for tomorrow morning. I don't even want to *look* at that junk. The first thing I did was get in the shower." He pictured her naked under a hot spray, rubbing her breasts with soap. "Man, it sure feels good to be clean again. Now I've got Ben-Gay from head to foot."

"Bet you smell terrific."

"The fumes make my eyes water. And my nightgown's sticking to me." He pictured her in a flannel nightgown. Of course, it probably wasn't flannel. Not in the middle of summer. Something light and transparent, and clinging to her breasts. He wondered if she'd put any Ben-Gay on her breasts. ". . . like a real person again," she said. "The Long Hike almost did me in."

"Almost did us all in."

"How's Heather getting along?"

"Not bad. The doctor says she'll be sore for a couple of weeks, but it's nothing to worry about. Mom's got her in the kitchen, soaking it."

"Maybe she oughta try some Ben-Gay."

"Yeah. Couldn't hurt."

"At first it's pretty hot, but you get used to it."

"Maybe I'll try some. After my shower."

"You're still yucky, huh?"

"Yeah. I got last shot at the bathtub. I'm still waiting for Rose to get done. She takes forever."

"Just as well. What if I'd called while you were in the shower?"

"I would've called back."

"I might've been in bed by then."

"Wouldn't you have waited up?"

"Maybe, maybe not. A girl's gotta get her beauty sleep."

"Good thing I wasn't in the shower, then."

"A very good thing."

There was a long silence. Nick suspected she was getting ready to hang up. He clutched the phone tightly.

"Well . . ." she said.

His heart was thudding and his mouth was parched.

". . . I guess I'd better let you—"

"Julie?"

"Yes?" she asked in a hushed voice.

"Look, I want to see you." There. It was out.

"That would be nice," she said.

"Tomorrow? Tomorrow night? Maybe we could go to a movie or something."

"I'd really like that."

"Great." He let out a nervous laugh. "This is so weird."

"What's weird?"

"Asking you for a date. I mean, like we were almost strangers or something."

"We're the same people who were in the mountains, Nick."

"I know. I guess so."

"You guess so?" She laughed softly.

"It's just that, you know, now we're back. It's strange."

"I haven't changed. I still feel the same about you."

A smile trembled on Nick's lips. "I feel the same, too. I really miss you. How about seven o'clock?"

"Fine. Just let me check with Dad. Hold on a minute."

Nick waited. He took a deep, shaky breath. He'd done it, he'd asked her and she'd seemed as eager as he was. *I still feel the same about you.* It was almost too good to believe. He was already nervous, anticipating the date.

"Okay," she said. "It's all set. Tomorrow night at seven?"

"Great. I'll see you then."

"Do you know how to find the house?"

"No, but Dad . . ." He didn't want to lose the sound of Julie's voice. "Maybe you'd better tell me."

There was blue terry cloth under Karen's face. Her lungs felt on fire, pain blasting through her body as a spasm of coughing shook her. Someone's hand was rubbing her back. As she lifted her head, nausea swept through her. She managed to get to her knees and twist around, briefly meeting Meg's worried eyes before scurrying to the toilet and vomiting.

When she finished, she sat on the toilet seat, sobbing and coughing, gasping for breath. Through teary eyes, she watched Meg fold up the bloody bathmat. She unrolled some tissue, wiped her eyes, her mouth and chin.

"How's the noggin?" Meg asked in her low, husky voice.

Karen groaned. She drew fingers through her wet hair, and felt a lump above her ear.

"Thank God I heard you yell. I was about to turn on the TV." Meg opened the medicine cabinet. She took down a box, slid a tampon out, and tore off its wrapper. She handed it to Karen.

While Karen inserted it, Meg pulled the bathtub stopper. "I tell you, kiddo, you scared the shit out of me. How're you feeling? Should I run you over to emergency?"

"I'm okay," she muttered.

"I was gonna give you about ten more seconds to wake up, and then I was gonna call the paramedics."

"How long was I out?"

Meg shook her head. "No idea. Maybe three or four minutes, I don't know. I just knew your ticker was still ticking and you were breathing. I figured you'd come around, sooner or later, but I started to have my doubts."

"What a mess."

"The bathmat's a goner. I'll clean up the rest after you're in bed."

"No, I'll—"

"You're in no condition to do anything, kiddo."

Karen looked down at herself, wrinkled her nose, and un-rolled more toilet paper. As she rubbed away streaks of blood, she said, "I've gotta take another shower."

"I suppose you do. Sit tight for a second." Meg hurried from the bathroom. Karen continued to clean herself. Soon, Meg returned with a spool of tape. Reaching up, she worked at securing the shower curtain to its rod. "Think it was the curse?" she asked.

"I *know* it was the curse."

Meg chuckled.

"A week early."

"Stress'll do that. On the bright side, at least you know the bastard didn't knock you up."

"I knew that before," she said.

When the curtain was in place, Meg ran the water. Karen clung to her arm for support, and staggered on wobbly legs to the tub. At her friend's urging, she didn't try to stand while she washed. She sat under the hot spray. With Meg waiting on the other side of the curtain, she shampooed and soaped herself and rinsed.

Meg stood by, hands out to catch her, while she climbed from the tub and dried. "Safe now?"

"Yeah. Thanks."

"You finish drying. I'll get us a little something."

"A little what?"

"I'll surprise you."

Left alone, Karen wrapped herself in the towel. She washed down two aspirin tablets with a glassful of cold water. She brushed her teeth. Then she drew a comb through her hair, wincing as she snagged tangles.

"In your room," Meg called from the hallway.

Karen went to her bedroom. Meg, just inside, greeted her with a wink. The covers of her bed had been pulled back, showing her flowered blue sheets. Her chair had been dragged close to the bedside. On its seat rested a tray adorned with crackers, a wedge of cheddar, a small wheel of Gouda, and a cheese knife. Two wine goblets stood on the lamp table, and beside them was an open bottle of white wine.

In spite of her aches, Karen managed a smile.

"Medicine," Meg said. "Cheese and crackers to settle your gut. A Masson Sauvignon Blanc to help you sleep."

"You're really fantastic."

"I know."

Karen put on her nightgown. She climbed into bed, pulled up the top sheet, and eased herself against the headboard. Meg poured the wine. She set the tray across Karen's lap, and sat on the chair.

They lifted their glasses. "Here's how," Meg said.

"Here's to you," Karen said. "You saved my life."

Meg blushed. "What are roommates for?"

They clinked their glasses, and drank.

CHAPTER TWENTY-SEVEN

"A decent meal," Arnold proclaimed, pulling up his chair to the breakfast table. He sniffed his plateful of bacon and fried eggs, and sighed loudly. "Ah, the comforts of home."

Smiling, Alice set a plate down in front of Heather. "I didn't see you turning up your nose at your other breakfasts."

"You even wanted mine," Rose reminded him.

"I'll eat anything in the mountains. But this, now—this is real food."

"I wonder what's keeping Nick," Alice said.

"He's probably getting ready for his big date."

"At nine in the morning?"

Arnold laughed, and started to cut his bacon.

Alice carried the final two plates to the table, then went to the kitchen doorway and called for Nick.

"Right there!" he yelled.

"Your egg'll get cold," Alice warned. She returned to the table, sat down, and sighed, glad to be off her feet. She didn't look forward to grocery shopping, walking the aisles with stiff legs and blistered feet. There wasn't much choice, though. Not if they wanted supper tonight.

She heard the shuffle of Nick's moccasins on the kitchen floor. He came up behind her, and sat at the table. He gave her a quick smile. His eyes had a jittery look. "Are you all right?" Alice asked.

"Sure. I didn't sleep too well, is all."

"Nervous about the big date?" Arnold asked.

Shrugging, Nick picked up his fork. It quivered in his shaky hand. He started to cut his eggs with the edge of it. Alice felt uneasy watching him, as if his tension were contagious. She started to eat, but barely noticed the taste of her food. Obviously, the boy was bothered by more than anxiety over tonight's date with Julie. He'd been through a nightmare, and she couldn't begin to guess how deeply it might've affected him. Julie might help take his mind off the rest of it.

"Where'll you be taking her?" she asked.

Nick shrugged. "I don't know. I'll have to check the paper. There're all kinds of movie theaters in the Valley."

"Plenty of drive-ins," Arnold said.

"I don't want you taking her to a drive-in."

"Why not?" Rose asked. "They're neat."

"Nick knows why not."

"*We* go," Rose persisted.

"That's different."

"Why?"

"Just you never mind, young lady."

"We used to call them passion pits."

"Arnold!"

Rose tilted back her head and smiled, showing a mouthful of chewed bacon. "Oh, I get it."

"What?" Heather asked.

"Mom doesn't want 'em making out."

"Some of my fondest memories . . ." Arnold started.

"That's enough." She turned to Nick. He was staring at his plate as if oblivious to the conversation, swabbing up the last of his egg yolk with a bit of toast. "You will not take Julie to a drive-in. I'm sure her father wouldn't approve, either."

"I'm not arguing," Nick said.

"Especially on a first date—"

"He's not arguing," Arnold interrupted.

"Okay. I'm not one to nag. I just want to be sure we understand each other."

"I understand," Nick said.

"So," Arnold said, "what's on the agenda for today?"

"I, for one, have to go grocery shopping." Alice got up from the table. "Who wants to come along?" She picked up the coffeepot.

"Me," Rose blurted.

"Me, too," said Heather.

"You'd better stay home," Arnold told her, "and keep off your feet."

"Oh, Dad."

"He's right," Alice said, stepping around the table to refill his mug. "The more you stay off that foot, the quicker it'll heal."

"Time heals all heels," Nick said, and smiled. His first real smile of the morning.

Alice poured him more coffee, then refilled her own mug and took the pot back to the counter. "Anything special I need to pick up at the store?"

"Vodka and Dos Equis," Arnold said.

"Of course." She sat down and took a sip of hot coffee, pleased that she'd turned the conversation to a less objectionable direction. "I think I'll pick up a new Ace bandage. The old one's a disgrace."

"I used up the Ben-Gay last night," Nick said.

Arnold sniffed. "So that's what I smell. Thought it was Rose's breath."

The girl make a face at him, and Heather laughed.

"I think I lost my comb," Nick said.

"Better buy him two or three," Flash said. "A young man in love is lost without his combs."

Rose made an O with her mouth. Heather giggled. Nick's face turned as red as a ripe tomato. "Jeez, Dad," he muttered.

Arnold was beaming. "Oh, did I say something wrong?"

"How's your dandruff shampoo holding out?" Alice asked her husband.

"Fine," he said. "A little low on the pit-slick, though."

"May I be excused now?" Nick asked. "I want to air out the sleeping bags."

"Just throw them over the line," Arnold said.

Nick left the kitchen. Arnold met Alice's gaze, and shrugged. "You embarrassed the boy half to death," she said.

"Is he really in love?" Heather whispered.

"Your father was just being his usual obnoxious self." Arnold chuckled.

"I bet he is," Rose said.

"Regardless," Alice warned. "It's nothing to poke fun at. Being in love is a very serious matter."

"Especially when you're seventeen," Arnold added.

"Come on, Rose, help me clear the table. I want to beat the crowds to the supermarket."

Benny held a plate under the kitchen faucet, and watched the steaming water melt away the clumps of sugar left over from the cinnamon rolls. When the plate looked clean, he handed it to Tanya. She put it into the dishwasher, and he grabbed another plate. "Do you think they'd let a kid use the library?" he asked.

"What library?" his cousin asked.

"At the college."

"What is it you're looking for? Maybe I could find it for you."

"Just some stuff."

Tanya set two coffee mugs upside down in the machine, and stared at him. She raised a dark eyebrow. "Occult stuff?" she asked.

"Yeah," he admitted. "Witches and things."

"Did you try your bedroom?"

"Yeah, last night. I haven't got that much, though. Nothing with the details. And the public library stinks."

"They probably don't want to corrupt the youth."

"Anyway, what I was thinking was that maybe I could go along with you and take a look around while you're in class."

"For two and a half hours? Aren't you afraid you'll get bored?"

"I never get bored. Dad says boredom's a sign of a weak mind."

Tanya grinned, brushed a lock of hair away from her forehead, and took the plate from Benny. "Well, you're welcome to come along, if that's what you want. But you'd better check with your dad first. He might have some chores for you. Go on ahead. I'll finish with the dishes."

"Thanks," he said, and hurried outside. His father, in his faded blue swimming trunks, was down on one knee beside the pool, checking the thermometer. "Hey, is it okay if I go over to the college with Tanya? It's all right with her if it's all right with you."

"Fine with me. What's up?"

"Nothing. I just want to fool around in the library."

Dad's mouth curved in a half smile. "The only known copies of the *Necronomicon* are said to reside in the Miskatonic University library and—"

Benny laughed. "You know about that?"

"You'd be surprised what your old dad knows. I ain't completely illiterate, boy. Anyway, go ahead if you want. Be warned, though. Karen'll be showing up in an hour or so."

Benny's eagerness faded. He didn't want to miss Karen. On the other hand, this was too important to delay. Maybe he wouldn't find anything helpful in the college library, but he had to give it a try. "Well," he said, "I'd better go anyway. We'll be back around one."

"Karen should still be here. She's staying for supper, I imagine. Good hunting."

CHAPTER TWENTY-EIGHT

They were on a quiet, tree-shadowed lane no more than six blocks from home, Rose fooling with the radio dial to bring in a rock station, when a German shepherd wandered out from behind a parked car. Alice gasped. She threw an arm across Rose's chest, knocking the girl backward as her foot shot down on the brake pedal. The tires shrieked. The dog swung its head around, seemed to glare at Alice, made no move to get out of the way. The hood hid it from view an instant before it was struck. The impact jolted the station wagon. Alice whimpered as the left front tire bumped over the dog.

"Oh, Mom!" Rose cried. She had a look of horror in her eyes.

Alice glanced at the rearview mirror. The shadowy lane was deserted behind them. She didn't know what to do. She wanted to drive on and get far away from it all, but she couldn't do that without a rear tire passing over the dog. The thought of that sickened her. Her right leg, still stretched out and mashing the brake pedal to the floor, started to bounce in a frenzy as if its muscles had all gone berserk.

Rose fumbled with her seat belt.

"Just wait a—"

"We've gotta help it, Mom!" She flung open her door and leaped out.

"Rose! Damn it!"

The girl, paying no attention, was running around the front of the car. With a shaky hand, Alice turned off the ignition. She set the emergency brake, struggled to free herself from the seat belt, and shoved open her door. Her jumpy right leg started to collapse when she put weight on it. She hung onto the door to hold herself up. "Rose!"

It was too late. The girl was standing rigid by the front tire, staring down, her pretty features twisted hideously, palms pressed to her ears as if to block out a terrible noise.

Alice glanced down at the crushed remains of the dog. She raised her eyes quickly to Rose. "There!" she snapped. "Are you happy? I *told* you not to look!" She hadn't, not really, but she'd tried. "I wish, damn it, just once, you'd *listen* to me when I tell you something!"

The girl kept staring at the dog. "Oh, Mom," she muttered, and dropped her hands to her sides.

"Did you hear anything I told you?"

"We've gotta help it," Rose said again, and started to cry.

"Oh, Rose, Rose." Alice hugged her daughter fiercely. She started to cry. "I'm sorry, honey. I'm sorry I yelled. I just didn't want you to see. I'm sorry."

"We've gotta help it."

"It's beyond our help, honey. It's with God now."

"No. Please. It can't be dead."

"I'm sorry, honey."

"We've gotta take it to a vet."

"It's dead. There's nothing a vet can do for it."

"Please. If we don't try . . . We've gotta *try!*"

"Trouble?" someone called.

Alice spotted a young, bearded man striding down the nearest driveway. Please, she thought, don't let it be his dog. "It ran out," she said. "I couldn't stop in time. It just . . . ran right out in front of me."

He stepped past the front of the car, and looked down. "You sure creamed it, all right. What a mess."

Alice wiped her eyes. "Do you know who it belongs to?"

"Never seen it before." He crouched down close to the remains. "Doesn't seem to have a collar. A stray maybe."

"We're gonna take it to a vet," Rose said.

The man raised his eyebrows. "You want to put *that* in your car?"

"No—"

"Yes! We have to, Mom. Please."

"Honey, it's dead."

"No, it's not!"

"Looks pretty dead to me," the man said. He sounded a bit amused. "I'm no authority, but the way its guts are spread around—"

"Stop that!" Alice snapped.

"Sorry. I didn't . . . Tell you what. If you really want to take it with you, I'll give you a hand. Let's not mess up your car, though. You want to hang on a minute, I've got some Hefty bags out in the garage. Go ahead and open your tailgate. I'll be back in two shakes."

Alice stood mute while he hurried away. She didn't want the awful thing in her car. But she felt trapped. She couldn't drive away without running over it again—not unless she first dragged it out from under the car. Besides, Rose would never forgive her.

She supposed that she did have a certain responsibility for the poor creature. She couldn't blame herself for killing it— she'd been driving under the speed limit and it had stepped out right in front of her and nobody could've stopped in time. But she had been the one to kill it, even if it weren't her fault. As much as she hated the idea, she supposed that hauling its corpse to a veterinary hospital would be the right thing to do.

Let them dispose of it properly.

They could leave it here for the Department of Animal Regulation to pick up. But other cars might . . . Maybe the man would move it out of the road.

Hell, she might as well take it. Make Rose happy. Unless

she was mistaken, there was a veterinary hospital on Wilshire, just a block from their dentist's office.

She saw the man striding down his driveway with a garbage bag and a shovel. A *shovel*. "Get in the car, honey."

As the girl obeyed, Alice took the keys from the ignition and stepped to the rear of the station wagon. She lowered the tailgate. Hearing a car behind her, she rushed to the driver's door and shut it. The car swung into the other lane. Alice looked down so she wouldn't see those inside the car as it passed. She was relieved that it didn't stop. Once it was gone, the road was clear.

"You sure you want to take this thing?" the man asked. "I could drag it over to the curb, have the pound come for it."

"No, that's all right. My daughter—"

"Yeah. Kids. You're always better off going along with them. Hey, they're usually right anyway."

He spread the plastic bag flat on the pavement, its edge an inch from the blood puddle. Standing on it, he put on a pair of garden gloves. He spread his feet wide, pinning down the bag, and dragged the dog forward by its front paws. Horrified, Alice saw that some of its insides stayed behind, as if glued to the street. She gagged and turned away. She heard crinkling plastic, then the raspy scrape of the shovel. "There y'go," the man said. To the dog? "You hanging in there? Ma'am? You all right?"

Alice nodded.

"Do you think you can lend a hand? We don't want the bag to tear."

"Of course," she muttered. She faced the man, and tried not to look at the dog. "What should I do?"

"Let's drag it to the back. If you can lift that end of the bag a bit, take some of the weight off . . ."

She stepped around the man. Crouching, she grabbed the edge of filmy plastic. The man lifted his end and waddled backward, dragging the awful load. The dog was very heavy. To keep from looking at it, Alice focused on the man's head.

Though he appeared no older than thirty, his black hair was thin on top. That explains the beard, she thought: balding men often wore beards.

Finally, they reached the rear of the station wagon.

"Lift?" he asked.

"I'll try."

"Got a good grip on it?"

She adjusted her hold. "Okay," she said.

"*Now.*"

They lifted. She felt the plastic stretch as if melting over her fingertips and knuckles. It spread and tore, but then the weight was gone, the dog supported by the tailgate.

The man crawled into the rear of the wagon. He tugged the bag, sliding the dog in after him. Turning away, he climbed into the backseat and left through a passenger door.

Alice shoved the tailgate shut.

"Okay," the man said. He plucked off his gloves and picked up his shovel. "All set. You can probably get someone at the vet's to take it out for you."

"Well, thank you so much for helping." She wondered if she should offer him money. That would be embarrassing, especially if he refused. "We really appreciate it."

"Anytime," he said, and made a wry smile. "Hey, if it pulls through, let me know."

Sick, Alice thought. "I will," she muttered.

Then the man was walking away with a sprightly step, the shovel over one shoulder. She half expected him to start whistling like one of the Seven Dwarfs.

"Hurry, Mom," Rose called.

She climbed in behind the steering wheel. The girl was on her knees, looking over the back of the seat toward the dog. She was sniffing, dabbing at her nose with a wad of blue Kleenex. "Turn around and strap yourself in," Alice said. While Rose sat down and fastened her safety harness, she buckled herself in and started the car.

She drove forward slowly to the end of the block. At the

stop sign, she checked the intersection carefully before proceeding.

"Drive faster, Mom. Please!"

"There's no hurry," she said.

"Yes there is!"

On the front lawn of a house just ahead, a boy in overalls was cavorting with a cocker spaniel. Alice watched them as she approached. Thank God it had been a dog, she thought, and not a child. That was too awful even to contemplate. What was wrong with the mother of this boy, letting him romp unattended in the front yard? The spaniel suddenly made a lunge toward the road. Alice shot her foot to the brake pedal, but the dog stopped at the sidewalk, wheeled around, and scampered back into the yard. Sighing with relief, Alice drove past.

The steering wheel was slick under her sweaty hands. She let go, one hand at a time, and wiped them on her skirt.

The shopping trip, she decided, was out of the question. After this ordeal, she was in no condition to face the supermarket. It could wait, or Arnold could go. Either way, she had no intention of leaving the house again today. When she got home, she would shut herself up in the bedroom with the new Sidney Sheldon book and not come out until . . .

From behind Alice came a low, rumbling growl. The back of her neck prickled.

"It *is* alive!" Rose blurted joyously, starting to turn around.

In the rearview mirror, Alice saw the German shepherd, forepaws on top of the backseat, fangs bared, bloody saliva hanging in strings from its snout. With a raging snarl, it sprang forward. Rose shrieked. Alice jammed on the brake pedal. The car lurched to a stop, throwing them both into their harnesses, slamming Alice's forehead against the steering wheel. The dog tumbled onto the cushion beside her, its entrails slopping down after it, teeth snapping shut on Rose's wrist as the screaming girl tried to unbuckle her safety belt. It released her wrist and lunged at her throat.

Alice fumbled with her own buckle. She flung the straps aside and threw herself onto the huge beast, hooking an arm around its neck as Rose cowered against the door and shrieked and tried to hold off its snapping jaws. Alice squeezed the thick, furry neck in the crook of her elbow. She shoved her other hand into its mouth, cried out as the teeth tore into her, but clutched the snout and pulled it toward her, away from Rose. Then she was falling backward, the squirming dog heavy on her chest, the teeth still grinding into her hand. "Rose!" she yelled. "Get out!"

The dog writhed and jerked, trying to roll but unable to free itself from Alice's grip. If she let go, she knew it would flip over and go for her throat. Her hand was afire with pain, her fingers weakening, but still she held on.

The door behind her head swung open.

Rose, standing above her, grabbed one of the dog's kicking forelegs. "Let go!" she cried.

"Rose!"

"Let go!"

She opened her fingers, felt the teeth release her. The dog stretched its head up, trying to snap at Rose.

Rose was trying to pull it out of the car! Didn't she realize . . .

"No!" Alice yelled. The wet fur of the dog's back muffled her outcry.

It was half out of the car, and didn't Rose realize it would go for her? Alice wrapped her arms around its open belly, trying to keep the beast from getting out.

The body suddenly quaked as a thudding, crushing sound filled Alice's ears. The car rocked a bit. The sound came again. Again. Each time, the car swayed and the dog jerked and trembled.

Then it was motionless on top of her.

"Mom? Are you okay?"

As the body was dragged off Alice, she realized what the thudding sound had been—*her daughter slamming the car door three times on the German shepherd's head.*

CHAPTER TWENTY-NINE

"What've they got him for?" Benny asked as a young man standing beside a guard shack waved them ahead.

Tanya smiled at the man, and drove slowly past him. "He's supposed to keep out undesirables," she said. "People who don't have any business being here. You get all kinds of crazies hanging around if you aren't careful. Flashers, rapists, that kind of thing. It's because there are so many women around. Every college has trouble like that."

"Really?" Benny asked.

"Sure. Berkeley had about a dozen rapes when I was there. That's one reason my folks were so eager to have me transfer down here and live with you guys."

"I didn't know that," Benny admitted. "I thought you did it just to help Dad."

"Oh, that was part of it, too." She swung into an empty space next to a VW van. "There were all kinds of reasons," she said. She reached for the spiral notebook and the heavy volume of Shakespeare plays on the seat beside her, but Benny grabbed them first.

"I'll carry them for you," he said.

Tanya smiled, and Benny felt a blush spread over his face. She really was so beautiful. Not as beautiful as Karen, though. He wished he could be home when Karen arrived.

He climbed from the car and joined Tanya on a walkway that led down the side of the parking lot. Not far ahead, he saw several buildings: some looked low and modern, all stucco and windows like his junior high; others were ancient, square structures of red brick. The buildings were far apart, separated by broad lawns with more trees than a park. In fact, Benny decided, the campus looked very much like a park. There were even benches. "This is nice," he said.

"I like it," Tanya told him.

"Better than Berkeley?"

She shrugged.

"Not as much?" he persisted.

"I don't know," she said. "I think I like this better. Berkeley was so huge, I felt lost. There'd be a couple of hundred students in some of my lecture classes. You know this Shakespeare class? Fourteen students. It's great." She glanced at her wristwatch, and groaned. "Cutting it close," she said. Instead of hurrying, she stopped. She nodded to the right. "My class is over that way. You'd better go on to the library without me, or I'll be late. I'll meet you there when class is over, so we can check out any books you want. Okay?"

"Fine."

She pointed straight ahead. "See the third building down? That's the library."

Benny flipped up his clip-on sunglasses and counted the structures. "The one with the pillars?"

"That's it. Kind of a dreary place. If you get sick of it, the student union's directly across the quad. You can get yourself a Coke or something. I'd better get moving." Benny gave her the notebook and the thick text. "Good luck," she said, and hurried away. She cut across the grass, walking quickly, her rump shifting inside her tight blue shorts. Then she waved and called out, "Steve!" A guy climbing the stairs of a distant building turned around, waved back, and waited for her. Tanya jogged forward to meet him.

Benny watched until they disappeared through a glass door. Feeling abandoned, he lowered his sunglasses into place and started toward the library. The few students he passed on the walkway seemed to be in no hurry. Apparently, they were between classes. A young couple was sitting on a bench, holding hands and talking. On a rise off to his left, a girl in shorts and a halter was lying on a towel, sunbathing while she read a paperback. A Frisbee landed near her. She ignored both the Frisbee and the shirtless guy who raced up and scooped it from the ground. The guy sailed it over Benny's head, and ran across the walkway to rejoin his friends.

Benny was glad that nobody seemed to notice him. He felt out of place here among these college kids, an intruder in their special world. He half expected someone to challenge him and throw him out.

A skinny, middle-aged woman in a pantsuit approached, scowling through her tinted glasses. "Excuse me, young man," she said in a sharp voice.

His heart quickened. "Me?"

"Yes, of course you. Which way is the administration building?"

"Gee, I don't know."

"You don't know," she said with disgust. "The *administration* building," she repeated, more loudly this time as if to penetrate his deafness or stupidity. "Weller Hall."

"I don't know him, either," Benny said. The whiny sound of his voice embarrassed him.

"It's not a *he*, young man. *Weller Hall*. It's the name of the administration building."

"Oh."

She huffed through her nose, and Benny eyed her nostrils, expecting snot to fly out.

"I don't know where anything is," he admitted. "Just the library and the parking lot."

"If I'd wanted the library or parking lot, I would've asked. I'm looking for—"

"Weller Hall," Benny interrupted.

"Are you being smart with me, young man?"

"No, ma'am."

"See that you're not," she snapped, and hurried off.

Shaken by the encounter, Benny quickened his pace. What was she, crazy? Couldn't she tell, just by looking, that he didn't belong here? Crazy old bag.

Crazy old bag. Somebody—Julie?—had used those words about the mountain woman. The witch.

Benny glanced back.

Gone! She was nowhere in sight. A creepy feeling scurried up his spine.

Probably she just went into the building back there.

But what if she is the witch? What if she followed us down from the mountains, followed us home?

As he climbed the steps toward the library door, he pictured the witch in the dark with her arms high, shouting her curse over the noise of the wind and rain. He tried to imagine how she might look in a gray pantsuit, wearing fashionable glasses, her hair fixed up. With a sick feeling, he realized she might look very much like the woman he'd just met. If only he'd had a better look at the witch's face.

"Don't be dumb," he said to himself out loud.

Then he took off his clip-ons and pulled open the library door. Carpet silenced his footsteps as he walked toward the circulation desk, where a young woman was reading. She held a felt-tipped pen. She wore a white blouse with a frilly collar, and had golden hair like Karen. Benny saw nothing threatening about her. She looked up as he approached, and smiled. "Hello," she said.

"Hi," Benny whispered. "Is it all right if I look around for a while? I'm waiting for my cousin. She's in class."

"Certainly. No problem. If you want to look at some magazines, the periodical room's over behind those stacks." She pointed to the right.

"Thank you."

"Help yourself. If you have any questions, I'll be right here."

Benny thanked her again, and walked over to the card catalog. Nobody else was using it. Except for a few students seated nearby at long tables, reading or scribbling notes, the big room was deserted.

He studied the drawer labels. Finding one marked WIK–WIZ, he slid the drawer open. He flipped through the cards toward the back of it. Soon, he came to a card marked *Witchcraft in Salem Village*. Behind it was *Witchcraft Through the Ages*, then *Witchery Ditchery Doc*, a novel. No good to him. He flicked that card forward. *Witches and Warlocks*. That sounded useful. But the next card set his heart racing: *Witch's Spells and Potions*.

He looked at the call number, and frowned. Instead of Dewey decimal numbers, which he understood, there was a series of letters.

Well, the librarian *had* offered to help.

Taking the ballpoint from his shirt pocket, he started to write the letters on the heel of his hand. The pen skipped badly. Then he noticed a small tray of scrap paper on top of the catalog. He took down a piece, and wrote out the call letters, author, and title.

Then he returned to the circulation desk. The woman finished marking a passage with her yellow felt-tipped pen, and smiled up at him.

"I'm sorry to bother you again," Benny said, "but do you know where I can find this book?"

She glanced at the paper. "Oh, that'll be downstairs. Are you familiar with the Library of Congress system?"

"No, I—"

"Well, you just go alphabetically along the shelves. They're all labeled. Then, when the books are all lettered the same, you go by the numbers underneath. It's pretty simple, really."

"Fine. Thank you. Uh . . . it's downstairs?"

Nodding, she swiveled her chair around and pointed. "Right through those double doors."

"Thank you," he said again. Taking the scrap paper, he walked alongside the counter and pulled open one of the doors. It swung shut behind him. The landing was dimly lit. Benny looked up at the fixture, a globe with the debris of dead bugs showing through its frosted glass. Wrinkling his nose, he started down the stairs. They seemed to be concrete, but rang under his footsteps as if there was metal inside.

The echo made him uneasy. He tried to descend more quietly. As he neared the next landing, he imagined taking off his shoes to muffle the noise. That would be dumb. And what if somebody saw him? "Hey, kid, put your shoes on. What're you trying to pull?" Besides, why should he worry about making a little noise?

When he reached the landing, he looked down the final flight of stairs and hesitated.

It was dark down there.

The globe overhead cast its light on the first few steps, faded, and left the lower ones in murky gloom. The fixture below was a dull, gray ball, its bulb either turned off or dead.

He'd seen a movie last summer, where a monster lurked under a staircase. He leaned over the railing and peered down. There did appear to be an open space beneath the stairs.

Don't be a jerk, he told himself. He took a deep breath and charged down into the darkness, more certain with each clamoring footfall that he was not alone in the stairwell. The bottom of the stairs took him by surprise. He thought there was one more step, but there wasn't. His right foot pounded down hard on the floor, sending pain up his leg. He stumbled forward, his shoulder driving open the door, and fell sprawling as the door slammed the wall with a stunning crash.

He picked up his glasses and glanced at the lenses. They hadn't broken. He put them on, and slid the clip-ons back into his shirt pocket. Then he got to his feet. Rubbing his sore knee, he looked down the long aisle ahead of him. He glanced to the sides, down narrow lanes between bookshelves. He saw no one. More important, no one had seen him; he felt like a clumsy idiot.

Klutz.

It was like the night he'd tripped Heather.

Good thing Julie wasn't here to ride him about it.

On the other hand, he almost wished she *was* here. Except for a buzzing sound from the fluorescent lights, the

room was silent. It's supposed to be silent, he reminded himself. This is a library. But somehow it seemed too silent. He
strongly suspected that nobody was down here but him.

With a glance at the lettering on the shelves to his left,
he realized that the witchcraft book was probably somewhere down that aisle. He should find it, grab it, and hurry
upstairs. But the thought of the stairwell sent a shudder
through him.

Sooner or later, he would have to face it. Unless he
waited down here long enough for Tanya to come. The librarian knew where he was. She'd tell Tanya, or maybe
she'd come down herself in a while. Or some students might
show up and . . . For all Benny knew, there might already be
students down here, silently searching the shelves. If he
found one, he could follow him out.

This is really dumb, he thought, as he started walking
slowly up the center aisle. He glanced each way into the narrow spaces between the shelves.

There's nothing in the stairwell. I'm just yellow.

So I'm yellow. If there just happens to be someone else
down here and I just happen to see him leaving, I'll just happen to follow along. No harm in that. Nobody has to know
what I'm doing. Nobody will ever know, if I don't tell.

He was halfway to the end of the aisle without spotting
anyone when he noticed a sound like someone panting. He
froze. The sound seemed to come from his right, somewhere
not far ahead. Between those shelves. If he took just one
big step, he could probably see.

It was a quick, harsh gasping sound that someone might
make after running hard. Then a moan that made his skin
prickle.

He knew he should take that single step forward. Or better yet, stride boldly by and just happen to glance over as he
passed. But he couldn't. Instead, he backed silently away.

After several paces, he ducked into the stacks to the left.
Hidden by the ceiling-high shelves, he made his way quickly
to the far wall. There, he turned left and rushed back the

way he'd come. He passed between the final set of shelves. Crouching at the end, he peered down the center aisle. He saw no one. He glanced behind him at the door to the stairs, only a couple of yards away.

Maybe he should run for it. The stairwell frightened him, but now it seemed no worse than the room itself. He had to get out of here before . . . The book. He needed the book. If he left without it, all this would've been for nothing.

He eased backward. The scrap paper was a crumpled, sodden ball in his hand. He picked it open, spread it out, and compared the series of call letters to those on a book near his shoulder.

He must be close. Standing, he sidestepped away from the aisle and scanned the labeled spines. The search led him deeper into the stacks, farther and farther from the door. As his eyes moved over the books, he listened intently, ready to bolt. He heard nothing but the buzz of the fluorescent lights.

On tiptoes, head tilted far back, he squinted at the top row of books. He couldn't quite make out the lettering. It's probably up there, he thought. If it is, I'll have to climb for it. The shelves were metal, about four feet long, deep enough to hold books on both sides, secured at each corner to upright rods. They looked very sturdy. Benny grabbed a forward edge, and tugged it. There was no wobble at all. He wouldn't try climbing, though, until he was sure he had to.

He stepped to the left, dropped to his knees, and stared at the bottom row of books. The first line of letters was right, but the numbers below . . . Turning his head, he read the titles: *Black Magic*, *A Practical Guide to Sorcery*, *Step into Darkness*, *Tarot Made Easy*, *Witches and Warlocks*, *Witch's Spells and Potions*.

Great!

He didn't see much use for the tarot book, and he had no idea what *Step into Darkness* might be about. A glance at the table of contents . . . No, he could do that once he was safe upstairs. He'd take it, and the other four.

As he reached for them, the books shot forward, knocking into his hands and tumbling against his knees. A bony, blue-veined hand snatched him by the wrist.

The lights went out.

Shrieking, he thrust his other hand forward, ramming books from the higher shelf into the darkness, hearing volumes fall on the other side. He tried again, this time finding the shelf's edge, shoving at it, trying to brace himself as the fierce grip drew his lower hand forward.

She wants to drag me through!

With all the strength in his left arm, he tried to hold himself back. "Let go!" he yelled. "*Help!*" The tugging grew more powerful until he felt as if it might rip his arm from the socket. His other arm gave out. He flew forward, head bashing the edge of the upper shelf, then fell onto his back.

"No!" he cried as he was dragged between the shelves.

In a frenzy of panic, he reached out with his left hand, felt the dry stiff fingers clutching his other wrist, pried one away. There was no yell of pain. Just the sharp brittle *pop*, like the snap of a twig, as the finger broke off. The grip loosened. He jerked his wrist free, whipped his arms down, and grabbed the bookshelf edge above his chest. With a quick yank, he thrust himself out. The metal edge scraped the top of his head as he sat up.

He lunged to his feet, turning in the direction of the door—he hoped. To the left? Yes! It had to be! He reached through the darkness, slapping at the books to keep his bearings. Then the books stopped. He threw himself against the wall, felt along it, found the door. He flung it open and plunged into the stairwell.

Clawing blindly, he smashed his forearm on the banister. He grabbed the railing. Hand over hand, he followed it upward. The entire stairwell was dark. At the first landing, he dared to glance back. Only blackness. He blinked to be sure his eyes were open. He heard nothing but his own rasping breath and thudding heart, but a chill spread over his skin like a spray of ice water. She's there, she's coming!

He charged up the next flight of stairs, trying not to scream, and saw a thin strip of light from under the door. He shouldered the door open.

The librarian flinched, swiveled in her chair, and opened her mouth. She said nothing, though, as Benny sprinted past the desk in his mad race for the exit.

He shoved open the glass door. He ran down the steps to the walkway, and he didn't stop running until he reached the car.

Chapter Thirty

Benny was lying across the backseat, sweltering in the locked car, when Tanya finally arrived. She opened the driver's door, and looked down at him. "Are you all right?" she asked.

Nodding, he sat up.

"I got worried when I didn't see you in here. Thought I'd lost you."

"Sorry," he muttered. He climbed out. After the oven of the car, the air outside felt fresh and cool. He mopped the sweat off his face, and put on his shirt. Tanya, leaning across the front seat, unlocked the passenger door for him. He opened it, and rolled down the window before getting in.

She handed him a small, black book. Benny stared at the cover. *Witch's Spells and Potions.* "You got it?" he asked, amazed.

"Kristi did. What went on anyway?"

"Huh?"

"At the library."

"I had some trouble," he muttered.

"So I heard. When I showed up, Kristi said you'd run off like a bat out of hell. What were you doing down there? She said the lights were off, and you'd thrown books all over the floor. She was a little ticked."

"I didn't do it."

Tanya glanced at him with disappointment, reached forward, and started the car. "Nobody else was down there, according to Kristi."

"Somebody was," he said, trembling now with the memory

of it. He held his right hand toward Tanya. His wrist was ringed with faint bruises, raw furrows where fingernails had raked his skin.

Tanya stared at the injuries. "Who did that to you?"

He shrugged.

"My God, Benny! You should've told someone. Who did it? Did he try to—"

"She."

"We'd better tell campus security."

"They won't find her. She's a witch."

"That's crazy, Benny, and you know it."

"Yeah," he muttered. "I figured you'd say that."

"We can't tell security that a witch—"

"I'm not gonna tell 'em anything. They'll just say I'm crazy, too."

With a sigh, Tanya shifted to reverse and backed out the car. She started driving toward the parking lot exit. The air coming through the open windows felt good to Benny. "I know you're not crazy," Tanya told him. "But you've got witches on the brain, and a very active imagination."

"Did I imagine this?" he asked, holding up his hand.

"Of course not."

"You think I did it to myself?"

"Did you?"

"No."

"Okay, I believe you. Now why don't you tell me what happened down there?"

"All right."

"And then her finger broke off," Benny said. "Right in my hand."

"Broke *off*?" Scott asked. "Are you sure?"

"Yeah."

"Bullshit," Julie muttered.

Scott frowned at her, and glanced at Karen. She was staring into her Bloody Mary, a look of disgust on her bruised face. "Okay," Scott said. "Then what happened?"

"Well, she let go and I got away."

"You never saw her at all?"

"It was pitch-black."

Scott leaned back in his lounge chair. He wiped the wet bottom of his cocktail glass on his trunks, but it dripped anyway as he took a sip. On the sun-heated skin of his chest, the splash of icy water felt like a knife prick. He rubbed it with his fingertips. "Sounds like you had a rough time of it, pal."

The words of sympathy seemed to hit Benny hard. His chin started to shake. He pressed his lips into a tight line.

"You sure all this really happened?" Julie asked. "You weren't just dreaming or something?"

"It wasn't a dream," he mumbled.

Tanya, sitting cross-legged with her back to the pool, said, "The library worker went down to look around after Benny took off. She told me the lights were off and there were books on the floor. She thought Benny did it. According to her, nobody else was down there."

"I wonder how well she looked," Karen said.

"Did she happen to find a finger?" Julie asked.

"A finger doesn't normally just break off," Scott said. "Even if the bone . . . there are muscles, tendons, flesh."

"And blood," Julie added. "There'd be blood all over the place."

Shaking his head, Benny turned his hands over as if looking for stains. He said nothing.

Scott sipped his Bloody Mary. "Well," he said, "whatever happened, it was pretty bizarre. I don't know what to think. But at least you're okay, Benny. That's what really counts."

"What if it happens again?" he asked in a hushed voice.

"I don't imagine . . . well . . ."

"You should be all right," Karen said, "as long as you're with someone. Just don't go anywhere alone for a while, if you can help it. That way, if something funny happens again, you won't have to face it by yourself."

"Maybe he needs a bodyguard," Julie suggested.

Benny stared at her, blinking rapidly. "You won't think it's so funny when it happens to you."

"Spare me."

"It was the curse," he blurted, "and you're part of the curse, too. All of us are, except Tanya. She's gonna try to get us all."

"Who, Tanya?" Julie asked, smirking.

"The witch! She's got our stuff and I *said* we've gotta get it back and nobody listened. I'm just a crazy little kid and there's no such thing as witches and curses. Only there is, and she put a curse on us and it's gonna get us all if we don't *do something!*" He shoved himself off the chair and raced into the house.

Julie blew softly through her pursed lips. "He oughta see a shrink."

"That'll be enough out of you," Scott snapped. "The kid's been through God-knows-what and what he *doesn't* need is lip from you."

Julie flinched, her smirk falling away. "Excuse me," she muttered, and walked toward the house.

Tanya, looking embarrassed, stood up and brushed off the seat of her shorts. "I'll see how Benny's doing."

"Thanks." When she was gone, Scott turned to Karen. "I shouldn't have lost my temper like that."

"Happens to the best of us. God knows, it was mild compared to some of my tirades at school. I've been known to go totally berserk."

Feeling better, Scott turned his chair to face her. She was leaning back, bare legs outstretched and crossed at the ankles, one hand curled around the glass resting on her belly. The front of the oversized, faded blue shirt she wore over her swimsuit had a patch of darkness from the glass's moisture.

"You deal with teenaged kids all the time," he said. "What do you make of my two?"

"I'd say, for starters, that Julie's scared, probably very upset about what happened to Benny."

"Has a funny way of showing it."

"The sarcasm's just a defense mechanism. She seems to use it all the time when she has trouble facing things. I don't think she's callous or insensitive. If anything, maybe she cares too much. The sarcasm's like a safety valve for her."

"All right. I'll give you an A for that one. She's always been that way, hiding behind it. Just gets hard to take sometimes."

"Look on the bright side—at least she doesn't go hysterical."

"I guess that's a blessing, of sorts. Okay. What about Benny?"

"I'd say he's extremely imaginative and sensitive, and handling the situation remarkably well. I'd be a total basket case if I'd gone through what he did. So would most people. They'd freak out totally."

"Do you think it really happened?"

"Yes."

"All of it?"

"Yes."

"How do you explain—"

She shook her head. "I can't explain any of it. That's why I would've freaked out if it'd happened to me. I think Benny's fortunate, in a way, that he can blame the curse. It gives him a frame of reference that lets him deal with it. In terms of curses and magic, anything can happen, nothing is illogical."

"*You* don't believe in that stuff?"

"The important thing is that Benny does. It's part of his reality. So this business in the library makes sense to him. Otherwise, God knows how he might've reacted."

"Look, we don't believe in that nonsense. *I* don't, anyway. How am I supposed to figure out what happened?"

Karen grinned mischievously. "Just keep telling yourself there's got to be a logical explanation. Write it fifty times on the blackboard."

"What do you think?"

"There's got to be a logical explanation."

"Like what?"

"Damned if I know."

Scott laughed. "You're a lot of help."

She drained the last of her Bloody Mary.

"Refill?" Scott asked.

"Sure. Why not? While you're gone, maybe I can dream up a theory."

"Try," he said. "Try very hard. I would appreciate a good, solid, down-to-earth explanation."

"Right. I'll work on it."

He took Karen's glass. Bending over her, he kissed her gently on the lips. Then he went into the house. Instead of turning toward the kitchen, he walked down the hall to Julie's room. Her door was open. She was lying on her bed under a Bruce Springsteen poster, staring at the ceiling, wearing her earphones. When she saw him enter, she pulled off the headset. "Hey," Scott said, "I'm sorry I yelled at you."

She answered with a shrug.

"I guess we're all kind of edgy."

"It's okay," she muttered.

"Why don't you give Nick a call, see if he'd like to come over early and have dinner with us? Say around five? I'll be doing steaks on the barbecue."

"Okay," she said, smiling slightly. "That'd be nice. I'll check with him."

"Fine."

In the kitchen, Scott took an extra steak from the freezer. Then he prepared the Bloody Marys. He carried them outside. After the air-conditioning of the house, the hot sun felt good. Karen was standing, taking off her shirt as he walked up behind her. She wore the same skimpy black swimsuit she'd taken camping. Except for crisscrossing straps, her back was bare to the waist.

"Ready for a dip?" Scott asked.

She grinned over her shoulder at him. "Ready for a sip," she said. She draped her shirt over the back of the chair.

Scott handed a drink to her, and they both sat down. "I dig your outfit," he said.

"Does it flatter my contusions?"

The bruises were yellow-green blotches on the tanned skin of her shoulders and breasts and arms. The teeth marks were darker than the discolored skin surrounding them. Looking at them brought back the horrible night—finding her motionless in the tent, the dread when he didn't know whether she was alive or . . .

"Do you have to stare?"

"Can't help myself," he said, managing a smile. "You're damn near naked."

"You're staring at the bruises."

"Nope, at your full, firm breasts."

She laughed and took a sip of her drink, shutting her eyes as her face tilted toward the sun.

"I talked to Julie. She's inviting Nick over to have dinner with us."

"Oh, that'll be nice."

"Even nicer that they're going out tonight. Now, if I can just get Tanya to take Benny to a movie or something . . ."

"Do you think that'd be a good idea?"

"Sure. We'd have the house to ourselves for a few hours."

"He might be better off staying home."

"Ah, you don't *want* to be alone with me."

"I'm serious, Scott. He went through a hellish experience this morning. If I were him, I wouldn't want to go out tonight. I'd want to stay here safe with my dad."

"Yeah, I guess I shouldn't push it. With you here, he wouldn't want to leave anyway. In fact, when he found out you'd be coming over, he almost didn't go to the library." Scott raised his hand, forefinger and thumb a quarter inch apart. "He was that close to staying home. If I'd just—"

Karen shook her head, stopping him. "There are always those ifs when something goes wrong. We can't blame ourselves. It's just a bunch of little choices that don't mean anything till the shit hits the fan, and then you look back and see how you got there. And you find a whole string of ifs going back forever."

"I suppose. But if Benny'd stayed home this morning—"

"He wouldn't have needed to go looking for a witchcraft book at all if we'd never gone camping. And we wouldn't have gone if you and I hadn't met."

"There's an if I'd hate to change," Scott said.

She smiled at him. "Me, too. But you've got to admit it's one of the links in the chain. If we hadn't met, Benny wouldn't have been attacked this morning."

You wouldn't have been beaten and raped, he thought. From the somber look on Karen's face, he wondered if she were thinking the same thing. If we'd never met . . .

Frowning, she took a drink. Scott watched a drop of water fall from her glass, splash the glossy skin of her chest, and roll down between her breasts. She wiped it away. "Anyhow," she said, "it gets slightly ridiculous when you think about it too much. The ifs are endless."

"I suppose so," Scott admitted. "So, have you come up with any marvelous theories about what happened to Benny?"

"I thought of something. He said the lights went out a second after the hand grabbed him. Unless we want to accept magic as the explanation, there must've been another person involved—someone to turn off the lights while the other attacked him."

"I wonder if it might've been a practical joke," Scott said. "A couple of students figuring it'd be a kick to throw a scare into him. After he ran off, they hid themselves somewhere."

"That still doesn't explain the finger."

"Well, if it didn't actually break off . . . Benny must've been in a panic, disoriented. He could've just bent it back, maybe even broken it, but only *imagined* it came off."

"He sounded pretty sure."

Scott sighed. "I just don't—" He heard a door slide open behind him. Looking over his shoulder, he saw Julie step out. She walked forward, frowning down at the concrete deck. She'd left the door open, but she seemed lost in thought, troubled, so Scott didn't tell her to shut it. She turned a deck chair toward him and Karen, and sat down without speaking.

"What is it?" Scott asked.

"I called Nick," she said in a distracted, barely audible voice. She was hunched over, elbows braced on the armrests of her chair, staring down with half-shut eyes.

"Can't he make it?" Scott asked.

"Maybe. He's not sure. He's . . . gotta stay home with Heather. His dad's at the hospital."

"Flash? My God, what happened to him?"

Julie shook her head. "Not him. They got a call, and he went over. It's Alice and Rose." She looked up at Scott with confusion in her eyes. "They were attacked by a dog. This morning. It was supposed to be dead, I guess. Alice hit it with the car, and she was driving it to a vet's to have it . . . taken care of. Then it attacked them. I guess it bit them."

"Jesus," Karen muttered.

"How bad are they?" Scott asked.

"Nick said they're operating on his mom's hand. It got her worse than Rose. They're in pretty good shape, I guess, except for bites on their hands and arms. Nick said they'd probably be home this afternoon."

"Alice is in surgery?"

"Just for her hand. Some tendons or muscles or something have to be fixed."

"Well . . ." Sighing, Scott gazed at the shiny surface of his drink. "Thank God it's nothing worse."

Julie rubbed her face with both hands, and leaned back in her chair as if exhausted. "Maybe Benny's right," she mumbled.

"It's just coincidence, honey."

"Is it?"

"Of course. Come on, you don't actually believe that a curse—"

"I don't want to believe it," she said in a tired voice. "But Benny, and now this."

"I admit it's a bit weird, both things happening the same day, but it's just a freakish coincidence."

"Two is a coincidence," Karen said, frowning down at her Bloody Mary. "Three is . . . I nearly died last night."

Scott gazed at her, stunned.

"I realize accidents happen all the time, people falling in the bathtub, but I've never done it before. Oh, I've slipped a couple of times, but last night I took a real header. If Meg hadn't pulled me out when she did . . ." Karen smiled crookedly. She stirred her drink with a forefinger, the cubes clinking on the sides of the glass. "I was out cold under the water when she found me. A couple more minutes . . ." She shrugged a bare shoulder. "I wonder if they really put a tag on your big toe. It seems so *ludicrous*, doesn't it? I suppose they do. Who's gonna object, right?"

"My God, Karen."

"Are you all right?" Julie asked.

"Well, I'm here to tell the tale. Yeah, I'm okay." Looking at Scott, she raised her eyebrows. "What do you think?"

He felt dazed. He could think of nothing to say. He shook his head.

"Coincidence or the curse?" she prodded.

"I . . . I just don't know."

"She said she'd get us," Julie muttered.

"On the bright side," Karen said, "at least nobody's been seriously hurt or killed."

"Not yet."

"Look," Scott said, "curse or no curse, sometimes you have bad luck and accidents. These things just happen. We'll only make matters worse if we start thinking that woman's causing it all."

"But what if she *is*?" Julie asked. "What if this is just the beginning?"

"I don't know," Scott said. "What's your answer? If you're so sure it is the curse, what do you suggest we do about it? Hide? Stop taking showers? Stay home the rest of our lives? Maybe you'd better forget about going to the movies with Nick tonight. The curse might get you."

"You don't have to get nasty."

"I mean it. Where does it take us? Do I quit my job? God knows, I'd damn well better not take up an L1011 with three hundred passengers aboard if this gal's put a whammy on me."

"When's your next flight?" Karen asked. She looked serious.

"Come on, I was just—"

"When is it, next week?"

"Tuesday. I'm taking the eight forty to Kennedy."

"This is Thursday. If things keep happening—"

"They won't."

"One way or the other," Karen continued, "we should have a pretty good idea where we stand by then."

"You sound like you're already convinced."

"I'm getting there fast."

"What about you, Julie?"

"I'm going on my date, no matter what."

CHAPTER THIRTY-ONE

Benny finished his grilled-cheese sandwich and Coke in the kitchen with Tanya, then excused himself. He carried his book into the den. Through the sliding glass door he saw the others outside. His father and Karen were just beyond the door, Dad reading while Karen was stretched out on a lounge.

Her hands were folded under her head. Her eyes were shut. Her skin looked slick and shiny from her suntan oil. Benny stared at her breasts, only their middles covered by the taut fabric of her swimsuit, their glossy sloping sides clearly visible. They were beautiful except for the bruises. The bruises gave Benny a sick feeling. He wished they were gone.

The black suit clung like skin, showing the curves of her ribs, her flat belly, even the small depression of her navel. It left her hipbones bare, and slanted in sharply down to her groin. Benny stared at the smooth hollows where her legs joined her body. One of the hollows creased as she raised her knee.

He knew that if he watched much longer, he might lose control. So he turned away. He moved a chair so he could still see Karen, and sat down. The view wasn't very good from here. But he felt guilty about spying on her, especially about getting aroused. By crossing a leg, he eased the tight feeling. He opened the book.

Really lucky that the librarian had remembered the title. He'd thought she was nice, from the start, but it took a very

special person to bring the book upstairs for him in spite of
the way he'd run off leaving such a mess.

His mind returned to the attack. He felt his penis shrink
as if trying to hide. As the fear tightened its grip, he forced
himself to read the title page.

*Witch's Spells and Potions: A Handbook for Witches and War-
locks* by Jean Du Champes. He turned to the table of contents, and ran his eyes down the chapter headings:

Chapter 7, on countermagic, sounded as if it might be
what he wanted. Maybe he should start at the beginning,
though, and work his way up to it. He riffled through the
pages, glimpsing weird diagrams and charts, a strange drawing that looked like a tree woman, lists like recipes, all kinds
of poems and chants. He flipped back to the page with the
tree woman. It was labeled MANDRAGORE. A leafy bush
seemed to grow out of her head. Her body, with outstretched
arms and legs, was formed by the root. Benny gazed at the
crudely drawn breasts and vagina. Then he was staring out
the glass door at Karen, trying to imagine how she would
look without her swimsuit. A couple of times he'd acciden-
tally seen Julie naked. But that was different; she was his sister. To see Karen . . . He forced himself to look away from
her, and turned to the end of the book. The last page was
numbered 264.

He was not a fast reader. At about twenty-five pages an hour, it would take him at least ten hours to wade through the whole volume. He'd better start with the important chapter. Later, if he had time, he would go back and read it all. That part about love spells. Maybe he could . . . No! This is bad stuff. It's wrong to mess with it. Dangerous, too. It's okay to use magic to fight the curse, but to put a spell on Karen . . . The idea excited him, but gave him a heavy, disgusted feeling.

I won't! No matter what!

He flipped back to the table of contents, checked the page number for the countermagic chapter, and quickly turned to it. He found the end of the section. Thirty pages long. With a sigh, he began to read:

Beware! Sooner or later, as you tread through the dark passages of magic, you are bound to arouse the enmity of practitioners unfriendly to your art, who will use their powers to foil you. Taken unaware, you will be totally at the mercy of your adversary, open to potent attacks that might prove injurious, even fatal. To insure your safety, you must take precautious that will throw a curtain of safety around yourself, your loved ones, and your home.

The protective spell required that he walk around the outside of the house during a new moon carrying a chalice of purified water, chanting about an earth goddess named Habondia. On completing the circle, he was to sprinkle some of the water in each room of the house. He should see chapter 3 for instructions on how to purify water. But there would be some moon tonight, so he didn't bother checking on that. He kept on reading.

He could hang a holystone on the hearth. If he had one. Or he could protect himself with a lodestone or a cross-stone. But where was he supposed to find such things?

The more he read, the more frustrated he grew. Every

spell, every amulet or talisman or potion, called for strange
rocks, herbs he'd never heard of, or planetary positions that
made no sense to him. He slammed the book shut.

Then he opened it again. He'd only read ten pages of the
countermagic chapter. He would read the rest of it. There
had to be something in it that would help.

Had to be.

CHAPTER THIRTY-TWO

When Julie woke up, the towel beneath her was sodden. She used a corner to wipe her face, and lifted her head. Down at the end of the pool, Karen was stretched out on a chaise longue, apparently asleep. Her father, sitting nearby, was reading a book.

Julie reached down at her sides, found the dangling cords of her bikini top, and tied them behind her back. Sweat streamed down her hot skin as she sat up. The concrete apron of the pool seared her feet. She slipped into thongs, and walked toward her dad. In a soft voice, so she wouldn't wake Karen, she asked the time.

Dad checked his wristwatch. "A little after three. Nick phoned while you were asleep."

"Oh, no! Jeez, why didn't somebody wake me up?"

"He just left a message with Tanya, said he'll be here at five."

"How's his mom?"

"He didn't say. Things must be going all right, though, or I doubt if he'd be coming."

"Yeah, I guess so." She sighed, disappointed about missing the call. "Anyway, are you gonna be sticking around for a while?"

"Yep. Why?"

"Nothing. Just thought I'd go in for a dip to cool off." With a casual shrug, she added, "Don't let me drown, huh?"

Dad raised his eyebrows. "If you're so concerned, maybe you should stay out of the pool."

The remark hurt. "Jeez, I was just kidding, for God's sake."

As she walked away, he said, "I'll keep an eye on you."

"Thanks," she muttered. At the edge of the pool, she kicked off her thongs and stepped down the stairs into the shallow end. The water felt cool and refreshing as it wrapped around her legs. She waded forward, sucking in her breath when the water touched her groin, wondering how she'd managed to stand the icy lake in the mountains. When the level reached her belly, she eased forward and left her feet. The chill water closed over her. After the first mild shock, it felt good. She swam beneath the surface to the far end, came up for air in the shadow of the diving board, and glanced at her father as she made her turn. The book was closed on his lap. He was watching her.

She backstroked slowly, keeping an eye on the pool side, trying to judge her distance so she wouldn't bump her head when she reached the end. Stopping, she glanced over her shoulder and found the wall two yards away. She sighed, annoyed with herself for being overly cautious, and plunged forward. Her muscles, sore from hiking, ached as they flexed and stretched. It was a good feeling. When she reached the deep end, she thrust herself away from the wall with such force that the water tugged her bikini pants down a couple of inches. She pulled them up and kept on swimming. When she reached the shallow end, she pushed off more gently.

If nobody else were here, she could forget about the suit and speed through the water naked. It was such a fine, wild feeling. Especially at night. Hell, though, if she were alone, she'd probably be afraid to go in the pool at all. That damn curse. Probably just bull, but how do you explain what happened to Benny, to Alice and Rose, even to Karen? Okay, Karen slipped in her tub. That happens to everyone. But what about . . .

She touched the wall at the deep end, and tucked. Her feet found the tile. Gripping her pants with one hand, she shoved. She skimmed through the water, let go, and began to stroke. With her first kick, a muscle spasm locked her right leg. Crying out silently into the water, she clutched her cramped thigh. She rubbed it hard, pounded it. Though the pain was bad and her lungs started to burn, she was rather pleased that she felt no panic. She'd had leg cramps before. She was only a few yards from a side of the pool. The main thing was to ignore the pain, use her arms and her good leg to surface, and get the hell to one of the walls. Forcing herself to release her thigh, she paddled upward and kicked. With a shock of agony, her left leg froze. Both legs were drawn up, paralyzed. Her weight shifted backward as she clawed her way up. Her arms broke the surface, slapped it hard, but without enough force to bring her head out. Through inches of frothy water, she saw the diving board wavering above her. Though she flailed her arms, she kept sinking. The board became a hazy blur. Even her fingertips no longer could reach the surface.

This is insane!

Shit, I'm really . . .

Something stopped her right arm. Another cramp? No, this felt different, like a tight cuff around her wrist. Pulling. In an instant, her head popped through the surface. Gasping for air, she turned and saw her father in the pool, one hand clutching her, the other hanging onto the edge. Beyond him, Karen was kneeling, face twisted with fear.

Dad eased her forward. She hung onto the concrete lip of the pool while he climbed out. Together, he and Karen pulled her from the water. She lay on her side, rubbing her stricken thighs.

"Cramps?" her father asked.

"Yeah."

"Both legs?"

She nodded.

"God," Karen muttered.

"It's crazy," she said.

"You were pushing it pretty hard, honey." Crouching beside her, Dad started to knead her right thigh. Karen worked on the other. Soon, the pain began to ease. The muscles loosened, and Julie straightened out her legs.

"I guess I'm okay now."

"You'd better lie down for a while," Dad said. He and Karen helped her stand up. Holding her by the arms, they walked her toward the lounge chair. Her legs were trembling and weak.

When she was stretched out on the cushion, Dad bent over her. He stroked her forehead, smoothing aside wet strands of hair. "Are you sure you're all right?"

She nodded. "I guess I shouldn't have gone in after all."

"You just pushed it too hard."

"I guess so. Hey, thanks for pulling me out."

He pressed his lips together tightly, and nodded. His eyes were red and wet. He patted her cheek. "Take a little nap now. I'll wake you up in time for Nick."

"Let me know at four, okay?"

"Sure."

Karen gave her shoulder a gentle squeeze, and smiled down at her. Then she and Dad walked toward their recliners, talking quietly.

Julie shut her eyes against the sunlight. She flexed her leg muscles, and felt them tremble. Then she relaxed. She was drained of energy. The heat was a comforting blanket. She tried to think about what had happened to her, but her mind strayed. She was stretched out on a hot granite slab by the lake, Nick's body wet against her, his lips caressing her mouth.

A hand shook her awake. "It's just past four," Dad said.

"Thanks," she murmured. She lay motionless for a little while after he left. She felt groggy, and weighted down by the heat of the sun. Then thoughts of Nick's arrival pushed away her weariness. She sat up, sweat trickling down her body, small puddles spilling from the hollows of her throat and her navel. She looked for her thongs. They were still at the shallow end of the pool where she'd left them. Clutching her towel, she raced over the burning concrete to the house.

Benny, seated in the den, looked up from his book as she slid open the door and entered. He wrinkled his nose to hold his glasses up. "Are you okay?" he asked.

"Sure. Dad tell you about it?"

"Yeah. I was in the john when it happened. Wish I'd seen it."

"Too bad. It was quite a spectacle—your sister nearly drowning. You'd better keep on your toes so you don't miss any more fun."

"I just meant maybe I could've helped."

"Sure." Chilled by the air-conditioning, she wrapped herself in the towel. "Where's Tanya?"

"I think she's in her room studying."

Julie left the den and went to Tanya's bedroom. She found the older girl at the desk, bent over her big volume of Shakespeare. "How do you feel?"

"Not bad."

Tanya shook her head. "Can't believe it. *Both* legs seized up on you?"

"Dad says I was pushing it."

"Benny thinks it's the curse."

"What else is new?"

"He's in there, boning up on remedies."

"Looking for a hex remover?"

"Something like that."

"It's just a lot of bull."

"You still think so?" Tanya asked.

"Hell, I've had leg cramps before. But since there does seem to be an epidemic of accident proneness going around, I was just wondering . . ." She sighed, wondering how to proceed. Tanya waited, eyebrows raised. "Nick's coming over pretty soon, and I've gotta get cleaned up. I need to take a quick shower. Did you hear about Karen falling in her tub last night?"

"You're kidding."

"No, she almost drowned, but her roommate got to her just in time."

"There *is* an epidemic."

"I'll say. Anyway, I was wondering if you'd mind taking a little break from your Shakespeare and kind of keeping an eye on me while I shower."

Tanya frowned up at her. "You really *are* worried."

"Well, I'm still a little shaky on my feet. I guess it's kind of ridiculous. I mean, I'm not spooked or anything. I just thought, to be on the safe side . . ." She stopped fumbling with words as Tanya set her pen down on the open book and pushed her chair back. "I'll be quick, I promise."

"No, that's all right. You can take your time. I'm pretty Shakespeared out."

"I really appreciate it." With a grin, she added, "I'll do the same for you sometime."

"Hey, forget it. There's no curse on *me*." She made a playful scowl. "You don't suppose it's contagious?"

"You'd have to ask Benny about that."

In her own bedroom, Julie tossed her damp pool towel onto her bed. She grabbed her robe, and hurried down the hallway to the bathroom. Tanya was already there, waiting on the toilet seat. "Maybe you've had your run of bad luck for the day."

"I sure hope so," Julie said. She crouched and ran water into the tub. When it felt right, she turned the shower on and slid the glass door shut. She took off her bikini, blushing slightly as Tanya watched.

"Think you got enough sun today?"

"Too much, probably. Hope I don't peel."

"Put some lotion on, afterward."

She nodded. She pulled the door partway open, tested the water with her hand, then carefully stepped into the tub. A foot slipped. She clung to the door.

"Christ, be careful!"

"I'm all right." Then she was standing in the tub with the door shut, the spray hot on her back. Through the frosted glass, Tanya was a vague, blurred shape. "Hope you know CPR," Julie called.

She couldn't quite hear Tanya's reply over the noise of the shower.

"You know, maybe I'd better take a fall, just to make this look good. I'm gonna feel like a jerk if nothing happens."

She turned slowly, enjoying the feel of the water as it splashed her body and streamed down. There was no stinging sensation, so she knew she wasn't badly sunburned. Her tanned skin had a glossy look, a slight reddish hue. Even her breasts looked rosy, but that was from the shower, not the sun. If she could find more time to sunbathe naked . . . In a way, though, she rather liked the contrast, the white places surrounded by bronze skin.

Remembering her promise to be quick, she ducked her head under the nozzle. When her hair was soaked, she shampooed it. She rinsed out the suds, then used a soapy washcloth on her face and ears. "So far so good," she called.

Hearing no answer, she peered through the glass. Her heart suddenly thumped hard. Her stomach knotted. She tugged open the door. Blinking water from her eyes, she stared through the stream at the vacant seat of the toilet.

"What's wrong?" Tanya asked.

Through the thick drifting steam, she saw her cousin near the closed bathroom door. Naked. Standing on her head.

"What the hell are you doing?"

"Relaxing."

"Good Christ."

"It's very pleasant. You should try it sometime."

Julie laughed. "Sure thing," she said; and shut the door. She soaped herself down, rinsed, and turned off the water. As she stepped onto the bathmat, Tanya's legs dropped forward. She landed lightly on the balls of her feet and stood up. Julie reached for her towel. "Gee, I always knew you were level-headed. I guess that comes from standing on it."

Tanya came forward, feeling the top of her head with both hands. Her body was slim, like Julie's, but her breasts were much larger and swayed slightly as she walked. "It's not flat," she said.

"*Level*. Nothing about you is flat."

"Let me by, smart-ass."

Julie shuffled sideways to make room, and Tanya knelt by the tub. She turned the faucets on.

"You're gonna take a shower?"

"A bath, actually."

"Gee, I thought you just stripped to show off your boobs."

"Magnificent, huh?"

"Want to trade?"

Tanya stoppered the drain, then looked over her shoulder. Her eyes settled on Julie's breasts. Julie resisted an urge to hide them behind the towel. "As a matter of fact, I wouldn't mind. I'd throw all my bras away."

"Come on, mine aren't *that* bad."

Tanya laughed. "What do you want? I *told* you I'd trade."

"I wear bras."

"Ah, but that's for decorum, not necessity."

"I don't know about that."

"If I had a set like yours, you wouldn't catch me dead in a bra. Especially in summer. And on dates. I tell you, you wouldn't believe the troubles I've had on dates. The thing's always in the way. Guys get frustrated fooling with the hooks and I have to unfasten it. It takes a Houdini to get out of the shoulder straps without taking off your blouse, which you might not want to do if you're messing around at a drive-in or something, so you end up half the time with the cups in your face. It's a colossal drag."

Smiling, Julie said, "I wouldn't know about that."

"Really? You mean you've never—"

"Never. You're looking at pristine tits." Except for . . . She suddenly saw the man on top of her, felt the tight squeeze of his hand. The memory of it made a cold, hard place in her stomach. She realized, vaguely, that Tanya was laughing at her quip.

"Untouched by human hands, huh? Well, a bra can do that for you, if that's what you want."

"I've just never gone out with a guy I cared enough about."

"That'll change. Let me tell you."

"I guess."

"You can bet on it," Tanya said, and climbed into the tub.

Still upset by the shock of remembering the attack, Julie quickly finished drying herself. She put on her robe. "Thanks for, you know, sticking around."

"Any time. It was a kick. Pristine tits."

Julie left the hot, steamy bathroom. The corridor felt cool. In her bedroom, she shut the door. She opened her robe. Stepping close to the full-length mirror, she stared at her left breast. The pale skin was stippled with goose bumps; the darker flesh was puckered around the jut of her nipple. It looked little different from her right breast. She stroked them both. The touch of her fingers felt the same on each. She remembered the burning hurt. There might even have been a bruise, though she hadn't noticed one before. Her breast looked fine now.

Hardly pristine, though.

Slightly used.

She shut her robe and glanced at the alarm clock by her bed. Four thirty-five. "Gads," she muttered. Sitting cross-legged on the carpet, she blow-dried and brushed her hair. The lock chopped off an inch short across her brow looked bad. "Bitch," she muttered, and got up to find scissors. Her sore legs reminded her of the near miss in the pool. Maybe you've had your run of bad luck for the day. If anything should happen to spoil the date . . . Nick, at least, didn't have the curse on him. The old bitch didn't get his hair or blood. What the hell am I thinking? There is no curse!

Sitting down with the scissors, she did her best to even out the sweep of hair. Try not to poke your eye out, she thought.

By the time she finished with her hair, the clock showed

ten before five. She flung her robe onto the bed, took a pair of fresh, pink panties from her drawer, and stepped into them. She pulled out a bra and started to put it on. *You wouldn't catch me dead . . . Guys get frustrated . . . It's a colossal drag.* Heart pounding fast, she plucked the bra off and hurried to her closet. Her hands trembled as she removed her blouse from the hanger. She put it on, held it shut, and looked down. Through the shiny, bright yellow fabric, her dark nipples were clearly visible. "No way," she said. Not in front of everyone. Even if it were just Nick, she doubted that she would dare.

By five o'clock, she was ready. She gave herself a final check in front of the mirror, approving of the cheery, fresh way she looked in the yellow blouse, the skirt of forest green, and sandals. Her choker of thin gold chain was a nice touch. The bra was the right touch: the lacy pattern of its cups, instead of her nipples, showed through the clinging blouse. "Decorum," she said. She grinned at herself and left her room.

Benny was no longer in the den. Through the sliding glass door she saw him outside, sitting with Karen at the table. They were both staring in the same direction, their faces rigid.

Julie tugged the door open and stepped outside. The heat of the afternoon enveloped her. Her father, a few yards away, squirted fuel into the barbecue.

"My God, be careful," Karen warned him.

"Never fear. I've done this a thousand times."

"Famous last words," Julie said.

Dad noticed her, and smiled. "Say, you look terrific."

"Thanks."

He took a book of matches from the pocket of his blue Aloha shirt. "If you go up in flames," Julie said, "it'll ruin your pretty shirt."

"Always the wise guy."

"Let me light it," Karen said. She started to get up, but Benny reached out and grabbed her hand.

"Don't," he told her.

"This is ridiculous." Dad tore a match loose.

Julie walked quickly to his side.

"Stand back, honey."

"See, you *are* worried."

"You people are driving me crazy. What are we gonna do, stop eating? If I don't get the fire started before long—"

"I've got an idea," Julie said. "Let's wait for Nick."

"Yeah!" Benny blurted. "He's okay. Nothing'll go wrong if he lights it."

"Oh, for Pete's sake."

"Let's wait for him," Karen said.

Dad shook his head. Somehow, he looked both dismayed and amused. "You want us to sit around here like four loonies waiting for the Great Uncursed One to arrive and light the charcoal? Is that the picture?"

"Yep," Julie said.

Benny nodded.

"We don't have to sit around like loonies," Karen explained. "We could sit around like sensible people."

"I'm not so sure," Dad said. But he tossed the unlighted match onto the charcoal, and returned with Julie to the table.

Chapter Thirty-three

"We'd better get going," Julie said. "It's a twenty-minute drive to the theater, and there might be a line." As she started to get up, Nick pushed back his own chair and stood.

He thanked Julie's father for the dinner.

"Any time," Scott said. "I'm glad you could make it. Maybe, if your mother is feeling up to it, you can all come over tomorrow."

"That'd be great."

"You can bring your suits. We'll make a day of it."

"I'll check when I get home."

"That's all right. I'll give your dad a call tonight."

Nick made his good-byes to the others. Scott walked alongside him toward the gate. "You two are sure you wouldn't rather stay here?"

"*Dad.*"

"We've got some spare trunks around, Nick."

"We can swim all we want tomorrow," Julie said. "Tonight we want to go to the movies. You *said* I could."

"I know. And I won't stand in the way. I was simply offering a suggestion."

"I wouldn't mind staying," Nick said.

"We've got a date," she told him, looking hurt. She frowned at Scott. "Besides, I'd like to know what's so safe about this place. If you're worried about the curse—which you keep claiming you don't believe in anyway—it can get me here just as easily as somewhere else. This is where I almost drowned, you know."

"I realize that."

"We'll be very careful," Nick assured him.

"Besides," Julie added, "Nick'll be driving, and he'll be with me the whole time, and he's the Great Uncursed One, as you put it so nicely."

Scott smiled, but he still looked uneasy.

"I won't let her out of my sight, I promise."

Scott gave him a pat on the back. "Okay. What time does the movie let out?"

"It's a double feature," Julie said. "The second show's over at about ten thirty."

"I'll expect you around eleven, then."

"Dad!" Julie looked appalled. "What if we want to go someplace afterward?"

"I think you'd better come straight home."

"For God's sake."

"I mean it, Julie. I don't know what's going on—if it's just been a lot of bad luck or what—but I think we all need to be especially careful until things settle down a bit. So eleven o'clock, or you can stay home. That's final."

"Thanks," she muttered.

"I'll have her back by eleven," Nick said.

"Fine. Well, have a good time, you two."

"Sure thing," Julie muttered, and pulled open the gate.

Nick followed her down the walkway alongside the house. "I'm sorry about all that," she said, looking back at him.

"It's all right. Your dad's just worried. I guess everyone is. Man, I had no idea all this stuff's been going on. It was bad enough, what happened to Mom and Rose, but Karen and then Benny and then *you* . . ."

"It's looking kind of hairy, isn't it."

"Maybe we should stay here."

Julie grinned. "Scared to be out with me?"

"Naw." He stepped up beside her as they cut across the front lawn.

Julie spotted the red Mustang at the curb. Her eyebrows raised. "Not too shabby."

He opened the passenger door for Julie, then went to the other side and climbed in. The heat inside the closed-up car was stifling. He turned the ignition. As the engine kicked over with a throaty grumble, he pressed switches to lower the windows. It didn't help much until he pulled away from the curb. Then a mild breeze came in, pushing the hot air out. He glanced at Julie. She was fastening her safety harness, her head turned down, her golden hair blowing slightly.

"You sure look nice," he said.

The buckle snapped into place. She raised her head and smiled. "Thank you. So do you. We sort of match."

"Yeah." His yellow knit shirt was not as bright as her blouse, his slacks a lighter shade of green than her skirt. His gaze lingered on her knees.

"You'd better watch where you're going," she said.

"Where *am* I going? You'd better give me directions."

"You want to make a left at the next stop sign."

He followed her instructions, but couldn't stop himself from stealing glances as he drove. All through dinner, he'd been astonished by her appearance. Even now, he couldn't get over how different she looked in a skirt. He'd seen her in shorts, he'd seen her in a bikini, but somehow the skirt transformed her, made her seem softer, more mysterious and exciting. The way it draped her thighs. The way it left her knees bare.

"Go right, up here at Ventura," she said.

Nick made the turn.

Except for giving directions, Julie remained silent. Her hands lay open and motionless on her legs. She seemed a little tense. Nick wished he weren't so nervous himself. Ever since their phone conversation last night, he'd been looking forward to this with a mixture of eagerness and dread.

Our first date.

What if something goes wrong? What if something *doesn't* go wrong?

The way she looked in her skirt was no help at all.

At least he didn't have to worry about taking her someplace

after the movies. That was a relief. A disappointment. If only he'd known last night, he might've been saved the fevered tossing and turning in bed as his mind spun images of him and Julie parked on a dark road kissing, embracing, fumbling under clothes for hidden flesh. There would be none of that tonight after all.

Maybe it wouldn't have happened anyway.

At any rate, he should be able to relax and enjoy the evening more, knowing he had no choice but to take her straight home after the movies.

"There it is," Julie said. "If you make a left at the next light, there's a big parking lot behind the theater."

"Okay."

She looked at him strangely. "Are you all right?"

"What do you mean?"

"Is something the matter?"

"No, I'm fine. How about you?"

"I don't feel so hot, as a matter of fact."

He signaled, and made the turn. "What's wrong? Should we go back?"

"That wouldn't help."

"Are you sick?"

She didn't answer. Nick swung into the lot, pulled to a stop in a parking space, and frowned at Julie. "What's wrong?"

"I asked you first."

"I'm fine. Well, maybe a little nervous."

"About the curse?"

He shook his head. He had a tight feeling in his throat. "No. Just about . . . going out with you. I mean, this is our first time really being together, you know? It feels a little strange."

"Is that all that's bothering you?"

"I think so."

"Well." She unfastened her buckle and pushed the harness aside. "I'm a little nervous, too. But you know what'll make it all better?" Reaching out, she curled a hand behind his neck and drew him closer. They kissed. Her lips were parted and moist, brushing against his mouth, then pressing firmly. Her other hand rubbed his chest, moved lower, caressed his belly, dropped to his left thigh. She kneaded his leg, squeezed and stroked it as if unaware of the way her wrist sometimes pushed against his groin. Then the hand went away. The lips went away. She stared into his eyes. "Feel better?" she asked.

"Are you kidding?"

"Not so nervous anymore?"

"I feel great."

"Me, too. Let's see the movie."

Outside the car, he took Julie's hand. They walked together through the early evening sunlight. The kiss had worked, just as she'd said it would. It had ended the strangeness, made their closeness real again. Nick felt relaxed and fine. Reluctantly, he let go of her hand to buy the tickets. Though the films were R-rated, the girl in the booth didn't question their ages.

"Would you like popcorn?" Nick asked as they entered the air-conditioned lobby.

"Not right now. I'm stuffed."

"Me, too. Maybe at intermission."

Julie smiled strangely, as if she knew something he didn't. "Maybe," she said.

The theater wasn't crowded. They chose seats near the center with no one to block their view. When the lights darkened, Julie leaned closer to Nick. She smiled, and nudged his elbow off the armrest. "Pushy," he whispered.

"That's me."

He stared at the screen. An ad for the *Los Angeles Times* was showing. His arm, pressed by Julie's shoulder, hung down across his leg. It felt awkward and useless. His nervousness came back. He should put the arm around Julie.

Come on, what're you waiting for?

He felt quivery and dry-mouthed.

The title of the feature film, *Getting It*, appeared over a scene of teenaged girls playing basketball in a school gymnasium. As the credits finished, the teacher blasted her whistle and the girls ran for the locker room.

Come on, arm! Now!

He couldn't force himself to lift it.

On the screen, the girls were trotting into the locker room, their shouts and giggles echoing.

"You oughta go for this," Julie whispered.

Her voice took away the worry. He put his arm across her shoulders. Amazing how easy it was. He let out a trembling breath as she snuggled against him. Why had he even hesitated? Well, it didn't matter now. He caressed her shoulder, making the fabric slide over the smoothness of her skin, the narrow band of her bra strap.

Some of the girls were showering now. The camera gave glimpses of their nudity. Then three boys rushed into the shower room, whooping and hollering, wearing only jockstraps. While most of the girls screamed, a slim attractive blonde laughed and attacked. She tackled a chubby guy. His friends fled. Other girls joined in. By the time he made his escape, the main girl was waving his jockstrap like a flag.

The scene changed. She paraded into a classroom wearing the jock on her head. Julie gasped, "Oh, no!" and the audience roared. The matronly teacher looked aghast. The girl walked up to the chubby boy's desk, plucked the jock from her head, and pulled it down over his face.

The boy's name was Ralph. The girl was Cindy. She was captain of the cheerleading squad, the most popular girl in school, and she wanted nothing to do with Ralph. Ralph wanted "in her pants."

As the movie went on, following his antics, Nick continued to caress Julie's shoulder and upper arm. Her blouse was getting damp from his hand. His arm was getting numb. Finally, he lowered it. He rested his hand on his leg. Julie reached down, took hold of it, and squeezed it.

Ralph, in the dark outside Cindy's house, serenaded her, playing "Lady of Spain" on a sousaphone. She went to her bedroom window and mooned him.

With his free hand, Nick stroked Julie's forearm, barely

touching it, feeling the soft light brush of its hair, the sleek skin.

Though he and Julie laughed at some of the film's raunchy antics, he began to get annoyed. The movie showed sex as a crude joke, not as something beautiful and strange, the way it should be, the way he wanted it to be with Julie. The kids were "copping feels," trying to "get it on," to "lay pipe," to "fuck their brains out." There was no tenderness, no caring, no *making love*. Nick began to wish they'd chosen a different movie. At least this one seemed to be nearing an end. The next feature, a spy thriller, should be a real improvement.

Julie lifted their hands over the armrest. She lowered them onto her leg. Nick felt the heat of it through the thin fabric of her skirt.

Though Cindy was doing a striptease for Ralph, the sight of her naked breasts and writhing body seemed not nearly so exciting to Nick as the feel of Julie's leg under his hand. If he inched their locked hands down a bit, he might get past the hem to her bare knee. While he tried to work up the nerve, Julie slid their hands to the very place he wanted. She loosened her grip. As his fingers closed gently over her leg, she stroked the back of his hand. His mouth was parched, his heart racing.

Cindy, done with the striptease, flopped naked onto the bed. Ralph had finally earned a "toss" with her by dumping a truckload of manure on her unfaithful boyfriend and his new girlfriend while the two were "scoring" in the backseat of his new convertible. Face flushed, eyes bulging, Ralph tossed off his clothes. "Come and get it!" Cindy called. With a whoop of delight, Ralph dived at her sprawled body. A freeze-frame caught him in midair. The words "The End" flashed across his rump.

Nick gave Julie's leg a gentle squeeze as the final credits rolled. Then he took his hand away. When the lights came on, she smiled at him. "Well," she said, "what did you think?"

"The movie? It was all right."

"A real gross-out, huh?"

"That's for sure."

"Well, I'm glad poor Ralph finally got his wish. He sure worked hard enough for it."

The words excited Nick. He wiped his sweaty hands on his pants. "Are you ready for some popcorn or something?"

Julie got that mysterious look on her face. "That depends."

"On what?"

"How badly do you want to see the next movie?"

The question stunned Nick. He stared at her. "What do you mean?"

"Dad says I have to be home by eleven. It's only eight thirty. If we leave now . . ." She raised her eyebrows. "What do you think?"

"Are you serious?"

"If you'd rather stay for the movie . . ."

"No. I don't care about that. I . . . uh . . . I don't think we'd win any points with your dad."

"He doesn't have to know."

"Jeez, Julie."

"Are you game?"

He let out an uneasy laugh. "Yeah, sure, I guess so."

"Great. Let's get out of here." She slung her purse strap over her shoulder, and stood up.

They sidestepped toward the aisle. Nick felt tight and jittery. We shouldn't do this, he thought. But he wanted to. He was scared, but he wanted to.

Where'll we go? Park someplace. Oh, my God.

In the lobby, she squeezed his hand. "Right back," she said, and pushed through a restroom door.

He remembered his promise not to let her out of his sight. Well, he couldn't follow her into the ladies' room. Ralph might, but not him.

He hurried to the men's room. One of the urinals was vacant. He stepped up to it. The underside of his penis felt wet and slick. Either the movie or Julie had excited him a lot. He didn't think it was the movie.

In the lobby again, he looked for Julie. He didn't see her. Apparently, she was still in the restroom. He waited. Slowly, the line at the refreshment stand dwindled. An usher in a red blazer shut the doors to the auditorium, signaling the start of the second feature.

Nick paced. He stared at the restroom door.

It finally opened, but the girl who came out wasn't Julie.

What was taking her so long?

Had something gone wrong?

The girl behind the refreshment counter was pumping butter flavoring onto a tub of popcorn for the last customer. Maybe, when she finished, Nick would ask her to check on Julie. That could turn out embarrassing.

He'd give Julie a couple more minutes.

He gazed at the second hand of the wall clock behind the counter. It moved quickly, sweeping past the numbers. He watched it make three circuits of the face. Still, he hesitated to interfere.

The restroom door stayed shut.

Come on, Julie! What's wrong?

CHAPTER THIRTY-FOUR

"Can I turn it up?" Rose asked.

"*May* I durn'd up," Alice corrected, her speech thick from too much wine.

"Go ahead," Flash said. He could hardly hear himself think, much less hear the television. The helicopter was making another pass low over the house. It had been circling the neighborhood for the past ten minutes, the whapping noise of its rotors deafening at times, then receding, then growing to a roar as it came back.

He watched Rose crawl to the television, reach up with her bandaged arm, and turn up the volume. She crawled backward to the place where she'd been sitting on the carpet. She crossed her legs.

Alice stared at the ceiling. She looked as if she might cry. "Why dudn' he go 'way," she said.

"Must be looking for a prowler. This time, at least, it's not three o'clock in the morning." That's when the police helicopter usually put in its appearance—seemed like once a month—waking them up, circling for half an hour, sometimes as long as an hour, hovering low over the houses, its searchlight sweeping the lawns and streets. It was a nuisance. A little frightening, too. It reminded him of 'Nam, and it wasn't used for routine patrols. Its presence meant that a suspect was out there. Somewhere close. You always wondered who he was, what he'd done, where he might be lurking.

Alice, beside him on the couch, leaned forward and

reached out with her left hand. Her fingertips bumped the wineglass, knocked it over. Chablis sloshed out onto the table.

Heather, in a rocking chair across the room, looked up from her book and frowned.

Alice saw her. "*You* try'n use yer lef' han'," she blurted. Her face was puckered and red.

Flash rubbed the back of Alice's neck. The tense muscles felt like iron. "It's okay, honey. We all have little accidents. I'll clean it up."

She nodded. Her lips were pressed together. She stared down at her right arm, wrapped in a cast from fingertips to shoulder, held against her chest by a sling. Her mouth started to tremble.

"I'll get you some more wine, too," Flash said as he pushed himself off the couch.

Heather put down her book. She followed him to the kitchen and leaned against the stove, watching him take a fresh bottle of wine and a can of Budweiser from the refrigerator. Her pale eyebrows were drawn together.

"Don't let your face freeze that way," Flash said.

"She's bombed," Heather said.

"Don't say that."

"Well, she is."

"So what," he snapped.

Heather flinched and blinked. She looked as if she might start bawling.

"I'm sorry," Flash said. "It's all this damn *noise*."

"You shouldn't let her drink so much."

"If she wants to get plastered out of her skull tonight, that's fine by me. Normally, I'd . . ." He realized he didn't need to talk so loudly; the roar of the chopper had faded a bit. "Normally, I'd be right with you, honey. It's not good to drink too much. But your mother went through a terrifying experience this morning. She and Rose both."

"Rose isn't getting bombed."

"She can if she wants."

Heather looked as if she thought her father had gone crazy.

"Why don't you wipe off the coffee table for me?"

With a shrug of her delicate shoulders, she limped over to the counter. She tore a yard of paper towels off the roll.

"How's the ankle?"

"It hurts some." She grinned. "Can I get bombed?"

"Do you want to?"

"No," she said. She arched an eyebrow. "I'll keep my wits about me, thank you." Then she hobbled out of the kitchen, the towels fluttering behind her like a streamer.

Flash uncorked the wine bottle. He popped the tab of his beer can. As he carried them into the living room, the telephone rang, adding its clamor to the noise of the approaching helicopter.

"The phone," Alice said.

"I'll get it," he told her. It rang two mores times as he filled her glass.

"Might be Nick," she said, a look of fear in her eyes.

Taking the beer with him, he rushed back into the kitchen and snatched up the receiver. "Hello?"

"Hi, Flash, it's Scott."

"Anything wrong?"

"The kids are . . ." The roar of the helicopter drowned him out.

"What was that? We've got one of those fucking cop choppers raising Cain."

"I was just saying the kids are off to the movies. How're Alice and Rose doing?"

"Aaah. Who knows? Okay, I guess. Nick fill you in?"

"Yeah. He said the operation went fine."

"She'll be in a cast for a while. They don't think there'll be any permanent damage, but they aren't making any promises. You know doctors."

"I sure hope it turns out all right. Look, one reason I called, I was wondering if you'd like to bring the bunch over tomorrow. Nick thought it sounded like a pretty good idea."

"I bet he did," Flash said. Chuckling, he took a swig of beer. "Those two sure hit it off, huh?"

"I'd say so."

"Well, sounds real good to me. I'll have to check with the general, but if I don't call back, you can expect us. Around what time?"

"If you want to make a day of it, drop in around ten or eleven. Bring your suits."

"Want us to bring anything else?"

"Just your thirsts and appetites."

"Real fine, Scott."

"Have you heard anything from the cops?"

"Their fucking chopper." He realized that the noise was fading a bit.

"About the situation."

"Yeah. I know what you mean." He swallowed some more beer. "I got a call a couple hours ago. Some deputies and a ranger went in on horses. Couldn't find the body or the woman. They brought out our tents, though. Said we can pick 'em up at the Black Butte ranger station if we're so inclined."

"I'm not."

"Me neither. Not just yet. But anyway, everything's just up in the air, since they didn't get the body. Won't be an inquest or anything."

"Nick seems to be holding up pretty well."

"I guess we can thank your daughter for that. How's Karen getting along?"

"She's here now. She's doing pretty well. But that's another thing I wanted to talk to you about. She had an accident last night." Flash listened, his concern for Karen turning to uneasy confusion when Scott told of the attack on Benny at the library, and Julie's leg cramps in the pool.

"Add in that dog attack on Alice and Rose," he continued, "and we've got four incidents in the past twenty-four hours."

"What do you make of it?" Flash asked.

"I honestly don't know what to think. If it was just Karen falling in the tub and Julie's problem in the pool, I wouldn't be too concerned. I'd say it was just bad luck. But the dog attack . . ."

"Alice insists the thing was dead when it went for 'em."

"Yeah, Nick mentioned that. And I haven't been able to figure out any logical explanation for what happened to Benny. Both those situations have me pretty worried. You can't just put them down as bad luck. They were actual assaults."

Flash frowned at the wall. He took a sip of beer.

"Every one of those incidents could've turned out fatal. I'd say we've been damn lucky so far."

"You thinking it's that old bag's hex?"

"That seems to be the consensus around here. I hate to go along with it, but I'm starting to wonder."

"What're we gonna do?"

"One thing about it—we're certainly not powerless. In each case, some quick action has saved the day. All I can suggest, for now, is that we keep on our toes and watch out."

"I guess your kid was right, huh? Benny. We should've grabbed that bitch when we had the chance."

"I don't know. Maybe. I'm not convinced she has anything to do with all this. If she is behind it, though—I mean, if it's really a curse—apparently you and Nick might be in the clear."

"'Cause she didn't cut us?"

"Right."

The chopper was returning. Flash set his beer can on the floor.

"She seemed to think she needed blood and hair from her victims to make it work. As far as we know, she didn't get to you or Nick."

"As far as we know?" Flash asked. He pushed a forefinger into his left ear to muffle the outside noise.

"Well, I've been talking to Benny about this. He thinks you two are probably all right, unless she got something we don't know about. Apparently, it doesn't have to be blood or hair. A piece of your clothing will do. Fingernail parings. Benny was a little embarrassed to mention it, but if she dug around after we left and came up with some feces . . ."

Flash grimaced. "A guy can't even take a crap."

"Did you?"

"As a matter of fact, no. I didn't cut my toenails, either. Does that mean I'm safe?"

"Could be. Assuming we are dealing with a curse. We can't be completely certain in any case. Who the hell knows? None of us are exactly experts on . . ."

In spite of the finger plugging his ear, he couldn't hear Scott's words. The din of the helicopter was too great. "I can't hear you," Flash said. "It's no use. Thanks for calling. And the invitation. See you tomorrow, huh? So long." He hung up.

The air around him, the house itself, seemed to be shaking. What's that asshole up to? Trying to land on the goddamn roof? He took a step away from the wall, and kicked over his beer can. "Shit!"

"YOU BEHIND THE TREE," a voice boomed. "THROW YOUR WEAPON TO THE GROUND AND STEP INTO THE LIGHT WITH YOUR HANDS ABOVE YOUR HEAD."

Flash charged into the living room. Alice was pushing herself off the couch, her good arm stretched toward Rose, who was rushing for the front door. "Stop!" he shouted at the girl.

"I REPEAT, THROW YOUR WEAPON TO THE GROUND AND . . ."

Flash caught Rose by the shoulder as she reached for the doorknob. He yanked her back. "When I tell you to stop—"

The boom of a gunshot broke through the noise.

Flash threw open the door.

"No!" Alice cried.

He lunged outside and stopped on the lawn. As he'd thought, the copter was hovering low over the house. The white beam of its searchlight was fixed on the trunk of an elm near the street. Behind the elm crouched a man with a revolver. The gun was aimed high. It jumped, blasting another shot at the chopper.

A patrol car, siren blaring, lights spinning red and blue, hurled around the corner at the end of the block.

The man fired again. Flash heard the slug smack into metal.

"You bastard!" he cried out as he raced at the man. The rotor blades threw a hot wind down on him.

In 'Nam, he'd felt the same hot wind as an army gunship descended to pick him up. It meant safety. Survival. In seconds, if a VC bullet didn't chop him down, he'd be airborne after six days of hiding, dodging enemy patrols. No bullets found him, that morning, but a rocket found the gunship as it hovered closer, and it tumbled in flames, shaking the jungle floor as it hit.

If that fucker falls on the house . . .

But the gun wasn't aimed at the chopper anymore. It was lowering toward Flash as he ran at the man, as the patrol car skidded to a stop, as the chopper soared over him, no longer threatening the house. It's all right now, he thought. And heard a gunshot.

CHAPTER THIRTY-FIVE

Nick, pacing the theater lobby, looked jumpy. He seemed to sag, as if worn out, when Julie approached him. His eyes stayed on her face, and she didn't think he'd noticed, yet, what she'd done.

"What's wrong?" she asked.

"I was just . . . You were in there so long."

"Sorry about that." She took his hand. "Did I worry you?"

"I was starting to wonder if . . ." He shrugged.

"Nothing happened," she said. They crossed the lobby and left the theater. "I'm sorry if you were worried. There was only one stall with a door on it. Seemed like everybody was waiting for that one. Me included."

"Oh. Well. I'm just glad nothing went wrong."

In spite of the night's warmth, Julie was trembling as they strolled along the sidewalk. She felt excited and daring.

"Where do you want to go?" Nick asked when they reached the car. He sounded very nervous. "Do you want a sundae or something?"

"Why don't we just drive around for a while?"

"Sure. Okay."

He started the car and drove out of the parking lot. Julie wished she could scoot over and snuggle against him, but the bucket seats would make it awkward. Deciding to wait, she fastened her safety belt. The pressure of the harness across her breast sent a pleasant tingle through her.

"Anyplace, special?" Nick asked.

"No. I'll know it when I see it. Why don't you make a left up here?"

He turned, leaving behind the traffic of Ventura Boulevard. Except for occasional streetlamps, the road was dark. Lights shone in the windows of houses, but Julie saw nobody wandering about. Dark, empty cars sat in driveways and lined the curbs. At a Y in the road, Julie suggested they go left. The road narrowed as it climbed into the hills. There were fewer streetlights, fewer houses. As headlights appeared on the curve ahead, Nick swung in behind a parked Toyota to make room. A Mercedes eased by, and he pulled out again. He drove forward, slowing at each bend.

Julie spotted a steep lane to the left. "Why don't we try that one?"

"It's not a through street," Nick told her.

She nodded as she read the sign. "That's okay."

"Hope you don't get us lost."

"All we've gotta do is point the car downhill."

"You're the navigator." He turned, and started up the grade. There were no streetlights. They passed a few driveways on the right, apparently leading to houses nestled unseen on the wooded slopes above the road. To the left, beyond the guardrails, the hillside dropped away. The lights of scattered houses were visible across the ravine.

"This is nice," Julie said. "Why don't you park along here someplace so we can enjoy the view?"

"Okay," he said in a whisper she could barely hear. A few moments later, he eased the car to the right. The right-side tires crunched over the ground. The branches of a bush on the slope scratched against Julie's window. Nick killed the headlights. He turned off the engine, and a heavy silence filled the car. He stared out the window. "Not much of a view from here," he whispered.

"This is fine," Julie said. Her mouth was dry.

Nick took off his safety harness. He glanced at the side mirror, the rearview mirror.

"Anyone coming?"

He shook his head. "I wonder if we're off the road far enough."

"I think it's all right." She opened her seat belt and pushed it out of the way. "Besides, there's not a whole lot of traffic."

"Pretty isolated up here, isn't it?"

"Yeah. Dark, too." With a smile, she asked, "You scared?"

"Nah. Are you? We can go someplace else if you want."

"This is just fine," Julie said.

Nick turned in his seat. Though light from the half-moon spilled in through the windshield, shadows hid his face. His eyes were patches of darkness, but Julie felt his gaze like a warm caress. She saw him lick his lips. He wiped his hands on his slacks. Then he reached out with one hand and gently stroked her cheek. Turning her head, she kissed his palm. The hand lingered for a moment, then curled around the back of her neck and urged her closer.

She wrapped her arms around Nick. She kissed him. He caressed her face, her hair, her shoulders.

He was too far away from her. They were both turned sideways on the bucket seats, twisted awkwardly and leaning in across the gap. She was uncomfortable and frustrated. Finally, she whispered, "I wasn't made to bend this way."

"Oh," Nick let go of her. "I'm sorry. Did I hurt you?"

"Don't be silly." She brushed her lower lip against his mouth. "Let's get in the backseat."

"You want to?" Straightening up, he looked up and down the road, as if to make sure the coast was clear. Then he shoved open the door. He muttered, "Damn it," as the interior light came on. Julie shielded her eyes against its sudden brightness. Then she crawled over the driver's seat and climbed out after Nick. He thrust forward the seat back. Julie ducked into the car. Nick scooted in beside her and pulled the door shut. As he locked it, Julie snuggled against him, rubbed his chest, kissed the side of his neck.

He cringed. "Hey, that tickles."

"Does it?" She nibbled his neck, making him squirm. "I

vahnt your blood," she intoned in her best Bela Lugosi accent. Then she pulled him down across the seat. Kneeling above him, she probed his ribs, his belly. He giggled and writhed, tried to protect himself, and finally dug wiggling fingers into Julie's armpits. With a squeal, she forced his hands away. She pinned them to the cushion. Then she kissed him. She let go of his hands. They went around her back, caressing.

She was half off the seat, toes on the floor, knees pressed against the cushion's edge. "I'm coming up," she whispered. She swung a leg over Nick, pushed with the other, squirmed, and finally found herself on top of him. Her legs were wide apart to make space for his upraised knees. "Am I mashing you?" she asked.

"No."

For a long time, they kissed. Julie relaxed a little, savoring the closeness, the intimate joining of their mouths, the feel of him under her body, the touch of his hands. His hands roamed over her shoulders and back, rubbing her through the thin fabric of her blouse. He always stopped at the waistband of her skirt. Though her blouse had come untucked, he never felt beneath it.

Straddling him this way, Julie could barely move. She wanted to hold him, stroke him, not merely lie on him and kiss. "Maybe if we sit up," she finally said. She climbed off Nick.

He sat up straight. Facing him, Julie knelt over his lap and lowered herself. Nick leaned forward slightly. They embraced each other tightly. "This is much better," Julie whispered.

"Yeah."

She rubbed his back. He rubbed hers. Heart beating faster, she eased her hands under his shirt. She slid them up his smooth skin. He hesitated for a while, then followed her lead. His hands went under the back of her blouse, and glided up her bare skin. They curved over her shoulders, moved down her sides in a way that made her shiver, then swept in again toward her spine.

Julie leaned away. Nick's hands dropped to her thighs. They rested there, motionless, while Julie raised his knit shirt. She rubbed his bare chest, thumbs pressing his nipples. He was squirming slightly under her, as if uncomfortable.

"Are you all right?" she asked.

He nodded.

"Do you know what I did in the john?"

"I have a pretty good idea."

"What?"

"I think . . . you took something off."

"Is that what you think?"

"Yeah." Nick lifted one hand from her thigh. It was half shut in a loose fist. It moved slowly higher. Julie's heart felt like a sledgehammer as the curled fingers pressed against her blouse just below her left breast. He brushed the underside of her breast, followed the curve upward. She caught her breath as he found her rigid nipple. The hand opened, and held her. Then his other hand closed around her right breast. "God, Julie," he whispered.

She clung to his shoulders and arched her back. She quivered as he explored her through the blouse, sliding the fabric over her skin, cupping her, squeezing gently, fingertips tracing her nipples. Finally, he opened the buttons. He spread the front of her blouse. He stared.

"Take a picture," Julie said. "It lasts longer."

Laughing softly, Nick pulled her forward. Her naked breasts pushed against his chest. He covered her face with kisses. His hands went under the back of her blouse, moved up and down as if hungry for the feel of her bare skin.

He went over sideways, holding her, guiding her down. Then she was on her back. One leg hung off the seat and the other was stretched out between Nick's legs. His thigh was a heavy pressure on her groin. She writhed against it, gasping. His chest was on one breast. His hand fondled the other, squeezed it, stroked its swollen nipple. Moaning, squirming with need, Julie thrust Nick's face away from her. She forced his head lower. He kissed her nipple. He licked it. He took it into his mouth. He sucked on it, and Julie whimpered. He tried to raise his head, as if worried, but she forced it down and held it there. He sucked hard. It hurt and it sent shocks of pleasure through her body.

Then it wasn't his thigh against her groin. It was his hand. Outside her skirt, but rubbing. "No," she gasped. "Nick, no." It didn't go away. She thrust herself against it. "No. Stop." She reached down for it, and clutched his wrist, intending to push his hand away. Instead, she pressed it to her.

His penis was rigid against her thigh. She shoved at his hip. He raised himself slightly and Julie touched him. He felt hard and hot through his pants. And very big. She wondered how it would feel inside her. The thought of that, the way it felt in her hand, the way Nick was massaging and sucking—all of it was too much. Crying out, she bucked and twisted. She clutched Nick. His penis throbbed against her hand and the agony of Julie's desire broke in a flood of release.

Then they lay beside each other, panting, kissing gently. "I love you so much," Nick whispered.

"I love you more."

"No you don't."

"Yes I do," she said. "And I want to stay here forever. I don't ever want to move."

"We'll have to move, sooner or later."

"What time is it?"

He checked his wristwatch. "About ten till ten."

"Already?" She sighed. She hugged him tightly. They kissed. They caressed each other. "I feel so peaceful and nice," she said.

"Me, too." Nick yawned.

"Am I boring you?"

He laughed, his breath warm on her face.

Julie yawned, too. She snuggled against him. "What if we fall asleep and don't wake up till midnight?"

"Or morning?"

"What time is it?"

"Ten twenty."

"Oh, no."

"Oh, yes."

"I don't want to leave."

"We'd better. We don't want your dad to get worried."

"Yeah, I know."

They sat up. As Nick straightened his shirt, Julie looked out the windows. Except for patches of moonlight, the street was dark. She saw no one.

Nick turned away from her. The bright ceiling light came on when he opened the door. While he climbed out, Julie took off her blouse. She tossed it onto the front seat.

Nick leaned into the car and stared.

"Something wrong?"

"My God, Julie."

She scooted across the seat, and climbed out. A warm breeze drifted against her.

"You nuts?" Nick asked.

"Yep." She raised her arms, and Nick stepped into them. His hands ran up and down her back as he kissed her. Then she eased him away. "We'd better go," she said.

"You're so beautiful."

"But nuts?"

"Yeah."

With a grin, she turned away. She crawled across the driver's seat, and sat down. Nick climbed in. He left the door slightly ajar to keep the light on while Julie lifted her purse from the floor. She took her bra out.

"Wait," Nick said. Leaning toward her, he slid a hand over her breast. His fingers curled around it, holding it firmly. Then he let go.

He continued to gaze at Julie while she put on her bra, fastened it, and slipped into her blouse. As she buttoned it, he tugged his door shut. He started the car. He turned on the headlights. He shifted to first gear, and released the emergency brake. The car started to roll forward. Its sluggish motion felt strange to Julie. Nick struggled with the steering wheel. Then he turned off the engine.

"What's wrong?" Julie asked.

"I don't know." He got out. He crouched by the front tire, stood up, and stepped around to the other side. He crouched again. Then he stood, and stared through the windshield at Julie.

"Oh, no," she muttered. A chill, sick feeling spread through her. She scurried across the seat and climbed out of the car.

The front tire was flat.

"This one over here, too," Nick said. He sounded grim.

"How could it happen?"

He walked slowly toward her, holding out his hand. "Look."

She peered at the small, dark object resting on his palm. "What is it?"

"Part of a valve stem."

"I don't get it," she muttered.

"Both front tires. Somebody cut off the valve stems."

"Oh, Jesus! While we were . . ."

Nick answered with a nod.

Chapter Thirty-six

Julie's legs went weak. She leaned against the side of the car. She felt crawly with gooseflesh. As she rubbed her arms, her eyes searched the darkness. The narrow, moonlit road looked deserted. There were no streetlights, no parked cars. Bushes along the guardrail looked like silent, watching men.

Nick patted her arm. "Don't worry."

"Who's worried?"

Leaning into the car, he shut off the headlights. He came out with the keys, and swung the door shut. Julie followed him to the trunk. "Can you change the tires?" she asked.

"I've only got one spare." He removed the tire iron.

"Then what's that for?"

"Just in case." He shut the trunk.

"Oh, man," Julie muttered.

"Let's go."

"Where?"

"To a telephone. We've gotta call the auto club." He took her hand, and they started down the road. They looked over their shoulders as they walked.

"There won't be a public phone," Julie said, "till we get to Ventura Boulevard."

"Probably not."

"I'm really sorry I got you into this, Nick."

"It's not your fault."

"Oh, yeah? It wouldn't have happened if we'd stayed at the movies. Me and my great ideas."

He squeezed her hand. "It was a great idea. It was . . . No matter what happens, I'll never regret it."

"No matter what happens. Oh, wonderful. What are you expecting?"

"I don't know. This is all part of it, though, isn't it?"

"The curse, you mean?"

"I guess that's what I mean."

"Oh, man."

Striding around a bend, they came upon a steep, narrow drive. To one side of it, half hidden behind bushes, stood a mailbox. The number on the box was 21; the name, FISH. The lane slanted up the slope, curving, disappearing in the darkness. "It must be a driveway," Julie said. "Should we give it a try?"

"Call from someone's house?"

"If we don't, we've got an awfully long walk ahead of us. What time is it?"

"Ten thirty-five."

"We couldn't possibly get to Ventura by eleven. Dad'll start going crazy."

"Guess we'd better do it then."

With a final look at the bleak, deserted road behind them, they started up the driveway. Trees blocked out the moonlight. The night was full of familiar sounds: an airliner, the honk of a car, a man's shout, a door slamming. But they all came from far away, as if they belonged to a different world. Only the chirping of crickets came from nearby. And their own noises: the scuff of their shoes on the concrete, their heavy breathing.

"This is one long driveway," Nick whispered.

"It's almost like we're back in the mountains."

"No packs, at least."

Julie looked back. Nobody there. The road they'd left was out of sight, hidden beyond a bend in the driveway.

Nick dropped behind her. He pressed his hand to her back, and pushed as she walked. "Oh, that's better."

"Glad to be of service."

They trudged around a curve in the driveway, and Nick's hand fell away. He stepped up beside her. They stood motionless, breathing hard, staring at the house.

With its rough stone walls and steep tile roof, it looked vaguely foreign to Julie.

"Hansel and Gretel time," Nick whispered.

She gave his arm a soft jab.

Except for a single post lamp along the walkway to the door, there were no lights. A monstrous, ancient Cadillac was parked near the garage.

"What do you think?" Nick asked.

"We came this far."

"It doesn't look very . . . inviting."

"Let's give it a shot, Hansel."

They walked to the door. There didn't seem to be a bell, just a brass knocker shaped like a fist. Nick lifted it, and rapped three times. Quickly, he propped the tire iron against the doorframe. Julie wiped her sweaty hands on her skirt. "Sure hope they have a phone," she whispered.

They waited. No sounds came from inside the house.

"Should we try again?" Julie asked.

"Maybe they're asleep."

She lifted the heavy knocker and the door swung open, pulling it from her hand. She flinched. The brass fell with a clamor.

A man looked out at them. He was not old and gnarled, as Julie had somehow expected. He appeared to be about forty. He was bald, and very fat. His blue kimono, sashed at the waist, was shiny in the glow of the foyer lamp. It reached nearly to his knees. His legs were bare. He wore dark socks. He stared, and said nothing. He was frowning slightly, but seemed more curious than angry.

"I'm sorry we disturbed you," Nick said. "Our car broke down, and we were wondering if we could use your phone."

With a nod, he gestured for them to enter. Julie followed

Nick over the threshold, and shut the door. The man walked ahead of them, limping slightly. He entered a dark room off the foyer, and turned on a lamp. He waved them in.

The shadowy room looked, to Julie, like a parlor from a century ago. Her eyes took in the Persian rug, the overstuffed, plush sofa and armchairs adorned with doilies, the pedestal, tables cluttered with figurines, the shelves of leather-bound books. She saw no telephone.

She breathed through her nose to avoid the room's musty smell.

The man swept a hand toward the purple sofa, as if inviting them to sit down. Julie glanced at Nick. He shrugged. "Sir," he said, "do you have a telephone we might use?"

His bald head nodded. He motioned for them to be seated.

What's going on? Julie thought. The man's odd behavior and the old-fashioned look of the parlor were making her uneasy. Why doesn't he say something?

She followed Nick to the sofa. She sank into its cushion and sat forward, rigid, gripping her knees.

The man smiled and nodded. Turning away, he bent over to turn on the portable television. The rear of his satin kimono rode up. Julie glimpsed bare rump. She looked at Nick. He shook his head and rolled his eyes upward.

Stepping back, the man stared at the television. It made a loud humming sound. The voices filled the room, and a black and white picture fluttered onto the screen. The man faced Julie. He smiled. "May I offer you tea?" he asked in a high-pitched voice.

So he *can* talk, she thought.

"We'd rather use your phone, if we may," Nick said.

His head bobbed.

"I'd better call Dad first," Julie said. "Tell him we'll be late."

The man lowered himself onto a chair near the end of the sofa. He folded his hands on his lap, and stared at her. He seemed very pleased, almost eager about something. He squirmed a bit.

"May I use your phone?" Julie asked.

He pointed at a curtained-off archway across the room, just to the left of the television. "In there?" Julie asked. He nodded. She pushed herself off the sofa and went to the archway. Sweeping the curtain aside, she peered in. By the dim light from the parlor, she saw a small alcove, apparently a passageway into another room. A curtain hung at the other end. Against the wall was a rolltop desk. She spotted the black shape of a telephone on its work top. A floor lamp stood beside the desk.

Reaching under its shade, she switched on a bulb. She let the curtain fall across the entry, took a single step to the desk, and picked up the phone. As she dialed, she heard voices from the parlor television.

Poor Nick, she thought, sitting out there with that weirdo.

The phone rang three times before it was picked up. "Hello?"

"Hi, Dad. It's me."

"Julie? Where are you? What's wrong?"

"We had some car trouble. Everything's fine, but we're kind of stuck."

"What happened?"

"We got a couple of flats."

"A *couple of flats?*" He sounded shocked.

"Yeah. We're gonna call the auto club, but I thought I'd better let you know we'll be late."

"*Two flat tires?* Did somebody let the air out, or what?"

"The valve stems were cut off."

He was silent for a few moments. "The auto club won't be able to fix that. They'll have to tow you."

"I was afraid of that."

"Look, I'd better come pick you up. The car can wait till morning. Where are you calling from?"

"We're at this guy's house." She remembered the mailbox at the foot of the driveway. "His name's Fish. He's up in the hills just south of Ventura Boulevard."

"What the *hell* are you doing up there!"

"Well . . ."

"Never mind. We'll discuss it later. What's his address?"

"Twenty-one something. Hang on a second, I'll ask." She set down the receiver, stepped away from the desk, and hooked back the curtain.

The man smiled over the top of Nick's head. He was behind the sofa, leaning over its back, a thick arm squeezing Nick's throat. Nick's face was deep red. He was kicking and struggling.

"No!" Julie cried out. Lurching into the parlor, she glanced from side to side. She needed a weapon. Nothing looked right. With a yell, she flung the television off its stand. It crashed to the floor.

The man's face twisted. He let go of Nick. He stared at the smoking, sizzling remains of the TV as Nick dropped onto the sofa, rolled, and tumbled off. The man's lips moved, but no words came out. His narrow eyes shifted to Julie. Roaring, he threw himself over the sofa.

Julie spun around. She dashed through the curtain, through the alcove, into the dark room beyond.

The man, still roaring, followed.

Scott, clutching the phone to his ear, yanked open the counter drawer. He jerked out a telephone directory.

"*What is it?*" Karen asked.

"I don't . . . Quick, look up 'Fish.'" He thrust the book at her.

Karen slipped it down on the counter. Her hands shook badly as she raced through the pages.

"'Fish,'" Scott said. "A man's name."

She found the F's, flicked the pages until she found *Fi*. She traced the columns with her fingertip. "God, there's a couple dozen Fishes."

"It's twenty-one something. The address."

Half the entries seemed to be for food: Fish Diner, Fish Kitchen, Fish Market. "Here! Fish, Marvin, Twenty-one Vista Terrace. Tarzana."

"Gotta be it. Write it down. Tanya!" he yelled.

As Karen scribbled the address on a notepad, Tanya came rushing into the kitchen. Benny was close behind her. They both looked alarmed.

"Julie!" Scott called into the phone. Then he hung up and tugged a Thomas street atlas from the drawer. "Julie's in trouble," he told Tanya. "I want you to call the police. Send them to this address."

Karen ripped off the note and pressed it into the girl's hand.

"Tell them it's an emergency."

"What's going on?" Benny asked.

"Stay here with Tanya." He looked at Karen. "Will you come with me?"

"Of course."

"Gotta find that street on the map," he said. He gave her the Thomas guide. "Meet you at the car," he said, and dashed from the kitchen.

Karen hurried outside. Her car was parked at the curb, but she figured he would want to take his Cutlass. It was in the driveway. She tried the passenger door. Locked.

Scott came running from the house, a pistol in his hand.

The man whipped the curtain aside and Julie, standing at the wall, swung the chair down as he lunged through the archway. The edge of the seat smacked his head. His legs buckled. His knees hammered the floor. He clutched the top of his head, and ducked. Julie raised the chair high and swung it down with all her strength. The wooden legs slammed across his back. Squealing, he fell facedown. He rolled over as she lifted the chair again. His knees were up, his kimono open.

"Pig!" Julie shrieked, and drove the chair down.

He caught two of its legs, wrenched it from her grip, and hurled it away.

Julie leaped for the curtain. As she shouldered through it, a kick pounded her ankle. Her feet tangled. She fell sprawling into the alcove. She scurried over its floor, thrust herself up, and staggered through the curtain to the parlor. Nick was lying motionless in front of the sofa.

She crouched, grabbed the broken television, and hurled it as the man's shape bulged the curtain. It struck him at knee level. He cried out. He tore the curtain down and tumbled into the room. In the lamplight, Julie saw that his bald scalp was bleeding badly. His face was a red, dripping mask. As he got to his hands and knees, she kicked. She'd lost her sandal. A shock of pain streaked up her foot, but the man yelped and grabbed his face. He fell on his side and started to roll away from her. He was on his back, whimpering and holding his face. Julie jumped. She brought her knees up high and shot her legs down, driving both feet into his soft bare belly. His breath whooshed out. She windmilled for a moment, then fell, hitting the floor flat on her back. She lay there stunned, fighting for breath, terrified that the man might recover before she could.

Finally, she pushed herself up. The man was still on his back. His knees were up. He was hugging his stomach and wheezing.

Nick was rolling over.

He's alive!

Julie got to her feet. She flung aside the fallen curtain, and lifted the television. Staggering toward the man, she raised it high. Her arms trembled as she held it above his face. She stared down at him. "No," he gasped. "Don't. I'm sorry. I couldn't help it."

Her arm muscles shuddered with the weight.

He pressed his hands to his bloody face, and started to sob.

Twisting sideways, Julie dropped the television. It crashed to the floor just above his head. "Leave us alone," she muttered, and went to Nick.

"Here it is," Karen said. "Vista Terrace. Go right on Ventura to Avenida del Sol. Then it's a left."

Scott turned a knob, and the ceiling light went off.

Karen held the atlas on her lap. She grabbed the dashboard with her other hand as the car skidded around a corner. "They'll be all right," she said.

"I shouldn't have let them go."

"You couldn't have known."

"God*damn* it!"

"Nick's with her. They'll be all right."

She saw a stop sign ahead. Scott didn't slow down. As he sped toward the intersection, Karen spotted headlights to the right. "Look out!"

He accelerated, the thrust of the car shoving her against the seat. Light glared through her window. A horn blasted. She hugged her head. Then the brightness was gone, the noise of the horn fading behind them.

"Scott!"

He didn't answer. He was hunched over the steering wheel, speeding up the center of the deserted road.

Karen tried to keep her voice calm. "It won't do Julie any good if we get ourselves killed."

"Fucking curse."

"*It's on us, too, Scott.*"

Julie flung open the front door. Dropping to a crouch, she snatched up the tire iron. She rushed into the parlor and gave it to Nick. The man was lying facedown now, holding his head and crying softly. "If he tries anything, beat the crap out of him."

She left Nick kneeling beside the man, and hurried into the alcove. The phone was beeping loudly. She pushed its plungers, lifted the handset off the desk, and got a tone. Quickly, she dialed.

It rang once. "Hello?" Benny's voice.

"It's me."

"Julie! Are you okay?"

"Is Dad there?"

"No. He's on the way to pick you up. The cops are on the way, too."

"They know where we are?"

"Yeah."

"How long ago did Dad leave?"

"I don't know, five minutes? What happened?"

"Some nut tried to kill us."

"It's the curse."

"Brilliant deduction, Bonzo." She hung up.

They sped west on Ventura Boulevard, Scott weaving through the traffic. He accelerated to make it through a yellow light, but was forced to stop at the next main intersection because the cars ahead of him blocked the way. He pounded a fist on the steering wheel. "Come on, come on, come on," he muttered.

Tilting the atlas to catch the light from the streetlamps, Karen drew a finger along the thick line of Ventura. "Avenida del Sol," she said, "should be two blocks up."

"I make a left," he said.

"Yeah. Then it's a few blocks. We'll come to a Y. You stay to the left. It'll run into Vista Terrace."

"Which way on Vista?"

"Left again. It doesn't go the other way."

The traffic began to move. He stayed in the left-hand lane, hissing through clenched teeth, pounding the wheel and muttering about the slowness of the car ahead.

"The police are probably there by now," Karen said.

"God, I hope so."

The car sprang out as if escaping, and swung across three lanes of oncoming traffic. The force of the turn shoved Karen against her door. Horns blared. Then they were speeding along Avenida del Sol. The residential road was dark except for a few streetlamps. There were no cars approaching. Scott steered up the center line.

"Don't let them see the gun," Karen warned.

"Huh?"

"The cops. If they see you with the gun, they might shoot."

Julie flinched as a clamor resounded through the house. "I'll get it," she said. Pushing against Nick's shoulder, she rose from her knees and rushed out of the parlor.

In the dim foyer, she grabbed the doorknob. She hesitated. "Who is it?" she called.

"Police officers."

She opened the door, and let out a sigh of relief at the sight of the two uniformed patrolmen.

"Here's the Y," Karen said. "Veer left. We're almost there."

He slowed down slightly as the road narrowed, and then Karen saw taillights through the thick bushes to the right. Scott hit the brakes and horn before she yelled. He swerved away, but the car speeding down the driveway slammed into them just ahead of Karen with a deafening crunch of metal. The impact threw her against the door.

Their headlights jarred over a hedge across the road. Then they were crashing through the bushes, skidding down a slope. Karen thrust her hands against the ceiling as the car rolled over. The windshield shattered. The roof quavered. She thought it would cave in but it held as the car slid and wobbled to a stop.

She was upside down, the harness cutting into her shoulder and lap.

Just like before.

Only now it was Scott, not Frank, hanging unconscious beside her as smoke started spilling from under the hood.

PART THREE

Chapter Thirty-seven

There were four of them.

They came down the trail from Carver Pass at dusk, walking single file.

Ettie, crouched behind an outcropping near her cave, could see only their vague shapes in the distance. But she knew who they were. She knew why they'd come.

They were the survivors.

They'd come to kill her.

She was pleased there were only four.

CHAPTER THIRTY-EIGHT

Karen slipped on the loose earth of the footpath, landed on her rump, and skidded. She dug in the heels of her boots to stop herself. The tingling pain of her scraped buttocks brought tears to her eyes. She wiped them away. Nick and Benny took her by the arms and helped her up.

She followed them to the bottom of the path, with Julie staying behind her. They walked along the lakeshore toward the stand of pine where they'd camped that Monday night, but were still a good distance away when Benny sat on the ground.

Karen stopped beside him. She dropped her pack, and kneeled in front of it. A breeze chilled the back of her sweaty blouse as she unstrapped a side pocket and took out Scott's .45 automatic. She jacked a cartridge into the chamber, switched the safety on, and sat down. She leaned back against her pack, and rested the heavy pistol on the lap of her jeans.

Benny was lying on his back with his knees in the air. Julie was settled against her pack. They were sweaty, gasping for breath. Nick, crouching over his open pack, took out a hatchet. Scott's hatchet. The sheriff still had Nick's. He sat down, and took off its leather sheath.

Karen shut her eyes. Her heart was racing and she felt nauseated. Sweat streamed down her face. She wiped it with her bare forearm, and let the shaking arm fall to her lap. Her wristbone hit the pistol, and she whimpered.

"Let's get moving," Nick said. His sudden voice made Karen flinch.

"I can't," Julie said. "Let's wait."

"A little while."

Karen heard movement. Through half-open eyelids, she watched Julie crawl over to Nick and hold him. He stroked her hair. For a moment, he looked as if he might cry.

He'd done some crying in the station wagon today—no, yesterday. It was all so confused in Karen's mind, as if she'd been in a daze ever since pulling Scott's unconscious body from the wreck. That was two nights ago. Last night was Juniper Lake and horrible dreams that kept waking her until Benny crawled into her sleeping bag and they embraced and finally fell asleep in each other's arms.

When she woke up in the morning, Benny was snug against her and snoring. Julie's sleeping bag was empty. She was with Nick. She crawled out naked in the frigid morning air, and Karen saw a smear of dried blood on one thigh. As she knelt beside her sleeping bag, she saw Karen watching. The girl glared as if daring Karen to chastise her. "Go back to him," Karen said. "Stay with him." The hard look fell away from Julie's face. Her chin trembled. She nodded, and returned to Nick's sleeping bag.

Later, no one spoke of the incident. But Karen caught Julie staring at her, from time to time, with a curious look on her face.

"How you doing, Benny?" Nick asked.

"I think I'm gonna die," he said.

Karen winced. Did he have to mention death?

"We're all gonna die," Nick said. "But not tonight. It's someone else's turn tonight."

"Damn right," Julie said.

"Karen?"

She nodded, and lifted the pistol off her lap.

"Okay," he said. "Let's haul ass."

Haul ass. He sounded just like Flash. Karen's throat

tightened, and tears came to her eyes. God, she'd hardly known the man. But he'd seemed like a good fellow. He was Scott's friend and Nick's father, and she supposed the tears were for them and for Alice, for Rose and Heather.

She pushed herself up. Her legs trembled under her weight, and her blistered feet burned. As the others stood up, she untucked her blouse. She lifted it, sucked in her belly, and pushed the pistol barrel down the waistband of her jeans. It was hard and cool against her skin.

"We'll circle this lake," Nick said. "Then we'll circle Upper Mesquite."

"Flashlights," Karen said.

"Yeah. It'll be dark in a few mintues."

"And cold," Benny added.

They searched through their packs. Benny put on his parka. Karen was shivering, and her own parka seemed too bulky. She left it in her pack, but took out her gray sweatshirt. Turning away from the others, she took off her cold, damp blouse. She wadded it. She used it to wipe the sweat off her face, the back of her neck, her sides. Then she tossed it into the pack, and put the sweatshirt on. It felt soft and warm. It made her think of Scott, the night he'd worn it back to his tent.

If only he were here . . .

Benny was gaping at her when she turned around. He looked down quickly at his flashlight, switched it on, and shined it on his face to see that it worked.

Karen took out her own flashlight and tested it.

Nick pointed with his hatchet to the left. "We'll go that way, head around the back side of the lake till we get to the ridge."

They started to walk, Nick in the lead with Julie close behind him. Karen let Benny go ahead of her. She didn't want him bringing up the rear; it seemed too vulnerable a position for the boy.

They followed the shoreline back the way they'd come. Where it curved at the northern end, they made their way up the broken granite blocks of the slope until they were thirty or forty feet above the water. Every step was an agony for Karen—for the others as well, she supposed. But nobody protested.

Probably, they could have just waited at the campsite. But they'd discussed it many times on the way in, and agreed to this. Everyone felt it would be better than waiting for the woman to make a first move. Also, there was a chance they might discover her hiding place, come upon her unawares. It was a slim chance, since the deputies hadn't been able to find her, but worth a try anyway. They agreed she must have a hiding place somewhere on the slopes above the lakes. They had enough food for four days. If they didn't find her tonight, if she stayed away from them, they would keep searching until the food ran out.

No one thought it would come to that.

If she was still at the lake, she would try for them. "She wants me," Nick had said. "I'm the one who killed her son. She can't get me with the curse. She doesn't have my blood and stuff."

"She got your dad," Julie had reminded him, taking his hand.

"That was an accident. He got in the way of it to save Mom and the girls. He would've been all right, except . . . She has to come for me. That's when we'll nail her."

"What if the curse doesn't end when she's dead?" Julie asked.

"It has to," Benny said, and explained that without her psychic power directing it the curse would dissipate.

"What makes you so sure?" Julie asked.

"The book said so."

"Let's hope the book's right," Karen said.

"Let's hope she's still at the lake," Julie said.

"She will be," Nick assured them. "She will be. She wants me dead."

Nick pointed up the slope, stirring Karen from her thoughts. He spoke to Julie. The girl nodded. Sitting on a boulder, she twisted around to watch him climb. Karen followed Benny across the rocks, and joined her.

"Where's he going?" Karen asked.

Julie pointed. Some distance above Nick was a dark crevice in the rocks. "He wants to check that out. We're supposed to wait here."

They watched Nick make his way higher, leaping from rock to rock, striding up an angled slab, finally reaching the shadowed gap. He shined his flashlight inside, then turned around and shook his head and started down.

Karen lowered herself onto a rock. It felt cool and lumpy through the seat of her jeans, and the pistol dug into her until she leaned back. She braced herself up on her elbows.

The water below, gray in the dim light, was ruffled by the wind. Directly across the lake was the clearing where they'd left their packs. The fireplace, a distance to the left, was intact and surrounded by the stumps and rocks they'd used for seats. Even a pile of firewood remained—wood they had gathered after swimming. She remembered the good, cold feel of the water. Flash whistling at her before she went in. Had the madwoman and her son been watching, spying on them from up here someplace? Maybe if they hadn't gone swimming, if the man hadn't seen her and Julie in their suits . . . Those ifs again. It was pointless to think that way. You can't go back and change anything, so why worry about it?

If they'd just listened to Benny that night and gone after the woman and taken her pouch . . .

Nick leaped down and joined them. "Just a crack in the rocks," he said. "It didn't go anywhere."

They started walking again. Soon, the last of the evening light faded out. Under the half-moon, the rocks ahead looked gray and bleak, like a dirty snowfield. A snowfield gouged with black shadows. The shadows, all around, made Karen uneasy. She reached under her sweatshirt and pulled out the automatic.

Benny looked back at her. "What's wrong?"

"Nothing much."

"Did you see something?"

"It's what I don't see that's got me worried."

"I wish Dad was here."

"So do I."

"Do you think he'll be mad when he finds out?"

"No. I think he'll be very proud. Especially if we do what we came for."

With a nod, Benny looked forward again. He switched on his flashlight, shined it on Julie's back, then down to the rocks in front of his feet.

Karen turned her own flashlight on, but its brightness seemed to deepen the dark around her. Following close behind Benny, she shot its beam up the slope, swept it over the rocks, probed the black crevices. Her back felt exposed. She twisted around, but the tunnel of light showed only rocks and fluttering shadows behind her. Nobody there, she thought. Nobody creeping up.

"Yeeeh!" The sharp outcry came from Benny. She sprang forward as the boy ducked and covered his head and a coyote leaping from above slammed him over. He tumbled toward the edge. Karen lunged across the boulder. Her jarring beam showed Benny's legs kicking high, flipping backward. She flung the flashlight and pistol from her hands. She stretched for him. Her fingertips brushed a cuff of his jeans, and then he was falling. Karen staggered, her momentum thrusting her toward the edge. She teetered there. Her sweatshirt went taut across her chest, and she was tugged to a stop.

Benny dropped to the rocks ten feet below. He cried out as he hit. With a yelp, the coyote raced away.

Julie let go of Karen's sweatshirt and stepped beside her. "Benny!"

They boy raised his head.

A crouched figure with a hatchet scurried toward him over the moonlit rocks.

"Look out!" Karen yelled.

"It's just Nick," Julie said.

As they climbed down, Karen heard Benny whimper, "My arm, my arm."

Karen knelt beside him. He was gasping, holding his right forearm.

"I think it might be broken," Nick said.

Karen stroked the boy's sweaty forehead. "Where else do you hurt?" she asked.

"Everywhere."

"You took a pretty good fall."

"I tried to duck, but it—"

Julie said, "Is anything else broken or sprained?"

"I don't know," he said. "I don't think so."

He flinched and sobbed as they sat him up. They carefully removed his parka. Julie shined a light on his arm while Nick rolled his right sleeve up above the elbow. The forearm was swollen and discolored, but the skin wasn't broken. "We need something to splint it," Nick said.

"Knives?" Karen suggested.

"Let's give it a try."

Julie opened her belt and took off her leather-cased knife. From hilt to tip, it was nearly a foot long.

"That'll do for one," Nick said.

Benny had a similar knife.

Karen held them in place, one on each side of the arm, while Nick strapped them tight with Benny's belt. "I guess that'll have to do until we find something better."

"Hope we don't need those things," Julie said.

Nick ruffled Benny's hair. "Now you're better armed than any of us."

"My *gun*," Karen muttered.

She and Julie climbed up the rocks to look for it. With Nick's flashlight, she searched the area where she'd let it fall. Her beam swept the gray surfaces, sought out dark corners, dug into fissures. Julie located the lost flashlight. It was broken. They kept on looking.

"It has to be here someplace," Julie said.

"You'd think so."

They went over the same area time and again.

"Maybe it's down there," Julie said, stepping close to the edge.

"Any luck?" Nick called to her.

"No."

They climbed down and searched the base of the rock cluster.

Julie glanced at her brother. "You're not sitting on it, are you?"

"No," he said.

"I'll try looking," Nick said.

Julie handed over her flashlight. She stayed below, while Karen led Nick back up the broken rocks to the place where she had dropped the gun. "Right about here," she said, standing a yard from the edge.

"Did you throw it, or just let it fall?"

"I just opened my hand so I could grab for Benny."

"Maybe you kicked it."

"I might've. If I did, it didn't register."

She showed him where Julie had found the flashlight. They searched there. They crisscrossed the craggy mound of granite, walking shoulder to shoulder.

"It might've gone down one of these cracks," Nick finally said.

"Wherever it is," Karen told him, "I don't think we're gonna find it. Not tonight anyway. Why don't we come back in the morning when we've got some light on the subject?"

"Morning will be too late," Nick said.

They climbed down, and spent some time searching the area around Benny and Julie.

"Might as well forget it," Julie said.

Karen took off her belt and made a sling for Benny's arm. Then they helped the boy to his feet.

"What now?" Julie asked.

"Let's just get back to our packs," Nick said. "There's aspirin in my first-aid kit. Maybe that'll help Benny's pain."

"Build a nice, warm fire," Julie added.

"And eat," Benny said. "I'm starving."

They were near the south end of the lake. Karen, with one of the flashlights, took the lead. Nick followed, supporting Benny. The boy could walk all right, though he winced with each limping step. Julie, carrying the hatchet and the other working flashlight, brought up the rear.

Karen tried to pick out the easiest route. Her beam probed the darkness ahead, swept the slope to her left. She felt very vulnerable without the gun.

By losing it, she'd put everyone in terrible danger. Nobody had criticized her and she tried not to blame herself, but damn it, she'd thrown away their main defense, the only weapon they had that could reach out and knock someone down at a safe distance. The pocketknife in her jeans was little comfort. The two big knives were belted around Benny's arm. Nick still had a sheath knife at his side, and Julie had the hatchet. A pitiful collection of weapons. Christ, why didn't I hang onto the gun!

Rounding the end of the lake, she came upon the feeder stream from Upper Mesquite. Her light shimmered on its rushing surface, followed the water upward to the low ridge, swept back and forth over both rocky shores. She saw rocks and lurching shadows and flowing water. Nothing more. She crouched. She cupped some cold, fresh water to her mouth. Then she jumped to the other side, and held her light on the stream.

Nick and Benny waded across, the water swirling over their boots, soaking their pants legs almost to the knees.

Julie leaped over the stream. "Now you two'll come down with pneumonia."

Nick made a sound resembling a laugh. "Better than *old-monia*."

Karen crossed the slope, heading downward, closer to the lake. And then her boot pressed springy earth, not rock. It felt like a cushion. It felt wonderful. The layer of pine needles made soft crunching sounds as she walked.

She took a twisting route to avoid trees and clumps of

rock. Then she saw the clearing just ahead. She spotted the fireplace, the stumps and rocks surrounding it like stools, the pile of wood. She was swept by a feeling of pleasure and relief, as if returning home after a long trip.

She staggered forward. She lowered herself onto the flat surface of a stump, stretched out her pulsing legs, and sighed.

"What the shit!" Nick blurted. "Where'd our packs go?"

Karen shined her flashlight into the darkness. The packs were gone.

CHAPTER THIRTY-NINE

Benny felt useless. He sat on a rock shivering, his arm throbbing with pain, while Nick and Julie searched for the backpacks. Karen sat on a stump close to him. She held an open pocketknife. "You can help them look if you want," he said.

"That's okay."

"You don't have to stay and guard me."

She smiled slightly. "Sure I do."

"Boy, I really messed things up."

"No you didn't. It could've happened to any of us." She wrapped her arms around herself.

"Are you cold?" Benny asked.

"I'm one giant goose bump."

"Do you want my parka?"

"No, thanks. It wouldn't fit anyway."

"You could put it over your back."

"No. You keep it. Really. You need it more than me. Didn't you know that women have an extra layer of fat?"

"Not you."

She laughed. "It's gonna be a rough night if they don't find the packs. We'll freeze our buns."

"And starve. Like the Donner party."

"Hardly like the Donner party. We can hike out of here in a day if we have to. We've done it before."

"We can't leave without . . . We've gotta kill the witch first."

"At least we know she's here," Karen said. "She has to

be the one who took our packs. That's something any-way."

"I knew she would be. She brought us here."

"What?"

"She brought us here. With her magic."

"That's a pleasant thought. What makes you think so?"

"We're here, aren't we?"

"We chose to come."

"Why didn't we have a wreck on the way up? We didn't even have a close call."

"Nick was driving. As your dad said, he's the Great Un-cursed One."

"Nothing's happened to any of us since Thursday. Nothing happened till we got here. She wanted us here."

"So she could get Nick?"

"And us. When we're out of the way, she'll go ahead and finish off Dad and Heather and Rose and Mrs. Gordon. She can finish them with the curse."

"We won't let her. Unless we freeze to death."

"Maybe we should make a fire."

"With what?"

"I've got matches," Benny told her.

"*You do?*"

"Sure." With his left hand, he fumbled open the button of a shirt-pocket flap.

"Oh, you're a life saver. I wish you'd mentioned that five minutes ago."

"It'll mess up our night vision," he said, taking out a book of matches.

"Who cares?" She stood and held out a shaky hand. Benny gave her the matches. She rushed toward the trees. Crouching, she gathered pine needles. As she returned, Benny swiveled around to face the fireplace. He remem-bered building it, collecting the rocks by himself and stack-ing them to form a low, circular wall, the afternoon they arrived at the lake and everyone was mad at him because it was his fault they had to stay here.

Karen, on her knees, tore off the matchbook cover. She tucked it into a small pile of pine needles, and carefully stacked kindling on top.

"It's all my fault," he said.

She looked over her shoulder at him. "What is?"

"Everything. If I hadn't tripped on Heather and hurt her foot, we would've gone to Wilson Lake and none of this stuff would've happened."

"Bullshit."

"It's true."

"You sound just like your dad, you know that? Blaming yourselves. It must run in the family."

"But it's true."

"Save the blame for that bitch and her son. We're just victims, Benny. We happened to be at the wrong place at the wrong time. A million things could've changed that. And we would've been just fine, camping here, if that sick maniac hadn't decided to rape me."

"He . . . he *raped* you?"

Karen hesitated. Then she said, "Yes."

Benny felt as if he'd been punched hard in the stomach. He hunched over. The movement sent pain pounding through his arm. He started to cry.

Karen stood up. She stepped close to him and pressed his head gently against her. The sweatshirt was soft. It smelled good. He rubbed his face against it, feeling her belly through the material. It was the sweatshirt she'd worn last night in her sleeping bag when she held him and she was so warm and he could feel her breasts against him and worried so badly that she might notice his hard-on. Then she'd whispered, "Don't worry about it," and he'd wanted to die with shame. But just for a minute. After that, it had been fine and peaceful. "Are you gonna marry Dad?" he'd asked.

"Maybe."

"I hope so."

"Why?"

"Because I love you."

"I love you, too, Benny."

He'd snuggled against her. He'd never felt so good before in all his life. Thinking about it eased the hurt.

"You okay?" she asked, stroking his hair.

"I . . . I feel so bad he did that to you."

"He's dead."

"I wish I'd killed him."

"No you don't."

"Oh yes I do."

She backed away. Crouching, she kissed him lightly on the mouth. "Let's get this fire going before we freeze." Turning around, she struck a match and lit the piece of cardboard. Flames curled up. The pine needles smoked and crackled and caught fire, igniting the twigs. Karen added bigger sticks from the nearby pile. The blaze grew high, dancing and throwing out heat. "*Now* we're cooking," she said.

Nick and Julie came up from behind. They huddled close to the fire.

"No luck?" Karen asked.

"We think she might've thrown them in the lake," Julie said.

"If she did," Nick said, "they'd have to be close to shore. We shouldn't have much trouble finding them."

"We're gonna take a look," Julie added. She was bent over the fire, the flashlight clamped between her knees, rubbing her hands together as if washing them in the flames.

"Where'd you find the matches?" Nick asked.

"They're Benny's," Karen said.

"Good going, Ben."

"Yeah." Julie smiled at him. "You're not a complete waste."

He smiled back at her. "No kidding."

Nick stepped away from the fire. "Okay, we'll take a look at the lake."

"Want to go with them?" Karen asked Benny.

"Yeah."

"It's better that way," she told the other two. "It's better if we stay together."

Benny stood up, wincing as the movement hurt his arm. The rest of his body felt stiff and sore, but he was glad to be included. Karen stayed close to his side as they headed for the lake.

Nick and Julie had the only working flashlights. They walked slowly along the shoreline, sweeping their beams over the water. The lights bent off to new angles where they penetrated. Through shallow water murky with swirling specks, Benny could see the bottom. The rocks down there were mossy. Patches of seaweed swayed with the currents. Farther out, the beams couldn't reach the bottom. They stopped a couple of feet below the surface, as if too weak to drive deeper into the gloom.

"Well," Nick said, "I still think they're out there. I'm going in."

"No, that's crazy," Julie said.

"Let's wait till morning," Karen suggested. "Even if you find them, the sleeping bags'll be soaking."

"Most of the food should be okay," Nick said. "I don't know about you guys, but I'm starved."

"Nick, you'll freeze."

"We've got a good fire." They followed him to the place where they'd left the packs. "If she threw them in, she probably took them straight over from here." He sat on the ground, put down the hatchet, and started to untie his boots.

Julie sat down beside him. "If you're going in, so am I."

"There's no point in both of us getting wet."

"I don't care."

"Julie." His voice was firm. "I mean it. You wait here."

She looked at him. Her mouth opened. Then it shut. Her shoulders slumped a bit. "Okay," she muttered. "If you don't want me to."

With his boots and socks off, he stood up and took off his flannel shirt. He lowered his jeans and stepped out of them. He left his jockey shorts on, and walked stiffly to the edge of the lake. He rubbed his arms. "Well," he said, "here goes."

He charged forward, feet slapping into the water, splashing it high until he was knee-deep. Then he dived, hitting the surface flat out. Karen and Julie kept flashlights on him as he slid along silently below the waves. After a few seconds, he came up. He swung around, and wiped water off his face.

"You standing up?" Julie asked.

"Yeah." The waves reached his chest.

"How is it?"

He answered with a groan of pain. Then he started walking.

Julie's light stayed on him. Karen aimed hers at the water just ahead of him. They walked slowly along the shore, keeping to his pace.

He stopped. His shoulders wobbled slightly. "What do you know!" he said. Then he ducked below the surface. His back was visible for a moment, pale in the flashlight beams, rippling and quivering. Then it sank out of sight. Benny stared at the murky water. He counted silently to ten, and then Nick burst to the surface holding a gray bundle in front of him. He raised it from the water. It was Karen's pack. "They're all right here," he said.

"Fantastic," Julie called.

He lifted the pack overhead, and took a step forward, and just behind him the water seemed to explode. His eyes bulged. His mouth sprang open. The pack fell from his hands. It pounded down on his head, driving him under the surface.

The flashlights clattered to the rocks. Karen and Julie, side by side, dashed into the lake. One flashlight was out. Benny snatched up the other. He saw Karen dive. She swam out fast, vanished under the surface, and came up pulling Nick by his arm. Julie splashed to his other side, grabbed his other arm. Nick's head came out of the water. They pulled him along between them. He was conscious. He was choking. When they reached shallow water, Benny saw that his legs were working.

"What happened?" Benny asked.

Nobody answered. Supporting Nick, the two women walked him onto dry land and lowered him to his knees. They eased him down flat.

The shiny red handle of a pocketknife jutted from his back.

CHAPTER FORTY

"Oh, my God," Julie muttered. "Oh, my God." She tugged the knife. Nick went rigid and cried out, but the blade, embedded a few inches below his right shoulder, wouldn't come out. She pulled harder. The handle slipped from her wet grip.

"I'll try," Karen said.

"It must be in the bone," Julie said. "It's awfully deep."

"Keep an eye on the lake, Benny." Karen rubbed her right hand on her sweatshirt and clutched the knife. She pressed her left hand against Nick's bloody back.

"Aaaah!" He shuddered and dug his fingers into the earth as she yanked on the knife. She worked it back and forth and jerked it free. Nick's muscles unclenched. He lowered his face to the ground. He was gasping and sobbing.

"Let's get over to the fire," Karen said.

He pushed himself to his hands and knees. Julie and Karen, gripping his arms, lifted him. He staggered between them as if his legs were too weak to support his weight. When they reached the fire, they sat him down on a stump with his back to the blaze. Julie plucked at the knot of the wet bandanna around her neck. She loosened it, took off the kerchief, and squeezed out the water. Gently, she patted the wound. The gash was less than an inch in length. It bled freely, but the blood wasn't pumping out.

Karen said, "It doesn't look too bad."

"It doesn't feel too good," Nick said. His voice sounded tight and shaky.

Julie folded the bandanna into a thick pad and pressed it firmly against the wound. Nick flinched.

"I'll get his clothes," Karen said. She hurried away. Benny went with her.

Holding the pad in place, Julie leaned close to him. She pressed her face against his wet hair, kissed the top of his head. Her free hand reached down and rubbed his chest. He was trembling badly.

"I guess I lucked out," he said.

"Real luck," Julie muttered.

"She couldn't get the knife out. She blew it."

"Sure."

"This time," he added.

Karen returned, holding Nick's clothes bundled in her arms. Benny had the hatchet.

"You did luck out," Julie said. "You've got dry clothes."

"We've gotta rig something to keep the bandage tight," Karen said. "Won't be easy. It's in a bad place." She tugged Nick's belt from its loops. "You'll have to keep your arm down." She wrapped the belt around his upper back. Julie pressed it to the bandanna while Karen slipped one end under his left armpit. She pulled the other end over his right arm just below his shoulder, and buckled it tightly at his chest. "How's that?"

"It's okay if I don't lift my arm."

"Don't lift your arm."

"Okay. Unless I have to."

"I'll get him dressed," Julie said.

"Fine." Karen and Benny stepped away.

Karen sat on a rock so close to the fire that steam curled off the wet legs of her jeans. The heat felt very good, but it only warmed her front. The back of her sweatshirt and pants were frigid against her skin.

Benny, on the other side of the fire, stared at her through the flashing lenses of his glasses.

"Keep a sharp eye out," she told him. "We don't want anyone sneaking up."

Nodding, he swung his legs sideways and stared toward the lake.

Karen stood up. She turned away from the fire, and peeled off her sweatshirt. She sighed as the warmth soothed her back. Scanning the darkness beyond the fire's glow, she wrung water from her sweatshirt. When she finished, she glanced over her shoulder at Benny. He was watching her. He quickly looked away, and she turned around. She held her sweatshirt over the flames. Steam rolled off it like smoke and was whipped away by the breeze.

Nick, to her left, had his flannel shirt draped over his back. One arm was in its sleeve. He stood up. Julie, crouching in front of him, pulled down his jockey shorts. He held onto her shoulder to steady himself while she pulled the shorts off his feet and helped him into his jeans.

Karen turned her eyes to Benny. He was staring at her. "No fair peeking," she warned, and he looked away.

The sweatshirt was still damp when she put it on, but at least it felt warm. For the moment. Sitting on the rock, she took off her boots and socks. She opened her jeans, and drew them down along with her panties.

Julie was putting socks on Nick.

The rock felt cold and gritty under Karen's buttocks, but she stayed seated as she wrung out her panties. She held them close to the fire while Benny continued to scan the shoreline and Julie finished with Nick's socks and boots. Then Karen stood, brushed some grit off her rump, and stepped into her panties. They felt warm and dry.

She turned around to heat up her back, and did her best to twist the water out of her jeans. The stiff material was difficult to work with. Finally, she gave up. She faced the fire and held them over the flames.

Nick swung around toward the fire. With his right arm inside the shirt, Julie hadn't been able to button it.

"How you doing?" Karen asked him.

"A little better. Kind of sick."

Benny looked over his shoulder. Karen nodded to him, and he brought his legs around. He leaned close to the fire.

"Guess she's trying to whittle us down," Nick said.

"Apt phrase, that," Karen told him.

"I think she's planning to freeze us to death," Julie said. She stepped to the fire. Karen could see her shaking. "What the hell," she said. "Since I'm freezing anyway, I might as well go ahead and get the packs."

Nick gaped at her.

"Why not? I'm already soaked."

"Let's just leave them till morning," Karen said.

"We don't even know for sure our sleeping bags are wet. They're in stuff bags. They might be fairly dry. Besides, there's the food, the first-aid kit. Especially the first-aid kit. It's got disinfectant. We can put a real bandage on you, Nick. It'd sure be better than keeping you all strapped up."

"You can't do it," he said.

"We know right where the packs are."

"What if *she's* there?" Benny said.

"You think she's gonna stay in the lake all night, just hoping we'll go back in?"

"Maybe she knows. Maybe she's *willing* you."

"Don't be a dork."

Karen sighed. "It's not a smart idea, Julie. She could be waiting."

"If she is, she hasn't got a knife."

"We don't know that for sure," Nick said.

"If she had another one, she would've used it on you."

"You don't need a knife to kill someone," Karen said.

"Killing can go both ways," Julie said. She stepped over to Nick and lifted the sheath knife from his lap. He clutched her wrist.

"You can't," he said.

"We need those packs. Don't tell me no, or I'd just have to go against you."

"Julie."

She leaned closer and kissed his mouth. Then she whispered to him. He whispered back, and released her wrist. "Keep the fire hot for me," she said. "I'll need it."

She moved closer to the flames. She pulled off her belt and slid the sheath onto it. Sitting on a rock beside Benny, she took off her boots and socks. She stripped down to her bra and panties. "You want to heat these up for me?" she asked, offering the wet clothes to Karen.

"I'm going with you."

"You don't have to."

Karen smiled. "Sure I do."

"We'll all go," Nick said.

"You and Benny aren't wet."

"We can stay on shore. At least we'll be close by in case something happens."

Julie nodded. She strapped the belt around her waist, and slid the knife to her hip. While Nick and Benny got to their feet, she arranged her clothing on rocks near the fire.

Karen spread her jeans over the rock where she'd been sitting.

"Let's get this show on the road," Julie said.

Julie cringed as she stepped into the water. Earlier, when she'd rushed in to help Nick, she'd been so overwhelmed by the urgency of getting to him that she'd hardly noticed the cold. Now, her whole body trembled as she waded deeper.

"Dive under fast," Nick suggested.

"Easy for you to say," she called back.

Karen, just ahead of her and thigh-deep, was pulling up the bottom of her sweatshirt to keep it out of the water. She turned to face Julie. Her small pocketknife was clamped between her teeth. She took it out. "This good?" she asked. Her voice was pitched higher than usual.

"Fine."

"It'll be quicker if we both dive for 'em."

"We'd just get tangled." Julie moved past Karen. She took

a sharp breath when the frigid water lapped her groin. With another step, she was covered to the waist. She sucked in her belly as if to draw it away from the painful touch. "*God*," she gasped. She turned around. "I'll pass you three. Take the last one myself."

"Right," Karen said.

"Then we'll get our asses over to the fire."

"I'm for that."

"Here goes!" she called to the others.

Nick, standing at the edge of the lake, waved his hatchet overhead. Benny, beside him, shined the flashlight in her eyes. The glare hurt. She flinched away from it and muttered, "Thanks a lot."

Then she waded out farther. The icy water soaked through her bra, washed over her shoulders. She turned to the right, and began searching. The water buoyed her up so her feet hardly touched the slippery rocks. She took long, slow steps, stroking the water with her arms to propel herself forward.

Then she toed something that wasn't rock. She explored it with her foot. It was a backpack. "Got one," she said.

Karen, waiting a couple of yards away in water up to her waist, nodded and clamped the knife between her teeth. Julie took a deep breath. Then she dived. She kept her eyes open, but saw only black as she clutched the sides of the pack, planted her feet on the slick rocks, and lifted. The pack felt nearly weightless.

She surfaced, and filled her lungs with air. Hugging the pack, she took a few slow-motion strides toward Karen. The woman reached out, took it from her, turned away, and started wading for shore.

Julie swung around. She swam a few strokes. Lowering her legs, she searched with her feet. As they swept over the rocks, she glanced to the side. Karen was ashore, bending down, lowering the pack.

Her toes caught a strap. She plunged and gripped it with

her right hand. It felt like leather. Must be Karen's Bergen. She pulled against it, and felt the pack start to rise as she brought her legs down toward the bottom.

Someone kicked her. The toenails raked her thigh. Ow! What's Karen doing *under* me?

It's not Karen!

A hand clawed her behind the shoulders, pulling her down. Another dug into her back. They held her tight against a bare, twisting body while legs hooked around her. Teeth ripped at her shoulder. Jerking with pain, she grasped long ropes of hair and tugged. The teeth held. They clamped harder. Her shoulder burned with agony. She wanted to cry out, but kept her lips clenched. The teeth released her. She tried to keep the head back, but it darted in, hair sliding through her fingers, and the teeth snapped shut on her collarbone.

She remembered Karen's warning. *You don't need a knife to kill someone.*

Just teeth. Rip out the jugular.

Knife.

The teeth let go.

Now for the throat.

She bent her head sideways and thrust her shoulder toward her ear. The teeth nipped her cheek, tried to get under her jaw. Then a spasm shook the woman as Julie rammed the six-inch blade into her back. Her fingernails pierced Julie's skin. She bucked and squirmed. Julie yanked the knife out and drove it in. She shoved a hand against the woman's face, pushed her away, and thrust the blade into her belly. Feet on the lake bottom, she clutched the knife with both hands and forced it upward.

Benny shined his flashlight on the water where Julie had gone under. The surface looked more turbulent there. She'd been down for a long time. Longer than it should take to lift up a pack.

Nick was watching, though. He didn't seem worried.

Karen was wading out quickly, but not as if she thought anything was wrong.

Then a head broke the surface. The beam of Benny's light reached to a face that sent a shock through him. The eyes were rolled up so that only the whites showed. The mouth was wide open, lips peeled back in a grimace. Blood spilled down the chin.

A scream filled Benny's throat. She was rising as if about to soar from the lake. Her shoulders burst from the surface. Her arms flapped wildly. Her bare breasts shook.

Then a pair of hands came up, clutching her belly. No, not exactly. But she wasn't about to fly, she was being lifted by those hands and then a head appeared below her.

It had to be Julie.

For just a moment, the woman—the witch—was above Julie's head, out of the water entirely, her naked body writhing and beating the air. Julie bent as she swung the body over her. It hit the water headfirst and threw up a frothy shower.

Chapter Forty-one

Nick stared, frozen with shock, as the body surged up out of the lake. The twisted face was not Julie's. The squirming figure kicked at the sky, and vanished with a huge splash.

Karen lunged forward, knife in her upraised hand.

Rushing in, Nick saw her reach down. Julie was gone. Where? Was she hurt, drowning? He was waist-deep and wading against the heavy push of the water when her head popped to the surface.

Off to Nick's side, Karen's left arm came up. Her hand was wrapped with black hair. She raised the woman's head. Water and blood spilled from the gaping mouth. As the shoulders appeared, she drew back her knife to strike. She hesitated. She lowered the knife. She looked at Nick. "Dead?"

"Looks that way."

Julie waded toward them. "She dead?"

"What happened?" Nick asked.

"Got her with your knife." As Julie approached, the water level dropped. The flashlight beam found her. She squinted and turned her face away. Nick groaned at the sight of her torn, bloody jaw and shoulder.

"God, Julie."

"I'm okay. Let's take her ashore."

"I've got her," Karen said.

"Good, 'cause I've got one of the packs."

Nick waited for them to trudge past, Karen towing the body by its hair. It was facedown in the water, floating along, its back and outstretched legs pale in the moonlight. Nick held the hatchet in his left hand, ready for use, but he saw no signs of life.

Julie was the first to reach the shore. She dropped the pack and returned. She and Karen each took an arm. They dragged the body onto dry land. Benny shined his light on it. Kneeling down, Nick looked at the wounds on its back, two raw pulpy gashes that slowly filled with blood.

"You sure got her," Benny muttered.

Julie turned the body over, and Nick recoiled at the sight. Benny gasped. Karen turned away, clutching her mouth. Julie muttered, "*Jesus.*"

The torso was split from just above the mons almost to the rib cage. Entrails had spilled from the opening. They looked like a pile of dead snakes.

Julie backed away, shaking her head. Nick went to her. He dropped the hatchet and drew her against him. She put her arms around him. She felt wet and cold. She was shaking badly. "It's all right," Nick said.

"I did that," she muttered.

"You had to."

"Doesn't make it any better."

"I know. I've been through it. Remember?"

"Yeah." She pressed her face to the side of his neck. He felt the brush of her eyelashes. His right hand, still pinned low by the belt, caressed the chilly skin of her flank.

"Let's go to the fire," he said.

"I want to get the other packs."

"Are you nuts?"

"Yeah. But you love me anyway, right?"

"I sure do." He kissed her mouth. She hugged him fiercely, apparently forgetting about his wound until he flinched with pain.

"I'm sorry."

"That's okay. I hurt *you* last night."

She smiled up at him. "You sure did. And don't you forget it."

"I'll never forget it."

"Do you still respect me?"

"No."

She laughed softly.

Nick squeezed her rump through the damp, silky fabric of her panties, and she squirmed against him. He felt a warm surge of pleasure.

"Don't make me feel too good," she warned. "I won't want to go back in."

"I don't want you to go back in."

"Duty calls." After a final, brief kiss, she eased herself away.

Karen was crouched near the shore, Benny holding the light for her as she rummaged through one of the packs. She took out a plastic case. "First-aid kit," she said. She raised it toward Nick. "Why don't you take Julie over to the fire and patch her up?"

"I'm all right," Julie said.

"You're bleeding all over yourself."

"I'm gonna get the other packs."

"I'll do that," Karen told her. "You and Nick go over and take care of yourselves."

"Are you sure?"

"Yeah. Go on."

"Thanks," Nick said.

He took Julie's hand, and they walked side by side toward the glow of the campfire.

"Maybe you'd better not," Benny said.

Karen pulled a dripping T-shirt from her pack, and stood up. "Why's that?" she asked.

"I don't like it."

"She's dead, Benny. It's over."

He turned aside and shined his beam on the body. It was still there. It hadn't moved at all.

Karen covered his hand. She pressed his thumb, sliding it back, switching off the light. "Don't look at it," she said. "Why don't you go on over to the fire? I'll be along in a few minutes."

"I want to stay with you."

"Okay, but keep the light off."

"I won't look at her."

"At me, either?"

"Huh?"

"I don't want my sweatshirt any wetter than it already is," she said. She wrung out the white T-shirt. Turning away, she pulled off her sweatshirt. Benny swallowed hard. He felt a little breathless as he stared at her moonlit back. The panties looked like a dim shadow across her buttocks. When she raised her arms to pull the T-shirt on, he glimpsed the side of a breast. He felt guilty about looking, but couldn't help himself. Just as he hadn't been able to keep his eyes away when she'd been at the fire.

She pulled the T-shirt down to her waist and turned to him. The way it clung, he wanted to shine the light on her. But he didn't.

"Okay," she said. "I'm going in."

"Hurry."

He watched her wade out into the lake. She was pale against the black water. She looked as if her legs were gone, as if they'd been chopped off just below the surface. The image made him uneasy. He glanced at the body of the witch, only a couple of yards from where he stood, then turned away. He switched on his flashlight, and played it over the ground until he spotted the hatchet where Nick had let it drop. He went to it. He put the flashlight into a pocket of his parka, and bent over. Pain throbbed through his arm, but faded to a dull ache as he straightened up with the hatchet in his left hand.

He stared out at Karen. She was moving slowly to the side, only her head and pale shoulders visible above the black.

Stepping close to the shore, he looked down at her sweatshirt draped over one of the packs. He remembered the soft feel of it when he snuggled with her last night. Then he pictured the way she'd looked in the glow of the firelight when she heated it over the flames and didn't know he was watching. *No fair peeking*, she'd said.

The witch is naked.

She's ugly and she's dead. It'd be perverted to look at her.

But he did. Her breasts, lit by the moon, were gray like stones. The nipples looked almost black.

He glanced toward the campfire. Julie was seated facing the fire. Nick, behind her, was bandaging her shoulder.

He checked the lake. Karen's head ducked under the surface, and she was gone.

With a few quick steps, he was standing over the witch. He pressed the hatchet between his knees. He took the flashlight from his pocket. He shined it down on her. In the pale glow, her breasts looked smooth. They were dingy white. He could see a network of blue veins through the skin. The nipples were very large. Their red-brown flesh had an odd, blue tinge. His heart was thundering. He felt an erection growing. He felt dirty, nauseated. But he couldn't look away.

He had never touched a woman's naked breast. He wondered what one would feel like.

No! She's dead!

Or maybe she isn't dead, and she's willing me.

He switched off the light and took a quick step backward. The hatchet dropped from between his knees.

He crouched to pick it up, and he was down close to her, gazing at her moonlit breasts. He reached out his trembling left hand.

She grabbed it by the wrist.

Nick slammed against Julie's back, knocking her forward off the stump. She flung up an arm to protect her head. It rammed the fireplace stones, caving them in. The weight left her back. Raising her head, she saw Nick tumble through the fire in a shower of sparks, a filthy naked man clinging to his back. They were only in the flames for an instant before they rolled through the other low wall. Julie shoved herself up. Nick was on his hands and knees, the man straddling his back, choking him with a forearm just as Fish had choked him.

Julie grabbed a rock. It seared her fingers and fell.

Nick rolled onto his side. She glimpsed the face of the man, and gasped as she recognized it. He was the man who had raped Karen, who had tried to rape her. He was the man Nick had killed nearly a week ago.

Behind her, a twig snapped. She spun around. A teenaged girl was lurching toward her. The girl's tangled hair was full of dirt. Soil clung to her gray skin. Bite marks marred her shoulders and breasts.

Julie leaped away from the reaching hands. The girl turned and kept coming. "Get away!" Julie cried out.

And then she saw a man staggering out of the darkness behind the girl. His head was down, hanging loosely, swaying and wobbling with each step.

She heard herself whimpering as she backed away. Her heel came down on a rock, and she nearly fell. Catching her balance, she crouched and grabbed the rock. It was warm from the fire, heavy, with jagged edges. She hurled it at the girl. It struck her nose and wide-open mouth. Her head was knocked back by the impact, but she didn't cry out or wince or even blink her eyes. The rock bounced off her face. It left her nose torn, her upper lip mashed, her teeth broken. There was no bleeding.

Silently, she bent over and picked up the rock.

The man was at her side.

Julie thrust her hand into the fire. She grabbed a stick by its unburnt end and yanked it out. The other end blazed like a torch. She swung it back and forth in front of the two, but they kept coming as if they didn't care. She backed away. Lurching to the side, she shoved the torch hard against the back of the man on top of Nick. It had no effect. She jabbed his head with it. His tangled hair caught fire. It blazed. But he stayed on Nick's squirming body and kept on choking him.

She flung her burning stick at the others. It missed the man's hanging head as he ducked to pick up a rock. Julie glimpsed the wound at the back of his neck—as if a wedge had been chopped out.

She grabbed a foot of the man on Nick. She wrapped

both hands around its cold ankle and pulled, straining backward, dragging him. Nick pried the arm away and shoved the man off him.

Julie yelped as a rock hammered her bandaged shoulder. She dropped the foot and whirled around. The girl swung again. The rock slammed the side of Julie's face. Her head burst with pain. She stumbled backward, stepped on a leg of the man sprawled behind her, and fell on him. His arms latched around her waist. They squeezed her breath out. She felt the heat of his charred scalp against her back.

The girl bent over her with the rock. Julie kicked at her. The man with the drooping head shoved her aside and threw himself onto Julie. She thrust her hands at him, but her arms folded. He smashed down on her, forehead pounding her face. Through her daze, she heard a yell. She felt a crushing weight for a moment. Then it was gone. She opened her eyes. The man was still on her but his head was gone. Nick had it hugged to his chest as he rolled. He flung it away and got to his hands and knees. His terrified eyes met Julie's. Then the girl pounced on his back, driving him down.

"No!" Julie shrieked as the girl swung her rock at Nick's head.

He threw his arms behind his head, and they took the blow.

Something hit Julie's ear. She cried out and held it, and pain erupted in her fingers as the headless man pounded her again with his rock. The arms around her middle let go. With a burst of hope, she thrust at the man's shoulders, forcing him up a bit. He dropped the rock. He clenched her throat with both hands. She gazed at the pulpy stump of his neck as he forced her down.

She felt a tug at her chest. Heard ripping cloth. Felt icy hands.

The corpse under Julie fondled and squeezed her breasts while the one on top strangled her.

The hand snatching Benny's wrist had caught him off balance. Numb with horror, he tried to jerk loose. The fingers held him tight. They yanked, and he fell forward onto the witch. He screamed as his face shoved against a breast. His broken arm burst with pain.

As he lay across her, kneeing the ground, she forced his left arm up behind his back. She grabbed the wrist with her other hand. There was a sudden tug, a thrust at his elbow. He heard a ripping, popping sound as his arm was wrenched out of its shoulder socket. He shrieked and passed out.

Karen was wading backward, chest-deep in the lake, dragging both packs by their straps when she heard an outcry from shore. She swung around. She stared. The straps slid from fingers suddenly gone numb.

She didn't know, couldn't believe what she was seeing.

Silhouettes of tangled bodies squirming on the ground near the scattered campfire.

A moonlit struggle near the shore.

She lunged forward and swam, clawing the water, kicking with all her strength. Her mind reeled as she raced for shore. What the hell was going on? Where had all those people come from? What if she couldn't help? What if she got there only to find the others dead? Oh, God, no. Please!

Her plunging hand raked the rocky bottom. She shoved herself to her feet and dashed, splashing the water high. She glanced toward the fire. What's happening? Then she fixed her gaze on the strange shapes just ahead of her. She felt dry ground under her feet.

It was the woman—the witch—sprawled on her back. Motionless legs stuck out from her side Benny? The hands were on his head, pushing his face to her torn belly, smothering him.

Karen grabbed Benny by the hips and yanked him back. As she dragged him clear, the woman rolled, snarling, clutched the hatchet, and crawled toward them. Karen leaped over Benny. She stomped the hatchet flat against the ground and slammed her other foot into the woman's face. The head snapped backward. Karen grabbed the chin, the base of the skull. She twisted hard. The body flipped onto its back. As the head lifted, she drove her heel down, crashing the head against the rocky earth, smashing the nose. The body went limp.

Grabbing the hatchet, she whirled around. Benny raised his head. "Hang in there," she gasped. "Gotta . . . the others . . . all hell . . ." She started toward the fire.

"Karen!" the boy yelled.

She looked back at him as she ran. He had turned himself onto his back, was sitting up.

"Come back!" he shouted. "Listen to me! I know!"

Karen raced back to him.

"Kill the witch!" he blurted. "Quick!"

"She can't—"

"She's not dead!"

If we'd listened to him before . . .

Karen ran, dropped to her knees. The woman below her was mumbling, staring up at the sky.

"Quick!" Benny yelled.

Nick had thrust himself up to his hands and knees, but the girl stayed on his back. The rock pounded his head. He threw himself over, rolled onto her. Her legs encircled his hips. An arm crossed his throat. A hand reached up over his face holding the jagged rock and he knew he couldn't get his arms up in time to block the blow.

Karen swung the hatchet down. It broke through the woman's forehead. The body jumped and twitched. She raised the hatchet, and chopped again.

The rock fell. It bounced off Nick's forehead. The arm at his throat went limp. The legs dropped away from his sides.

He flung himself clear of the girl. She was motionless on the ground. He pushed himself to his feet. As he staggered over to her, Julie, pressed between the two naked men, tore the clutching hands of the headless one away from her throat. She was gasping and sobbing. Nick grabbed the man's shoulder and hip, and rolled him off. As the body tumbled aside, a pair of hands slid away from Julie's breasts.

She raised her arms to Nick.

He gripped her wrists, and pulled her up.

They stepped away from the bodies. Nick eased her against him. For a long time, they held each other gently and wept.

Chapter Forty-two

Scott heard a soft knocking on the door of his hospital room. "Come in," he said. He lay his book aside, and watched the door swing open.

Karen stepped in. She tilted her head to one side, and raised her eyebrows. "Could you use a little company?"

"Get over here," he said, trying to sound gruff.

She looked lovely, her hair soft and glowing around her face, brushing her bare shoulders as she approached. Her dress had spaghetti straps. Its silken blue fabric clung to her breasts, was drawn in at the waist by a gold chain belt, floated around her thighs.

At his bedside, she flicked a finger against one of his hoisted casts. "How you been?"

"Lonely. *Where* you been?"

"On an outing." She set her purse on the floor, and bent over him. She stroked his cheek.

"Looks like you got some sun," he said. He fingered a tiny curl of peeling skin on the side of her nose.

"I missed you," she said.

"I kept waiting for you at visiting hours."

"I'm sorry."

"No you. No Julie, no Benny. Tanya came by a few times, but it wasn't quite the same."

She kissed him. Her lips felt chapped, but they felt very good and he wrapped his arms around her and caressed her. He seemed to sink into her, as if joining with a part of himself that had vanished and left him empty and returned.

Returned from an outing.

He released her.

She sat on the edge of the bed, and held herself steady with a hand on his chest as she drew a leg up beneath her. He stroked her bare thigh. "This outing," he said.

"We didn't want you to worry."

"You went back to the mountains?"

She nodded. "Julie, Benny, Nick, and me."

"Everyone's all right?"

"We survived. Julie and Benny are waiting in the hall. Julie thought I should see you first."

"The kid's got style."

"That she does. You've got a couple of great kids."

"They have their moments. How's Nick?"

"You know about Flash?"

"Yeah. Tanya told me." He sighed. He squeezed Karen's knee. "He was a good guy."

"Nick's very proud of him. Nick's also madly in love with your daughter."

"Of course," Scott said.

She laced her fingers with his.

"O'Tooles are a lovable sort," he added.

"Don't I know it."

He stared into her eyes. "God, I'm glad you're back."

"Me, too."

"You shouldn't have gone without me."

"You would've done us a lot of good. Two broken legs. Old gimpy."

"How'd it go out there?"

"It got hairy."

"I assume the good guys won."

"You assume correctly. The witch is vanquished. The curse went with her."

"Want to tell me about it?"

"Nope. Benny wants to tell you about it. He's very insistent on that point. If it weren't for him, things might've gone . . . a bit sour."

"He saved the day, huh?"

"I'd say so." Karen slipped her hand free. She bent over and lifted her purse from the floor. As she opened it, Scott slid his hand up the smooth bare skin of her thigh. She took a felt-tipped pen from her purse. She didn't try to stop his hand. She caught her breath and arched her back.

"Well now," he said.

"Take the pen," she whispered.

"And what should I do with it?"

"Autograph your son's casts."

"*Casts?*"

"In the plural."

"Oh, no."

"Oh, yes."

He took the pen from her hand. "Any more surprises?"

"Not at the moment."

"Then give me another kiss."

"The kids are waiting."

"We'll make it brief."

"But not too brief?"

He drew her down to him and held her and kissed her moist, parted lips, and wanted never to stop.

"Christ, gang!" Julie called from the doorway. "Break it up!"

CHAPTER ONE

EDDIE, IN HIS VAN, HAD THE ROAD TO HIMSELF.

Except for the bicycle.

When he first saw the bike from the crest of the hill, it was below him and far ahead. At such a distance, he couldn't tell much about the rider.

He knew it wasn't a kid.

The bike was one of those high, streamlined jobs, not like you see kids pedaling around on. And the rider looked big enough to fit the bike.

Could be a teenager, Eddie thought.

Could be a gal.

Squinting, he leaned toward the windshield. The bottom of the steering wheel sank into his belly, filling the crease between his rolls of fat.

Could be a gal, he thought.

With the back of his hand, Eddie wiped his mouth.

He was halfway down the hill by now, picking up speed and closing the gap between his van and the bike.

The rider's brown hair was somewhat long. That didn't prove much. A lot of men wore their hair that long and longer.

But you don't see a lot of guys in red shorts.

Eddie sped closer.

Close enough to see how the rider's hips flared out from a small waist.

A gal, all right.

On both sides of the road were fields with trees here and there. No buildings. No people. The road ahead to where it curved and vanished was deserted. Eddie checked his side mirrors. Behind him, the road was clear.

"Her it is," he said.

He pressed the gas pedal to the floor.

Though the rider didn't look back, she must have heard the rising engine sound. Her bike moved to the right, gliding away from the middle of the lane and taking up a new position a yard from the road's edge.

Eddie bore down on her.

She was hunched over her handlebars. She kept pedaling.

Her T-shirt was so tight that Eddie could see the bumps of her spine. Bare skin showed between the bottom of her shirt and the elastic band of her shorts.

Her left arm swung out. She waved Eddie by.

At the last instant, she looked back. Eddie was near enough to see that her eyes were blue.

She was very pretty.

He turned his van toward her.

I like the pretty ones.

Her front wheel jerked right.

Pretty and young and tender.

He waited for her to meet the windshield.

But she was being hurled the wrong way—forward and to the right. She was no longer on the bike. She was above it, legs kicking overhead, as Eddie's van smashed through it.

No problem, Eddie thought.

She won't go far.

I'll get her. Oh, yes.

His right-side tires bounced over the gravel shoulder of the road and he was about to steer back onto the pavement when he came upon a bridge.

He hadn't even noticed it before.

He glimpsed the sign as he sped past it.

Weber Creek.

Not much of a creek.

Not much of a bridge—but it had a concrete guard wall four feet high.

CHAPTER TWO

"ARE YOU ALL RIGHT?"

"Do I *look* all right?"

She was sitting on the ground with her back to the road, her head turned to look up at him. Above her right eyebrow, the skin was scraped off to her hairline. The raw place was striped with beaded threads of blood. It was dirty, and a few bits of straw-colored weeds clung to the stickiness.

Jake sat down beside her on the edge of the ditch.

Both her knees and the front of her right thigh were in the same condition as her forehead. Her right arm hung between her legs, knuckles against the ground. She held the arm with her other hand while it shook. She didn't appear to be trying to hold it still. The other hand seemed meant to soothe it the way someone might lay a hand on an injured pet.

"Do you think it's broken?" Jake asked.

"I wouldn't know."

Jake took out a notepad. "Could I have your name?"

"Jamerson," she said. The corner of her mouth twitched.

Jake wrote. "And your first name?"

"Celia."

"Thanks."

She turned her head to look at him again. "Shouldn't you be doing something about *that*?" Her eyes shifted toward the blazing van fifty or sixty feet to her left.

"The fire truck's on the way. My partner's keeping an eye on things."

"What about the . . . driver?"

"We can't do much for him."

"Is he dead?"

A shish kebab, Chuck had remarked when he saw the driver's remains hanging out the windshield.

"Yes," Jake said.

"He tried to hit me. I mean it. He had the whole road to himself. I'm over by the shoulder and I signal him to go around, and I look back and he's actually swerving right at me. He's grinning and he swerves right at me. Must've been going sixty." Her face had a puzzled expression as if she were listening to a bizarre joke and waiting for Jake to feed her the punch line. "That guy meant to kill me," she said. "He creamed my bike."

She nodded toward it. The bike with its twisted wheels lay in the weeds on the far side of the ditch.

"What happened, I turned quick to get out of his way and it flipped on me. Just before he hit it, I guess. The van never touched me. Next thing I knew, I was landing in the ditch and there was this crash. Bastard. That's what he gets, going around trying to . . . what'd I ever do to *him*?"

"Did you know him?" Jake asked.

"I've heard of these guys, they'll run down dogs just for laughs. Hey, maybe he thought I was a dog." She tried to laugh and came out with a harsh sobbing noise.

"Had you ever seen the man before?"

"No."

"Did you do anything that might've angered him?"

"Sure, I flipped him the bird. What is this? Is it suddenly my fault?"

"*Did* you flip him off?"

"No, damn it. I didn't even see him till he was about a foot off my tail."

"As far as you're concerned, then, his action was totally unprovoked?"

"That's right."

"You say that you heard the crash just after you landed in the ditch?"

"Maybe I hadn't hit yet. I really don't know."

"What happened next?"

"I think I conked out. Yeah, I'm pretty sure I did. Then what happened, I heard your siren. That's when I got up and . . ."

"Hey, Jake!"

Jake looked over his shoulder. Chuck, fire extinguisher in one hand, was standing by the open rear door of the flaming van and waving him over. "I'd better see what he wants. Sit tight, there should be an ambulance on the way."

Celia nodded.

Jake stood up, brushed off his seat, and walked over to his partner.

"Take a look-see here," Chuck said, pointing to the ground.

The pale dirt of the road's shoulder was speckled with a few dark blotches. Jake crouched for a closer look.

"Looks like blood to me," Chuck said.

"Yeah."

"Was the girl over here?"

"Not according to what she told me."

"We better find out for sure. Cause if she wasn't . . . know what I mean?"

Jake heard a distant siren. He saw a smear of blood on the gray asphalt of the road. The fire truck or ambulance wasn't in sight yet, so he rushed across both lanes. Chuck trotted along beside him, still hanging onto the fire extinguisher.

"How'd someone survive a crash like that?" Chuck said.

Jake shook his head. "Just lucky."

"Yeah, I guess it can happen. You hear about folks making it through airline crashes. *There*." He pointed.

"I see it."

A slick of blood on a blade of crabgrass.

Jake stepped into the weeds. He scanned the ditch and the field beyond it. Both were overgrown with weeds that had flourished and bloomed under the recent spring rains. The uneven terrain of the field was dotted with clumps of bushes. There were a few trees scattered around.

He saw no one.

Chuck cupped his hands to the sides of his mouth and yelled, "Hello! Hey, out there!"

Jake, standing beside him, could barely hear his voice over the noise of the siren.

The siren died. Chuck called out again. Jake heard the groan of air brakes, the tinny crackle of a radio. He looked back and saw the town's bright yellow pump truck.

"How come you suppose he wandered off?" Chuck asked. "It was me got banged up, I'd stick around and wait for help."

"Maybe he's in shock and doesn't know what he's doing. More likely, though, he wanted to haul ass out of here. The girl says she was riding her bike along, minding her own business, and the van tried to run her down on purpose. Which would mean the guy's not a model citizen. You take care of matters here, I'll see if I can dig him up."

"Don't take all day, huh? I'm getting the hungries and my stockpile's dry."

The stockpile was the cache of Twinkies, chips and candy bars that Chuck kept in the patrol car.

"You'll live," Jake said. He slapped Chuck's paunch, then climbed down into the ditch.

After looking for traces of blood, he climbed out of the ditch on its far side.

Back on the road, the firemen were blasting at the flames with chemical extinguishers. Chuck was walking over to Celia, who was standing now, though bent over a bit and still holding her right arm.

Jake wondered if she was from the university. She was the right age, and he probably would've known her if she was a local. Also, there was her wise-guy attitude. *Do I look all right?*

Don't hold it against her, he told himself. She was hurting.

A good-looking woman, even with her face scraped up.

Came damn close to getting her ticket canceled.

He turned away and continued searching.

Two in the van, one bought the farm and the other guy got away. The dead guy was obviously the driver. The survivor must've been in the back of the van, or he would've gone out the windshield, same as the driver. And Celia didn't mention seeing anyone in the passenger seat.

If he was in the back, maybe he wasn't part of it.

No, he *was* part of it, or he would've stuck close to the van after the crash.

Wandering back and forth, Jake spotted a dandelion with a broken stem, a smear of blood on its blossoms. It was a few yards north of where he'd come out of the ditch. In his mind, Jake connected the two points and extended the line across the field. It led to a low rise a couple of hundred yards to the northwest. The high ground was shaded by a stand of eucalyptus trees. He headed that way.

From behind him came the blare of another siren. That would be the ambulance.

Nice response time, he thought.

He checked his wristwatch. 3:20 P.M. He and Chuck had spotted the smoke at 3:08. They'd reached the accident site two minutes later and called in. So the ambulance had taken ten minutes.

Good thing nobody's life was depending on it.

Jake waded into Weber Creek, peering up and down the narrow band of water. On the other side, he stopped long enough to check the area for signs. The weeds were nearly knee-high. He couldn't find any traces of blood or trampled foliage. Maybe the guy had changed course. Looking back, though, Jake could only make out the faintest sign of his own passage.

I'm hardly the world's greatest tracker, he thought.

And if the guy had made any effort to be careful, he could've skirted the places with high weeds and stuck to areas where the ground cover was sparse. Or maybe followed the creek.

Maybe I already passed him. If he stretched out flat . . .

Sneaking up on me . . .

Jake whirled around.

Nobody there.

His gaze swept over the field, then back toward the road. The van was still smoking, but he couldn't see any flames. Chuck was standing close to Celia. An ambulance attendant was heading their way.

Jake continued toward the rise, but he'd begun to feel that he'd lost the suspect. He didn't like that. In spite of the blood, it was apparent that the man hadn't been severely injured. Hurt, sure, but not incapacitated.

A potential killer.

Jake didn't want to lose him.

What kind of man pulls a stunt like that—tries to run down a total stranger in broad daylight? He wasn't driving, of course, but he was an accomplice, Jake was sure of that.

Maybe they never intended to kill her, just run her off the road, rack her up enough to take the fight out of her, and snatch her. That Jake could understand. A good-looking woman, get her into the van, have their fun with her, dump her later on, maybe dead.

If Celia's account was accurate, though, they actually tried to smash her with the van. It would've killed her for sure. And messed her up pretty good. Hardly your typical MO for a pair of traveling rapists.

They wanted her dead first?

Sick.

Outlandish, too. There just aren't that many necrophiles running around; the odds against two of them linking up must be staggering.

It could happen.

More likely, though, they just would have left her.

Thrill killers.

Combing the roads in a van, looking for suitable victims.

If I lose this guy . . .

Jake turned slowly, scanning the entire expanse of the field. He trudged to the top of the rise and made a quick circuit around the trees. Nobody there. On the other side, the ground sloped down to a narrow road. Beyond the road, the field continued. The foliage and trees were heavier on that side. Plenty of places for a man to conceal himself.

Jake spent a long time watching the area. Turning around, he gazed at the field he had crossed.

You lost him, all right.

Get up a search party, go over the area inch by inch. The logical step, but not very practical. How do you get together enough men on short notice to do the job properly?

He leaned against a tree. He kicked a small rock and sent it flying down the slope. It landed in a clump of bushes, and he imagined his suspect crying out, "Ouch!" and making a run for it.

Dream on, Corey.

Shit.

He looked up the side road. It led only to the Oakwood Inn. The old restaurant had been closed for years, but a couple from Los Angeles was planning to reopen it. He saw a station wagon parked in front. The folks must be there, fixing the place up.

I'd better warn them.

The damned restaurant only looked like it was a quarter of a mile away. Weary and discouraged—and gnawed by guilt for letting the creep slip away—Jake shoved himself away from the tree and made his way down the slope. He waded through the weeds. Once he reached the road, the walking was easier.

He kept a lookout, though he no longer expected to find the suspect.

Suspect, my ass, he thought.

This guy's into wasting random victims.

And I lost him.

Maybe the accident, losing his partner, took some of the starch out of him.

Right.

Goddamn it.

I lost him and it'll be my fault if he . . .

The distant sound of a car engine broke into Jake's thoughts.

Chuck coming to fetch him?

He turned and realized that the sound came from the direction of the Oakwood Inn. He remembered the station wagon.

Snapped his head forward.

He was standing in a dip.

He saw only the road.

From the noise, the car was speeding.

And he knew.

He'd been slow—he should've guessed it the instant he saw the car sitting there, vulnerable, in front of the restaurant.

Your van is totaled, you're on foot and hurt, you spot an unattended vehicle . . .

Heart racing, mouth gone dry, Jake Corey snatched out his .38, planted his feet on each side of the faded yellow centerline of the road, lowered himself into a shooting crouch, and waited.

He aimed at the road's crest fifty yards away.

"Come on, you mother."

Jake wished he had a .357 like the one Chuck carried. With that, he'd be able to kill a car.

Jake would have to go for the driver.

He had never shot anyone.

But he knew this was it. He couldn't let the bastard get away.

Six slugs through the windshield.

That should do it.

The car burst into view, bounced on loose shocks as it hit the down slope, sped toward him.

Wait till he's almost on you, blow him away, dive for safety.

Jake's finger tightened on the trigger.

Brakes shrieked. The car skidded, fishtailed, and stopped thirty feet in front of him.

Jake couldn't believe it.

"Let me see your hands!" he yelled.

The driver, a thin and frightened-looking man of about thirty, stared at Jake through the windshield.

"I want to see your hands *right now*! Grab the steering wheel *right now*!"

The hands appeared. They gripped the top of the wheel.

"Keep 'em there!"

Jake kept his revolver pointed at the man's face while he approached the car. The head turned, eyes following him as he stepped to the driver's door.

No one else in the car.

Jake pulled the door open and stepped back. Crouching slightly, he had a full view of the man.

Who wore a blue knit shirt, and Bermuda shorts, and who didn't appear to be injured in any way.

"What's going on, Officer?"

"Place your hands on top of your head and interlace your fingers."

"Hey really . . ."

"Do it!"

Why are you keeping this up? Jake wondered. Because you don't know. Not yet. Not for sure.

The man put his hands on top of his head.

"Okay. Now climb out."

As he followed orders, Jake got a look at his back. No blood or sign of injury there, either.

"Turn around slowly." Jake made circular motions with his left forefinger. The man turned. Jake looked for bulges. The knit shirt was skintight. The only bulge was at the rear pocket of his shorts—a wallet. Good. Jake didn't want to frisk him.

"Will you tell me what's going on?"

Jake holstered his weapon.

"Could I see your driver's license, please?"

The man took out his wallet. He knew enough to remove the license from its plastic holder. Probably been stopped for traffic violations.

Jake took the card. His hand was trembling. It reminded him of Celia's shaking arm. The name on the license was Ronald Smeltzer. The photo matched the face of the man in front of him. The home address was on Euclid, in Santa Monica, California. "Thank you, Mr. Smeltzer," he said, and returned the license. "I'm sorry about stopping you that way."

"A wave would've sufficed."

"I was expecting trouble. I assume you're the new owner of the Oakwood."

"That's right. Could you tell me what's going on? I realize I was taking the road a bit fast, but . . ." Smeltzer shrugged. He was obviously upset, but showing no belligerence. Jake appreciated his attitude.

"I was on my way to speak with you—to warn you, actually. We just had an incident over on Latham Road."

"We were wondering. We heard the sirens."

"On your way to investigate?"

"No, no. As a matter of fact, we haven't got ice. My wife and I have been working all day, trying to get the place in shape. No refrigerator, yet. It's supposed to be delivered tomorrow. We thought we'd relax over cocktails for a while, but . . ." He shrugged. He looked as if he felt a little foolish. "No ice. What can I say?"

"Your wife is back at the restaurant?" Jake asked. The man nodded. "I don't think you want to leave her alone just now. We've got a situation. Give me a lift to your restaurant and I'll explain."

The two men climbed into the car. Smeltzer turned it around and headed back up the road at a moderate speed.

"Pick it up," Jake told him. "I know you can do better than this."

Smeltzer stepped on the gas.

As the car raced toward the restaurant, Jake explained about the attempt to run down Celia Jamerson, the blood behind the van, and his search for the injured passenger. Smeltzer listened, asking no questions but shaking his head a couple of times and frequently muttering, "Oh, man."

The car lurched to a stop at the foot of the restaurant's stairs. Smeltzer flung open his door. At the same moment, a door at the top of the stairs swung wide.

A woman stood in the shadows. She stepped out onto the porch as Smeltzer and Jake climbed from the car. Her perplexed expression altered into a frown of concern——probably as she realized that Jake was a cop.

She had nice legs. She wore red shorts. This is my day for beautiful women in red shorts, Jake thought. The front of her loose gray jersey jiggled nicely as she trotted down the stairs. The jersey had been cut off, halfway up. Any higher, Jake thought, and he'd be seeing what made the jiggles.

"Ron?" she asked, stopping in front of the car.

"Honey, this is Officer. . . ." He looked at Jake.

"Jake Corey."

"I ran into him on my way out. Almost literally." He gave Jake a sheepish glance.

"Some kind of trouble?"

Jake let Smeltzer explain. His wife nodded. She didn't say, "Oh, man," after each of his sentences. She didn't say anything. She just frowned and nodded and kept glancing over at Jake as if expecting him to interrupt. "Is this true?" she finally asked him.

"He covered it pretty well."

"You think there might be a killer hanging around here?"

"He didn't kill anyone today, but it wasn't for lack of trying. Have either of you seen anyone?"

She shook her head.

"But we've been working inside," Smeltzer added.

"You folks have a home in town, don't you?" Jake asked. He seemed to remember hearing that they'd bought the Anderson house.

"I was on my way there," Smeltzer said, "for the ice."

"It's certainly your decision, but if I were you, I'd close up here for today and go on back to your house. There's no point in taking unnecessary risks."

Husband and wife exchanged a look.

"I don't know," Smeltzer said to her. "What do you think?"

"We've got to get this place in shape before they bring in the equipment."

"I guess we could come in early tomorrow."

"It's up to you," the wife said.

"This guy does sound like he might be dangerous."

"Whatever you say, Ron. It's your decision."

"You'd rather stay," Ron said.

"Did I say that?"

"I think we'd be smart to leave."

"Okay. It's settled, then." She smiled at Jake. It was a false smile. *See? You got your way.*

Hey lady, he wanted to tell her, sorry. Just thought you might want to know there's an asshole in the neighborhood and maybe you're his type. Forgive me.

Smeltzer turned to Jake. "Could we give you a lift?"

"Yeah, thanks. I could use a ride back to the road."

"Fine. We'll just be a minute. We need to lock up."

He and his wife headed up the porch stairs.

Jake glanced at the woman's rear end. He didn't find it especially interesting. She was a fine-looking package, beautifully wrapped, but Jake had the idea that he wouldn't like what he found inside.

So much for lust.

They were inside the restaurant for longer than Jake expected. At first, he assumed they were probably delayed by a heated discussion about leaving ahead of schedule. Then he began to worry.

What if the guy from the van was in there and got them?

Not very likely.

But the possibility stayed with Jake. He counted to thirty, slowly, in his mind.

They still weren't out.

He went for the stairs, took them three at a time, and reached for the door handle.

The door swung away from him.

"Sorry it took so long," Smeltzer said. "Had to use the john."

"No problem." Jake turned away, not even trying for a glimpse of the wife, and trotted down the stairs.

From behind him came her voice. "This really *is* the pits."

"Better safe than sorry," Smeltzer said.

"Of course."

EDWARD LEE

Author of *Brides of the Impaler*

From the bones of the dead…from a long-buried secret …through an ancient ritual…they rise to kill. What was first created to protect has now been perverted and twisted into servants of evil, commanded to exact a bloody, brutal vengeance. The original golem was molded from clay centuries ago to serve and defend the innocent. But today new golems will stalk the night to bring terror and death to the quiet Maryland coast. For one young couple, their dream home will become a slaughterhouse when they discover that nothing can stop the relentless walking horror known as…

THE GOLEM

"The living legend of literary mayhem. Read him if you dare!"
— Richard Laymon, Author of *Beware*

ISBN 13: 978-0-8439-5808-9

DAVID ROBBINS

Doomsday. The end of all things.
Dreaded by many, scoffed at by skeptics.
And now it has come to pass.

At a remote site in Minnesota, filmmaker Kurt Carpenter has built a secure compound and invited a select group of people to bunker down until the worst is over. The world into which they reemerge is like nothing they've ever seen. At first they think they're the only ones left. But they soon find out how wrong they are. In the wasteland of what used to be America, their battle to survive is only just beginning...

ENDWORLD

DOOMSDAY

ISBN 13: 978-0-8439-6232-1

RAY GARTON

Author of *Ravenous* and *Live Girls*

Something very strange is happening in the coastal California town of Big Rock. Several residents have died in unexplained, particularly brutal ways, many torn apart in animal attacks. And there's always that eerie howling late at night...

You might think there's a werewolf in town. But you'd be wrong. It's not just one werewolf, but the whole town that's gradually transforming. Bit by bit, as the infection spreads, the werewolves are becoming more and more powerful. In fact, humans may soon be the minority, mere prey for their hungry neighbors. Is it too late for the humans to fight back? Did they ever have a chance from the start?

BESTIAL

"Garton has a flair for taking veteran horror themes and twisting them to evocative or entertaining effect."
—*Publishers Weekly*

ISBN 13: 978-0-8439-6185-0

GORD ROLLO

AUTHOR OF *THE JIGSAW MAN*

The small town of Dunnville is no stranger to fear. Evil has stalked its dark streets once before. These days, no one in the town likes to talk about it much. Some folks deny it ever happened....

But four boyhood friends are about to discover the truth, though no one will believe them. Their parents think they've been listening to too many scary stories. But what the boys have released from an icy well is no legend, and it will soon terrify Dunnville to its very core. Unspeakable horror is running free...and the nightmares of the past are about to begin again.

CRIMSON

ISBN 13: 978-0-8439-6195-9

Master of terror

RICHARD LAYMON

has one word of advice for you:

BEWARE

Elsie knew something weird was happening in her small supermarket when she saw the meat cleaver fly through the air all by itself. Everyone else realized it when they found Elsie on the butcher's slab the next morning—neatly jointed and wrapped. An unseen horror has come to town, and its victims are about to learn a terrifying lesson: what you can't see can very definitely hurt you.

ISBN 13: 978-0-8439-6137-9

✂ ☐ **YES!**

Sign me up for the Leisure Horror Book Club and send my FREE BOOKS! If I choose to stay in the club, I will pay only $8.50* each month, a savings of $7.48!

NAME: _____

ADDRESS: _____

TELEPHONE: _____

EMAIL: _____

☐ I want to pay by credit card.

☐ **VISA**   ☐ MasterCard.   ☐ DISCOVER

ACCOUNT #: _____

EXPIRATION DATE: _____

SIGNATURE: _____

Mail this page along with $2.00 shipping and handling to:
Leisure Horror Book Club
PO Box 6640
Wayne, PA 19087
Or fax (must include credit card information) to:
610-995-9274
You can also sign up online at **www.dorchesterpub.com**.
*Plus $2.00 for shipping. Offer open to residents of the U.S. and Canada only.
Canadian residents please call 1-800-481-9191 for pricing information.
If under 18, a parent or guardian must sign. Terms, prices and conditions subject to change. Subscription subject to acceptance. Dorchester Publishing reserves the right to reject any order or cancel any subscription.

GET FREE BOOKS!

You can have the best fiction delivered to your door for less than what you'd pay in a bookstore or online. Sign up for one of our book clubs today, and we'll send you *FREE* BOOKS* just for trying it out... **with no obligation to buy, ever!**

As a member of the Leisure Horror Book Club, you'll receive books by authors such as **RICHARD LAYMON, JACK KETCHUM, JOHN SKIPP, BRIAN KEENE** and many more.

As a book club member you also receive the following special benefits:
- **30% off all orders!**
- **Exclusive access to special discounts!**
- **Convenient home delivery and 10 days to return any books you don't want to keep.**

Visit www.dorchesterpub.com or call 1-800-481-9191

There is no minimum number of books to buy, and you may cancel membership at any time.
*Please include $2.00 for shipping and handling.